D0259132

# ALL TOGETHER
# DEAD

*Also by Charlaine Harris from Gollancz Romancz:*

Definitely Dead
Dead as a Doornail

Grave Sight
Grave Surprise
An Ice Cold Grave

# ALL TOGETHER DEAD

CHARLAINE
HARRIS

GOLLANCZ

LONDON

Copyright © Charlaine Harris 2007
All rights reserved

The right of Charlaine Harris to be identified as the author
of this work has been asserted by her in accordance with the
Copyright, Designs and Patents Act 1988.

First published in Great Britain in 2008 by
Gollancz
An imprint of the Orion Publishing Group
Orion House, 5 Upper St Martin's Lane, London WC2H 9EA

A CIP catalogue record for this book is available
from the British Library

ISBN 978 0 57508 3 905 (cased)
ISBN 978 0 57508 3 912 (export trade paperback)

1 3 5 7 9 10 8 6 4 2

Printed in Great Britain by Mackays of Chatham plc, Chatham, Kent

www.orionbooks.co.uk

The Orion Publishing Group's policy is to use papers that are natural,
renewable and recyclable products and made from wood grown in
sustainable forests. The logging and manufacturing processes are expected to
conform to the environmental regulations of the country of origin.

*This book is dedicated to a few of the women I'm proud to call "friend": Jodi Dabson Bollendorf, Kate Buker, Toni Kelner, Dana Cameron, Joan Hess, Eve Sandstrom, Paula Woldan, and Betty Epley. All of you have meant something different to me, and I feel grateful to know you.*

# ACKNOWLEDGMENTS

There are a few people I've thanked before and need to thank again: Robin Burcell, former cop and present writer, and FBI Agent George Fong, who were great about answering my questions about security and bomb disposal. I appreciate the input of Sam Saucedo, the former newscaster and now writer, who explained a few things about border politics to me. I also need to thank S. J. Rozan, who was happy to answer my questions about architecture, though the vampire part was a distinct shock. I may have misused the information given me, but it was in a good cause. As always, I owe a great debt to my friend Toni L. P. Kelner, who read my first draft without laughing in my face. And my new continuity person, Debi Murray, gets a tip of the hat; from now on if I make mistakes, I have someone to blame. I owe a lot to the many wonderful readers who visit my website (www.charlaineharris.com) and leave messages of encouragement and interest. Beverly Batillo, my fan club president, has given me a boost many a time when I was down in the dumps.

# 1

THE SHREVEPORT VAMPIRE BAR WOULD BE OPENING late tonight. I was running behind, and I'd automatically gone to the front door, the public door, only to be halted by a neatly lettered sign, red Gothic script on white cardboard: WE'LL BE READY TO GREET YOU WITH A BITE TONIGHT, AT EIGHT O'CLOCK. PLEASE EXCUSE OUR DELAYED OPENING. It was signed "The Staff of Fangtasia."

It was the third week in September, so the red neon FANGTASIA sign was already on. The sky was almost pitch-black. I stood with one foot inside my car for a minute, enjoying the mild evening and the faint, dry smell of vampire that lingered around the club. Then I drove around to the back and parked beside several other cars lined up at the employee entrance. I was only five minutes late, but it looked like everyone else had beaten me to the meeting. I rapped on the door. I waited.

I'd raised my hand to knock again when Pam, Eric's second-in-command, opened the door. Pam was based at the bar, but she had other duties in Eric's various business dealings. Though vampires had gone public five years ago and turned their best face to the world, they were still pretty secretive about their moneymaking methods, and sometimes I wondered how much of America the undead actually owned. Eric, the owner of Fangtasia, was a true vampire in the keeping-things-to-himself department. Of course, in his long, long existence he'd had to be.

"Come in, my telepathic friend," Pam said, gesturing dramatically. She was wearing her work outfit: the filmy, trailing black gown that all the tourists who came into the bar seemed to expect from female vampires. (When Pam got to pick her own clothing, she was a pastels-and-twinset kind of woman.) Pam had the palest, straightest blond hair you ever saw; in fact, she was ethereally lovely, with a kind of deadly edge. The deadly edge was what a person shouldn't forget.

"How you doing?" I asked politely.

"I am doing exceptionally well," she said. "Eric is full of happiness."

Eric Northman, the vampire sheriff of Area Five, had made Pam a vampire, and she was both obliged and compelled to do his bidding. That was part of the deal of becoming undead: you were always in sway to your maker. But Pam had told me more than once that Eric was a good boss to have, and that he would let her go her own way if and when she desired to do so. In fact, she'd been living in Minnesota until Eric had purchased Fangtasia and called her to help him run it.

Area Five was most of northwestern Louisiana, which until a month ago had been the economically weaker half of the state. Since Hurricane Katrina, the balance of power in

Louisiana had shifted dramatically, especially in the vampire community.

"How is that delicious brother of yours, Sookie? And your shape-shifting boss?" Pam said.

"My delicious brother is making noises about getting married, like everyone else in Bon Temps," I said.

"You sound a bit depressed." Pam cocked her head to one side and regarded me like a sparrow eyeing a worm.

"Well, maybe a tad wee bit," I said.

"You must keep busy," Pam said. "Then you won't have time to mope."

Pam *loved* "Dear Abby." Lots of vampires scrutinized the column daily. Their solutions to some of the writers' problems would just make you scream. Literally. Pam had already advised me that I could only be imposed on if I permitted it, and that I needed to be more selective in picking my friends. I was getting emotional-health counseling from a vampire.

"I am," I said. "Keeping busy, that is. I'm working, I've still got my roommate from New Orleans, and I'm going to a wedding shower tomorrow. Not for Jason and Crystal. Another couple."

Pam had paused, her hand on the doorknob of Eric's office. She considered my statement, her brows drawn together. "I am not remembering what a wedding shower is, though I've heard of it," she said. She brightened. "They'll get married in a bathroom? No, I've heard the term before, surely. A woman wrote to Abby that she hadn't gotten a thank-you note for a large shower gift. They get . . . presents?"

"You got it," I said. "A shower is a party for someone who's about to get married. Sometimes the shower is for the couple, and they're both there. But usually only the bride is the honoree, and all the other people at the party are women. Everyone brings a gift. The theory is that this way the couple can start life with everything they need. We do the same thing when a couple's expecting a baby. Course, then it's a baby shower."

"Baby shower," Pam repeated. She smiled in a chilly way. It was enough to put frost on your pumpkin, seeing that up-curve of the lips. "I like the term," she said. She knocked on Eric's office door and then opened it. "Eric," she said, "maybe someday one of the waitresses will get pregnant, and we can go to a *baby shower*!"

"That would be something to see," said Eric, lifting his golden head from the papers on his desk. The sheriff registered my presence, gave me a hard look, and decided to ignore me. Eric and I had issues.

Despite the fact that the room was full of people waiting for his attention, Eric lay down his pen and stood to stretch his tall and magnificent body, perhaps for my benefit. As usual, Eric was in tight jeans and a Fangtasia T-shirt, black with the white stylized fangs that the bar used as its trademark. "Fangtasia" was written in jazzy red script across the white points in the same style as the neon sign outside. If Eric turned around, the back would read "The Bar with a Bite." Pam had given me one when Fangtasia first got into marketing its own stuff.

Eric made the shirt look good, and I remembered all too well what was underneath it.

I tore my gaze away from Eric's stretch to look around the room. There were lots of other vampires crammed into the smallish space, but till you saw them you didn't know they were there, they were so still and silent. Clancy, the bar manager, had claimed one of the two visitor chairs before the desk. Clancy had just barely survived the previous year's Witch War, but he hadn't come out unscathed. The witches had drained Clancy near to the point of no return. By the time Eric discovered Clancy, tracing his smell to a Shreveport cemetery, Clancy was one Vacutainer short of dead. During his long recovery, the red-haired vamp had grown bitter and snappish. Now he grinned at me, showing some fang. "You can sit in my lap, Sookie," he said, patting his thighs.

I smiled back, but not like my heart was in it. "No, thanks, Clancy," I said politely. Clancy's flirting had always had an edge to it, and now that edge was razor sharp. He was one of those vamps I'd rather not be alone with. Though he ran the bar capably, and he had never laid a finger on me, he still set off warning bells. I can't read vampire minds, which was why I found it refreshing to hang with them, but when I felt that tingle of warning, I did find myself wishing I could just dip into Clancy's head and find out what was going on in there.

Felicia, the newest bartender, was sitting on the couch, along with Indira and Maxwell Lee. It was like the vampire Rainbow Coalition meeting. Felicia was a happy mixture of African and Caucasian, and she was almost six feet tall, so there was more loveliness to appreciate. Maxwell Lee was one of the darkest men I'd ever seen. Little Indira was the daughter of Indian immigrants.

There were four more people in the room (using the term "people" loosely), and each one of them upset me, though in varying degrees.

One of them was someone I didn't acknowledge. I'd taken a page from the Were rule book and treated him like an outlawed member of my pack: I abjured him. I didn't speak his name, I didn't speak to him, I didn't recognize his existence. (Of course, this was my ex, Bill Compton—not that I recognized that he was in the room, brooding away in a corner.)

Leaning against the wall next to him was ancient Thalia, who was possibly even older than Eric. She was as small as Indira and very pale, with tightly waving black hair—and she was extremely rude.

To my amazement, some humans found that a complete turn-on. Thalia actually had a devoted following who seemed thrilled when she used her stilted English to tell them to fuck off. I'd discovered she even had a website, established and maintained by fans. Go figure. Pam had told me that when Eric had agreed to let Thalia live in Shreveport, it was the equivalent of keeping a badly trained pit bull tethered in the yard. Pam had not approved.

These undead citizens all lived in Area Five. To live and work under Eric's protection, they'd all sworn fealty to him. So they were required to devote a certain amount of their time to doing his bidding, even if they didn't work at the bar. There were a few extra vampires in Shreveport these days, since Katrina; just like a lot of humans, they had to go somewhere. Eric hadn't decided what to do about the undead refugees, and they hadn't been invited to the meeting.

Tonight there were two visitors in Fangtasia, one of whom outranked Eric.

Andre was the personal bodyguard of Sophie-Anne Leclerq, the Queen of Louisiana. The queen, at present, was an evacuee in Baton Rouge. Andre looked very young, maybe sixteen; his face was baby-smooth, his pale hair was thick and heavy. Andre had lived a long existence caring only for Sophie-Anne, his maker and savior. He was not wearing his saber tonight, because he wasn't acting as her bodyguard, but I was sure Andre was armed with something—knife or gun. Andre himself was a lethal weapon, with or without an aid.

Just as Andre was about to speak to me, from beyond his chair a deep voice said, "Hey, Sookie." Our second visitor, Jake Purifoy. I made myself hold still when every impulse I had was telling me to get out of the office. I was being an idiot. If I hadn't run screaming at the sight of Andre, Jake shouldn't make me think of bolting. I forced myself to nod to the nice-looking young man who still looked alive. But

I knew my greeting didn't look natural. He filled me with a terrible blend of pity and fear.

Jake, born a Were, had been attacked by a vampire and bled to the point of death. In what had been perhaps a mistaken gesture of mercy, my cousin Hadley (another vampire) had discovered Jake's nearly lifeless body and brought Jake over. This might have been considered a good deed; but as it turned out, no one had really appreciated Hadley's kindness . . . not even Jake himself. No one had ever heard of a turned Were before: Weres disliked and distrusted vampires, and the feeling was heartily reciprocated. The going was very rough for Jake, who occupied a lonely no-man's-land. The queen had given him a place in her service, since no one else had stepped forward.

Jake, blind with bloodlust, had gone after me as his first vampire snack. I had a still-red scar on my arm as a result.

What a wonderful evening this was turning out to be.

"Miss Stackhouse," said Andre, rising from Eric's second guest chair. He bowed. This was a true tribute, and it lifted my spirits a bit.

"Mr. Andre," I said, bowing back. Andre swept his hand to indicate his politely vacated seat, and since that solved my placement problem, I accepted.

Clancy looked chagrined. He should have given me his chair, since he was the lower-ranked vampire. Andre's action had pointed that out as clearly as a blinking neon arrow. I tried hard not to smile.

"How is Her Majesty?" I asked, trying to be just as courteous as Andre had been. It would be stretching it to say I liked Sophie-Anne, but I sure respected her.

"That's part of the reason I am here tonight," he said. "Eric, can we get started now?" A gentle chiding for Eric's time-wasting tactics, I thought. Pam folded to the floor beside my chair, crouched on the balls of her feet.

"Yes, we're all here. Go ahead, Andre. You have the floor," Eric said with a little smile at his own modern terminology. He slumped back down into his chair, extending his long legs to rest his feet on the corner of his desk.

"Your queen is living in the Area Four sheriff's house in Baton Rouge," Andre said to the little assemblage. "Gervaise was very gracious in extending his hospitality."

Pam cocked an eyebrow at me. Gervaise would have lost his head if he *hadn't* extended his hospitality.

"But staying at Gervaise's place can only be a temporary solution," Andre continued. "We've been down to New Orleans several times since the disaster. Here's a report of our property's condition."

Though none of the vampires moved, I felt their attention had heightened.

"The queen's headquarters lost most of its roof, so there was extensive water damage on the second floor and in the attic area. Furthermore, a large piece of someone else's roof landed inside the building, causing a pileup of debris and some holes in walls—problems like that. While we're drying the inside, the roof is still covered with blue plastic. One reason I came up this way is to find a contractor who will start reroofing immediately. So far, I haven't had any luck, so if any of you have personal influence with some human who does this kind of work, I need your help. On the ground floor, there was a lot of cosmetic damage. Some water came in. We had some looters, too."

"Maybe the queen should remain in Baton Rouge," Clancy said maliciously. "I'm sure Gervaise would be overwhelmed with delight at the prospect of hosting her permanently."

So Clancy was a suicidal idiot.

"A delegation of New Orleans leaders came to visit our

queen in Baton Rouge to ask that she return to the city," Andre said, ignoring Clancy completely. "The human leaders think that if the vampires will return to New Orleans, tourism will pick up again." Andre fixed Eric with a cold gaze. "In the meantime, the queen has talked to the four other sheriffs about the financial aspect of restoring the New Orleans buildings."

Eric gave an almost imperceptible inclination of the head. Impossible to say what he felt about being taxed for the queen's repairs.

New Orleans had been the place to go for vampires and those who wanted to be around them ever since Anne Rice had been proven right about their existence. The city was like Disneyland for vamps. But since Katrina, all that had gone to hell, of course, along with so much else. Even Bon Temps was feeling the storm's effect, and had been ever since Katrina had hit land. Our little town was still crowded with people who had fled from the south.

"What about the queen's entertainment estate?" asked Eric. The queen had bought an old monastery at the edge of the Garden District for entertaining large numbers of people, both vamp and non-vamp. Though surrounded by a wall, the estate was not considered easily defensible (since it was a registered building, historic and unchangeable, the windows couldn't be blocked up), so the queen couldn't actually live there. I thought of it as her party barn.

"It didn't suffer much damage," Andre said. "There were looters there, too. Of course, they left a trace of their smell." Vampires were second only to Weres in their tracking abilities. "One of them shot the lion."

I felt sorry for that. I'd liked the lion, sort of.

"Do you need help with the apprehension?" Eric asked.

Andre arched an eyebrow.

"I only ask because your numbers are low," Eric said.

"No, already taken care of," Andre said, and smiled just a tad.

I tried not to think about that.

"Aside from the lion and the looting, how was the estate?" Eric said to get the discussion of the storm damage back on track.

"The queen can stay there while she views the other properties," Andre continued, "but at the most for a night or two only."

There were tiny nods all around.

"Our loss of personnel," Andre said, moving on in his agenda. All the vampires tensed a bit, even Jake, the newbie. "Our initial assessment was modest, as you know. We assumed some would come forward after the impact of the storm was absorbed. But only ten have surfaced: five here, three in Baton Rouge, two in Monroe. It seems that we have lost thirty of our number just in Louisiana. Mississippi has lost at least ten."

There were tiny sounds and movements all over the room as the Shreveport vampires reacted to the news. The concentration of vamps, both resident and visiting, had been high in New Orleans. If Katrina had visited Tampa with that much force, the number of dead and missing would have been much lower.

I raised my hand to speak. "What about Bubba?" I asked when Andre nodded at me. I hadn't seen or heard of Bubba since Katrina. You'd know Bubba if you saw him. Anyone on earth would know him; at least, anyone over a certain age. He hadn't quite died on that bathroom floor in Memphis. Not quite. But his brain had been affected before he was brought over, and he wasn't a very good vampire.

"Bubba's alive," said Andre. "He hid in a crypt and survived on small mammals. He isn't doing too well mentally, so the queen has sent him up to Tennessee to stay with the Nashville community for a while."

"Andre has brought me a list of those that are missing," Eric said. "I'll post it after the meeting."

I'd known a few of the queen's guards, too, and I would be glad to find out how they'd fared.

I had another question, so I waved my hand.

"Yes, Sookie?" Andre asked. His empty gaze fixed me in place, and I was sorry I'd asked to speak.

"You know what I wonder, y'all? I wonder if one of the kings or queens attending this summit, or whatever you all call it, has a—like a weather predictor, or something like that on staff."

Plenty of blank stares were aimed my way, though Andre was interested.

"Because, look, the summit, or conference, or whatever, was supposed to take place in late spring originally. But— delay, delay, delay, right? And then Katrina hit. If the sum-mit had started when it was supposed to, the queen could have gone in a powerful position. She would have had a big war chest and a full quiver of vamps, and maybe they wouldn't have been so anxious to prosecute her for the king's death. The queen would have gotten anything she asked for, probably. Instead, she's going in as"—I started to say "a beggar," but I considered Andre just in time— "much less powerful." I'd been afraid they'd laugh or maybe ridicule me, but the silence that followed was intensely thoughtful.

"That's one of the things you'll need to look for at the summit," Andre said. "Now that you've given me the idea, it seems oddly possible. Eric?"

"Yes, I think there is something in that," Eric said, star-ing at me. "Sookie is good at thinking outside the box."

Pam smiled up at me from beside my elbow.

"What about the suit filed by Jennifer Cater?" Clancy asked Andre. He'd been looking increasingly uncomfortable in the chair he'd thought he was so clever to snag.

You could have heard a pin drop. I didn't know what the hell the red-haired vampire was talking about, but I thought it would be better to find out from the conversation than to ask.

"It's still active," Andre said.

Pam whispered, "Jennifer Cater was in training to become Peter Threadgill's lieutenant. She was in Arkansas managing his affairs when the violence erupted."

I nodded to let Pam know I appreciated her filling me in. The Arkansas vampires, though they hadn't gone through a hurricane, had undergone quite a reduction in their own ranks, thanks to Louisiana's group.

Andre said, "The queen has responded to the suit by testifying that she had to kill Peter to save her own life. Of course, she offered reparation to the common fund."

"Why not to Arkansas?" I whispered to Pam.

"Because the queen maintains that since Peter is dead, Arkansas goes to her, according to the marriage contract," Pam murmured. "She can't make reparation to herself. If Jennifer Cater wins her suit, not only will the queen lose Arkansas, she'll have to pay Arkansas a fine. A huge one. And make other restitution."

Andre began to drift around the room soundlessly, the only indication that he was unhappy about the topic.

"Do we even have that much money after the disaster?" Clancy asked. It was an unwise question.

"The queen hopes the suit will be dismissed," Andre said, again ignoring Clancy. Andre's permanently teenage face was quite blank. "But apparently the court is prepared to hear a trial. Jennifer is charging that our queen lured Threadgill to New Orleans, away from his own territory, having planned all along to start the war and assassinate him." This time Andre's voice came from behind me.

"But that wasn't what happened at all," I said. And Sophie-Anne hadn't killed the king. I'd been present at his death. The vampire standing behind me right at this moment had killed Threadgill, and I'd thought at the time he was justified.

I felt Andre's cold fingers brush my neck as I sat there. How I knew the fingers were Andre's, I couldn't tell you; but the light touch, the second of contact, made me suddenly focus on an awful fact: I was the only witness to the death of the king, besides Andre and Sophie-Anne.

I'd never put it to myself in those terms, and for a moment, I swear, my heart stopped beating. At that skipped beat, I drew the gaze of at least half the vamps in the room. Eric's eyes widened as he looked at my face. And then my heart beat again, and the moment was over as if it never had been. But Eric's hand twitched on the desk, and I knew that he would not forget that second, and he would want to know what it meant.

"So you think the trial will be held?" Eric asked Andre.

"If the queen had been going to the summit as the ruler of New Orleans—New Orleans as it was—I believe the sitting court would have negotiated some kind of settlement between Jennifer and the queen. Maybe something involving Jennifer being raised to a position of power as the queen's deputy and getting a large bonus; something like that. But as things are now . . ." There was a long silence while we filled in the blanks. New Orleans wasn't as it had been, might never be so again. Sophie-Anne was a lame duck right now. "Now, because of Jennifer's persistence, I think the court will pursue it," Andre said, and then fell silent.

"We know there's no truth to the allegations," a clear,

cold voice said from the corner. I'd been doing a good job of ignoring the presence of my ex, Bill. But it didn't come naturally to me. "Eric was there. I was there. Sookie was there," the vampire (Nameless, I told myself ) continued.

That was true. Jennifer Cater's allegation, that the queen had lured her king to her party barn in order to kill him, was completely bogus. The bloodbath had been precipitated by the decapitation of one of the queen's men by one of Peter Threadgill's.

Eric smiled reminiscently. He'd enjoyed the battle. "I accounted for the one who started it," he said. "The king did his best to trap the queen in an indiscretion, but he didn't, thanks to our Sookie. When his plot didn't work, he resorted to a simple frontal attack." Eric added, "I haven't seen Jennifer in twenty years. She's risen fast. She must be ruthless."

Andre had stepped to my right and within my line of vision, which was a relief. He nodded. Again, all the vampires in the room made a little group movement, not quite in unison but eerily close. I had seldom felt so alien: the only warmblood in a room full of animated dead creatures.

"Yes," Andre said. "Ordinarily the queen would want a full contingent there to support her. But since we're forced to practice economy, the numbers going have been cut." Again, Andre came near enough to touch me, just a brush of my cheek.

The idea triggered a kind of mini-revelation: *This was how it felt to be a normal person.* I hadn't the slightest idea of the true intentions and plans of my companions. This was how real people lived every day of their lives. It was frightening but exciting; a lot like walking through a crowded room blindfolded. How did regular people stand the suspense of day-to-day living?

"The queen wants this woman close to her in meetings, since other humans will be there," Andre continued. He was speaking strictly to Eric. The rest of us might as well not have been in the room. "She wants to know their thoughts. Stan is bringing his telepath. Do you know the man?"

"I'm sitting right here," I muttered, not that anyone paid any attention but Pam, who gave me a sunny smile. Then, with all those cold eyes fixed on me, I realized that they were waiting for me, that Andre had been addressing me directly. I'd become so used to the vamps talking over and around me that I'd been taken by surprise. I mentally replayed Andre's remarks until I understood he was asking me a question.

"I've only met one other telepath in my life, and he was living in Dallas, so I'm supposing it's the same guy—Barry the Bellboy. He was working at the vamp hotel in Dallas when I picked up on his, ah, gift."

"What do you know about him?"

"He's younger than me, and he's weaker than me—or at least he was at the time. He'd never accepted what he was, the way that I had." I shrugged. That was the sum total of my knowledge.

"Sookie will be there," Eric told Andre. "She is the best at what she does."

That was flattering, though I faintly recalled Eric saying he'd encountered only one telepath previously. It was also infuriating, since he was implying to Andre that my excellence was to Eric's credit instead of my own.

Though I was looking forward to seeing something outside of my little town, I found myself wishing I could think of a way to back out of the trip to Rhodes. But months ago I'd agreed to attend this vampire summit as a paid employee of the queen's. And for the past month, I'd been working long hours at Merlotte's Bar to bank enough time so the other barmaids wouldn't mind covering for me for a week. My boss, Sam, had been helping me keep track of my overage with a little chart.

"Clancy will stay here to run the bar," Eric said.

"This human gets to go while I have to remain?" the red-haired manager said. He was really, really unhappy with Eric's decision. "I won't get to see any of the fun."

"That's right," Eric said pleasantly. If Clancy had thought of saying something else negative, he took one look at Eric's face and clamped down on it. "Felicia will stay to help you. Bill, you will stay."

"No," said that calm, cool voice from the corner. "The queen requires me. I worked hard on that database, and she's asked me to market it at the summit to help recoup her losses."

Eric looked like a statue for a minute, and then he moved, a little lift of his eyebrows. "Yes, I'd forgotten your computer skills," he said. He might have been saying, "Oh, I'd forgotten you can spell *cat*," for all the interest or respect he showed. "I suppose you need to be with us, then. Maxwell?"

"If it's your will, I will stay." Maxwell Lee wanted to make it clear that he knew a thing or two about being a good underling. He glanced around at the assemblage to underscore his point.

Eric nodded. I guessed that Maxwell would get a nice toy for Christmas, and Bill—whoops, Nameless—would get ashes and switches. "Then you'll remain here. And you, too, Thalia. But you must promise me that you will be good in the bar." Thalia's required tour of duty in the bar, which simply consisted of sitting around being mysterious and vampiric a couple of evenings a week, did not always go by without incident.

Thalia, perpetually sullen and broody, gave a curt nod. "I don't want to go, anyway," she muttered. Her round black eyes showed nothing but contempt for the world. She had seen too much in her very long life, and she hadn't enjoyed herself in a few centuries, was the way I read it. I tried to avoid Thalia as much as possible. I was surprised she'd even hang with the other vamps; she seemed like a rogue to me.

"She has no desire to lead," Pam breathed into my ear. "She only wants to be left in peace. She was thrown out of Illinois because she was too aggressive after the Great Revelation." The Great Revelation was the vampire term for the night that they'd gone on television all over the world to let us know that they actually existed and, furthermore, that they wanted to come out of the shadows and into the economic and social flow of human society.

"Eric lets Thalia do what she wants as long as she follows the rules and shows up on time for her hours at the bar," Pam continued in her tiny whisper. Eric was ruler of this little world, and no one was forgetting it. "She knows what the punishment will be if she steps out of line. Sometimes she seems to forget how little she would like that punishment. She should read Abby, get some ideas."

If you weren't getting any joy out of your life, you needed to . . . oh, do something for others, or take up a new hobby, or something like that, right? Wasn't that the usual advice? I flashed on Thalia volunteering to take the night shift at a hospice, and I shuddered. The idea of Thalia knitting, with two long, sharp needles, gave me another frisson of horror. To heck with the therapy.

"So, the only ones attending the summit are Andre, our queen, Sookie, myself, Bill, and Pam," Eric said. "Cataliades the lawyer and his niece as his runner. Oh, yes, Gervaise from Four and his human woman, a concession since Gervaise has been hosting the queen so generously. Rasul, as driver. And Sigebert, of course. That's our party. I know some of you are disappointed, and I can only hope that next year will be a better year for Louisiana. And for Arkansas, which we now consider part of our territory."

"I think that's all that we needed to talk about with all of you present," Andre said. The rest of the stuff he and Eric had to discuss would be done in private. Andre didn't touch me again, which was a good thing. Andre scared me down to my polished pink toenails. Of course, I should feel that way about everyone in the room. If I'd had good sense, I would move to Wyoming, which had the lowest vamp population (two; there'd been an article about them in *American Vampire*). Some days I was sorely tempted.

I whipped a little notepad out of my purse as Eric went over the date of our departure, the date of our return, the time our chartered Anubis Airline plane was arriving from Baton Rouge to pick up the Shreveport contingent, and a rundown of the clothes we would need. With some dismay, I realized I would have to go borrowing from my friends again. But Eric added, "Sookie, you wouldn't need these clothes if it wasn't for the trip. I've called your friend's store and you have credit there. Use it."

I could feel my cheeks redden. I felt like the poor cousin until he added, "The staff has an account at a couple of stores here in Shreveport, but that would be inconvenient for you." My shoulders relaxed, and I hoped he was telling the truth. Not one flicker of an eyelid told me any different.

"We may have suffered a disaster, but we won't go in looking poor," Eric said, being careful to give me only a fraction of his stare.

"Don't look poor," I made a note.

"Is everyone clear? Our goals for this conference are to support the queen as she tries to clear herself of these ridiculous charges, and to let everyone know that Louisiana is still a prestigious state. None of the Arkansas vampires who came to Louisiana with their king survived to tell the tale." Eric smiled, and it wasn't a pleasant smile.

I hadn't known that before this night.

Gosh, wasn't that convenient.

## 2

"Halleigh, since you're marrying a policeman, maybe you'll be able to tell me . . . just how big is a cop's nightstick?" Elmer Claire Vaudry asked.

I was sitting beside the bride-to-be, Halleigh Robinson, since I'd been given the all-important task of recording each gift and its giver as Halleigh opened all the white-and-silver wrapped boxes and flowered gift bags.

No one else seemed the least surprised that Mrs. Vaudry, a fortyish grade school teacher, was asking a bawdy question at this firmly middle-class, church lady event.

"Why, I wouldn't know, Elmer Claire," Halleigh said demurely, and there was a positive chorus of disbelieving sniggers.

"Well, now, what about the handcuffs?" Elmer Claire asked. "You ever use those handcuffs?"

A fluttering of southern lady voices rose in the living

room of Marcia Albanese, the hostess who'd agreed to let her house be the sacrificial lamb: the actual shower site. The other hostesses had had the lesser problems of bringing the food and the punch.

"You are just *something*, Elmer Claire," Marcia said from her spot by the refreshments table. But she was smiling. Elmer Claire had her role as the Daring One, and the others were glad to let her enjoy it.

Elmer Claire would never have been so vulgar if old Caroline Bellefleur had been present at the shower. Caroline was the social ruler of Bon Temps. Miss Caroline was about a million years old and had a back stiffer than any soldier. Only something extreme would keep Miss Caroline home from a social event of this importance to her family, and something extreme had happened. Caroline Bellefleur had suffered a heart attack, to the amazement of everyone in Bon Temps. To her family, the event had not been a tremendous surprise.

The grand Bellefleur double wedding (Halleigh and Andy's, Portia and her accountant's) had been set for the previous spring. It had been organized in a rush because of Caroline Bellefleur's sudden deterioration in health. As it happened, even before the hurried-up wedding could be held, Miss Caroline had been felled by the attack. Then she'd broken her hip.

With the agreement of Andy's sister, Portia, and her groom, Andy and Halleigh had postponed the wedding until late October. But I'd heard Miss Caroline was not recovering as her grandchildren had hoped, and it seemed unlikely she ever would be back to her former self.

Halleigh, her cheeks flushed, was struggling with the ribbon around a heavy box. I handed her a pair of scissors. There was some tradition about not cutting the ribbon, a tradition that somehow tied into predicting the number of children the bridal couple would produce, but I was willing to bet that Halleigh was ready for a quick solution. She snipped the ribbon on the side closest to her so no one would notice her callous disregard for custom. She flashed me a grateful look. We were all in our party best, of course, and Halleigh looked very cute and young in her light blue pantsuit with pink roses splashed on the jacket. She was wearing a corsage, of course, as the honoree.

I felt like I was observing an interesting tribe in another country, a tribe that just happened to speak my language. I'm a barmaid, several rungs below Halleigh on the social ladder, and I'm a telepath, though people tended to forget about it since it is hard to believe, my outside being so normal. But I'd been on the guest list, so I'd made a big effort to fit in sartorially. I was pretty sure I'd succeeded. I was wearing a sleeveless tailored white blouse, yellow slacks, and orange-and-yellow sandals, and my hair was down and flowing smoothly past my shoulder blades. Yellow earrings and a little gold chain tied me all together. It might be late September, but it was hot as the six shades of hell. All the ladies were still dressed in their hot-weather finery, though a few brave souls had donned fall colors.

I knew everyone at the shower, of course. Bon Temps is not a big place, and my family has lived in it for almost two hundred years. Knowing who people are is not the same as being comfortable with them, and I'd been glad to be given the job of recording the gifts. Marcia Albanese was sharper than I'd given her credit for being.

I was certainly learning a lot. Though I was trying hard not to listen in, and my little task helped in that, I was getting a lot of mental overflow.

Halleigh was in hog heaven. She was getting presents, she was the center of attention, and she was getting married to a great guy. I didn't think she really knew her groom that well, but I was certainly willing to believe that there were

wonderful sides to Andy Bellefleur that I'd never seen or
heard. Andy had more imagination than the average middle-
class man in Bon Temps; I knew that. And Andy had fears
and desires he'd buried deeply; I knew that, too.

Halleigh's mother had come from Mandeville to attend
the shower, of course, and she was doing her smiling best to
support her daughter. I thought I was the only one who
realized that Halleigh's mother hated crowds, even crowds
this small. Every moment she sat in Marcia's living room
was very uncomfortable for Linette Robinson. At this very
moment, while she was laughing at another little sally by
Elmer Claire, she was wishing passionately that she was
home with a good book and a glass of iced tea.

I started to whisper to her that it would all be over in (I
cast a glance at my watch) another hour, hour-fifteen at the
outside—but I remembered in time that I'd just freak her out
worse than she already was. I jotted down "Selah Pumphrey—
dish towels," and sat poised to record the next gift. Selah
Pumphrey had expected me to give her a Big Reaction when
she'd sailed in the door, since for weeks Selah had been dating
that vampire I'd abjured. Selah was always imagining I'd
jump on her and whack her in the head. Selah had a low opinion of me, not that she knew me at all. She certainly didn't
realize that the vampire in question was simply off my radar
now. I was guessing she'd been invited because she'd been
Andy and Halleigh's real estate agent when they'd bought
their little house.

"Tara Thornton—lace teddy," I wrote, and smiled at my
friend Tara, who'd selected Halleigh's gift from the stock at
her clothing store. Of course, Elmer Claire had a lot to say
about the teddy, and a good time was had by all—at least on
the face of it. Some of the assembled women weren't comfortable with Elmer Claire's broad humor, some of them were
thinking that Elmer Claire's husband had a lot to put up

with, and some of them just wished she would shut up. That group included me, and Linette Robinson, and Halleigh.

The principal at the school where Halleigh taught had given the couple some perfectly nice place mats, and the assistant principal had gotten napkins to match. I recorded those with a flourish and stuffed some of the torn wrapping paper into the garbage bag at my side.

"Thanks, Sookie," Halleigh said quietly, as Elmer Claire was telling another story about something that had happened at her wedding involving a chicken and the best man. "I really appreciate your help."

"No big," I said, surprised.

"Andy told me that he got you to hide the engagement ring when he proposed," she said, smiling. "And you've helped me out other times, too." Then Andy had told Halleigh *all* about me.

"Not a problem," I said, a little embarrassed.

She shot a sideways glance at Selah Pumphrey, seated two folding chairs away. "Are you still dating that beautiful man I saw at your place?" she asked rather more loudly. "The handsome one with the gorgeous black hair?"

Halleigh had seen Claude when he dropped me off at my temporary lodging in town; Claude, the brother of Claudine, my fairy godmother. Yes, really. Claude *was* gorgeous, and he could be absolutely charming (to women) for about sixty seconds. He'd made the effort when he'd met Halleigh, and I could only be thankful, since Selah's ears had pricked up just like a fox's.

"I saw him maybe three weeks ago," I said truthfully. "But we're not dating now." We never had been, actually, because Claude's idea of a good date was someone with a little beard stubble and equipment I'd never possess. But not everyone had to know that, right? "I'm seeing someone else," I added modestly.

"Oh?" Halleigh was all innocent interest. I was getting fonder of the girl (all of four years younger than me) by the second.

"Yes," I said. "A consultant from Memphis."

"You'll have to bring him to the wedding," Halleigh said. "Wouldn't that be great, Portia?"

This was another kettle of fish entirely. Portia Bellefleur, Andy's sister and the other bride-to-be in the double Bellefleur wedding, had asked me to be there to serve alcohol, along with my boss, Sam Merlotte. Now Portia was in a bind. She would never have invited me other than as a worker. (I sure hadn't been invited to any showers for *Portia*.) Now I beamed at Portia in an innocent, I'm-so-happy way.

"Of course," Portia said smoothly. She had not trained in the law for nothing. "We'd be delighted if you'd bring your boyfriend."

I had a happy mental picture of Quinn transforming into a tiger at the reception. I smiled at Portia all the more brightly. "I'll see if he can come with me," I said.

"Now, y'all," Elmer Claire said, "a little bird told me to write down what Halleigh said when she unwrapped her gifts, cause you know, that's what you'll say on your wedding night!" She waved a legal pad.

Everyone fell silent with happy anticipation. Or dread.

"This is the first thing Halleigh said: 'Oh, what pretty wrapping!'" A chorus of dutiful laughter. "Then she said, let's see: 'That's going to fit; I can hardly wait!'" Snickers. "Then she said, 'Oh, I needed one of those!'" Hilarity.

After that, it was time for cake and punch and peanuts and the cheese ball. We'd all resumed our seats, carefully balancing plates and cups, when my grandmother's friend Maxine opened a new topic of discussion.

"How's your new friend, Sookie?" Maxine Fortenberry asked. Maxine was clear across the room, but projecting was no problem for Maxine. In her late fifties, Maxine was stout and hearty, and she'd been a second mother to my brother, Jason, who was best friends with her son Hoyt. "The gal from New Orleans?"

"Amelia's doing well." I beamed nervously, all too aware I was the new center of attention.

"Is it true that she lost her house in the flooding?"

"It did sustain quite a bit of damage, her tenant said. So Amelia's waiting to hear from the insurance company, and then she'll decide what to do."

"Lucky she was here with you when the hurricane hit," Maxine said.

I guess poor Amelia had heard that a thousand times since August. I think Amelia was pretty tired of trying to feel lucky. "Oh, yes," I said agreeably. "She sure was."

Amelia Broadway's arrival in Bon Temps had been the subject of lots of gossip. That's only natural.

"So for right now, Amelia'll just stay on with you?" Halleigh asked helpfully.

"For a while," I said, smiling.

"That's just real sweet of you," Marcia Albanese said approvingly.

"Oh, Marcia, you know I got that whole upstairs that I never use. She's actually improved it for me; she got a window air conditioner put in up there, so it's much nicer. It doesn't put me out one bit."

"Still, lots of people wouldn't want someone living in their home that long. I guess I should take in one of the poor souls staying at the Days Inn, but I just can't bring myself to let someone else in my house."

"I like the company," I said, which was mostly true.

"Has she been back to check on her house?"

"Ah, only once." Amelia had to get in and out of New Orleans real quick, so none of her witch friends could track her down. Amelia was in a bit of hot water with the witch community of the Big Easy.

"She sure loves that cat of hers," Elmer Claire said. "She had that big old tom at the vet the other day when I took Powderpuff in." Powderpuff, Elmer Claire's white Persian, was about a million years old. "I asked her why she didn't get that cat neutered, and she just covered that cat's ears like he could hear me, and she asked me not to talk about it in front of Bob, just like he was a person."

"She's real fond of Bob," I said, not quite knowing whether I wanted to gag or laugh at the idea of the vet neutering Bob.

"You know that Amelia how?" Maxine asked.

"You remember my cousin Hadley?"

Everyone in the room nodded, except newcomer Halleigh and her mother.

"Well, when Hadley lived in New Orleans, she rented the upstairs of Amelia's house from her," I said. "And when Hadley passed away"—here there were solemn nods all around—"I went down to New Orleans to clean out Hadley's things. And I met Amelia, and we became friends, and she just decided she'd visit Bon Temps for a while."

All the ladies looked at me with the most expectant expressions, as if they couldn't wait to hear what would come next. Because there had to be more explanation, right?

There was indeed a lot more to the story, but I didn't think they were ready to hear that Amelia, after a night of great loving, had accidentally turned Bob into a cat during a sexual experiment. I'd never asked Amelia to describe the circumstances, because I was pretty sure I didn't want to get a visual on that scene. But they were all waiting for a little more explanation. Any explanation.

"Amelia had a bad breakup with her boyfriend," I said, keeping my tone low and confidential.

All the other ladies' faces were both titillated and sympathetic.

"He was a Mormon missionary," I told them. Well, Bob had *looked* like a Mormon missionary, in dark slacks and a white short-sleeved shirt, and he'd even arrived at Amelia's on a bicycle. He was actually a witch, like Amelia. "But he knocked on Amelia's door and they just fell in love." Actually, into bed. But you know—same thing, for the purposes of this story.

"Did his parents know?"

"Did his church find out?"

"Don't they get to have more than one wife?"

The questions crowded in too thick for me to deal with, and I waited until the attendees had subsided into their waiting mode again. I was not used to making up fabrications, and I was running out of truth to base the rest of the story on. "I really don't know much about the Mormon church," I told the last questioner, and that was the absolute truth. "Though I think modern Mormons aren't supposed to have more than one wife. But what happened to them was his relatives found out and got real mad because they didn't think Amelia was good enough for the man, and they snatched him away and made him go home. So she wanted to leave New Orleans to get a change of scene, forget about the past, you know."

They all nodded, absolutely fascinated by Amelia's big drama. I felt a twinge of guilt. For a minute or two, everyone gave her opinion about the sad story. Maxine Fortenberry summed it all up.

"Poor girl," said Maxine. "He should've stood up to them."

I passed Halleigh another present to open. "Halleigh, you know that won't happen to you," I said, diverting the conversation back to its proper topic. "Andy is just nuts about you; anyone can tell."

Halleigh blushed, and her mother said, "We all love

Andy," and the shower was back on track. The rest of the conversation veered from the wedding to the meals each church was taking in turn to cook for the evacuees. The Catholics had tomorrow night, and Maxine sounded a little relieved when she said the number to cook for had dropped to twenty-five.

As I drove home afterward, I was feeling a little frazzled from the unaccustomed sociability. I also faced the prospect of telling Amelia about her new invented background. But when I saw the pickup standing in my yard, all such thoughts flew out of my head.

Quinn was here—Quinn the weretiger, who made his living arranging and producing special events for the world of the weird—Quinn, my honey. I pulled around back and practically leaped out of my car after an anxious glance in my rearview mirror to make sure my makeup was still good.

Quinn charged out of the back door as I hurried up to the steps, and I gave a little jump. He caught me and whirled me around, and when he put me down he was kissing me, his big hands framing my face.

"You look so beautiful," he said, coming up for air. A moment later, he gasped. "You smell so good." And then he was back into the kissing.

We finally broke it off.

"Oh, I haven't seen you in so long!" I said. "I'm so glad you're here!" I hadn't seen Quinn in weeks, and then I'd been with him only briefly as he'd passed through Shreveport on his way to Florida with a load of props for the coming-of-age ceremony for a packleader's daughter.

"I've missed you, babe," he said, his big white teeth gleaming. His shaved head shone in the sunlight, which was coming at quite an angle this late in the afternoon. "I had a little time to catch up with your roomie while you were at the shower. How'd it go?"

"Like showers usually do. Lots of presents and lots of gossip. This was the second shower I've been to for this gal, plus I gave them a plate in their everyday china for a wedding present, so I've done them proud."

"You can go to more than one shower for the same person?"

"In a small town like this, yeah. And she went home to have a shower and a dinner party in Mandeville during the summer. So I guess Andy and Halleigh are set up pretty well."

"I thought they were supposed to get married last April."

I explained about Caroline Bellefleur's heart attack. "By the time she was getting over that and they were talking wedding dates again, Miss Caroline fell and broke her hip."

"Wow."

"And the doctors didn't think she'd get over *that*, but she survived that, too. So I think Halleigh and Andy and Portia and Glen are actually going to have the most-anticipated wedding of the Bon Temps year sometime next month. And you're invited."

"I am?"

We were heading inside by this time, since I wanted to take off my shoes and I also wanted to scout out what my housemate was up to. I was trying to think of some long errand I could send her off on, since I so seldom got to see Quinn, who was kind of my boyfriend, if at my age (twenty-seven), I could use that term.

That is, I thought he would be my boyfriend if he could ever slow down enough to latch on to me.

But Quinn's job, working for a subsidiary of Extreme(ly Elegant) Events, covered a lot of territory, literally and figuratively. Since we'd parted in New Orleans after our rescue from Were abductors, I'd seen Quinn three times. He'd been in Shreveport one weekend as he passed through on his way to somewhere else, and we'd gone out to dinner at

Ralph and Kacoo's, a popular restaurant. It had been a good evening, but he'd taken me home at the end of it since he had to start driving at seven the next morning. The second time, he'd dropped into Merlotte's while I was at work, and since it was a slow night, I'd taken an hour off to sit and talk to him, and we'd held hands a little. The third time, I'd kept him company while he was loading up his trailer at a U-RENT-SPACE storage shed. It had been in the middle of summer, and we'd both been sweating up a storm. Streaming sweat, lots of dust, storage sheds, the occasional vehicle trolling through the lot . . . not a romantic ambience.

And even though Amelia was now obligingly coming down the stairs with her purse over her shoulder and clearly planning to head into town to give us some privacy, it hardly seemed promising that we'd have to grab an instant to consummate a relationship that had had so little face time.

Amelia said, "Good-bye!" She had a big smile all over her face, and since Amelia has the whitest teeth in the world, she looked like the Cheshire cat. Amelia's short hair was sticking out all over (she says no one in Bon Temps can cut it right) and her tan face was bare of makeup. Amelia looks like a young suburban mom who has an infant seat strapped into the back of her minivan; the kind of mom who takes time off to run and swim and play tennis. In point of fact, Amelia did run three times a week and practiced tai chi out in my back-yard, but she hated getting in the water and she thought tennis was for (and I quote) "mouth-breathing idiots." I'd always admired tennis players myself, but when Amelia had a point of view, she stuck to it.

"Going to the mall in Monroe," she said. "Shopping to do!" And with an I'm-being-a-good-roommate kind of wave, she hopped into her Mustang and vanished . . .

. . . leaving Quinn and me to stare at each other.

"That Amelia!" I said lamely.

"She's . . . one of a kind," Quinn said, just as uneasy as I was.

"The thing is—" I began, just as Quinn said, "Listen, I think we ought—" and we both floundered to a halt. He made a gesture that indicated I should go first.

"How long are you here for?" I asked.

"I have to leave tomorrow," he said. "I could stay in Monroe or Shreveport."

We did some more staring. I can't read Were minds, not like regular humans. I can get the intent, though, and the intent was . . . intent.

"So," he said. He went down on one knee. "Please," he said.

I had to smile, but then I looked away. "The only thing is," I began again. This conversation would come much more easily to Amelia, who was frank to a very extreme point. "You know that we have, uh, a lot of . . ." I gestured back and forth with my hand.

"Chemistry," he said.

"Right," I said. "But if we never get to see any more of each other than we have the past three months, I'm not really sure I want to make that next step." I hated to say it, but I had to. I didn't need to cause myself pain. "I have big lust," I said. "Big, big lust. But I'm not a one-night-stand kind of woman."

"When the summit is over, I'm taking a long time off," Quinn said, and I could tell he was absolutely sincere. "A month. I came here to ask you if I could spend it with you."

"Really?" I couldn't help sounding incredulous. "Really?"

He smiled up at me. Quinn has a smooth, shaved head, an olive complexion, a bold nose, and a smile that makes these little dimples in the corners of his mouth. His eyes are purple, like a spring pansy. He is as big as a pro wrestler, and just as scary. He held up a huge hand, as if he were swearing an oath. "On a stack of Bibles," he said.

"Yes," I said after a moment's scan of my inner qualms to make sure they were minor. And also, I may not have a built-in truth detector, but I could have told if he'd been thinking, *I'm saying that to get in her pants.* Shifters are very hard to read, their brains are all snarly and semiopaque, but I would've picked up on that. "Then . . . yes."

"Oh, boy." Quinn took a deep breath and his grin lit up the room. But in the next moment, his eyes got that focused look men get when they're thinking about sex very specifically. And then, lickety-split, Quinn was on his feet and his arms were around me as tightly as ropes tying us together.

His mouth found mine. We picked up where we'd left off with the kissing. His mouth was a very clever one and his tongue was very warm. His hands began examining my topography. Down the line of my back to the curve of my hips, back up to my shoulders to cup my face for a moment, down to brush my neck teasingly with the lightest of fingertips. Then those fingers found my breasts, and after a second he tugged my top out of my pants and began exploring territory he'd only visited briefly before. He liked what he found, if "Mmmmm" was a statement of delight. It spoke volumes to me.

"I want to see you," he said. "I want to see all of you."

I had never made love in the daytime before. It seemed very (excitingly) sinful to be struggling with buttons before the sun had even set, and I was so grateful I'd worn an extra-nice white lace bra and little bitty panties. When I dress up, I like to dress up all the way down to the skin.

"Oh," he said when he saw the bra, which contrasted nicely with my deep summer tan. "Oh, *boy.*" It wasn't the words; it was the expression of deep admiration. My shoes were already off. Luckily that morning I'd dispensed with handy-but-totally-unsexy knee-high hose in favor of bare legs. Quinn spent some quality time nuzzling my neck and kissing his way down to the bra while I was struggling to undo his belt, though since he would bend while I was trying to deal with the stiff buckle, that wasn't working out fast enough.

"Take off your shirt," I said, and my voice came out as hoarse as his. "I don't have a shirt, you shouldn't have a shirt."

"Fine," he said, and presto, the shirt was off. You'd expect Quinn to be hairy, but he isn't. What he is, is muscular to the $n$th degree, and right at the moment his olive skin was summer-tan. His nipples were surprisingly dark and (not so surprisingly) very hard. Oh, boy—right at my eye level. He began dealing with his own damn belt while I began to explore one hard nub with my mouth, the other with my hand. Quinn's whole body jerked, and he stopped what he was doing. He ran his fingers into my hair to hold my head against him, and he sighed, though it came out more like a growl, vibrating through his body. My free hand yanked at his pants, and he resumed working on the belt but in an unfocused and distracted way.

"Let's move into the bedroom," I said, but it didn't come out like a calm and collected suggestion, more a ragged demand.

He swooped me up, and I latched my arms around his neck and kissed him on his beautiful mouth again.

"No fair," he muttered. "My hands are full."

"Bed," I said, and he deposited me on the bed and then simply fell on top of me.

"Clothes," I reminded him, but he had a mouthful of white lace and breast, and he didn't reply. "Oh," I said. I may have said "Oh" a few more times; and "Yes," too. A sudden thought yanked me right out of the flow of the moment.

"Quinn, do you have, you know . . ." I had never needed to have such items before, since vamps can't get a girl pregnant or give her a disease.

"Why do you think I still have my pants on?" he said, pulling a little package out of his back pocket. His smile this time was far more feral.

"Good," I said from my heart. I would have thrown myself from a window if we'd had to quit. "And you might take the pants off now."

I'd seen Quinn naked before but under decidedly stressful circumstances—in the middle of a swamp, in the rain, while we were being pursued by werewolves. Quinn stood by the bed and took off his shoes and socks and then his pants, moving slowly enough to let me watch. He stepped out of his pants, revealing boxer briefs that were suffering their own kind of stress. In one quick movement he eased them off, too. He had a tight, high butt, and the line from his hip to his thigh was just mouthwatering. He had fine, thin white scars striping him at random, but they seemed like such a natural part of him that they didn't detract from his powerful body. I was kneeling on the bed while I admired him, and he said, "Now you."

I unhooked my bra and slid it off my arms, and he said, "Oh, God. I am the luckiest man alive." After a pause, he said, "The rest."

I stood by the bed and eased the little white lacey things off.

"This is like standing in front of a buffet," he said. "I don't know where to begin."

I touched my breasts. "First course," I suggested.

I discovered that Quinn's tongue was just a bit raspier than a regular man's. I was gasping and making incoherent noises when he moved from my right breast to my left as he tried to decide which one he liked best. He couldn't make up his mind immediately, which was fine with me. By the time he settled on the right breast, I was pushing against him and making sounds that couldn't be mistaken for anything but desperate.

"I think I'll skip the second course and go right to dessert," he whispered, his voice dark and ragged. "Are you ready, babe? You sound ready. You feel ready."

"I am so ready," I said, reaching down between us to wrap my hand around his length. He quivered all over when I touched him. He rolled on the condom.

"Now," he growled. "Now!" I guided him to my entrance, thrust my hips up to meet him. "I dreamed of this," he said, and shoved inside me up to the hilt. That was the last thing either of us was able to say.

Quinn's appetite was as outstanding as his equipment.

He enjoyed dessert so much, he came back for seconds.

W E WERE IN THE KITCHEN WHEN AMELIA RETURNED.
I'd fed Bob, her cat, since she'd been so tactful earlier and
deserved some reward. Tact does not come naturally to
Amelia.

Bob ignored his kibble in favor of watching Quinn fry
bacon, and I was slicing tomatoes. I'd gotten out the cheese
and the mayonnaise and the mustard and the pickles, anything I could imagine a man might want on a bacon sandwich. I'd pulled on some old shorts and a T-shirt, while
Quinn had gotten his bag from his truck and put on his
workout clothes—a tank top and worn shorts made from
sweat material.

Amelia gave Quinn a top-to-bottom scan when he turned
back to the stove, and then she looked at me, grinning
broadly. "You guys have a good reunion?" she said, tossing
her shopping bags on the kitchen table.

"Up to your room, please," I said, because otherwise Amelia would want us to admire every single thing she'd bought. With a pout, Amelia snagged the bags and carried them upstairs, returning in a minute to ask Quinn if there was enough bacon for her.

"Sure," Quinn said obligingly, taking out some strips and putting a few more in the pan.

I liked a man who could cook. While I set out plates and silverware, I was pleasantly aware of the tenderness I felt south of my belly button and of my overwhelmingly relaxed mood. I got three glasses out of the cabinet but kind of forgot what I was doing on my way to the refrigerator, since Quinn stepped away from the stove to give me a quick kiss. His lips were so warm and firm, they reminded me of something else that had been warm and firm. I flashed on my astonished moment of revelation when Quinn had slid into me for the first time. Considering that my only previous sexual encounters had been with vampires, who are definitely on the cool side, you can imagine what a startling experience a breathing lover with a heartbeat and a warm penis would be. In fact, shape-shifters tended to run a bit warmer than regular humans. Even through the condom, I'd been able to feel the heat.

"What?" Quinn asked. "Why the look?" He was smiling quizzically.

I smiled. "I was just thinking of your temperature," I said.

"Hey, you knew I was hot," he said with a grin. "What about the thought reading?" he said more seriously. "How did that work out?"

I thought it was great that he'd even wondered. "I can't call your thoughts any trouble," I said, unable to suppress a huge grin. "It might be a stretch to count 'yesyesyesyespleasepleaseplease' as a thought."

"Not a problem then," he said, totally unembarrassed.

"Not a problem. As long as you're wrapped in the moment and you're happy, I'm gonna be happy."

"Well, hot damn." Quinn turned back to the stove. "That's just *great*."

I thought it was, too.

Just great.

Amelia ate her sandwich with a good appetite and then picked Bob up to feed him little bits of bacon she'd saved. The big black-and-white cat purred up a storm.

"So," said Quinn, after his first sandwich had disappeared with amazing quickness, "this is the guy you changed by accident?"

"Yeah," said Amelia, scratching Bob's ears. "This is the guy." Amelia was sitting cross-legged in the kitchen chair, which is something I simply couldn't do, and she was focused on the cat. "The little fella," she crooned. "My fuzzy wuzzy honey, isn't he? Isn't he?" Quinn looked mildly disgusted, but I was just as guilty of talking baby talk to Bob when I was alone with him. Bob the witch had been a skinny, weird guy with a kind of geeky charm. Amelia had told me Bob had been a hairdresser; I'd decided if that were true, he'd fixed hair at a funeral parlor. Black pants, white shirt, bicycle? Have you ever known a hairdresser who presented himself that way?

"So," Quinn said. "What are you doing about it?"

"I'm studying," Amelia said. "I'm trying to figure out what I did wrong, so I can make it right. It would be easier if I could . . ." Her voice trailed off in a guilty kind of way.

"If you could talk to your mentor?" I said helpfully.

She scowled at me. "Yeah," she said. "If I could talk to my mentor."

"Why don't you?" Quinn asked.

"One, I wasn't supposed to use transformational magic. That's pretty much a no-no. Two, I've looked for her online since Katrina, on every message board witches use, and I can't find any news of her. She might have gone to a shelter somewhere, she might be staying with her kids or some friend, or she might have died in the flooding."

"I believe you had your main income from your rental property. What are your plans now? What's the state of your property?" Quinn asked, carrying his plate and mine to the sink. He wasn't being bashful with the personal questions to-night. I waited with interest to hear Amelia's answers. I'd al-ways wanted to know a lot of things about Amelia that were just plain rude to ask: like, What was she living on now? Though she had worked part-time for my friend Tara Thorn-ton at Tara's Togs while Tara's help was sick, Amelia's outgo far exceeded her visible income. That meant she had good credit, some savings, or another source of income besides the tarot readings she'd done in a shop off Jackson Square and her rent money, which now wasn't coming in. Her mom had left her some money. It must have been a chunk.

"Well, I've been back into New Orleans once since the storm," Amelia said. "You've met Everett, my tenant?"

Quinn nodded.

"When he could get to a phone, he reported some dam-age to the bottom floor, where I live. There were trees and branches down, and of course there wasn't electricity or wa-ter for a couple of weeks. But the neighborhood didn't suffer as badly as some, thank God, and when the electricity was back on, I snuck down there." Amelia took a deep breath. I could hear right from her brain that she was scared to ven-ture into the territory she was about to reveal to us. "I, um, went to talk to my dad about fixing the roof. Right then, we had a blue roof like half the people around us." The blue plastic that covered damaged roofs was the new norm in New Orleans.

This was the first time Amelia had mentioned her family

to me, in more than a very general way. I'd learned more from her thoughts than I'd learned from her conversation, and I had to be careful not to mix the two sources when we talked. I could see her dad's presence in her head, love and resentment mixing in her thoughts to form a confused mishmash.

"Your dad is going to repair your house?" Quinn asked casually. He was excavating in my Tupperware box in which I stored any cookies that happened to cross my threshold— not a frequent occurrence, since I have a tendency to put on weight when sweets are in the house. Amelia had no such problem, and she'd stocked the box with a couple of kinds of Keebler cookies and told Quinn he was welcome to help himself.

Amelia nodded, much more fascinated by Bob's fur than she had been a moment before. "Yeah, he's got a crew on it," she said.

This was news to me.

"So who is your dad?" Quinn was keeping up the directness. So far it had worked for him.

Amelia squirmed on the kitchen chair, making Bob raise his head in protest.

"Copley Carmichael," she muttered.

We were both silent with shock. After a minute, she looked up at us. "What?" she said. "Okay, so he's famous. Okay, so he's rich. So?"

"Different last name?" I said.

"I use my mom's. I got tired of people being weird around me," Amelia said pointedly.

Quinn and I exchanged glances. Copley Carmichael was a big name in the state of Louisiana. He had fingers in all kinds of financial pies, and all those fingers were pretty dirty. But he was an old-fashioned human wheeler-dealer: no whiff of the supernatural around Copley Carmichael.

"Does he know you're a witch?" I asked.

"He doesn't believe it for a minute," Amelia said, sounding frustrated and forlorn. "He thinks I'm a deluded little wannabe, that I'm hanging with weird little people and doing weird little jobs to stick my tongue out at him. He wouldn't believe in vampires if he hadn't seen them over and over."

"What about your mom?" Quinn asked. I got myself a refill on my tea. I knew the answer to this one.

"Dead," Amelia told him. "Three years ago. That's when I moved out of my dad's house and into the bottom floor of the house on Chloe. He'd given it to me when I graduated from high school so I'd have my own income, but he made me manage it myself so I'd have the experience."

That seemed like a pretty good deal to me. Hesitantly I said, "Wasn't that the right thing to do? Get you to learn by doing?"

"Well, yeah," she admitted. "But when I moved out, he wanted to give me an allowance . . . at my age! I knew I had to make it on my own. Between the rent, and the money I picked up doing fortunes, and magic jobs I got on my own, I've been making a living." She threw up her head proudly.

Amelia didn't seem to realize the rent was income from a gift of her father's, not something she'd actually earned. Amelia was truly pleased as punch with her own self-sufficiency. My new friend, whom I'd acquired almost by accident, was a bundle of contradictions. Since she was a very clear broadcaster, I got her thoughts loud and clear. When I was alone with Amelia, I had to shield like crazy. I'd relaxed with Quinn around, but I shouldn't have. I was getting a whole mess from Amelia's head.

"So, could your dad help you find your mentor?" Quinn asked.

Amelia looked blank for a moment, as if she was considering that. "I don't see how," she said slowly. "He's a powerful guy; you know that. But he's having as much trouble in New Orleans since Katrina as the rest of the people are."

Except he had a lot more money and he could go somewhere else, returning when he pleased, which most of the inhabitants of the city could not. I closed my mouth to keep this observation to myself. Time to change the topic.

"Amelia," I said. "How well did you know Bob, anyway? Who's looking for him?"

She looked a little frightened, not Amelia's normal thing. "I'm wondering, too," she said. "I just knew Bob to speak to, before that night. But I do know that Bob had—has—great friends in the magic community. I don't think any of them know we got together. That night, the night before the queen's ball when the shit hit the fan between the Arkansas vamps and our vamps, Bob and I went back to my place after we'd left Terry and Patsy at the pizza place. Bob called in sick to work the next day, since we had celebrated so hard, and then he spent that day with me."

"So it's possible Bob's family has been looking for him for months? Wondering if he's dead or alive?"

"Hey, chill. I'm not that awful. Bob was raised by his aunt, but they don't get along at all. He hasn't had much contact with her for years. I'm sure he does have friends that are worrying, and I'm really, really sorry about that. But even if they knew what had happened, that wouldn't help Bob, right? And since Katrina, everyone in New Orleans has a lot to worry about."

At this interesting point in the discussion, the phone rang. I was closest, so I picked it up. My brother's voice was almost electric with excitement.

"Sookie, you need to come out to Hotshot in about an hour."

"Why?"

"Me and Crystal are getting married. Surprise!"

While this was not a total shock (Jason had been "dating" Crystal Norris for several months), the suddenness of the ceremony made me anxious.

"Is Crystal pregnant again?" I asked suspiciously. She'd miscarried a baby of Jason's not long ago.

"Yes!" Jason said, like that was the best news he could possibly impart. "And this time, we'll be married when the baby comes."

Jason was ignoring reality, as he was increasingly willing to do. The reality was that Crystal had been pregnant at least once before she was pregnant by Jason, and she had lost that child, too. The community at Hotshot was a victim of its own inbreeding.

"Okay, I'll be there," I said. "Can Amelia and Quinn come, too?"

"Sure," Jason said. "Crystal and me'll be proud to have them."

"Is there anything I can bring?"

"No, Calvin and them are getting ready to cook. It's all going to be outside. We got lights strung up. I think they'll have a big pot of jambalaya, some dirty rice, and coleslaw, and me and my buddies are bringing the alcohol. Just come looking pretty! See you at Hotshot in an hour. Don't be late."

I hung up and sat there for a minute, my hand still clutching the cordless phone. That was just like Jason: come in an hour to a ceremony planned at the last minute for the worst possible reason, and don't be late! At least he hadn't asked me to bring a cake.

"Sookie, you okay?" Quinn asked.

"My brother Jason's getting married tonight," I said, trying to keep my voice even. "We're invited to the wedding, and we need to be there in an hour." I'd always figured Jason wouldn't marry a woman I truly adored; he'd always shown a partiality to tough sluts. And that was Crystal, sure enough.

Crystal was also a werepanther, a member of a community that guarded its own secrets jealously. In fact, my brother was now a werepanther himself because he'd been bitten over and over by a rival for Crystal's attentions.

Jason was older than I, and God knows, he'd had his share of women. I had to assume he knew when one suited him.

I emerged from my thoughts to find that Amelia was looking startled and excited. She loved to go out and party, and the chances for that around Bon Temps were limited. Quinn, who'd met Jason when he was visiting me, looked at me with a skeptical raised eyebrow.

"Yeah, I know," I said. "It's crazy and dumb. But Crystal's pregnant again, and there's no stopping him. Do you two want to come along with me? You don't have to. I'm afraid I've got to get ready right now."

Amelia said, "Oh, goody, I can wear my new outfit," and sped upstairs to tear the tags off.

Quinn said, "Babe, do you want me to come?"

"Yes, please," I said. He came over to me and wrapped his heavy arms around me. I felt comforted, even though I knew Quinn was thinking what a fool Jason was.

I pretty much agreed with him.

# 4 ~

It was still warm at night, but not oppressively so, not this late in September. I wore a sleeveless white dress with red flowers on it, one I'd worn before when I had a date with Bill (whom I *wouldn't* think about). Out of sheer vanity, I put on my high-heeled red sandals, though they were hardly practical footwear for a wedding on a roughly paved road. I put on some makeup while Quinn was showering, and I wasn't displeased with my reflection. There's nothing like great sex to give you a glow. I came out of my room and glanced at the clock. We needed to leave pretty quickly.

Amelia was wearing a short-sleeved dress, beige with a tiny navy pattern. Amelia loved to buy clothes and considered herself a snappy dresser, but her taste was strictly suburban young matron. She wore little navy sandals with flowers on the straps, much more appropriate than my heels.

Just when I was beginning to worry, Quinn came out of my room wearing a brown silk dress shirt and khakis.

"What about a tie?" he asked. "I've got some in my bag."

I thought of the rural setting and vast lack of sophistication in the little community of Hotshot. "I don't think a tie will be necessary," I said, and Quinn looked relieved.

We piled into my car and drove west and then south. On the drive, I had a chance to explain to my out-of-town guests about the isolated band of werepanthers and their small cluster of houses grouped together in rural Renard Parish. I was driving, since that was just simplest. Once out of sight of the old railroad tracks, the country became increasingly unpopulated until for two or three miles we saw no lights of any kind. Then we saw cars and lights at a crossroads ahead. We were there.

Hotshot was out in the middle of nowhere, set in a long depression in the middle of gently rolling land, swells that were too ill-defined to be called hills. Formed around an ancient crossroads, the lonely community had a powerful vibration of magic. I could tell that Amelia was feeling that power. Her face became sharper and wiser as we got closer. Even Quinn inhaled deeply. As for me, I could detect the presence of magic, but it didn't affect non-supernatural me.

I pulled over to the side of the road behind Hoyt Fortenberry's truck. Hoyt was Jason's best friend and lifelong shadow. I spied him right ahead of us, trudging down the road to a well-lit area. I'd handed Amelia and Quinn a flashlight, and I kept one aimed at my feet.

"Hoyt," I called. I hurried to catch up with him, at least as much as was practical in the red heels. "Hey, are you okay?" I asked when I saw his downcast face. Hoyt was not a very good-looking guy, or very bright, but he was steady and tended to see past the moment to its consequences, something my brother had never mastered.

"Sook," Hoyt said. "I can't believe he's getting hitched. I guess I thought me and Jason would be bachelors forever." He attempted to smile.

I gave him a pat on the shoulder. Life would've been neat 'n' tidy if I could have fallen in love with Hoyt, thus attaching him to my brother forever, but Hoyt and I had never had the slightest interest in each other.

Hoyt's mind was radiating a dull misery. He was certain that his life was changing forever this night. He expected Jason to mend his ways completely, to stay in with his wife like a husband should, and to forsake all others.

I sure hoped Hoyt's expectations were right on the money.

On the edges of the crowd, Hoyt met up with Catfish Hennessy, and they began making loud jokes about Jason's breaking down and marrying.

I hoped the male bonding would help Hoyt get through the ceremony. I didn't know if Crystal truly loved my brother—but Hoyt did.

Quinn took my hand, and with Amelia in our wake we forged through the little crowd until we reached the center.

Jason was wearing a new suit, and the blue of it was only a bit darker than the blue of his eyes. He looked great, and he was smiling to beat the band. Crystal was wearing a leopard-print dress cut as low in the front as you could get and still term the garment a dress. I didn't know if the leopard motif was an ironic statement on her part or a simple expression of her fashion sense. I suspected the latter.

The happy couple was standing in the middle of an empty space, accompanied by Calvin Norris, leader of the Hotshot community. The crowd kept respectfully back, forming an uneven circle.

Calvin, who happened to be Crystal's uncle, was holding Crystal's arm. He smiled at me. Calvin had trimmed his beard and dug out a suit for the occasion, but he and Jason were the only men wearing ties. Quinn noticed that and thought relieved thoughts.

Jason spotted me right after Calvin did, and he beckoned to me. I stepped forward, suddenly realizing that I was going to have a part in the ceremony. I hugged my brother, smelling his musky cologne . . . but no alcohol. I relaxed a fraction. I had suspected Jason had fortified himself with a drink or two, but he was quite sober.

I let go of Jason and glanced behind me to see what had become of my companions, so I knew the moment when the werepanthers realized Quinn was there. There was a sudden hush among the two-natured, and I heard his name ripple through them like a little wind.

Calvin whispered, "You brought *Quinn?*" as if I'd arrived with Santa Claus or some other mythical creature.

"Is that okay?" I said, since I'd had no clue it would create such a stir.

"Oh, yes," he said. "He's your man now?" Calvin's face held such a mixture of startled reevaluation and speculation that I immediately began wondering what I didn't know about my new lover.

"Um, well, sorta," I said with sudden caution.

"We're honored to have him here," Calvin assured me.

"Quinn," Crystal breathed. Her pupils were dilating, and I felt her brain focus on my date with a sort of groupie longing. I wanted to kick her. *Here to marry my brother, remember?*

Jason looked as puzzled as I was. Since he'd been a panther only a few months, there was a lot about the hidden world of the two-natured he hadn't picked up on yet.

Me, too.

Crystal made an effort to quell herself and get back into

the moment. She was naturally enjoying being the center of attention, but she spared a moment to reassess her prospective sister-in-law. Her respect for me (pretty much nonexistent, heretofore) had just shot off the charts.

"What's the procedure?" I asked briskly, trying to get us all back on track.

Calvin reverted to his practical self. "Since we have human guests, we've adapted the ceremony," he explained in a very low voice. "Here's how it goes . . . you vouch for Jason as his closest living relative, because he ain't got no one older than you to do it. I'm Crystal's oldest living relative, so I vouch for her. We offer to take the penalty if either of them does wrong."

Ah-oh. I didn't like the sound of that. I darted a quick look at my brother, who (naturally) didn't seem to think twice about the commitment I was making. I shouldn't have expected anything else.

"Then the minister comes forward and the service proceeds just like any other wedding," Calvin said. "If there weren't outsiders here, it would be different."

I was curious about that, but this wasn't the time to ask lots of questions. However, there were a few that had to be answered. "What penalty am I promising to pay? What constitutes 'doing wrong'?"

Jason huffed a sigh, exasperated that I wanted to find out what I was promising. Calvin's calm yellow eyes met mine, and they were full of understanding.

"Here's what you're vowing," Calvin said in a voice that was quiet but intense. We huddled around him. "Jason, you listen hard. We went over this, but I don't think you were giving me your full attention." Jason was listening now, but I could feel his impatience.

"Being married here"—and Calvin waved a hand to indicate the little Hotshot community—"means being faithful to your mate, unless the mate has to breed to keep the group up. Since Crystal's pretty much out of the running on that, Jason, that means she has to be faithful to you, and you to her. You don't have mating obligations like the purebloods do." Jason flushed at this reminder that his status was lesser since he was only a shifter because he'd been bitten by one, not because he'd been born with the gene. "So if Crystal runs around on you and a member of the community can attest to it, and if she can't pay the price for some reason—pregnancy, or illness, or a kid to raise—I have to do it. We're not talking money here, you understand?"

Jason nodded. "You're talking physical punishment," he said.

"Yes," Calvin said. "Not only are you promising to be faithful, you're also swearing to keep our secret."

Jason nodded again.

"And to help out other members of the community if they're in need."

Jason scowled.

"Example?" I said.

"If Maryelizabeth's roof needs replacing, we might all chip in a bit to buy the material and we'd all make time to do the work. If a kid needs a place to stay, your home is open to that kid. We take care of each other."

Jason nodded again. "I understand," he said. "I'm willing." He would have to give up some of his buddy time, and I felt sad for Hoyt; and I confess I felt a little sad for myself. I wasn't gaining a sister; I was losing my brother, at least to some degree.

"Mean this from the heart or call it off now," I said, keeping my voice very low. "You're committing my life to this, too. Can you keep the promises you're making to this woman and her community, or not?"

Jason looked at Crystal for a long moment, and I had no

right to be in his head, so I pulled out and instead cast through the crowd for random thoughts. They were mostly what you'd expect: a bit of excitement at being at a wedding, a bit of pleasure at seeing the parish's most notorious bachelor shackled to a wild young woman, a bit of curiosity about the odd Hotshot ritual. *Hotshot* was a byword in the parish—"as weird as a guy from Hotshot" had been a saying for years, and Hotshot kids who attended the Bon Temps school often had a hard time of it until after the first few playground fights.

"I'll keep my promises," Jason said, his voice hoarse.

"I'll keep mine," Crystal said.

The difference between the two was this: Jason was sincere, though I doubted his ability to stick to his word. Crystal had the ability, but she wasn't sincere.

"You don't mean it," I said to her.

"The hell you say," she retorted.

"I don't usually say one way or another," I said, making the effort to keep my voice low. "But this is too serious to keep silent. I can see inside your head, Crystal. Don't you ever forget I can."

"I ain't forgetting nothing," she said, making sure each word had weight. "And I'm marrying Jason tonight."

I looked at Calvin. He was troubled, but in the end, he shrugged. "We can't stop this," he said. For a second, I was tempted to struggle with his pronouncement. *Why not?* I thought. *If I hauled off and slapped her, maybe that would be enough disruption to stall the whole thing.* Then I reconsidered. They were both grown-ups, at least theoretically. They would get married if they chose, either here and now or somewhere else on some other night. I bowed my head and sucked up my misgivings.

"Of course," I said, raising my face and smiling that

bright smile I got when I was really anxious. "Let's get on with the ceremony." I caught a glimpse of Quinn's face in the crowd. He was looking at me, concerned by the low-voiced argument. Amelia, on the other hand, was happily chatting with Catfish, whom she'd met at the bar. Hoyt was by himself right under one of the portable lights rigged up for the occasion. He had his hands thrust in his pockets, and he looked more serious than I'd ever seen him. There was something strange about the sight, and after a second I figured out why.

It was one of the few times I'd ever seen Hoyt alone.

I took my brother's arm, and Calvin again gripped Crystal's. The priest stepped into the center of the circle, and the ceremony began. Though I tried hard to look happy for Jason, I had a difficult time holding back my tears while my brother became the bridegroom of a wild and willful girl who had been dangerous from birth.

There was dancing afterward, and a wedding cake, and lots of alcohol. There was food galore, and consequently there were huge trash cans that filled up with paper plates, cans, and crumpled paper napkins. Some of the men had brought cases of beer and wine, and some had hard liquor, too. No one could say that Hotshot couldn't throw a party.

While a zydeco band from Monroe played, the crowd danced in the street. The music echoed across the fields in an eerie way. I shivered and wondered what was watching from the dark.

"They're good, aren't they?" Jason asked. "The band?"

"Yeah," I said. He was flushed with happiness. His bride was dancing with one of her cousins.

"That's why we hurried this wedding up," he said. "She found out she was pregnant, and we decided to go on and do it—just do it. And her favorite band was free for tonight."

I shook my head at my brother's impulsiveness. Then I reminded myself to keep visible signs of disapproval at a minimum. The bride's family might take issue.

Quinn was a good dancer, though I had to show him some of the Cajun steps. All the Hotshot belles wanted a dance with Quinn, too, so I had a turn with Calvin, and Hoyt, and Catfish. Quinn was having a good time, I could tell, and on one level I was, too. But around two thirty a.m., we gave each other a little nod. He had to leave the next day, and I wanted to be alone with him. Plus, I was tired of smiling.

As Quinn thanked Calvin for the wonderful evening, I watched Jason and Crystal dancing together, both apparently delighted with each other. I knew right from Jason's brain that he was infatuated with the shifter girl, with the subculture that had formed her, with the newness of being a supernatural. I knew from Crystal's brain that she was exultant. She'd been determined to marry someone that hadn't grown up in Hotshot, someone who was exciting in bed, someone able to stand up to not only her but her extended family . . . and now she had.

I made my way over to the happy couple and gave each of them a kiss on the cheek. Now Crystal was family, after all, and I would have to accept her as such and leave the two to work out their own life together. I gave Calvin a hug, too, and he held me for a second before releasing me and giving me a reassuring pat on the back. Catfish danced me around in a circle, and a drunken Hoyt took up where he'd left off. I had a hard time convincing the two that I really meant to leave, but finally Quinn and I began to make our way back to my car.

As we wended through the edges of the crowd, I spotted Amelia dancing with one of her Hotshot beaux. They were both in high spirits, both literally and libation-wise. I called to Amelia that we were leaving, and she yelled, "I'll get a ride with someone later!"

Though I enjoyed seeing Amelia happy, it must have been Misgiving Night, because I worried about her a little. However, if anyone could take care of herself, it was Amelia.

We were moving slow when we let ourselves into the house. I didn't check out Quinn's head, but mine was muzzy from the noise, the clamor of all the brains around me, and the extra surges of emotion. It had been a long day. Some of it had been excellent, though. As I recalled the very best parts, I caught myself smiling down at Bob. The big cat rubbed himself against my ankles, meowing in an inquiring kind of way.

Oh, geez.

I felt like I had to explain Amelia's absence to the cat. I squatted down and scratched Bob's head, and (feeling incredibly foolish) I said, "Hey, Bob. She's going to be real late tonight; she's still dancing at the party. But don't you worry, she'll be home!" The cat turned his back on me and stalked out of the room. I was never sure how much human was lurking in Bob's little feline brain, but I hoped he'd just fall asleep and forget all about our strange conversation.

Just at that moment, I heard Quinn call to me from my bedroom, and I put thoughts about Bob on hold. After all, it was our last night together for maybe weeks.

While I brushed my teeth and washed my face, I had one last flare of worry about Jason. My brother had made his bed. I hoped he could lie comfortably in it for some time. *He's a grown-up*, I told myself over and over as I went into the bedroom in my nicest nightgown.

Quinn pulled me to him, said, "Don't worry, babe, don't worry. . . ."

I banished my brother and Bob from my thoughts and this bedroom. I brought a hand up to trace the curve of Quinn's scalp, kept those fingers going down his spine, loved it when he shivered.

# 5

I WAS WALKING IN MY SLEEP. IT WAS A GOOD THING I knew every inch of Merlotte's like I knew my own house, or I'd have bumped into every table and chair. I yawned widely as I took Selah Pumphrey's order. Ordinarily Selah irritated the hell out of me. She'd been dating Nameless Ex-Lover for several weeks—well, months now. No matter how invisible Ex had become, she'd never be my favorite person.

"Not getting enough rest, Sookie?" she asked, her voice sharp.

"Excuse me," I apologized. "I guess not. I was at my brother's wedding last night. What kind of dressing did you want on that salad?"

"Ranch." Selah's big dark eyes were examining me like she was thinking of etching my portrait. She really wanted to know all about Jason's wedding, but asking me would be like surrendering ground to the enemy. Silly Selah.

Come to think of it, what was Selah doing here? She'd never come in without Bill. She lived in Clarice. Not that Clarice was far; you could get there in fifteen or twenty minutes. But why would a real estate saleswoman from Clarice be . . . oh. She must be showing a house here. Yes, the brain was moving slowly today.

"Okeydokey. Coming right up," I said, and turned to go.

"Listen," Selah said. "Let me be frank."

Oh, boy. In my experience, that meant, "Let me be openly mean."

I swung around, trying to look anything but massively irritated, which was what I actually was. This was not the day to screw with me. Among my many worries, Amelia hadn't come home the night before, and when I'd gone upstairs to look for Bob, I'd found that he'd thrown up in the middle of Amelia's bed . . . which would have been okay by me, but it had been covered with my great-grandmother's quilt. It had fallen to me to clean up the mess and get the quilt to soaking in the washing machine. Quinn had left early that morning, and I was simply sad about that. And then there was Jason's marriage, which had such potential to be a disaster.

I could think of a few more items to add to the list (down to the dripping tap in my kitchen), but you get that my day was not a happy one.

"I'm here working, Selah. I'm not here to have any personal chitchats with you."

She ignored that.

"I know you're going on a trip with Bill," she said. "You're trying to steal him back from me. How long have you been scheming about this?"

I know my mouth was hanging open, because I just hadn't gotten enough warning that was coming. My telepathy was affected when I was tired—just as my reaction time and thought processes were—and I was heavily shielded when I worked, as a matter of course. So I hadn't picked up on Selah's thoughts. A flash of rage passed through me, lifting my palm and raising it to slap the shit out of her. But a warm, hard hand took mine, gripped it, brought it down to my side. Sam was there, and I hadn't even seen him coming. I was missing everything today.

"Miss Pumphrey, you'll have to get your lunch somewhere else," Sam said quietly. Of course, everyone was watching. I could feel all the brains go on alert for fresh gossip as eyes drank in every nuance of the scene. I could feel my face redden.

"I have the right to eat here," Selah said, her voice loud and arrogant. That was a huge mistake. In an instant, the sympathies of the spectators switched to me. I could feel the wave of it wash over me. I widened my eyes and looked sad like one of those abnormally big-eyed kids in the awful waif paintings. Looking pathetic was no big stretch. Sam put an arm around me as though I were a wounded child and looked at Selah with nothing on his face but a grave disappointment in her behavior.

"I have the right to tell you to go," he said. "I can't have you insulting my staff."

Selah was never likely to be rude to Arlene or Holly or Danielle. She hardly knew they existed, because she wasn't the kind of woman who really looked at a server. It had always stuck in her craw that Bill had dated me before he'd met her. ("Dated," in Selah's book, being a euphemism for "had enthusiastic and frequent sex with.")

Selah's body was jerky with anger as she threw her napkin on the floor. She got to her feet so abruptly that her chair would have fallen if Dawson, a boulder of a werewolf who ran a motorcycle repair business, hadn't caught it with one huge hand. Selah grabbed up her purse to stalk out of the door, narrowly avoiding a collision with my friend Tara, who was entering.

Dawson was highly amused by the whole scene. "All that over a vamp," he said. "Them cold-blooded things must be something, to get fine-looking women so upset."

"Who's upset?" I said, smiling and standing straighter to show Sam I was unfazed. I doubt he was fooled, since Sam knows me pretty well, but he got my emotional drift and went back behind the bar. The buzz of discussion of this juicy scene rose from the lunch crowd. I strode over to the table where Tara was sitting. She had JB du Rone in tow.

"Looking good, JB," I said brightly, pulling the menus from between the napkin box and the salt and pepper shakers in the middle of the table and handing one to him and one to Tara. My hands were shaking, but I don't think they noticed.

JB smiled up at me. "Thanks, Sookie," he said in his pleasant baritone. JB was just beautiful, but really short on the brains. However, that gave him a charming simplicity. Tara and I had watched out for him in school, because once that simplicity was observed and targeted by other, less handsome boys, JB had been in for some rough patches . . . especially in junior high. Since Tara and I also both had huge flaws in our own popularity profiles, we'd tried to protect JB as much as we were able. In return, JB had squired me to a couple of dances I'd wanted to go to very badly, and his family had given Tara a place to stay a couple of times when I couldn't.

Tara had had sex with JB somewhere along this painful road. I hadn't. It didn't seem to make any difference to either relationship.

"JB has a new job," Tara said, smiling in a self-satisfied way. So that was why she'd come in. Our relationship had been uneasy for the past few months, but she knew I'd want to share in her pride at having done a good thing for JB.

That was great news. And it helped me not think about Selah Pumphrey and her load of anger.

"Whereabouts?" I asked JB, who was looking at the menu as if he'd never seen it before.

"At the health club in Clarice," he said. He looked up and smiled. "Two days a week, I sit at the desk wearing this." He waved a hand at his clean and tight-fitting golf shirt, striped burgundy and brown, and his pressed khakis. "I get the members to sign in, I make healthy shakes, and I clean the equipment and hand out towels. Three days a week, I wear workout clothes and I spot for all the ladies."

"That sounds great," I said, awestruck at the perfection of the job for JB's limited qualifications. JB was lovely: impressive muscles, handsome face, straight white teeth. He was an ad for physical health. Also, he was naturally good-natured and neat.

Tara looked at me, expecting her due praise. "Good work," I told her. We gave each other a high five.

"Now, Sookie, the only thing that would make life perfect is you calling me some night," JB said. No one could project a wholesome, simple lust like JB.

"Thanks so much, JB, but I'm seeing someone now," I said, not troubling to keep my voice down. After Selah's little exhibition, I felt the need to brag a little.

"Oooh, that Quinn?" Tara asked. I may have mentioned him to her once or twice. I nodded, and we did another high five. "Is he in town now?" she asked in a lower voice, and I said, "Left this morning," just as quietly.

"I want the Mexican cheeseburger," JB said.

"Then I'll get you one," I said, and after Tara had ordered, I marched to the kitchen. Not only was I delighted for JB, I was happy that Tara and I seemed to have mended our fences. I had needed a little upswing to my day, and I had gotten it.

When I reached home with a couple of bags of groceries, Amelia was back and my kitchen sparkled like an exhibit in a Southern Homes show. When she was feeling stressed or bored, Amelia cleaned, which was a fantastic habit to have in a housemate—especially when you're not used to having one at all. I like a neat house myself, and I get cleaning spurts from time to time, but next to Amelia I was a slob.

I looked at the clean windows. "Feeling guilty, huh?" I said.

Amelia's shoulders slumped. She was sitting at the kitchen table with a mug of one of her weird teas, steam rising from the dark liquid.

"Yeah," she said glumly. "I saw the quilt was in the washing machine. I worked on the spot, and it's hanging out back on the line now."

Since I'd noted that when I came in, I just nodded. "Bob retaliated," I said.

"Yeah."

I started to ask her who she'd stayed with, then realized it was really none of my business. Besides, though I was very tired, Amelia was a broadcaster of the first order, and within seconds I knew she'd stayed with Calvin's cousin Derrick and the sex hadn't been good; also, Derrick's sheets had been very dirty and that had made her nuts. Plus, when Derrick had woken up this morning, he'd indicated that in his mind, a night together made them a couple. Amelia had had a hard time getting Derrick to give her a ride back to the house. He wanted her to stay with him, in Hotshot.

"Weirded out?" I asked, putting the hamburger meat in the refrigerator drawer. It was my week to cook, and we were going to have hamburger steak, baked potatoes, and green beans.

Amelia nodded, lifting her mug to take a sip. It was a homemade hangover restorative she'd concocted, and she shuddered as she experimented on herself. "Yeah, I am. Those Hotshot guys are a little strange," she said.

"Some of them." Amelia had adjusted better to my telepathy than anyone I'd ever encountered. Since she was frank and open anyway—sometimes way too much—I guess she never felt she had secrets to hide.

"What are you gonna do?" I asked. I sat down opposite her.

"See, it's not like I'd been dating Bob for a long time," she said, jumping right into the middle of the conversation without bothering with preliminaries. She knew I understood. "We'd only gotten together that one night. Believe me, it was great. He really *got* me. That's why we began, ah, experimenting."

I nodded, tried to look understanding. To me, experimenting was, well, licking a place you'd never licked before, or trying a position that gave you a cramp in your thigh. Like that. It did not involve turning your partner into an animal. I'd never worked up enough nerve to ask Amelia what their goal had been, and it was one thing her brain wasn't throwing out.

"I guess you like cats," I said, following my train of thought to its logical conclusion. "I mean, Bob is a cat, but a small one, and then you picked Derrick out of all the guys who would have been thrilled to spend the night with you."

"Oh?" Amelia said, perking up. She tried to sound casual. "More than one?"

Amelia did have the tendency to think way too well of herself as a witch, but not enough of herself as a woman.

"One or two," I said, trying not to laugh. Bob came in and wreathed himself around my legs, purring loudly. It could hardly have been more pointed, since he walked around Amelia as if she were a pile of dog poop.

Amelia sighed heavily. "Listen, Bob, you've gotta forgive me," she said to the cat. "I'm sorry. I just got carried away.

A wedding, a few beers, dancing in the street, an exotic partner . . . I'm sorry. Really, really sorry. How about I promise to be celibate until I can figure out a way to turn you back into yourself?"

This was a huge sacrifice on Amelia's part, as anyone who'd read her thoughts for a couple of days (and more) would know. Amelia was a very healthy girl and she was a very direct woman. She was also fairly diverse in her tastes. "Well," she said, on second thought, "what if I just promise not to do any guys?"

Bob's hind end sat while his front end stood, and his tail wrapped around his front paws. He looked adorable as he stared up at Amelia, his large yellow eyes unblinking. He appeared to be thinking it over. Finally, he said, "Rohr."

Amelia smiled.

"You taking that as a yes?" I said. "If so, remember . . . I just do guys, so don't go looking my way."

"Oh, I probably wouldn't try to hook up with you anyway," Amelia said.

Did I mention Amelia is a little tactless? "Why not?" I asked, insulted.

"I didn't pick Bob at random," Amelia said, looking as embarrassed as it is possible for Amelia to look. "I like 'em skinny and dark."

"I'll just have to live with that," I said, trying to look deeply disappointed. Amelia threw a tea ball at me, and I caught it in midair.

"Good reflexes," she said, startled.

I shrugged. Though it had been ages since I'd had vampire blood, a trace seemed to linger on in my system. I'd always been healthy, but now I seldom even got a headache. And I moved a little quicker than most people. I wasn't the only person to enjoy the side effects of vamp blood ingestion. Now that the effects have become common knowledge, vampires have become prey themselves. Harvesting that blood to sell on the black market is a lucrative and highly perilous profession. I'd heard on the radio that morning that a drainer had disappeared from his Texarkana apartment after he'd gotten out on parole. If you make an enemy of a vamp, he can wait it out a lot longer than you can.

"Maybe it's the fairy blood," Amelia said, staring at me thoughtfully.

I shrugged again, this time with a definite drop-this-subject air. I'd learned I had a trace of fairy in my lineage only recently, and I wasn't happy about it. I didn't even know which side of my family had bequeathed me this legacy, much less which individual. All I knew was that at some time in the past, someone in my family had gotten up close and personal with a fairy. I'd spent a couple of hours poring over the yellowing family trees and the family history my grandmother had worked so hard to compile, and I hadn't found a clue.

As if she'd been summoned by the thought, Claudine knocked at the back door. She hadn't flown on gossamer wings; she'd arrived in her car. Claudine is a full-blooded fairy, and she has other ways of getting places, but she uses those ways only in emergencies. Claudine is very tall, with a thick fall of dark hair and big, slanted dark eyes. She has to cover her ears with her hair, since unlike her twin, Claude, she hasn't had the pointy parts surgically altered.

Claudine hugged me enthusiastically but gave Amelia a distant wave. They are not nuts about each other. Amelia has acquired magic, but Claudine is magic to the bone. Neither quite trusts the other.

Claudine is normally the sunniest creature I ever met. She is very kind, and sweet, and helpful, like a supernatural Girl Scout, because it's her nature and because she's trying to work her way up the magical ladder to become an angel. Tonight, Claudine's face was unusually serious. My heart sank. I wanted to go to bed, and I wanted to miss Quinn in private, and I wanted to get over the jangling my nerves had taken at Merlotte's. I didn't want bad news.

Claudine settled at the kitchen table across from me and held my hands. She spared a look for Amelia. "Take a hike, witch," she said, and I was shocked.

"Pointy-eared bitch," muttered Amelia, getting up with her mug of tea.

"Mate killer," responded Claudine.

"He's not dead!" shrieked Amelia. "He's just—different!"

Claudine snorted, and actually that was an adequate response.

I was too tired to scold Claudine for her unprecedented rudeness, and she was holding my hands too tight for me to be pleased about her comforting presence. "What's up?" I asked. Amelia stomped out of the room, and I heard her shoes on the stairs up to the second floor.

"No vampires here?" Claudine said, her voice anxious. You know how a chocoholic feels about chunky fudge ice cream, double dipped in dark chocolate? That's how vamps feel about fairies.

"Yeah, the house is empty except for me, you, Amelia, and Bob," I said. I was not going to deny Bob his person-hood, though sometimes it was pretty hard to recall, especially when his litter box needed cleaning.

"You're going to this summit?"

"Yes."

"Why?"

That was a good question. "The queen is paying me," I said.

"Do you need the money so badly?"

I started to dismiss her concern, but then I gave it some serious thought. Claudine had done a lot for me, and the least I could do for her was think about what she said.

"I can live without it," I said. After all, I still had some of the money Eric had paid me for hiding him from a group of witches. But a chunk of it had gone, as money seems to; the insurance hadn't covered everything that had been damaged or destroyed by the fire that had consumed my kitchen the winter before, and I'd upgraded my appliances, and I'd made a donation to the volunteer fire department. They'd come so quickly and tried so hard to save the kitchen and my car.

Then Jason had needed help to pay the doctor's bill for Crystal's miscarriage.

I found I missed that layer of padding between being solvent and being broke. I wanted to reinforce it, replenish it. My little boat sailed on precarious financial waters, and I wanted to have a towboat around to keep it afloat.

"I can live without it," I said, more firmly, "but I don't want to."

Claudine sighed. Her face was full of woe. "I can't go with you," she said. "You know how vampires are around us. I can't even put in an appearance."

"I understand," I said, a bit surprised. I'd never dreamed of Claudine's going.

"And I think there's going to be trouble," she said.

"What kind?" The last time I'd gone to a vampire social gathering, there had been big trouble, major trouble, the bloodiest kind of trouble.

"I don't know," Claudine said. "But I feel it coming, and I think you should stay home. Claude does, too."

Claude didn't give a rat's ass what happened to me, but Claudine was generous enough to include her brother in her kindness. As far as I could tell, Claude's benefit to the world was strictly as a decoration. He was utterly selfish, had no social skills, and was absolutely beautiful.

"I'm sorry, Claudine, and I'll miss you while I'm in Rhodes," I said. "But I've obligated myself to go."

"Going in the train of a vampire," Claudine said dismally. "It'll mark you as one of their world, for good. You'll never be an innocent bystander again. Too many creatures will know who you are and where you can be found."

It wasn't so much what Claudine said as the way she said it that made cold prickles run up my spine and crawl along my scalp. She was right. I had no defense, though I rather thought that I was already into the vamp world too deeply to opt out.

Sitting there in my kitchen with the late afternoon sun slanting through the window, I had one of those illuminations that changes you forever. Amelia was silent upstairs. Bob had come back into the room to sit by his food bowl and stare at Claudine. Claudine herself was gleaming in a beam of sunlight that hit her square in the face. Most people would be showing every unattractive skin flaw. Claudine still looked perfect.

I wasn't sure I would ever understand Claudine and her thinking about the world, and I still knew frighteningly little about her life; but I felt quite sure that she had devoted herself to my well-being, for whatever reason, and that she was really afraid for me. And yet I knew I was going to Rhodes with the queen, and Eric, and the abjured one, and the rest of the Louisiana contingent.

Was I just curious about what the agenda might be at a vampire summit? Did I want the attention of more undead members of society? Did I want to be known as a fangbanger, one of those humans who simply adored the walking dead? Did some corner of me long for a chance to be near Bill without seeking him out, still trying to make some emotional sense of his betrayal? Or was this about Eric? Unbeknownst to myself, was I in love with the flamboyant Viking who was so handsome, so good at making love, and so political, all at the same time?

This sounded like a promising set of problems for a soap opera season.

"Tune in tomorrow," I muttered. When Claudine looked at me askance, I said, "Claudine, I feel embarrassed to tell you I'm doing something that really doesn't make much sense in a lot of ways, but I want the money and I'm going to do it. I'll be back here to see you again. Don't worry, please."

Amelia clomped back into the room, began making herself some more tea. She was going to float away.

Claudine ignored her. "I'm going to worry," she said simply. "There is trouble coming, my dear friend, and it will fall right on your head."

"But you don't know how or when?"

She shook her head. "No, I just know it's coming."

"Look into my eyes," muttered Amelia. "I see a tall, dark man . . ."

"Shut up," I told her.

She turned her back to us, made a big fuss out of pinching the dead leaves off some of her plants.

Claudine left soon after. For the remainder of her visit, she didn't recover her normal happy demeanor. She never said another word about my departure.

6 ~

ON THE SECOND MORNING AFTER JASON'S WEDDING, I
was feeling much more myself. Having a mission helped. I
needed to be at Tara's Togs right after it opened at ten. I had
to pick out the clothes Eric said I needed for the summit. I
wasn't due at Merlotte's until five thirty or so that night, so
I had that pleasant feeling of the whole day stretching ahead
of me.

"Hey, girl!" Tara said, coming from the back of the shop
to greet me. Her part-time assistant, McKenna, glanced at
me and resumed moving clothes around. I assumed she was
putting misplaced items back into their correct positions;
clothing store employees seem to spend a lot of time doing
that. McKenna didn't speak, and unless I was much mistaken, she was trying to avoid talking to me at all. That
hurt, since I'd gone to see her in the hospital when she'd had

her appendix out two weeks ago, and I'd taken her a little present, too.

"Mr. Northman's business associate Bobby Burnham called down here to say you needed some clothes for a trip?" Tara said. I nodded, trying to look matter of fact. "Would casual clothes be what you needed? Or suits, something of a business nature?" She gave me an utterly false bright smile, and I knew she was angry with me because she was scared for me. "McKenna, you can take that mail to the post office," Tara told McKenna with an edge to her voice. McKenna scuttled out the back door, the mail stuffed under her arm like a riding crop.

"Tara," I said, "it's not what you think."

"Sookie, it's none of my business," she said, trying hard to sound neutral.

"I think it is," I said. "You're my friend, and I don't want you thinking I'm just going traveling with a bunch of vampires for fun."

"Then why are you going?" Tara's face dropped all the false cheer. She was deadly serious.

"I'm getting paid to go with a few of the Louisiana vamps to a big meeting. I'll act as their, like, human Geiger counter. I'll tell them if a human's trying to bullshit them, and I'll know what the other vamps' humans are thinking. It's just for this one time." I couldn't explain more fully. Tara had been into the world of the vampires more heavily than she needed to be, and she'd almost gotten killed. She wanted nothing more to do with it, and I couldn't blame her. But she still couldn't tell me what to do. I'd gone through my own soul searching over this issue, even before Claudine's lecture, and I wasn't going to permit anyone else to second-guess me once I'd made up my mind. Getting the clothes was okay. Working for the vamps was okay . . . as long as I didn't turn humans over to get killed.

"We've been friends for a coon's age," Tara said quietly. "Through thick and thin. I love you, Sookie, I always will; but this is a real thin time." Tara had had so much disappointment and worry in her life that she simply wasn't willing to undertake any more. So she was cutting me loose, and she thought she would call JB that night and renew their carnal acquaintance, and she would do that almost in memory of me.

It was a strange way to write my premature epitaph.

"I need an evening dress, a cocktail-type dress, and some nice day clothes," I said, checking my list quite unnecessarily. I wasn't going to fool with Tara anymore. I was going to have fun, no matter how sour she looked. She'd come around, I told myself.

I was going to enjoy buying clothes. I started off with an evening dress and a cocktail dress. And I got two suits, like business suits (but not really, since I can't see myself in black pinstripes). And two pants outfits. And hose and knee-highs and a nightgown or two. And a bit of lingerie.

I was swinging between guilt and delight. I spent more of Eric's money than I absolutely had to, and I wondered what would happen if Eric asked to see the things he'd bought. I'd feel pretty bad then. But it was like I'd been caught up in a buying frenzy, partly out of the sheer delight of it, and partly out of anger at Tara, and partly to deny the fear I was feeling at the prospect of accompanying a group of vampires anywhere.

With another sigh, this one a very quiet and private one, I returned the lingerie and the nightgowns to their tables. Nonessentials. I felt sad to part with them, but I felt better overall. Buying clothes to suit a specific need, well, that was okay. That was a meal. But buying underthings, that was something else entirely. That was like a MoonPie. Or Ding Dongs. Sweet, but bad for you.

The local priest, who had started attending Fellowship of the Sun meetings, had suggested to me that befriending vamps, or even working for them, was a way of expressing a death wish. He'd told me this over his burger basket the week before. I thought about that now, standing at the cash register while Tara rang up all my purchases, which would be paid for with vampire money. Did I believe I wanted to die? I shook my head. No, I didn't. And I thought the Fellowship of the Sun, which was the ultra right-wing anti-vampire movement that was gaining an alarming stronghold in America, was a crock. Their condemnation of all humans who had any dealings with vampires, even down to visiting a business owned by a vamp, was ridiculous. But why was I even drawn to vamps to begin with?

Here was the truth of it: I'd had so little chance of having the kind of life my classmates had achieved—the kind of life I'd grown up thinking was the ideal—that any other life I could shape for myself seemed interesting. If I couldn't have a husband and children, worry about what I was going to take to the church potluck and if our house needed another coat of paint, then I'd worry about what three-inch heels would do to my sense of balance when I was wearing several extra pounds in sequins.

When I was ready to go, McKenna, who'd come back from the post office, carried my bags out to my car while Tara cleared the amount with Eric's day man, Bobby Burnham. She hung up the phone, looking pleased.

"Did I use it all up?" I asked, curious to find out how much Eric had invested in me.

"Not nearly," she said. "Want to buy more?"

But the fun was over. "No," I said. "I've gotten enough." I had a definite impulse to ask Tara to take every stitch back.

Then I thought what a shabby thing that would be to do to her. "Thanks for helping me, Tara."

"My pleasure," she assured me. Her smile was a little warmer and more genuine. Tara always liked making money, and she'd never been able to stay mad at me long. "You need to go to World of Shoes in Clarice to get something to go with the evening gown. They're having a sale."

I braced myself. This was the day to get things done. Next stop, World of Shoes.

I would be leaving in a week, and work that night went by in a blur as I grew more excited about the trip. I'd never been as far from home as Rhodes, which was way up there by Chicago; actually, I'd never been north of the Mason-Dixon Line. I'd flown only once, and that had been a short flight from Shreveport to Dallas. I would have to get a suitcase, one that rolled. I'd have to get . . . I thought of a long list of smaller items. I knew that some hotels had hair dryers. Would the Pyramid of Gizeh? The Pyramid was one of the most famous vampire-oriented hotels that had sprung up in major American cities.

Since I'd already arranged my time off with Sam, that night I told him when I was scheduled to leave. Sam was sitting behind his desk in the office when I knocked on the door—well, the door frame, because Sam almost never shut the door. He looked up from his bill paying. He was glad to be interrupted. When he worked on the books, he ran his hands through his reddish blond hair, and now he looked a little electrified as a result. Sam would rather be tending bar than doing this task, but he'd actually hired a substitute for tonight just for the purpose of getting his books straight.

"Come in, Sook," he said. "How's it going out there?"

"Pretty busy; I haven't got but a second. I just wanted to tell you I'll be leaving next Thursday."

Sam tried to smile, but he ended up simply looking unhappy. "You have to do this?" he asked.

"Hey, we've talked about this," I said, sounding a clear warning.

"Well, I'll miss you," he explained. "And I'll worry a little. You and lots of vamps."

"There'll be humans there, like me."

"*Not* like you. They'll be humans with a sick infatuation with the vampire culture, or deaddiggers, looking to make a buck off the undead. None of these are healthy people with long life expectancies."

"Sam, two years ago I didn't have any idea of what the world around me was really like. I didn't know what you really were; I didn't know that vampires were as different from each other as we are. I didn't know that there were real fairies. I couldn't have imagined any of that." I shook my head. "What a world this is, Sam. It's wonderful and it's scary. Each day is different. I never thought I would have any kind of life for myself, and now I do."

"I'd be the last person in the world to block your place in the sun, Sookie," Sam said, and he smiled at me. But it didn't escape my attention that his statement was a wee bit ambiguous.

Pam came to Bon Temps that night, looking bored and cool in a pale green jumpsuit with navy piping. She was wearing navy penny loafers . . . no kidding. I hadn't even realized those were still for sale. The dark leather was polished to a high shine, and the pennies were new. She got plenty of admiring looks in the bar. She perched at a table in my section and sat patiently, her hands clasped on the table in front of her. She went into the vampire state of suspension that was so unnerving to anyone who hadn't seen it yet— her eyes open but not seeing, her body totally unmoving, her expression blank. Since she was having some downtime,

I waited on a few people before I went to her table. I was sure I knew why she was there, and I wasn't looking forward to the conversation.

"Pam, can I get you a drink?"

"What's with the tiger, then?" she asked, going straight for the conversational jugular.

"Quinn is who I'm seeing now," I said. "We don't get to stay together much because of his job, but we'll see each other at the summit." Quinn had been hired to produce some of the summit's expected ceremonies and rituals. He'd be busy, but I'd catch glimpses of him, and I was already excited about the prospect. "We're spending a month together after the summit," I told Pam.

Ah-oh, maybe I'd over-shared on that one. Pam's face lost its smile.

"Sookie, I don't know what strange game you and Eric have going, but it's not good for us."

"I have nothing going! Nothing!"

"You may not, but he does. He has not been the same since the time you two spent together."

"I don't know what I can do about that," I said weakly.

Pam said, "I don't either, but I hope he can resolve his feelings for you. He doesn't enjoy having conflicts. He doesn't enjoy feeling attached. He is not the carefree vampire he used to be."

I shrugged. "Pam, I've been as straight with him as I can be. I think maybe he's worried about something else. You're exaggerating my importance in Eric's scheme of things. If he has any kind of undying love for me, then he's sure not telling me about it. And I never see him. And he knows about Quinn."

"He made Bill confess to you, didn't he?"

"Well, Eric was there," I said uncertainly.

"Do you think Bill would ever have told you if Eric hadn't commanded him to?"

I'd done my best to forget that night altogether. In the back of my mind, I'd known the strange timing of Bill's revelation was significant, but I just hadn't wanted to think about it.

"Why do you think Eric would give a flying fuck what Bill had been ordered to do, much less reveal it to a human woman, if he didn't have inappropriate feelings for you?"

I'd never put it to myself quite like that. I'd been so ripped up by Bill's confession—the queen had planted him to seduce me (if necessary) to gain my trust—that I hadn't thought of why Eric had forced Bill into the position of telling me about the plot.

"Pam, I don't know. Listen, I'm working here, and you need to order something to drink. I gotta take care of my other tables."

"O-negative, then. TrueBlood."

I hurried to get the drink out of the cooler, and I warmed it up in the microwave, shaking it gently to make sure the temperature was even. It coated the sides of the bottle in an unpleasant way, but it certainly looked and tasted like real blood. I'd poured a few drops into a glass one time at Bill's so I could have the experience. As far as I could tell, drinking synthetic blood was exactly like drinking real blood. Bill had always enjoyed it, though he'd remarked more than once that flavor wasn't the thing; it was the sensation of biting into flesh, feeling the heartbeat of the human, that made being a vampire fun. Glugging out of a bottle just didn't do the trick. I took the bottle and a wineglass to Pam's table and deposited both before her, along with a napkin, of course.

"Sookie?" I looked up to see that Amelia had come in.

My roomie had come into the bar often enough, but I was surprised to see her tonight. "What's up?" I asked.

"Um . . . hi," Amelia said to Pam. I took in Amelia's pressed khakis, her neat white golf shirt, her equally white tennis shoes. I glanced at Pam, whose pale eyes were wider than I'd ever seen them.

"This is my roommate, Amelia Broadway," I told Pam. "Amelia, this is Pam the vampire."

"I am pleased to meet you," Pam said.

"Hey, neat outfit," Amelia said.

Pam looked pleased. "You look very nice, too," she said.

"You a local vamp?" Amelia asked. Amelia was nothing if not blunt. And chatty.

Pam said, "I'm Eric's second-in-command. You do know who Eric Northman is?"

"Sure," Amelia said. "He's the blond hunk of burning love who lives in Shreveport, right?"

Pam smiled. Her fangs popped out a little. I looked from Amelia to the vampire. Geez Louise.

"Perhaps you would like to see the bar some night?" Pam said.

"Oh, sure," Amelia said, but not as if she were particularly excited. Playing hard to get. For about ten minutes, if I knew Amelia.

I left to answer a customer beckoning from another table. Out of the corner of my eye, Amelia sat down with Pam, and they talked for a few minutes before Amelia got up and stood by the bar, waiting for me to return.

"And what brings you here tonight?" I asked maybe a little too abruptly.

Amelia raised her eyebrows, but I didn't apologize.

"I just wanted to tell you, you got a phone call at the house."

"Who from?"

"From Quinn."

I felt a smile spread across my face, a real one. "What did he say?"

"He said he'd see you in Rhodes. He misses you already."

"Thanks, Amelia. But you could've just called here to tell me, or told me when I got home."

"Oh, I got a little bored."

I'd known she would be, sooner or later. Amelia needed a job, a full-time job. She missed her city and her friends, of course. Even though she'd left New Orleans before Katrina, she'd suffered a little every day since the storm's aftermath had devastated the city. Amelia missed the witchcraft, too. I'd hoped she'd pal around with Holly, another barmaid and a dedicated Wiccan. But after I'd introduced the two and they'd had some conversations, Amelia had told me glumly that she and Holly were very different sorts of witches. Amelia herself was (she considered) a true witch, while Holly was a Wiccan. Amelia had a thinly veiled contempt for the Wiccan faith. Once or twice, Amelia had met with Holly's coven, partly to keep her hand in . . . and partly because Amelia yearned for the company of other practitioners.

At the same time, my houseguest was very anxious she might be discovered by the witches of New Orleans and made to pay a high price for her mistake in changing Bob. To add yet another emotional layer, since Katrina, Amelia feared for the safety of these same former companions. She couldn't find out if they were okay without them discovering her in return.

Despite all this, I'd known the day (or night) would come when Amelia would be restless enough to look outside my house and yard and Bob.

I tried not to frown as Amelia went over to Pam's table to visit some more. I reminded my inner worrier that Amelia could take care of herself. Probably. I'd been more certain the night before in Hotshot. As I went about my work, I switched my thoughts to Quinn's call. I wished I'd had my new cell phone (thanks to Amelia's paying me a little rent, I could afford one) with me, but I didn't think it was right to carry it at work, and Quinn knew I wouldn't have it with me and turned on unless I was at liberty to answer it. I wished Quinn would be waiting at home when I left the bar in an hour. The strength of that fantasy intoxicated me.

Though it would have been pleasant to roll in that feeling, indulging myself in the flush of my new relationship, I concluded was time to back down and face a little reality. I concentrated on serving my tables, smiling and chatting as needed, and refreshing Pam's TrueBlood once or twice. Otherwise, I left Amelia and Pam to their tête-à-tête.

Finally, the last working hour was over, and the bar cleared out. Along with the other servers, I did my closing-up chores. When I was sure the napkin holders and salt shakers were full and ready for the next day, I went down the little hall into the storeroom to deposit my apron in the large laundry basket. After listening to us hint and complain for years, Sam had finally hung a mirror back there for our benefit. I found myself standing absolutely still, staring into it. I shook myself and began to untie my apron. Arlene was fluffing her own bright red hair. Arlene and I were not such good friends these days. She'd gotten involved in the Fellowship of the Sun. Though the Fellowship represented itself as an informational organization, dedicated to spreading the "truth" about vampires, its ranks were riddled with those who believed all vampires were intrinsically evil and should be eliminated, by violent means. The worst among the Fellowship took out their anger and fear on the humans who consorted with vampires.

Humans like me.

Arlene tried to meet my eyes in the mirror. She failed.

"That vamp in the bar your buddy?" she asked, putting a very unpleasant emphasis on the last word.

"Yes," I said. Even if I hadn't liked Pam, I would have said she was my buddy. Everything about the Fellowship made the hair rise up on my neck.

"You need to hang around with humans more," Arlene said. Her mouth was set in a solid line, and her heavily made-up eyes were narrow with intensity. Arlene had never been what you'd call a deep thinker, but I was astonished and dismayed by how fast she'd been sucked into the Fellowship way of thinking.

"I'm with humans ninety-five percent of the time, Arlene."

"You should make it a hundred."

"Arlene, how is this any of your business?" My patience was stretched to its breaking point.

"You been putting in all these hours because you're going with a bunch of vamps to some meeting, right?"

"Again, what business of yours?"

"You and me were friends for a long time, Sookie, until that Bill Compton walked into the bar. Now you see vamps all the time, and you have strange people staying at your house."

"I don't have to defend my life to you," I said, and my temper utterly snapped. I could see inside her head, see all the smug and satisfied righteous judgment. It hurt. It rankled. I had babysat her children, consoled her when she was left high and dry by a series of unworthy men, cleaned her trailer, tried to encourage her to date men who wouldn't walk all over her. Now she was staring at me, actually surprised at my anger.

"Obviously you have some big holes in your own life if

you have to fill them with this Fellowship crap," I said. "Look at what sterling guys you pick to date and marry." With that unchristian dig, I spun on my heel and walked out of the bar, thankful I'd already gotten my purse from Sam's office. Nothing's worse than having to stop in the middle of a righteous walkout.

Somehow Pam was beside me, having joined me so quickly that I hadn't seen her move. I looked over my shoulder. Arlene was standing with her back flat against the wall, her face distorted with pain and anger. My parting shot had been a true one. One of Arlene's boyfriends had stolen the family silverware, and her husbands . . . hard to know where to start.

Pam and I were outside before I could react to her presence.

I was rigid with the shock of Arlene's verbal attack and my own fury. "I shouldn't have said anything about him," I said. "Just because one of Arlene's husbands was a murderer is no reason for me to be ugly." I was absolutely channeling my grandmother, and I gave a shaky hoot of laughter.

Pam was a little shorter than I, and she looked up into my face curiously as I struggled to control myself.

"She's a whore, that one," Pam said.

I pulled a Kleenex out of my purse to blot my tears. I often cried when I got angry; I hated that. Crying just made you look weak, no matter what triggered it.

Pam held my hand and wiped my tears off with her thumb. The tender effect was a little weakened when she stuck the thumb in her mouth, but I figured she meant well.

"I wouldn't call her a whore, but she's truly not as careful as she might be about who she goes with," I admitted.

"Why do you defend her?"

"Habit," I said. "We were friends for years and years."

"What did she do for you, with her friendship? What benefit was there?"

"She . . ." I had to stop and think. "I guess I was just able to say I had a friend. I cared about her kids, and I helped her out with them. When she couldn't work, I'd take her hours, and if she worked for me, I'd clean her trailer in return. She'd come see me if I was sick and bring me food. Most of all, she was tolerant of my differences."

"She used you and yet you felt grateful," Pam said. Her expressionless white face gave me no clue to her feelings.

"Listen, Pam, it wasn't like that."

"How was it, Sookie?"

"She really did like me. We really did have some good times."

"She's lazy. That extends to her friendships. If it's easy to be friendly, she will be. If the wind blows the other way, her friendship will be gone. And I'm thinking the wind is blowing the other way. She has found some other way to be an important person in her own right, by hating others."

"Pam!"

"Is this not true? I've watched people for years. I know people."

"There's true stuff you should say, and true stuff that's better left unsaid."

"There's true stuff you would *rather* I left unsaid," she corrected me.

"Yes. As a matter of fact, that's . . . true."

"Then I'll leave you and go back to Shreveport." Pam turned to walk around the building to where her car was parked in front.

"Whoa!"

She turned back. "Yes?"

"Why were you here in the first place?"

Pam smiled unexpectedly. "Aside from asking you questions about your relationship with my maker? And the bonus of meeting your delectable roommate?"

"Oh. Yeah. Aside from all that."

"I want to talk to you about Bill," she said to my utter surprise. "Bill, and Eric."

"I DON'T HAVE ANYTHING TO SAY." I UNLOCKED MY car and tossed my purse inside. Then I turned to face Pam, though I was tempted to get in the car and go home.

"We didn't know," the vampire said. She walked slowly, so I could see her coming. Sam had left two lawn chairs out in front of his trailer, set at right angles to the rear of the bar, and I got them out of his yard and set them by the car. Pam took the hint and perched in one while I took the other.

I drew a deep, silent breath. I had wondered ever since I returned from New Orleans if all the vamps in Shreveport had known Bill's secret purpose in courting me. "I wouldn't have told you," Pam said, "even if I had known Bill had been charged with a mission, because . . . vampires first." She shrugged. "But I promise you that I didn't know."

I bobbed my head in acknowledgment, and a little pocket of tension in me finally relaxed. But I had no idea how to respond.

"I must say, Sookie, that you have caused a tremendous amount of trouble in our area." Pam didn't seem perturbed by that; she was just stating a fact. I hardly felt I could apologize. "These days Bill is full of anger, but he doesn't know who to hate. He feels guilty, and no one likes that. Eric is frustrated that he can't remember the time he was in hiding at your house, and he doesn't know what he owes you. He's angry that the queen has annexed you for her own purposes, through Bill, and thus poached on Eric's territory, as he sees it. Felicia thinks you are the bogeyman, since so many of the Fangtasia bartenders have died while you were around. Longshadow, Chow." She smiled. "Oh, and your friend, Charles Twining."

"None of that was my fault." I'd listened to Pam with growing agitation. It's so not good to have vampires angry with you. Even the current Fangtasia bartender, Felicia, was much stronger than I would ever be, and she was definitely the low vamp on the totem pole.

"I don't see that that makes any difference," Pam said, her voice curiously gentle. "Now that we know you have fairy blood, thanks to Andre, it would be easy to write all this off. But I don't think that's it, do you? I've known many humans descended from the fae, and none of them have been telepathic. I think that's just you, Sookie. Of course, knowing you have this streak of fairy makes one wonder how you would taste. I certainly enjoyed the sip I got when the maenad maimed you, though that was tainted with her poison. We love fairies, as you know."

"Love them to death," I said under my breath, but of course Pam heard.

"Sometimes," she agreed with a little smile. That Pam.

"So what's the bottom line here?" I was ready to go home and just be human, all by myself.

"When I say 'we' didn't know about Bill's agreement with the queen, that includes Eric," Pam said simply.

I looked down at my feet, struggling to keep my face under control.

"Eric feels especially angry about this," Pam said. She was picking her words now. "He is angry at Bill because Bill made an agreement with the queen that bypassed Eric. He is angry that he didn't discern Bill's plan. He is angry at you because you got under his skin. He is angry at the queen because she is more devious than he is. Of course, that's why she's the queen. Eric will never be a king, unless he can control himself better."

"You're really worried about him?" I'd never known Pam to be seriously concerned about much of anything. When she nodded, I found myself saying, "When did you meet Eric?" I'd always been curious, and tonight Pam seemed to be in a sharing mood.

"I met him in London the last night of my life." Her voice was level, coming out of the shadowy darkness. I could see half her face in the overhead security light, and she looked quite calm. "I risked everything for *love*. You'll laugh to hear this."

I wasn't remotely close to laughing.

"I was a very wild girl for my times. Young ladies weren't supposed to be alone with gentlemen, or any males, for that matter. A far cry from now." Pam's lips curved upward in a brief smile. "But I was a romantic, and bold. I slipped out of my house late at night to meet the cousin of my dearest friend, the girl who lived right next door. The cousin was visiting from Bristol, and we were very attracted to each other. My parents didn't consider him to be my equal in social class, so I knew they wouldn't let him court me. And if

I were caught alone with him at night, it would be the end of me. No marriage, unless my parents could force him to wed me. So, no future at all." Pam shook her head. "Crazy to think of now. Those were the times women didn't have choices. The ironic part is, our meeting was quite innocent. A few kisses, a lot of sentimental claptrap, undying love. Yada yada yada."

I grinned at Pam, but she didn't look up to catch the smile.

"On my way back to my house, trying to move so silently through the garden, I met Eric. There was no way to slip silently enough to avoid *him*." For a long moment, she was quiet. "And it really was the end of me."

"Why'd he turn you?" I settled lower in my chair and crossed my legs. This was an unexpected and fascinating conversation.

"I think he was lonely," she said, a faint note of surprise in her voice. "His last companion had struck out on her own, since children can't stay with their maker for long. After a few years, the child must strike out on its own, though it may come back to the maker, and must if the maker calls."

"Weren't you angry with him?"

She seemed to be trying to remember. "At first, I was shocked," Pam said. "After he'd drained me, he put me in bed in my own room, and of course my family thought I'd died of some mysterious ailment, and they buried me. Eric dug me up, so I wouldn't wake up in my coffin and have to dig my own way out. That was a great help. He held me and explained it all to me. Up until the night I died, I'd always been a very conventional woman underneath my daring tendencies. I was used to wearing layers and layers of clothes. You would be amazed at the dress I died in: the sleeves, the trim. The fabric in the skirt alone could make you three dresses!" Pam looked fondly reminiscent, nothing more.

"After I'd awakened, I discovered being a vampire freed some wild thing in me."

"After what he did, you didn't want to kill him?"

"No," she said instantly. "I wanted to have sex with him, and I did. We had sex many, many times." She grinned. "The tie between maker and child doesn't have to be sexual, but with us it was. That changed quite soon, actually, as my tastes broadened. I wanted to try everything I'd been denied in my human life."

"So you actually liked it, being a vampire? You were glad?"

Pam shrugged. "Yes, I've always loved being what I am. It took me a few days to understand my new nature. I'd never even heard of a vampire before I became one."

I couldn't imagine the shock of Pam's awakening. Her self-proclaimed quick adjustment to her new state amazed me.

"Did you ever go back to see your family?" I asked. Okay, that was tacky, and I regretted it as soon as the words passed my lips.

"I saw them from a distance, maybe ten years later. You understand, the first thing a new vampire needed to do was leave her home area. Otherwise she ran the risk of being recognized and hunted down. Now you can parade around as much as you like. But we were so secret, so careful. Eric and I headed out of London as quickly as we could go, and after spending a little time in the north of England while I became accustomed to my state, we left England for the continent."

This was gruesome but fascinating. "Did you love him?"

Pam looked a little puzzled. There was a tiny wrinkle in her smooth forehead. "Love him? No. We were good companions, and I enjoyed the sex and the hunting. But love? No." In the glare of the overhead security lights, which cast curious dark shadows in the corners of the lot, I watched

Pam's face relax into its normal smooth lines. "I owe him my loyalty," Pam said. "I have to obey him, but I do it willingly. Eric is intelligent, ambitious, and very entertaining. I would be crumbled to nothing in my grave by now if he hadn't been watching me slip back to my house from meeting that silly young man. I went my own way for many, many years, but I was glad to hear from him when he opened the bar and called me to serve him."

Was it possible for anyone in the world to be as detached as Pam over the whole "I was murdered" issue? There was no doubt Pam relished being a vampire, seemed to genuinely harbor a mild contempt for humans; in fact, she seemed to find them amusing. She had thought it was hilarious when Eric had first exhibited feelings for me. Could Pam truly be so changed from her former self?

"How old were you, Pam?"

"When I died? I was nineteen." Not a flicker of feeling crossed her face.

"Did you wear your hair up every day?"

Pam's face seemed to warm a little. "Yes, I did. I wore it in a very elaborate style; my maid had to help me. I put artificial pads underneath my hair to give it height. And the underwear! You would laugh yourself sick to see me get into it."

As interesting as this conversation had been, I realized I was tired and ready to go home. "So the bottom line is, you're really loyal to Eric, and you want me to know that neither of you knew that Bill had a hidden agenda when he came to Bon Temps." Pam nodded. "So, you came here to-night to . . . ?"

"To ask you to have mercy on Eric."

The idea of Eric needing my mercy had never crossed my mind. "That's as funny as your human underwear," I said. "Pam, I know you believe you owe Eric, even though he killed you—honey, he *killed* you—but I don't owe Eric a thing."

"You care for him," she said, and for the first time she sounded a little angry. "I know you do. He's never been so entangled in his emotions. He's never been at such a disadvantage." She seemed to gather herself, and I figured our conversation was over. We got up, and I returned Sam's chairs.

I had no idea what to say.

Fortunately, I didn't have to think of anything. Eric himself walked out of the shadows at the edge of the lot.

"Pam," he said, and that one word was loaded. "You were so late, I followed your trail to make sure all was well."

"Master," she said, which was something I'd never heard from Pam. She went down on one knee on the gravel, which must have been painful.

"Leave," Eric said, and just like that, Pam was gone.

I kept silent. Eric was giving me that vampiric fixed stare, and I couldn't read him at all. I was pretty sure he was mad—but about what, at whom, and with what intensity? That was the fun part of being with vampires, and the scary part of being with vampires, all at the same time.

Eric decided action would speak louder than words. Suddenly, he was right in front of me. He put a finger under my chin and lifted my face to his. His eyes, which looked simply dark in the irregular light, latched on to mine with an intensity that was both exciting and painful. Vampires; mixed feelings. One and the same.

Not exactly to my astonishment, he kissed me. When someone has had approximately a thousand years to practice kissing, he can become very good at it, and I would be lying if I said I was immune to such osculatory talent. My temperature zoomed up about ten degrees. It was everything I could do to keep from stepping into him, wrapping my arms around him, and stropping myself against him. For a dead guy, he had the liveliest chemistry—and apparently all my hormones were wide awake after my night with Quinn. Thinking of Quinn was like a dash of cold water.

With an almost painful reluctance, I pulled away from Eric. His face had a focused air, as if he was sampling something and deciding if it was good enough to keep.

"Eric," I said, and my voice was shaking. "I don't know why you're here, and I don't know why we're having all this drama."

"Are you Quinn's now?" His eyes narrowed.

"I'm my own," I said. "I choose."

"And have you chosen?"

"Eric, this is beyond gall. You haven't been dating me. You haven't given me any sign that was on your mind. You haven't treated me as though I had any significance in your life. I'm not saying I would have been open to those things, but I'm saying in their *absence* I've been free to find another, ah, companion. And so far, I like Quinn just fine."

"You don't know him any more than you really knew Bill."

That sliced down where it hurt.

"At least I'm pretty damn sure he wasn't ordered to get me in bed so I'd be a political asset!"

"It's better that you knew about Bill," Eric said.

"Yes, it's better," I agreed. "That doesn't mean I enjoyed the process."

"I knew that would be hard. But I had to make him tell you."

"Why?"

Eric seemed stumped. I don't know any other way to put it. He looked away, off into the darkness of the woods. "It wasn't right," he said at last.

"True. But maybe you just wanted to be sure I wouldn't ever love him again?"

"Maybe both things," he said.

There was a sharp moment of silence, as if something big was drawing in breath.

"Okay," I said slowly. This was like a therapy session. "You've been moody around me for months, Eric. Ever since you were . . . you know, not yourself. What's up with you?"

"Ever since that night I was cursed, I've wondered why I ended up running down the road to your house."

I took a step or two back and tried to pull some evidence, some indication of what he was thinking, from his white face. But it was no use.

It had never occurred to me to wonder why Eric had been there. I'd been so astounded over so many things that the circumstances of finding Eric alone, half naked, and clueless, early in the morning on the first day of the New Year, had been buried in the aftermath of the Witch War.

"Did you ever figure out the answer?" I asked, realizing after the words had left my mouth how stupid the question was.

"No," he said in a voice that was just short of a hiss. "No. And the witch who cursed me is dead, though the curse was broken. Now she can't tell me what her curse entailed. Was I supposed to look for the person I hated? Loved? Could it have been random that I found myself running out in the middle of nowhere . . . except that nowhere was on the way to your house?"

A moment of uneasy silence on my part. I had no idea what to say, and Eric was clearly waiting for a response.

"Probably the fairy blood," I said weakly, though I had spent hours telling myself that my fraction of fairy blood was not significant enough to cause more than a mild attraction on the part of the vampires I met.

"No," he said. And then he was gone.

"Well," I said out loud, unhappy with the quiver in my voice. "As exits go, that was a good one." It was pretty hard to have the last word with a vampire.

8

"MY BAGS ARE PACKED . . ." I SANG.

"Well, I'm not so lonesome I could cry," Amelia said. She'd kindly agreed to drive me to the airport, but I should have made her promise to be pleasant that morning, too. She'd been a little broody the whole time I was putting on my makeup.

"I wish I was going, too," she said, admitting what had been sticking in her craw. Of course, I'd known Amelia's problem before she'd said it out loud. But there wasn't a thing I could do.

"It's not up to me to invite or not invite," I said. "I'm the hired help."

"I know," she said grumpily. "I'll get the mail, and I'll water the plants, and I'll brush Bob. Hey, I heard that the Bayou State insurance salesman needs a receptionist, since the mom of the woman who worked for him got evacuated from New Orleans and has to have full-time care."

"Oh, do go in to apply for that job," I said. "You'll just love it." My insurance guy was a wizard who backed up his policies with spells. "You'll really like Greg Aubert, and he'll interest you." I wanted Amelia's interview at the insurance agency to be a happy surprise.

Amelia looked at me sideways with a little smile. "Oh, is he cute and single?"

"Nope. But he has other interesting attributes. And remember, you promised Bob you wouldn't do guys."

"Oh, yeah." Amelia looked gloomy. "Hey, let's look up your hotel."

Amelia was teaching me how to use my cousin Hadley's computer. I'd brought it back with me from New Orleans, thinking I'd sell it, but Amelia had coaxed me to set it up here at the house. It looked funny on a desk in the corner of the oldest part of the house, the room now used as a living room. Amelia paid for an extra phone line for the Internet, since she needed it for her laptop upstairs. I was still a nervous novice.

Amelia clicked on Google and typed in "Pyramid of Gizeh hotel." We stared at the picture that popped up on the screen. Most of the vampire hotels were in large urban centers, like Rhodes, and they were also tourist attractions. Often called simply "the Pyramid," the hotel was shaped like one, of course, and it was faced with bronze-colored reflective glass. There was one band of lighter glass around one of the floors close to the base.

"Not exactly . . . hmmm." Amelia looked at the building, her head tilted sideways.

"It needs to slant more," I said, and she nodded.

"You're right. It's like they wanted to have a pyramid, but they didn't really need enough floors to make it look right. The angle's not steep enough to make it look really grand."

"And it's sitting on a big rectangle."

"That, too. I expect those are the convention rooms."

"No parking," I said, peering at the screen.

"Oh, that'll be below the building. They can build 'em that way up there."

"It's on the lakefront," I said. "Hey, I get to see Lake Michigan. See, there's just a little park between the hotel and the lake."

"And about six lanes of traffic," Amelia pointed out.

"Okay, that, too."

"But it's close to major shopping," Amelia said.

"It's got an all-human floor," I read. "I'll bet that's this floor, the one that's lighter. I thought that was just the design, but it's so humans can go somewhere to have light during the day. People need that for their well-being."

"Translation: it's a law," Amelia said. "What else is there? Meeting rooms, blah blah blah. Opaque glass throughout except for the human floor. Exquisitely decorated suites on the highest levels, blah blah blah. Staff thoroughly trained in vampires' needs. Does that mean they're all willing to be blood donors or fuck buddies?"

Amelia was so cynical. But now that I knew who her father was, that kind of made sense.

"I'd like to see the very top room, the tip of the pyramid," I said.

"Can't. It says here that that's not a real guest floor. It's actually where all the air conditioner stuff is."

"Well, hell. Time to go," I said, glancing at my watch.

"Oh, yeah." Amelia stared gloomily at the screen.

"I'll only be gone a week," I said. Amelia was definitely a person who didn't like to be by herself. We went downstairs and carried my bags to the car.

"I got the hotel number to call in case of emergency. I got your cell phone number, too. You pack your charger?" She maneuvered down the long gravel driveway and out onto Hummingbird Road. We'd go right around Bon Temps to get to the interstate.

"Yeah." And my toothbrush and toothpaste, my razor, my deodorant, my hair dryer (just in case), my makeup, all my new clothes and some extras, lots of shoes, a sleeping outfit, Amelia's traveling alarm clock, underwear, a little jewelry, an extra purse, and two paperbacks. "Thanks for loaning me the suitcase." Amelia had contributed her bright red roller bag and a matching garment bag, plus a carry-on I'd crammed with a book, a crossword puzzle compendium, a portable CD player, and a headset, plus a small CD case.

We didn't talk much on the drive. I was thinking how strange it was going to be, leaving Amelia alone in my family home. There had been Stackhouses in residence on the site for over a hundred and seventy years.

Our sporadic conversation died by the time we neared the airport. There didn't seem to be anything else to be said. We were right by the main Shreveport terminal, but we were going to a small private hangar. If Eric hadn't booked an Anubis charter plane weeks ago, he would've been up a creek, because the summit was definitely taxing Anubis's capabilities. All the states involved were sending delegations, and a big hunk of Middle America, from the Gulf to the Canadian border, was included in the American Central division.

A few months ago, Louisiana would have needed two planes. Now one would suffice, especially since a few of the party had gone ahead. I'd read the list of missing vampires after the meeting at Fangtasia, and to my regret, Melanie and Chester had been on it. I'd met them at the queen's New Orleans headquarters, and though we hadn't had time to become bosom buddies or anything, they'd seemed like good vamps.

There was a guard at the gate in the fence enclosing the hangar, and he checked my driver's license and Amelia's before he let us in. He was a regular human off-duty cop, but he seemed competent and alert. "Turn to the right, and there's parking by the door in the east wall," he said.

Amelia leaned forward a little as she drove, but the door was easy enough to see, and there were other cars parked there. It was about ten in the morning, and there was a touch of cool in the air, just below the surface warmth. It was an early breath of fall. After the hot, hot summer, it was just blissful. It would be cooler in Rhodes, Pam had said. She'd checked the temperatures for the coming week on the Internet and called me to tell me to pack a sweater. She'd sounded almost excited, which was a big deal for Pam. I'd been getting the impression that Pam was a wee bit restless, a bit tired of Shreveport and the bar. Maybe it was just me.

Amelia helped me unload the suitcases. Amelia had had to take a number of spells off the red Samsonite before she could hand it over to me. I hadn't asked what would have happened if she'd forgotten. I pulled up the handle on the rolling bag and slung the carry-on bag across my shoulder. Amelia took the hanging bag and opened the door.

I'd never been in an airplane hangar before, but it was just like the ones in the movies: cavernous. There were a few small planes parked inside, but we proceeded as Pam had instructed to the large opening in the west wall. The Anubis Air jet was parked outside, and the coffins were being loaded onto the luggage belt by the uniformed Anubis employees. They all wore black relieved only by a stylized jackal's head on the chest of the uniform, an affectation that I found irritating. They glanced at us casually, but no one challenged us or asked to see identification until we got to the steps leading up to the plane.

Bobby Burnham was standing at the foot of the steps

with a clipboard. Of course, since it was daylight, it was obvious Bobby wasn't a vamp, but he was nearly pale and stern enough to be one. I'd never met him before, but I knew who he was, and he certainly recognized me. I plucked that right from his brain. But his certainty didn't stop him from checking my ID against his damn list, and he was giving Amelia the big glare, like she couldn't turn him into a toad. (That was what Amelia was thinking.)

"He'd have to croak," I murmured, and she smiled.

Bobby introduced himself, and when we nodded, he said, "Your name is on the list, Miss Stackhouse, but Miss Broadway's isn't. I'm afraid you'll have to get your luggage up by yourself." Bobby was loving the power.

Amelia was whispering something under her breath, and in a rush Bobby blurted, "I'll carry the heavy bag up the stairs, Miss Stackhouse. Can you handle the other bag? If that's not something you want to do, I'll be back down in a minute and take them up for you." The astonishment on his face was priceless, but I tried not to enjoy it too much. Amelia was playing a slightly mean trick.

"Thanks, I can manage," I reassured him, and took the hanging bag from Amelia while he bumped up the stairs with the heavier piece of luggage.

"Amelia, you rascal," I said, but not too angrily.

"Who's the asshole?" she asked.

"Bobby Burnham. He's Eric's daytime guy." All vamps of a certain rank had one. Bobby was a recent acquisition of Eric's.

"What does he do? Dust the coffins?"

"No, he makes business arrangements, he goes to the bank, he picks up the dry cleaning, he deals with the state offices that are open only in the day, and so forth."

"So he's a gofer."

"Well, yeah. But he's an important gofer. He's Eric's gofer."

Bobby was coming back down the steps now, still looking surprised that he'd been polite and helpful. "Don't do anything else to him," I said, knowing that she was considering it.

Amelia's eyes flashed before she got the sense of what I was saying. "Yeah, petty of me," she admitted. "I just hate power-mad jerks."

"Who doesn't? Listen, I'll see you in a week. Thanks for bringing me to the plane."

"Yeah, yeah." She gave me a forlorn smile. "You have a good time, and don't get killed or bitten or anything."

Impulsively, I hugged her, and after a second's surprise, she hugged me back.

"Take good care of Bob," I said, and up the stairs I went.

I couldn't help feeling a little anxious, since I was cutting my ties with my familiar life, at least temporarily. The Anubis Air employee in the cabin said, "Choose your seat, Miss Stackhouse." She took the hanging bag from me and put it away. The interior of the aircraft was not like that of any human plane, or at least that was what the Anubis website had alleged. The Anubis fleet had been designed and outfitted for the transportation of sleeping vamps, with human passengers coming in second. There were coffin bays around the wall, like giant luggage bins, and at the front end of the aircraft there were three rows of seats, on the right three seats, and on the left two, for people like me . . . or, at least, people who were going to be helpful to the vamps at this conference in some capacity. At present, there were only three other people sitting in the seats. Well, one other human and two part-humans.

"Hi, Mr. Cataliades," I said, and the round man rose from his seat, beaming.

"Dear Miss Stackhouse," he said warmly, because that was the way Mr. Cataliades talked, "I am so very glad to see you again."

"Pleased to see you, too, Mr. Cataliades."

His name was pronounced Ka-TAL-ee-ah-deez, and if he had a first name, I didn't know it. Sitting next to him was a very young woman with bright red spiked hair: his niece, Diantha. Diantha wore the strangest ensembles, and tonight she'd topped herself. Maybe five feet tall, bony thin, Diantha had chosen orange calf-length leggings, blue Crocs, a white ruffled skirt, and a tie-dyed tank top. She was dazzling to the eye.

Diantha didn't believe in breathing while she talked. Now she said, "Goodtoseeya."

"Right back at ya," I said, and since she didn't make any other move, I gave her a nod. Some supes shake hands, others don't, so you have to be careful. I turned to the other passenger. With another human, I thought I was on firmer ground, so I held out my right hand. As if he'd been offered a dead fish, the man extended his own hand after a perceptible pause. He pressed my palm in a limp way and withdrew his fingers as if he could just barely refrain from wiping them on his suit pants.

"Miss Stackhouse, this is Johan Glassport, a specialist in vampire law."

"Mr. Glassport," I said politely, struggling not to take offense.

"Johan, this is Sookie Stackhouse, the queen's telepath," Mr. Cataliades said in his courtly way. Mr. Cataliades's sense of humor was as abundant as his belly. There was a twinkle in his eye even now. But you had to remember that the part of him that wasn't human—the majority of Mr. Cataliades—was a demon. Diantha was half-demon; her uncle even more.

Johan gave me a brief up-and-down scan, almost audibly sniffed, and returned to the book he had in his lap.

Just then, the Anubis stewardess began giving us the usual spiel, and I buckled myself into my seat. Soon after that, we were airborne. I didn't have a twinge of anxiety, because I was so disgusted by Johan Glassport's behavior.

I didn't think I'd ever encountered such in-your-face rudeness. The people of northern Louisiana may not have much money, and there may be a high teen pregnancy rate and all kinds of other problems, but by God, we're polite.

Diantha said, "Johan'sanasshole."

Johan paid absolutely no attention to this accurate assessment but turned the page of his book.

"Thanks, dear," Mr. Cataliades said. "Miss Stackhouse, bring me up to date on your life."

I moved to sit opposite the trio. "Not much to tell, Mr. Cataliades. I got the check, as I wrote you. Thanks for tying up all the loose ends on Hadley's estate, and if you'd reconsider and send me a bill, I'd be glad to pay it." Not exactly glad, but relieved of an obligation.

"No, child. It was the least I could do. The queen was happy to express her thanks in that way, even though the evening hardly turned out like she'd planned."

"Of course, none of us imagined it would end that way." I thought of Wybert's head flying through the air surrounded by a mist of blood, and I shuddered.

"You are the witness," Johan said unexpectedly. He slipped a bookmark into his book and closed it. His pale eyes, magnified behind his glasses, were fixed on me. From being dog poop on his shoe, I had been transformed into something quite interesting and remarkable.

"Yeah. I'm the witness."

"Then we must talk, now."

"I'm a little surprised, if you're representing the queen at this very important trial, that you haven't gotten around to talking to me before," I said in as mild a voice as I could manage.

"The queen had trouble contacting me, and I had to finish with my previous client," Johan said. His unlined face didn't exactly change expression, but it did look a bit tenser.

"Johan was in jail," Diantha said very clearly and distinctly.

"Oh, my goodness," I said, truly startled.

Johan said, "Of course, the charges were completely unfounded."

"Of course, Johan," Mr. Cataliades said with absolutely no inflection in his voice.

"Ooo," I said. "What were those charges that were so false?"

Johan looked at me again, this time with less arrogance. "I was accused of striking a prostitute in Mexico."

I didn't know much about law enforcement in Mexico, but it did seem absolutely incredible to me that an American could get arrested in Mexico for hitting a prostitute, if that was the only charge. Unless he had a lot of enemies.

"Did you happen to have something in your hand when you struck her?" I asked with a bright smile.

"I believe Johan had a knife in his hand," Mr. Cataliades said gravely.

I know my smile vanished right about then. "You were in jail in Mexico for knifing a woman," I said. Who was dog poop now?

"A prostitute," he corrected. "That was the charge, but of course, I was completely innocent."

"Of course," I said.

"Mine is not the case on the table right now, Miss Stackhouse. My job is to defend the queen against the very serious charges brought against her, and you are an important witness."

"I'm the only witness."

"Of course—to the actual death."

"There were several actual deaths."

"The only death that matters at this summit is the death of Peter Threadgill."

I sighed at the image of Wybert's head, and then I said, "Yeah, I was there."

Johan may have been lower than pond scum, but he knew his stuff. We went through a long question and answer session that left the lawyer knowing more about what had happened than I did, and I'd been there. Mr. Cataliades listened with great interest, and now and then threw in a clarification or explained the layout of the queen's monastery to the lawyer.

Diantha listened for a while, sat on the floor and played jacks for half an hour, then reclined her seat and went to sleep.

The Anubis Airline attendant came through and offered drinks and snacks from time to time on the three-hour flight north, and after I'd finished my session with the trial lawyer, I got up to use the bathroom. That was an experience; I'd never been in an airplane bathroom before. Instead of resuming my seat, I walked down the plane, taking a look at each coffin. There was a luggage tag on each one, attached to the handles. With us in the plane today were Eric, Bill, the queen, Andre, and Sigebert. I also found the coffin of Gervaise, who'd been hosting the queen, and Cleo Babbitt, who was the sheriff of Area Three. The Area Two sheriff, Arla Yvonne, had been left in charge of the state while the queen was gone.

The queen's coffin was inlaid with mother-of-pearl designs, but the others were quite plain. They were all of polished wood: no modern metal for these vamps. I ran my hand over Eric's, having creepy mental pictures of him lying inside, quite lifeless.

"Gervaise's woman drove ahead by night with Rasul to make sure all the queen's preparations were in place," Mr. Cataliades's voice said from my right shoulder. I jumped and shrieked, which tickled the queen's civil lawyer pink. He chuckled and chuckled.

"Smooth move," I said, and my voice was sour as a squeezed lemon.

"You were wondering where the fifth sheriff was."

"Yes, but you were maybe a thought or two behind."

"I'm not telepathic like you, my dear. I was just following your facial expressions and body language. You counted the coffins and began reading the luggage tags."

"So the queen is not only the queen, but the sheriff of her own area."

"Yes; it eliminates confusion. Not all the rulers follow that pattern, but the queen found it irksome to constantly consult another vampire when she wanted to do something."

"Sounds like the queen." I glanced forward at our companions. Diantha and Johan were occupied: Diantha with sleep, Johan with his book. I wondered if it was a dissection book, with diagrams—or perhaps an account of the crimes of Jack the Ripper, with the crime scene photographs. That seemed about Johan's speed. "How come the queen has a lawyer like him?" I asked in as low a voice as I could manage. "He seems really . . . shoddy."

"Johan Glassport is a great lawyer, and one who will take cases other lawyers won't," said Mr. Cataliades. "And he is also a murderer. But then, we all are, are we not?" His beady dark eyes looked directly into mine.

I returned the look for a long moment. "In defense of my own life or the life of someone I loved, I would kill an attacker," I said, thinking before every word left my mouth.

"What a diplomatic way to put it, Miss Stackhouse. I

can't say the same for myself. Some things I have killed, I tore apart for the sheer joy of it."

Oh, *ick*. More than I wanted to know.

"Diantha loves to hunt deer, and she has killed people in my defense. And she and her sister even brought down a rogue vampire or two."

I reminded myself to treat Diantha with more respect. Killing a vampire was a very difficult undertaking. And she could play jacks like a fiend.

"And Johan?" I asked.

"Perhaps I'd better leave Johan's little predilections un-spoken for the moment. He won't step out of line while he's with us, after all. Are you pleased with the job Johan is do-ing, briefing you?"

"Is that what he's doing? Well, yes, I guess so. He's been very thorough, which is what you want."

"Indeed."

"Can you tell me what to expect at the summit? What the queen will want?"

Mr. Cataliades said, "Let's sit and I'll try to explain it to you."

For the next hour, he talked, and I listened and asked questions.

By the time Diantha sat up and yawned, I felt a bit more prepared for all the new things I faced in the city of Rhodes. Johan Glassport closed his book and looked at us, as if he were now ready to talk.

"Mr. Glassport, have you been to Rhodes before?" Mr. Cataliades asked.

"Yes," the lawyer answered. "I used to practice in Rhodes. Actually, I used to commute between Rhodes and Chicago; I lived midway between."

"When did you go to Mexico?" I asked.

"Oh, a year or two ago," he answered. "I had some dis-agreements with business associates here, and it seemed a good time to . . ."

"Get the heck out of the city?" I supplied helpfully.

"Run like hell?" Diantha suggested.

"Take the money and vanish?" Mr. Cataliades said.

"All of the above," said Johan Glassport with the faintest trace of a smile.

9

It was midafternoon when we arrived in Rhodes. There was an Anubis truck waiting to onload the coffins and transport them to the Pyramid of Gizeh. I looked out the limo windows every second of the ride into the city, and despite the overwhelming presence of the chain stores we also saw in Shreveport, I had no doubt I was in a different place. Heavy red brick, city traffic, row houses, glimpses of the lake . . . I was trying to look in all directions at once. Then we came into view of the hotel; it was amazing. The day wasn't sunny enough for the bronze glass to glint, but the Pyramid of Gizeh looked impressive anyway. Sure enough, there was the park across the six-lane street, which was seething with traffic, and beyond it the vast lake.

While the Anubis truck pulled around to the back of the Pyramid to discharge its load of vampires and luggage, the limo swept up to the front of the hotel. As we daytime creatures scooted out of the car, I didn't know what to look at first: the broad waters or the decorations of the structure itself.

The main doors of the Pyramid were manned by a lot of maroon-and-beige uniformed men, but there were silent guardians, too. There were two elaborate reproductions of sarcophagi placed in an upright position, one on each side of the main lobby doors. They were fascinating, and I would have enjoyed the chance to examine both of them, but we were swept into the building by the staff. One man opened the car door, one examined our identification to make sure we were registered guests—not human reporters, curiosity seekers, or assorted fanatics—and another pushed open the door of the hotel to indicate we should enter.

I'd stayed in a vampire hotel before, so I expected the armed guards and the lack of ground floor windows. The Pyramid of Gizeh was making more of an effort to look a bit like a human hotel than Dallas's Silent Shore had; though the walls held murals imitating Egyptian tomb art, the lobby was bright with artificial light and horribly perky with piped-in music—"The Girl from Ipanema" in a vampire hotel.

The lobby was busier than the Silent Shore's, too.

There were lots of humans and other creatures striding around purposefully, lots of action at the check-in desk, and some milling around the hospitality booth put up by the host city's vampire nest. I'd gone with Sam to a bar supply convention in Shreveport once when he was shopping for a new pump system, and I recognized the general setup. Somewhere, I was sure, there would be a convention hall with booths, and a schedule of panels or demonstrations.

I hoped there would be a map of the hotel, with all events and locations noted, in our registration packet. Or were the vampires too snooty for such mundane aids? No, there was a hotel diagram framed and lit for the perusal of guests and scheduled tours. This hotel was numbered in reverse order. The top floor, the penthouse, was numbered 1. The bottom, largest floor—the human floor—was numbered 15. There was a mezzanine between the human floor and lobby, and there were large convention rooms in the annex to the northern side of the hotel, the rectangular windowless projection that had looked so odd in the Internet picture.

I eyed people scurrying through the lobby—maids, bodyguards, valets, bellmen. . . . Here we were, all us little human beavers, scurrying around to get things ready for the undead conventioneers. (Could you call them that, when this was billed as a summit? What was the difference?) I felt a little sour when I wondered why this was the order of things, when a few years ago, the vampires were the ones doing the scurrying, and that was back into a dark corner where they could hide. Maybe that had been the more natural way. I slapped myself mentally. I might as well go join the Fellowship, if that was how I really felt. I'd noticed the protesters in the little park across the street from the Pyramid of Gizeh, which some of the signs referred to as "The Pyramid of Geezers."

"Where are the coffins?" I asked Mr. Cataliades.

"They're coming in through a basement entrance," he said.

There had been a metal detector at the hotel door. I'd tried hard not to look when Johan Glassport had emptied his pockets. The detector had gone off like a siren when he'd passed through. "Do the coffins have to go through a metal detector, too?" I asked.

"No. Our vampires have wooden coffins, but the hardware on them is metal, and you can't empty the vampires out to search their pockets for other metal objects, so that wouldn't make any sense," Mr. Cataliades answered, for the first time sounding impatient. "Plus, some vampires have chosen the modern metal caskets."

"The demonstrators across the street," I said. "They have me spooked. They'd love to sneak in here."

Mr. Cataliades smiled, a terrifying sight. "No one will get in here, Miss Sookie. There are other guards that you can't see."

While Mr. Cataliades checked us in, I stood to his side and turned to look around at the other people. They were all dressed very nicely, and they were all talking. About us. I felt instantly anxious at the looks we were getting from the others, and the buzzing thoughts from the few live guests and staff reinforced my anxiety. We were the human entourage of the queen who had been one of the most powerful vampire rulers in America. Now she was not only weakened economically, but she was going on trial for murdering her husband. I could see why the other flunkies were interested—*I* would've found us interesting—but I was uncomfortable. All I could think about was how shiny my nose must be, and how much I wanted to have a few moments alone.

The clerk went over our reservations very slowly and deliberately, as if to keep us on exhibit in the lobby for as long as possible. Mr. Cataliades dealt with him with his usual elaborate courtesy, though even that was getting strained after ten minutes.

I'd been standing at a discreet distance during the process, but when I could tell the clerk—fortyish, recreational drug user, father of three—was just fucking us over to entertain himself, I took a step closer. I laid a hand on Mr. C's sleeve to indicate that I wanted to join in the conversation. He interrupted himself to turn an interested face toward me.

"You give us our keys and tell us where our vamps are, or I'll tell your boss that you're the one selling Pyramid of Gizeh items on eBay. And if you bribe a maid to even *touch* the queen's panties, much less steal 'em, I'll sic Diantha on you." Diantha had just returned from tracking down a bottle of water. She obligingly revealed her sharp, pointed teeth in a lethal smile.

The clerk turned white and then red in an interesting display of blood flow patterns. "Yes, ma'am," he stammered, and I wondered if he would wet himself. After my little rummage through his head, I didn't much care.

In very short order, we all had keys, we had a list of "our" vampires' resting places, and the bellman was bringing our luggage in one of those neat carts. That reminded me of something.

*Barry,* I said in my head. *You here?*

*Yeah,* said a voice that was far from the faltering one it had been the first time I'd heard it. *Sookie Stackhouse?*

*It's me. We're checking in. I'm in 1538. You?*

*I'm in 1576. How are you doing?*

*Good, personally. But Louisiana . . . we've had the hurricane, and we've got the trial. I guess you know all about that?*

*Yeah. You saw some action.*

*You could say that,* I told him, wondering if my smile was coming across in my head.

*Got that loud and clear.*

Now I had an inkling of how people must feel when they were faced with me.

*I'll see you later,* I told Barry. *Hey, what's your real last name?*

*You started something when you brought my gift out into the open,* he told me. *My real name is Barry Horowitz. Now I just call myself Barry Bellboy. That's how I'm registered, if you forget my room number.*

*Okay. Looking forward to visiting with you.*

*Same here.*

And then Barry and I both turned our attention to other

things, and that strange tickling feeling of mind-to-mind communication was gone.

Barry's the only other telepath I've ever encountered.

Mr. Cataliades had discovered that the humans—well, the non-vampires—in the party had each been put in a room with another person. Some of the vampires had roommates, too. He hadn't been pleased that he himself was sharing a room with Diantha, but the hotel was extremely crowded, the clerk had said. He may have been lying about a lot of other things, but that much was clearly true.

I was sharing a room with Gervaise's squeeze, and as I slid the card into the slot on the door, I wondered if she'd be in. She was. I'd been expecting a woman like the fangbangers who hang around at Fangtasia, but Carla Danvers was another kind of creature entirely.

"Hey, girl!" she said, as I entered. "I figured you'd be along soon when they brought your bags up. I'm Carla, Gerry's girlfriend."

"Nice to meet you," I said, shaking hands. Carla was a prom queen. Maybe she hadn't been, literally; maybe she hadn't made homecoming queen, either, but she'd surely been on the court. Carla had dark brown chin-length hair, and big brown eyes, and teeth that were so straight and white that they were an advertisement for her orthodontist. Her breasts had been enhanced, and her ears were pierced, and her belly button, too. She had a tattoo on her lower back, some black vines in a vee pattern with a couple of roses with green leaves in the middle. I could see all this because Carla was naked, and she didn't seem to have the slightest idea that her nudity was a little on the "too much information" side to suit me.

"Have you and Gervaise been going together long?" I asked to camouflage how uncomfortable I was.

"I met Gerry, let's see, seven months ago. He said it would be better for me to have a separate room because he might have to have business meetings in his, you know? Plus, I'm going shopping while I'm here—retail therapy! Big city stores! And I wanted someplace to store my shopping bags so he won't ask me how much it all costs." She gave me a wink I can only say was roguish.

"Okay," I said. "Sounds good." It really didn't, but Carla's program was hardly my business. My suitcase was waiting for me on a stand, so I opened it and started to unpack, noting that my hanging bag with my good dresses was already in the closet. Carla had left me exactly half the closet space and drawer space, which was decent. She had brought about twenty times more clothes than I had, which made her fairness all the more remarkable.

"Whose girlfriend are you?" Carla asked. She was giving herself a pedicure. When she drew up one leg, the overhead light winked on something metallic between her legs. Completely embarrassed, I turned away to straighten my evening dress on the hanger.

"I'm dating Quinn," I said.

I glanced over my shoulder, keeping my gaze high.

Carla looked blank.

"The weretiger," I said. "He's arranging the ceremonies here."

She looked marginally more responsive.

"Big guy, shaved head," I said.

Her face brightened. "Oh, yeah, I saw him this morning! He was eating breakfast in the restaurant when I was checking in."

"There's a restaurant?"

"Yeah, sure. Though of course it's tiny. And there's room service."

"You know, in vampire hotels there often isn't a restaurant," I said, just to make conversation. I'd read an article about it in *American Vampire*.

"Oh. Well, that makes no sense at all." Carla finished one set of toes and began another.

"Not from a vampire point of view."

Carla frowned. "I know they don't eat. But people do. And this is a people world, right? That's like not learning English when you emigrate to America."

I turned around to check out Carla's face, make sure she was serious. Yeah, she was.

"Carla," I said, and then stopped. I didn't have any idea what to say, how to get across to Carla that a four-hundred-year-old vamp really didn't care very much about the eating arrangements of a twenty-year-old human. But the girl was waiting for me to finish. "Well, it's good that there's a restaurant here," I said weakly.

She nodded. "Yeah, 'cause I need my coffee in the morning," she said. "I just can't get going without it. Course, when you date a vamp, your morning is liable to begin at three or four in the afternoon." She laughed.

"True," I said. I'd finished unpacking, so I went over to our window and looked out. The glass was so heavily tinted that it was hard to make out the landscape, but it was seeable. I wasn't on the Lake Michigan side of the hotel, which was a pity, but I looked at the buildings around the west side of the hotel with curiosity. I didn't see cities that often, and I'd never seen a northern city. The sky was darkening rapidly, so between that and the tinted windows I really couldn't see too much after ten minutes. The vampires would be awake soon, and my workday would begin.

Though she kept up a sporadic stream of chatter, Carla didn't ask what my role was at this summit. She assumed I was there as arm candy. For the moment, that was all right with me. Sooner or later, she'd find out what my particular talent was, and then she'd be nervous around me. On the other hand, now she was a little *too* relaxed.

Carla was getting dressed (thank God) in what I thought of as "classy whore." She was wearing a glittery green cocktail dress that almost didn't have a top to it, and fuck-me shoes, and what amounted to a see-through thong. Well, she had her working clothes, and I had mine. I wasn't too pleased with myself for being so judgmental, and maybe I was a little envious that my working clothes were so conservative.

For tonight, I had chosen a chocolate brown lace handkerchief dress. I put in my big gold earrings and slid into brown pumps, put on some lipstick, and brushed my hair really well. Sticking my keycard into my little evening purse, I headed to the front desk to find out which suite was the queen's, since Mr. Cataliades had told me to present myself there.

I had hoped to run into Quinn along the way, but I didn't see hide nor hair of him. What with me having a roommate, and Quinn being so busy all the time, this summit might not promise as much fun on the side as I'd hoped.

The desk clerk blanched when he saw me coming, and he looked around to see if Diantha was with me. While he was scrawling the queen's room number on a piece of notepaper with a shaking hand, I looked around me with more attention.

There were security cameras in a few obvious locations, pointed at the front doors and at the registration desk. And I thought I could see one at the elevators. There were the usual armed guards—usual for a vampire hotel, that is. The big selling point for any vampire hotel was the security and privacy of its guests. Otherwise, vampires could stay more cheaply and centrally in the special vampire rooms of mainstream hotels. (Even Motel 6 had one vampire room at almost every location.) When I thought about the protesters outside, I really hoped the security crew here at the Pyramid was on the ball.

I nodded at another human woman as I crossed the lobby to the central bank of elevators. The rooms got ritzier the higher up you went, I gathered, since there were fewer on the floor. The queen had one of the fourth floor suites, since she'd booked for this event a long time ago, before Katrina—and probably while her husband was still alive. There were only eight doors on her floor, and I didn't have to see the number to know which room was Sophie-Anne's. Sigebert was standing in front of it. Sigebert was a boulder of a man. He had guarded the queen for hundreds of years, as had Andre. The ancient vampire looked lonely without his brother, Wybert. Otherwise, he was the same old Anglo-Saxon warrior he'd been the first time I'd met him—shaggy beard, physique of a wild boar, missing a tooth or two in crucial places.

Sigebert grinned at me, a terrifying sight. "Miss Sookie," he said by way of greeting.

"Sigebert," I said, carefully pronouncing it "See-ya-bairt." "Are you doing okay?" I wanted to convey sympathy without dipping into too-sentimental waters.

"My brother, he died a hero," Sigebert said proudly. "In battle."

I thought of saying, "You must miss him so much after a thousand years." Then I decided that was exactly like reporters asking the parents of missing children, "How do you feel?"

"He was a great fighter," I said instead, and that was exactly what Sigebert wanted to hear. He clapped me on the shoulder, almost knocking me to the ground. Then his look got a little absent, as if he were listening to an announcement.

I'd suspected that the queen could talk to her "children" telepathically, and when Sigebert opened the door for me without another word, I knew that was true. I was glad she couldn't talk to me. Being able to communicate with Barry was kind of fun, but if we hung out together all the time I was sure it would get old in a hurry. Plus, Sophie-Anne was a heck of a lot scarier.

The queen's suite was lavish. I'd never seen anything like it. The carpet was as thick as a sheep's pelt, and it was off-white. The furniture was upholstered in shades of gold and dark blue. The slanting slab of glass that enclosed the outside wall was opaque. I have to say, the large wall of darkness made me feel twitchy.

In the midst of this splendor, Sophie-Anne sat curled on a couch. Small and extremely pale, with her shining brown hair swept up in a chignon, the queen was wearing a raspberry-colored silk suit with black piping and black alligator heels. Her jewelry was heavy, gold, and simple.

Sophie-Anne would have looked more age-appropriate wearing a Gwen Stefani L.A.M.B. outfit. She'd died as a human when she'd been maybe fifteen or sixteen. In her time, that would have made her a fully-grown woman and mother. In our time, that made her a mall rat. To modern eyes, her clothes were too old for her, but it would take an insane person to tell her so. Sophie-Anne was the world's most dangerous teenager, and the second most dangerous had her back. Andre was standing right behind Sophie-Anne, as always. When he'd given me a thorough look, and the door had closed behind me, he actually sat beside Sophie-Anne, which was some kind of signal that I was a member of the club, I guess. Andre and his queen had both been drinking TrueBlood, and they looked rosy as a result—almost human, in fact.

"How are your accommodations?" Sophie-Anne asked politely.

"Fine. I'm rooming with a . . . girlfriend of Gervaise's," I said.

"With *Carla*? Why?" Her brows rose up like dark birds in a clear sky.

"The hotel's crowded. It's no big thing. I figure she'll be with Gervaise most of the time, anyway," I said.

Sophie-Anne said, "What did you think of Johan?"

I could feel my face harden. "I think he belongs in jail."

"But he will keep me out of it."

I tried to imagine what a vampire jail would be like, gave up. I couldn't give her any positive feedback on Johan, so I just nodded.

"You are still not telling me what you picked up from him."

"He's very tense and conflicted."

"Explain."

"He's anxious. He's scared. He's fighting different loyalties. He only wants to come out alive. He doesn't care for anyone but himself."

"So how does that make him different from any other human?" Andre commented.

Sophie-Anne responded with a twitch of one side of her mouth. That Andre, what a comedian.

"Most humans don't stab women," I said as quietly and calmly as I could. "Most humans don't enjoy that."

Sophie-Anne was not completely indifferent to the violent death Johan Glassport had meted out, but naturally she was a little more concerned with her own legal defense. At least, that was how I read her, but with vampires, I had to go on subtle body language rather than the sure knowledge right out of their brains. "He'll defend me, I'll pay him, and then he's on his own," she said. "Anything might happen to him then." She gave me a clear-eyed look.

Okay, Sophie-Anne, I got the picture.

"Did he question you thoroughly? Did you feel he knew

what he was doing?" she asked, returning to the important stuff.

"Yes, ma'am," I said promptly. "He did seem to be really competent."

"Then he'll be worth the trouble."

I didn't even let my eyes flicker.

"Did Cataliades tell you what to expect?"

"Yes, ma'am, he did."

"Good. As well as your testimony at the trial, I need you to attend every meeting with me that includes humans."

This was why she was paying me the big bucks.

"Ah, do you have any schedule of meetings?" I asked. "It's just, I'd be ready and waiting if I had any idea when you needed me."

Before she could answer, there was a knock at the door. Andre rose and moved to answer it so smoothly and fluidly that you would have sworn he was part cat. His sword was in his hand, though I hadn't seen it before. The door opened a bit just as Andre reached it, and I heard Sigebert's bass rumble.

After they'd exchanged a few sentences, the door opened wider, and Andre said, "The King of Texas, my lady." There was only a hint of pleased surprise in his voice, but it was the equivalent of Andre doing cartwheels across the carpet. This visit was a show of support for Sophie-Anne, and all the other vampires would notice.

Stan Davis came in, trailing a group of vamps and humans.

Stan was a nerd's nerd. He was the kind of guy who you checked out for a pocket protector. You could see the comb marks in his sandy hair, and his glasses were heavy and thick. They were also quite unnecessary. I'd never met a vamp who didn't have excellent vision and very precise hearing. Stan was wearing a wash 'n' wear white shirt with a Sears brand logo and some navy Dockers. And brown leather moccasins. Hoo, boy. He'd been a sheriff when I'd met him, and now that he was king, he was maintaining the same low-key approach.

Behind Stan came his sergeant at arms, Joseph Velasquez. A short, burly Hispanic with spiky hair, Joseph never seemed to crack a smile. By his side was a red-haired female vamp named Rachel; I remembered her, too, from my trip to Dallas. Rachel was a savage one, and she didn't like cooperating with humans in the least. Trailing the two was Barry the Bellboy, looking good in designer jeans and a taupe silk T-shirt, a discreet gold chain around his neck. Barry had matured in an almost scary way since I'd last seen him. He'd been a handsome, gawky boy of maybe nineteen when I'd first spotted him working as a bellboy at the Silent Shore Hotel in Dallas. Now Barry had had a manicure, a very good haircut, and the wary eyes of someone who'd been swimming in the shark pool.

We smiled at each other, and Barry said, *Good to see you. Looking pretty, Sookie.*

*Thanks, and likewise, Barry.*

Andre was doing the proper vampire greeting thing, which did not include handshaking. "Stan, we are pleased to see you. Who have you brought to meet us?"

Stan gallantly bent to kiss Sophie-Anne's hand. "Most beautiful queen," he said. "This vampire is my second, Joseph Velasquez. And this vampire is my nest sister Rachel. This human is the telepath Barry Bellboy. Indirectly, I have you to thank for him."

Sophie-Anne actually smiled. She said, "Of course, I am always delighted to do you any sort of favor in my power, Stan." She gestured to him to sit opposite her. Rachel and Joseph took up flanking positions. "It's so good to see you here in my suite. I had been concerned that I wouldn't have any visitors at all."

("Since I'm under indictment for killing my husband, and since I've also sustained a staggering economic blow," was the subtext.)

"I extend my sympathies to you," Stan said with a completely inflectionless voice. "The losses in your country have been extreme. If we can help . . . I know the humans from my state have helped yours, and it's only right that the vampires do likewise."

"Thank you for your kindness," she said. Sophie-Anne's pride was hurting in a major way. She had to struggle to paste that smile back on her face. "I believe you know Andre," she continued. "Andre, you now know Joseph. And I believe all of you know our Sookie."

The phone rang, and since I was closest to it, I answered it.

"Am I speaking to a member of the Queen of Louisiana's party?" the gruff voice asked.

"Yes, you are."

"One of you needs to come down to the loading bay to get a suitcase that belongs to your party. We can't read the label."

"Oh . . . okay."

"Sooner the better."

"All right."

He hung up. Okay, that was a little abrupt.

Since the queen was waiting for me to tell her who had called, I relayed the request, and she looked equally puzzled for all of a millisecond. "Later," she said dismissively.

In the meantime, the light eyes of the King of Texas were focused on me like laser beams. I inclined my head to him, which I hoped was the correct response. It seemed to be adequate. I would have liked to have had time to go over the protocol with Andre before the queen began receiving guests, but truthfully, I hadn't expected there to be any, much less a powerful guy like Stan Davis. This had to mean something good for the queen, or maybe it was a subtle vampire insult. I was sure I'd find out.

I felt the tickle of Barry in my mind. *She good to work for?* Barry asked.

*I just help her out from time to time,* I said. *I still have a day job.*

Barry looked at me with surprise. *You kidding? You could be raking it in, if you go to a good state like Ohio or Illinois where there's real money.*

I shrugged. *I like where I live,* I said.

Then we both became aware that our vampire employers were watching our silent exchange. Our faces were changing expression, I guess, like faces do during a conversation . . . except our conversation had been silent.

"Excuse me," I said. "I didn't mean to be rude. I just don't see people like me very often, and it's kind of a treat to talk to another telepath. I beg your pardon, ma'am, sir."

"I could almost hear it," Sophie-Anne marveled. "Stan, he has been very useful?" Sophie-Anne could talk to her own children mentally, but it must be as rare an ability among vampires as it was among people.

"Very useful," Stan confirmed. "The day that your Sookie brought him to my attention was a very good day for me. He knows when the humans are lying; he knows what their ulterior motives are. It's wonderful insight."

I looked at Barry, wondering if he ever thought of himself as a traitor to humankind or just as a vendor supplying a needed good. He met my eyes, his own face hard. Sure, he was conflicted about serving a vampire, revealing human secrets to his employer. I struggled with that idea myself from time to time.

"Hmmm. Sookie only works for me on occasion." Sophie-Anne was staring at me, and if I could characterize her smooth face, I would say she was thoughtful. Andre had something going on behind his pink-tinged teenage facade, and it was something I had better watch out for. He wasn't just thoughtful, he was interested; engaged, for want of a better description.

"Bill brought her to Dallas," Stan observed, not quite asking a question.

"He was her protector at the time," Sophie-Anne said.

A brief silence. Barry leered at me hopefully, and I gave him an in-your-dreams look. Actually, I felt like hugging him, since that little exchange broke up the silence into something I could handle.

"Do you really need Barry and me here, since we're the only humans, and it might not be so productive if we just sat around and read each other's minds?"

Joseph Velasquez actually smiled before he could stop himself.

After a silent moment, Sophie-Anne nodded, and then Stan. Queen Sophie and King Stan, I reminded myself. Barry bowed in a practiced way, and I felt like sticking out my tongue at him. I did a sort of bob and then scuttled out of the suite. Sigebert eyed us with a questioning face. "The queen, she not need you?" he asked.

"Not right now," I said. I tapped a pager that Andre had handed me at the last minute. "The pager will vibrate if she needs me," I said.

Sigebert eyed the device mistrustfully. "I think it would be better if you just stayed here," he said.

"The queen, she says I can go," I told him.

And off I went, Barry trailing along behind me. We took the elevator down to the lobby, where we found a secluded corner where no one could sneak up on us to eavesdrop.

I'd never conversed with someone entirely in my head, and neither had Barry, so we played around with that for a while. Barry would tell me the story of his life while I tried to block out all the other brains around me; then I'd try to listen to everyone else *and* to Barry.

This was actually a lot of fun.

Barry turned out to be better than I was at picking out who was thinking what in a crowd. I was a bit better at hearing nuance and detail, not always easy to pick up in thoughts. But we had some common ground.

We agreed on who the best broadcasters in the room were; that is, our "hearing" was the same. He would point at someone (in this case it was my roommate, Carla) and we would both listen to her thoughts, then rate them on a scale of one to five, five being the loudest, clearest broadcast. Carla was a three. After that agreement, we rated other people, and we found ourselves reacting almost as one over that.

Okay, this was interesting.

*Let's try touching,* I suggested.

Barry didn't even leer. He was into this, too. Without further ado, he took my hand, and we faced in nearly opposite directions.

The voices came in so clearly, it was like having a full-voice conversation with everyone in the room, all at once. Like pumping up the volume on a DVD, with the treble and bass perfectly balanced. It was elating and terrifying, all at once. Though I was facing away from the reception desk, I clearly heard a woman inquiring about the arrival of the Louisiana vamps. I caught my own image in the brain of the clerk, who was feeling delighted at doing me a bad turn.

*Here comes trouble,* Barry warned me.

I swung around to see a vampire advancing on me with not a very pleasant expression on her face. She had hot hazel eyes and straight light brown hair, and she was lean and mean.

"Finally, one of the Louisiana party. Are the rest of you in hiding? Tell your bitch whore of a mistress that I'll nail her hide to the wall! She won't get away with murdering my king! I'll see her staked and exposed to the sun on the roof of this hotel!"

I said the first thing that came into my head, unfortunately. "Save the drama for your mama," I told her, just like an eleven-year-old. "And by the way, who the heck are you?"

Of course, this had to be Jennifer Cater. I started to tell her that her king's character had been really substandard, but I liked my head right where it sat on my shoulders, and it wouldn't take much to tip this gal over the edge.

She gave good glare, I'd say that for her.

"I'll drain you dry," she said, harshly. We were attracting a certain amount of attention by then.

"Ooooo," I said, exasperated beyond wisdom. "I'm so scared. Wouldn't the court love to hear you say that? Correct me if I'm wrong, but aren't vampires prevented by—oh, yes—the *law* from threatening humans with death, or did I just read that wrong?"

"As if I give a snap of my fingers for human law," Jennifer Cater said, but the fire was dying down in her eyes as she realized that the whole lobby was listening to our exchange, including many humans and possibly some vampires who'd love to see her out of the way.

"Sophie-Anne Leclerq will be tried by the laws of our people," Jennifer said as a parting shot. "And she will be found guilty. I'll hold Arkansas, and I'll make it great."

"That'll be a first," I said with some justification. Arkansas, Louisiana, and Mississippi were three poor states huddled together, much to our mutual mortification. We were all grateful for each other, because we got to take turns being at the bottom of almost every list in the United States: poverty level, teen pregnancy, cancer death, illiteracy. . . . We pretty much rotated the honors.

Jennifer marched off, not wanting to try a comeback. She was determined, and she was vicious, but I thought Sophie-Anne could outmaneuver Jennifer any day. If I were a betting woman, I'd put money on the French nag.

Barry and I gave each other a shrug. Incident over. We joined hands again.

*More trouble,* Barry said, sounding resigned.

I focused my brain where his was going. I heard a weretiger heading our way in a big, big hurry.

I dropped Barry's hand and turned, my arms out already and my whole face smiling. "Quinn!" I said, and after a moment where he looked very uncertain, Quinn swung me up in his arms.

I hugged him as hard as I could, and he returned the hug so emphatically that my ribs creaked. Then he kissed me, and it took all my strength of character to keep the kiss within social boundaries.

When we parted to breathe, I realized Barry was standing awkwardly a few feet away, not sure what to do.

"Quinn, this is Barry Bellboy," I said, trying not to feel embarrassed. "He's the only other telepath I know. He works for Stan Davis, the King of Texas."

Quinn extended a hand to Barry, who I now realized was standing awkwardly for a reason. We'd transmitted a bit too graphically. I felt a tide of red sweep over my cheeks. The best thing to do was pretend I hadn't noticed, of course, and that's what I did. But I could feel a little smile twitching the corners of my mouth, and Barry looked more amused than angry.

"Good to meet you, Barry," Quinn rumbled.

"You're in charge of the ceremony arrangements?" Barry asked.

"Yep, that's me."

"I've heard of you," Barry said. "The great fighter. You've got quite a rep among the vamps, man."

I cocked my head. Something I wasn't getting here. "Great fighter?" I said.

"I'll tell you about it later," Quinn said, and his mouth set in a hard line.

Barry looked from me to Quinn. His own face did some hardening, and I was surprised to see that much toughness in Barry. "He hasn't told you?" he asked, and then read the answer right from my head. "Hey, man, that's not right," he said to Quinn. "She should know."

Quinn almost snarled. "I'll tell her about it soon."

"Soon?" Quinn's thoughts were full of turmoil and violence. "Like now?"

But at that moment, a woman strode across the lobby toward us. She was one of the most frightening women I'd ever seen, and I've seen some scary women. She was probably five foot eight, with inky black curls that hugged her head, and she was holding a helmet under her arm. It matched her armor. The armor itself, black and lusterless, was very much like a rather tailored baseball catcher's outfit: a chest guard, thigh protectors, and shin guards, with the addition of thick leather braces that strapped around the forearms. She had some heavy boots on, too, and she carried a sword, a gun, and a small crossbow draped about her in appropriate holsters.

I could only gape.

"You are the one they call Quinn?" she asked, coming to a halt a yard away. She had a heavy accent, one I couldn't trace.

"I am," Quinn said. I noticed Quinn didn't seem to be as amazed as I was at the appearance of this lethal being.

"I'm Batanya. You are in charge of special events. Does

that include security? I wish to discuss my client's special needs."

"I thought security was your job," Quinn said.

Batanya smiled, and it would really make your blood run cold. "Oh, yes, that's my job. But guarding him would be easier if—"

"I'm not in charge of security," he said. "I'm only in charge of the rituals and procedures."

"All right," she said, her accent making the casual phrase into something serious. "Then whom do I talk to?"

"A guy named Todd Donati. His office is in the staff area behind the registration desk. One of the clerks can show you."

"Excuse me," I said.

"Yes?" She looked down an arrow-straight nose at me. But she didn't look hostile or snooty, just worried.

"I'm Sookie Stackhouse," I said. "Who do you work for, Miss Batanya?"

"The King of Kentucky," she said. "He has brought us here at great expense. So it's a pity there's nothing I can do to keep him from being killed, as things stand now."

"What do you mean?" I was considerably startled and alarmed.

The bodyguard looked like she was willing to give me an earful, but we were interrupted.

"Batanya!" A young vampire was hurrying across the lobby, his crew cut and all-black Goth ensemble looking all the more frivolous when he stood by the formidable woman. "The master says he needs you by his side."

"I am coming," Batanya said. "I know my place. But I had to protest the way the hotel is making my job much harder than it needs to be."

"Complain on your own dime," the youngster said curtly.

Batanya gave him a look I wouldn't have wanted to have earned. Then she bowed to us, each in turn. "Miss Stackhouse," she said, extending her hand for me to shake. I hadn't realized hands could be characterized as muscular. "Mr. Quinn." Quinn got the shake, too, while Barry got a nod, since he hadn't introduced himself. "I will call this Todd Donati. Sorry I filled your ears, when this is not your responsibility."

"Wow," I said, watching Batanya stride away. She was wearing pants like liquid leather, and you could see each buttock flex and relax with her movement. It was like an anatomy lesson. She had muscles in her butt.

"What galaxy did she come from?" Barry asked, sounding dazed.

Quinn said, "Not galaxy. Dimension. She's a Britlingen."

We waited for more enlightenment.

"She's a bodyguard, a super-bodyguard," he explained. "Britlingens are the best. You have to be really rich to hire a witch who can bring one over, and the witch has to negotiate the terms with their guild. When the job's over, the witch has to send them back. You can't leave them here. Their laws are different. Way different."

"You're telling me the King of Kentucky paid gobs of money to bring that woman to this . . . this dimension?" I'd heard plenty of unbelievable things in the past two years, but this topped them all.

"It's a very extreme action. I wonder what he's so afraid of. Kentucky isn't exactly rolling in money."

"Maybe he bet on the right horse," I said, since I had my own royalty to worry about. "And I need to talk to you."

"Babe, I gotta get back to work," Quinn said apologetically. He shot an unfriendly look at Barry. "I know we need to talk. But I've got to line up the jurors for the trial, and I've got to set up a wedding ceremony. Negotiations between the King of Indiana and the King of Mississippi have been concluded, and they want to tie the knot while everyone's here."

"Russell's getting married?" I smiled. I wondered if he'd be the bride or the groom, or a little bit of both.

"Yeah, but don't tell anyone yet. They're announcing it tonight."

"So when are we gonna talk?"

"I'll come to your room when the vamps are in bed for the day. Where are you?"

"I have a roommate." I gave him the room number anyway.

"If she's there, we'll find somewhere else to go," he said, glancing at his watch. "Listen, don't worry; everything's okay."

I wondered what I should be worrying about. I wondered where another dimension was, and how hard it would be to bring over bodyguards from it. I wondered why anyone would go to the expense. Not that Batanya hadn't seemed pretty damn effective; but the extreme effort Kentucky had gone to, that sure seemed to argue extreme fear. Who was after him?

My waist buzzed at me, and I realized I was being summoned back up to the queen's suite. Barry's pager went off, too. We looked at each other.

*Back to work,* he said, as we went toward the elevator. *I'm sorry if I caused trouble between you and Quinn.*

*You don't mean that.*

He glanced at me. He had the grace to look ashamed. *I guess I don't. I had a picture built up of how you and me would be, and Quinn kind of intruded on my fantasy life.*

*Ah . . . ah.*

*Don't worry—you don't have to think of something to say. It was one of those fantasies. Now that I'm really with you, I have to adjust.*

*Ah.*

*But I shouldn't have let my disappointment make me a jerk.*

*Ah. Okay. I'm sure Quinn and I can work it out.*

*So, I kept the fantasy screened from you, huh?*

I nodded vigorously.

*Well, at least that's something.*

I smiled at him. *Everyone's got to have a fantasy,* I told him. *My fantasy is finding out where Kentucky got that money, and who he hired to bring that woman here. Was she not the scariest thing you've ever seen?*

*No,* Barry answered, to my surprise. *The scariest thing I've ever seen . . . well, it wasn't Batanya.* And then he locked the communicating door between our brains and threw away the key. Sigebert was opening the door into the queen's suite, and we were back at work.

After Barry and his party left, I kind of waved my hand in the air to let the queen know I had something to say if she wanted to listen. She and Andre had been discussing Stan's motivation in paying the significant visit, and they paused in identical attitudes. It was just weird. Their heads were cocked at the same angle, and with their extreme pallor and stillness, it was like being regarded by works of art carved in marble: Nymph and Satyr at Rest, or something like that.

"You know what Britlingens are?" I asked, stumbling over the unfamiliar word.

The queen nodded. Andre just waited.

"I saw one," I said, and the queen's head jerked.

"Who has gone to the expense to hire a Britlingen?" Andre asked.

I told them the whole story.

The queen looked—well, it was hard to say how she looked. Maybe a little worried, maybe intrigued, since I'd garnered so much news in the lobby.

"I never knew how useful I'd find it, having a human servant," she said to Andre. "Other humans will say anything around her, and even the Britlingen spoke freely."

Andre was perhaps a tad jealous if the look on his face was any indication.

"On the other hand, I can't do a damn thing about any of this," I said. "I can just tell you what I heard, and it's hardly classified information."

"Where did Kentucky get the money?" Andre said.

The queen shook her head, as if to say she hadn't a clue and really didn't care that much. "Did you see Jennifer Cater?" she asked me.

"Yes, ma'am."

"What did she say?" asked Andre.

"She said she'd drink my blood, and she'd see you staked and exposed on the hotel roof."

There was a moment of utter silence.

Then Sophie-Anne said, "Stupid Jennifer. What's that phrase Chester used to use? She's getting too big for her britches. What to do . . . ? I wonder if she would accept a messenger from me?"

She and Andre looked at each other steadily, and I decided they were doing a little telepathic communication of their own.

"I suppose she's taken the suite Arkansas had reserved," the queen said to Andre, and he picked up the in-house phone and called the front desk. It wasn't the first time I'd heard the king or queen of a state referred to as the state itself, but it seemed a really impersonal way to refer to your former husband, no matter how violently the marriage had ended.

"Yes," he said after he'd hung up.

"Maybe we should pay her a visit," the queen said. She and Andre indulged in some of that silent to and fro that was their way of conversing. Probably like watching Barry and

me, I figured. "She'll admit us, I'm sure. There'll be something she wants to say to me in person." The queen picked
up the phone, but not as if that was something she did every
day. She dialed the room number with her own fingers, too.

"Jennifer," she said charmingly. She listened to a torrent
of words that I could hear only a bit. Jennifer didn't sound
any happier than she'd been in the lobby.

"Jennifer, we need to talk." The queen sounded much
more charming and a lot tougher. There was silence on the
other end of the line. "The doors are not closed to discussion
or negotiation, Jennifer," Sophie-Anne said. "At least, my
doors aren't. What about yours?" I think Jennifer spoke
again. "All right, that's wonderful, Jennifer. We'll be down
in a minute or two." The queen hung up and stood silent for
a long moment.

It seemed to me like going to visit Jennifer Cater, when
she was bringing a lawsuit against Sophie-Anne for murdering Peter Threadgill, was a real bad idea. But Andre nodded
approvingly at Sophie-Anne.

After Sophie-Anne's conversation with her archenemy, I
thought we'd head to the Arkansas group's room any second. But maybe the queen wasn't as confident as she'd
sounded. Instead of starting out briskly for the showdown
with Jennifer Cater, Sophie-Anne dawdled. She gave herself
a little extra grooming, changed her shoes, searched around
for her room key, and so on. Then she got a phone call about
what room service charges the humans in her group could
put on the room bill. So it was more than fifteen minutes
before we managed to leave the room. Sigebert was coming
out of the staircase door, and he fell into place with Andre at
the waiting elevator.

Jennifer Cater and her party were on floor seven. There
was no one standing at Jennifer Cater's door: I guessed she
didn't rate her own bodyguard. Andre did the knocking

honors, and Sophie-Anne straightened expectantly. Sigebert hung back, giving me an unexpected smile. I tried not to flinch.

The door swung open. The interior of the suite was dark. The smell that wafted from the door was unmistakable.

"Well," said the Queen of Louisiana briskly. "Jennifer's dead."

# 10

"Go see," the queen told me.

"What? But all y'all are stronger than I am! And less scared!"

"And we're the ones she's suing," Andre pointed out. "Our smell cannot be in there. Sigebert, you must go see."

Sigebert glided into the darkness.

A door across the landing opened, and Batanya stepped out.

"I smell death," she said. "What's happened?"

"We came calling," I said. "But the door was unlocked already. Something's wrong in there."

"You don't know what?"

"No, Sigebert is exploring," I explained. "We're waiting."

"Let me call my second. I can't leave Kentucky's door unguarded." She turned to call back into the suite, "Clovache!"

At least, I guess that was how it was spelled, it was pronounced "Kloh-VOSH."

A kind of Batanya Junior emerged—same armor, but smaller scale; younger, brown-haired, less terrifying . . . but still plenty formidable.

"Scout the place," Batanya ordered, and without a single question Clovache drew her sword and eased into the apartment like a dangerous dream.

We all waited, holding our breaths—well, I was, anyway. The vamps didn't have breath to hold, and Batanya didn't seem at all agitated. She had moved to a spot where she could watch the open door of Jennifer Cater's place and the closed door of the King of Kentucky. Her sword was drawn.

The queen's face looked almost tense, perhaps even excited; that is, slightly less blank than usual. Sigebert came out and shook his head without a word.

Clovache appeared in the doorway. "All dead," she reported to Batanya.

Batanya waited.

"By decapitation," Clovache elaborated. "The woman was, ah"—Clovache appeared to be counting mentally—"in six pieces."

"This is bad," the queen said at the same moment Andre said, "This is good." They exchanged exasperated glances.

"Any humans?" I asked, trying to keep my voice small because I didn't want their attention, but I did want to know, very badly.

"No, all vampires," Clovache said after she got a go-ahead nod from Batanya. "I saw three. They're flaking off pretty fast."

"Clovache, go in and call that Todd Donati." Clovache went silently into the Kentucky suite and placed a call, which had an electrifying effect. Within five minutes, the area in front of the elevator was crammed with people of all sorts and descriptions and degrees of living.

A man wearing a maroon jacket with *Security* on the pocket seemed to be in charge, so he must be Todd Donati. He was a policeman who'd retired from the force early because of the big money to be made guarding and aiding the undead. But that didn't mean he liked them. Now he was furious that something had happened so early in the summit, something that would cause him more work than he was able to handle. He had cancer, I heard clearly, though I wasn't able to discern what kind. Donati wanted to work as long as he could to provide for his family after he was gone, and he was resentful of the stress and strain this investigation would cause, the energy it would drain. But he was doggedly determined to do his job.

When Donati's vampire boss, the hotel manager, showed up, I recognized him. Christian Baruch had been on the cover of *Fang* (the vamp version of *People*) a few months ago. Baruch was Swiss born. As a human, he'd designed and managed a bunch of fancy hotels in Western Europe. When he'd told a vampire in the same line of business that if he was "brought over" (not only to the vampire life but to America), he could run outstanding and profitable hotels for a syndicate of vampires, he'd been obliged in both ways.

Now Christian Baruch had eternal life (if he avoided pointy wooden objects), and the vampire hotel syndicate was raking in the money. But he wasn't a security guy or a law enforcement expert, and he wasn't the police. Sure, he could decorate the hell out of the hotel and tell the architect how many suites needed a wet bar, but what good would he be in this situation? His human hireling looked at Baruch sourly. Baruch was wearing a suit that looked remarkably wonderful, even to inexperienced eyes like mine.

I was sure it had been made for him, and I was sure it had cost a bundle.

I had been pushed back by the crowd until I was pressed against the wall by one of the suite doors—Kentucky's, I realized. It hadn't opened yet. The two Britlingens would have to guard their charge extra carefully with this mob milling around. The hubbub was extraordinary. I was next to a woman in a security uniform; it was just like the ex-cop's, but she didn't have to wear a tie.

"Do you think letting all these people into this space is a good idea?" I asked. I didn't want to be telling the woman her business, but dang. Didn't she ever watch *CSI*?

Security Woman gave me a dark look. "What are *you* doing here?" she asked, as if that made some big point.

"I'm here because I was with the group that found the bodies."

"Well, you just need to keep quiet and let us do our work."

She said this in the snottiest tone possible. "What work would that be? You don't seem to be doing anything at all," I said.

Okay, maybe I shouldn't have said that, but she *wasn't* doing anything. It seemed to me that she should be—

And then she grabbed me and slammed me into the wall and handcuffed me.

I gave a kind of yelp of surprise. "That really wasn't what I meant you to do," I said with some difficulty, since my face was mashed against the door of the suite.

There was a large silence from the crowd behind us. "Chief, I got a woman here causing trouble," said Security Woman.

Maroon looked awful on her, by the way.

"Landry, what are you doing?" said an overly reasonable male voice. It was the kind of voice you use with an irrational child.

"She was telling me what to do," replied Security Woman, but I could tell her voice was deflating even as she spoke.

"What was she telling you to do, Landry?"

"She wondered what all the people were doing here, sir."

"Isn't that a valid question, Landry?"

"Sir?"

"Don't you think we should be clearing out some of these people?"

"Yes, sir, but she said she was here because she was in the party that found the bodies."

"So she shouldn't leave."

"Right. Sir."

"Was she trying to leave?"

"No, sir."

"But you handcuffed her."

"Ah."

*"Take the fucking handcuffs off her, Landry."*

"Yes, sir." Landry was a flat pancake by now, no air left in her at all.

The handcuffs came off, to my relief, and I was able to turn around. I was so angry I could have decked Landry. But since I would've been right back in the handcuffs, I held off. Sophie-Anne and Andre pushed through the crowd; actually, it just kind of melted in front of them. Vampires and humans alike were glad to get out of the way of the Queen of Louisiana and her bodyguard.

Sophie-Anne glanced at my wrists, saw that they really weren't hurt at all, and correctly diagnosed the fact that my worst injury was to my pride.

"This is my employee," Sophie-Anne said quietly, apparently addressing Landry but making sure everyone there heard her. "An insult or injury to this woman is an insult or injury to me."

Landry didn't know who the hell Sophie-Anne was, but

she could tell power when she saw it, and Andre was just as scary. They were the two most frightening teenagers in the world, I do believe.

"Yes, ma'am, Landry will apologize in writing. Now can you tell me what happened here just now?" Todd Donati asked in a very reasonable voice.

The crowd was silent and waiting. I looked for Batanya and Clovache and saw they were missing. Suddenly Andre said, "You are the chief of security?" in a rather loud voice, and as he did, Sophie-Anne leaned very close to me to say, "Don't mention the Britlingens."

"Yes, sir." The policeman ran a hand over his mustache. "I'm Todd Donati, and this is my boss, Mr. Christian Baruch."

"I am Andre Paul, and this is my queen, Sophie-Anne Leclerq. This young woman is our employee Sookie Stack-house." Andre waited for the next step.

Christian Baruch ignored me. But he gave Sophie-Anne the look I'd give a roast I was thinking of buying for Sunday dinner. "Your presence is a great honor to my hotel," he murmured in heavily accented English, and I glimpsed the tips of his fangs. He was quite tall, with a large jaw and dark hair. But his small eyes were arctic gray.

Sophie-Anne took the compliment in stride, though her brows drew together for a second. Showing fang wasn't an exactly subtle way of saying, "You shake my world." No one spoke. Well, not for a long, awkward second. Then I said, "Are you all going to call the police, or what?"

"I think we must consider what we have to tell them," Baruch said, his voice smooth, sophisticated, and making fun of rural-southern-human me. "Mr. Donati, will you go see what's in the suite?"

Todd Donati pushed his way through the crowd with no subtlety at all. Sigebert, who'd been guarding the open doorway (for lack of anything better to do), stood aside to let the human enter. The huge bodyguard worked his way over to the queen, looking happier when he was in proximity to his ruler.

While Donati examined whatever was left in the Arkansas suite, Christian Baruch turned to address the crowd. "How many of you came down here after you heard something had happened?"

Maybe fifteen people raised their hands or simply nodded.

"You will please make your way to the Draft of Blood bar on the ground level, where our bartenders will have something special for all of you." The fifteen moved out pretty quickly after that. Baruch knew his thirsty people. Vamps. Whatever.

"How many of you were not here when the bodies were discovered?" Baruch said after the first group had left. Everyone raised a hand except the four of us: me, the queen, Andre, Sigebert.

"Everyone else may feel free to leave," Baruch said as civilly as if he was extending a pleasant invitation. And they did. Landry hesitated and got a look that sent her hurtling down the stairs.

The area around the central elevator seemed spacious now, since it was so much emptier.

Donati came back out. He didn't look deeply disturbed or sick, but he did look less composed.

"There's only bits of them left now. There's stuff all over the floor, though; residue, I guess you'd call it. I think there were three of them. But one of them is in so many pieces, that it might be two of them."

"Who's on the registration?"

Donati referred to a palm-held electronic device. "Jennifer Cater, of Arkansas. This room was rented to the delegation of Arkansas vampires. The remaining Arkansas vampires."

The word *remaining* possibly got a little extra emphasis. Donati definitely knew the queen's history.

Christian Baruch raised a thick, dark brow. "I do know my own people, Donati."

"Yes, sir."

Sophie-Anne's nose might have wrinkled delicately with distaste. *His own people, my ass,* that nose said. Baruch was at most four years old, as a vampire.

"Who's been in to see the bodies?" Baruch asked.

"Neither of us," Andre said promptly. "We haven't set foot in the suite."

"Who did?"

"The door was unlocked, and we smelled death. In view of the situation between my queen and the vampires of Arkansas, we thought it was unwise to go inside," Andre said. "We sent Sigebert, the queen's guard."

Andre simply omitted Clovache's exploration of the suite. So Andre and I did have something in common: we could skirt the truth with something that wasn't quite a lie. He'd done a masterful job.

As the questions continued—mostly unanswered or unanswerable—I found myself wondering if the queen would still have to go to trial now that her main accuser was dead. I wondered whom the state of Arkansas belonged to; it was reasonable to assume that the wedding contract had given the queen some rights regarding Peter Threadgill's property, and I knew Sophie-Anne needed every bit of income she could claim, since Katrina. Would she still have those rights to Arkansas, since Andre had killed Peter? I hadn't thought through how much was hanging over the queen's head at this summit.

But after I'd finished asking myself all these questions, I realized that the most immediate issue had yet to be addressed. Who'd killed Jennifer Cater and her companions? (How many Arkansas vamps could be left, after the battle in New Orleans and today's slaughter? Arkansas wasn't that big a state, and it had very few population centers.)

I was recalled to the here and now when Christian Baruch caught my eyes. "You're the human who can read minds," he said so suddenly that I jerked.

"Yes," I said, because I was tired of sirring and ma'aming everyone.

"Did you kill Jennifer Cater?"

I didn't have to fake astonishment. "That's giving me a lot of credit," I said. "Thinking I could have gotten the drop on three vampires. No, I didn't kill her. She came up to me in the lobby this evening, talking trash, but that's the only time I ever even saw her."

He looked a little taken aback, as if he'd expected another answer or maybe a humbler attitude.

The queen took a step to stand beside me, and Andre mirrored her, so that I was bracketed by ancient vampires. What a warm and cozy feeling. But I knew they were reminding the hotelier that I was their special human and not to be harassed.

At that very opportune moment, a vampire flung open the door from the stairs and hurtled toward the death suite. But Baruch was just as swift, and he barred the way so that the new vampire bounced off him and onto the floor. The small vamp was up in a movement so quick my eyes couldn't break it down and was making a desperate effort to get Baruch out of the doorway.

But the newcomer couldn't, and finally he took a step away from the hotelier. If the smaller vampire had been human, he'd have been panting, and as it was his body shook with tremors of delayed action. He had brown hair and a short beard, and he was wearing a suit, a regular old JCPenney one. He looked like an ordinary guy until you saw his wide eyes and realized that he was some kind of lunatic.

"Is it true?" he asked, his voice low and intent.

"Jennifer Cater and her companions are dead," Christian Baruch said, not without compassion.

The small man howled, literally howled, and the hair on my arms stood up. He sank to his knees, his body swaying back and forth in a transport of grief.

"I take it you are one of her party?" the queen said.

"Yes, yes!"

"Then now I am your queen. I offer you a place at my side."

The howling stopped as if it had been lopped off by a pair of scissors.

"But you had our king killed," the vampire said.

"I was the spouse of your king, and as such, I'm entitled to inherit his state in the event of his death," Sophie-Anne said, her dark eyes looking almost benevolent, almost luminous. "And he is undoubtedly dead."

"That's what the fine print said," Mr. Cataliades murmured in my ear, and I barely suppressed a yelp of astonishment. I'd always thought that what people said about big men moving lightly was total bullshit. Big people move bigly. But Mr. Cataliades walked as lightly as a butterfly, and I had no idea he was nearby until he spoke to me.

"In the queen's wedding contract?" I managed to say.

"Yes," he said. "And Peter's attorney went over it very thoroughly indeed. The same applied in the event of Sophie-Anne's death, too."

"I guess there were a lot of clauses hanging on that?"

"Oh, just a few. The death had to be witnessed."

"Oh, gosh. That's me."

"Yes, indeed it is. The queen wants you in her sight and under her thumb for a very good reason."

"And other conditions?"

"There could be no second-in-command alive to take the state over. In other words, a great catastrophe had to occur."

"And now it has."

"Yes, it seems that it has." Mr. Cataliades appeared quite pleased about that.

My mind was tumbling around like one of those wire bins they draw bingo numbers from at the fair.

"My name is Henrik Feith," the small vamp said. "And there are only five vampires left in Arkansas. I am the only one here in Rhodes, and I am only alive because I went down to complain about the towels in the bathroom."

I had to slap a hand over my own mouth to keep from laughing, which would have been, shall we say, inappropriate. Andre's gaze remained fixed on the man kneeling before us, but somehow his hand wandered over and gave me a pinch. After that it was easy to not laugh. In fact, it was hard not to shriek.

"What was wrong with the towels?" Baruch said, completely sidetracked by this slur on his hotel.

"Jennifer alone used up three," Henrik began explaining, but this fascinating byway was cut short when Sophie-Anne said, "Enough. Henrik, you come with us to my suite. Mr. Baruch, we look forward to receiving updates from you on this situation. Mr. Donati, are you intending to call the Rhodes police?"

It was polite of her to address Donati as though he actually had a say in what was done. Donati said, "No, ma'am, this seems like a vampire matter to me. There's no body to examine now, there's no film since there's no security camera in the suite, and if you'll look up . . ." We all did, of course, to the corner of the hallway. "You'll notice that someone has very accurately thrown a piece of gum over the lens of the security camera. Or perhaps, if it was a vampire, he jumped up and planted the gum on the lens. Of course I'm going to review the tapes, but as fast as vampires can jump, it may well be impossible to determine who the individual is. At the moment, there aren't any vampires on the homicide squad in the Rhodes police force, so I'm not sure there's anyone we can call. Most human cops won't investigate vampire crime, unless they have a vampire partner to get their backs."

"I can't think of anything more we can do here," Sophie-Anne said, exactly as if she could not care less. "If you don't need us any longer, we'll go to the opening ceremony." She had looked at her watch a few times during this conversation. "Master Henrik, if you are up to it, come with us. If you're not up to it, which of course we would understand, Sigebert will take you up to my suite and you may remain there."

"I would like to go somewhere quiet," Henrik Feith said. He looked like a beaten puppy.

Sophie-Anne nodded to Sigebert, who didn't look happy about getting his marching orders. But he had to obey her, of course, so off he went with the little vampire who was one-fifth of all that was left of the Arkansas undead.

I had so much to think about that my brain went into a stall. Just when I believed nothing more could happen, the elevator dinged and the doors swept open to allow Bill to leap out. He didn't arrive as dramatically as Henrik, but he made a definite entrance. He stopped dead and assessed the situation. Seeing we were all standing there calmly, he gathered his composure around him and said, "I hear there has been trouble?" He addressed this to the air in between us, so anyone could answer him.

I was tired of trying to think of him as Nameless. Hell, it was Bill. I might hate every molecule in his body, but he was undeniably there. I wondered if the Weres really managed to keep the abjured off their radar, and how they dealt with it. I wasn't managing very well.

"There is trouble," the queen said. "Though I don't understand what your presence will achieve."

I'd never seen Bill looking abashed, but he did now. "I apologize, my queen," he said. "If you need me for something, I'll have returned to my booth in the convention hall."

In icy silence, the elevator doors slid shut, blocking out my first lover's face and form. It was possible that Bill was trying to show he cared about me by showing up with such haste when he was supposed to be doing business for the queen elsewhere. If this demonstration was supposed to soften my heart, it failed.

"Is there anything I can be doing to help you in your investigation?" Andre asked Donati, though his words were really aimed at Christian Baruch. "Since the queen is the legal heir of Arkansas, we stand ready to assist."

"I would expect nothing less of such a beautiful queen, one also well-known for her business acumen and tenacity." Baruch bowed to the queen.

Even Andre blinked at the convoluted compliment, and the queen gave Baruch a narrow-eyed look. I kept my gaze fixed on the potted plant, and I kept my face absolutely blank. I was in danger of snickering. This was brownnosing on a scale I'd never encountered.

There really didn't seem to be any more to say, and in subdued silence I got on the elevator with the vampires and Mr. Cataliades, who had remained most remarkably quiet.

Once the doors shut, he said, "My queen, you must marry again immediately."

Let me tell you, Sophie-Anne and Andre had quite a reaction to this bombshell; their eyes widened for all of a second.

"Marry anyone: Kentucky, Florida, I would add even Mississippi, if he were not negotiating with Indiana. But you need an alliance, someone lethal to back you up. Otherwise jackals like this Baruch will circle around, yipping for your attention."

"Mississippi's out of the running, thankfully. I don't think I could stand all the men. Once in a while, of course, but not day in, day out, scores of them," Sophie-Anne said.

It was the most natural and unguarded thing I'd ever heard her say. She almost sounded human. Andre reached out and punched the button to stop the elevator between floors. "I wouldn't advise Kentucky," he said. "Anyone who needs Britlingens is in enough trouble of his own."

"Alabama is lovely," Sophie-Anne said. "But she enjoys some things in bed that I object to."

I was tired of being in the elevator and also of being regarded as part of the scenery. "May I ask a question?" I said.

After a moment's silence, Sophie-Anne nodded.

"How come you get to keep your children with you, and you've gone to bed with them, and most vampires aren't able to do that? Isn't it supposed to be a short-term relationship, sire and child?"

"Most vampire children don't stay with their makers after a certain time," Sophie-Anne agreed. "And there are very few cases of children staying with their maker as long as Andre and Sigebert have been with me. That closeness is my gift, my talent. Every vampire has a gift: some can fly, some have special skills with the sword. I can keep my children with me. We can talk to each other, as you and Barry can. We can love each other physically."

"If all that's so, why don't you just name Andre the King of Arkansas and marry him?"

There was a long, total silence. Sophie-Anne's lips parted a couple of times as if she was about to explain to me why that was impossible, but both times she pressed them shut again. Andre stared at me with such intensity that I expected to see two spots on my face begin smoking. Mr. Cataliades just looked shocked, as if a monkey had begun to speak to him in iambic pentameter.

"Yes," said Sophie-Anne finally. "Why don't I do that? Have as king and spouse my dearest friend and lover." In the blink of an eye, she looked positively radiant. "Andre, the only drawback is that you will have to spend some time apart from me when you return to Arkansas to take care of the state's affairs. My oldest child, are you willing?"

Andre's face was transformed with love. "For you, anything," he said.

We had us a Kodak moment going. I actually felt a little choked up.

Andre pressed the button again and down we went.

Though I am not immune to romance—far from it—in my opinion, the queen needed to focus on finding out who'd killed Jennifer Cater and the remaining Arkansas vampires. She needed to be grilling Towel Guy, the surviving vampire—Henrik Whatever. She didn't need to be trailing around meeting and greeting. But Sophie-Anne didn't ask me what I thought, and I'd volunteered enough of my ideas for the day.

The lobby was thronged. Plunged into such a crowd, my brain would normally be going into overload unless I was very careful indeed. But when the majority of the beings with brains were vampires, I got a lobby full of nothing, just a few flutters from the human flunky brains. Watching all the movement and not hearing much was strange, like watching birds' wings beating and yet not hearing the movement. I was definitely working now, so I sharpened up and scanned the individuals who had circulating blood and beating hearts.

One male witch, one female. One lover/blood donor—in

other words, a fangbanger, but a high-class one. When I tracked him down visually, I saw a very handsome young man wearing everything designer down to his tighty whities, and proud of it. Standing beside the King of Texas was Barry the Bellboy: he was doing his job as I was doing mine. I tracked a few hotel employees going about their business. People aren't always thinking about interesting stuff like, "Tonight I'm in on a plot to assassinate the hotel manager," or something like that, even if they *are*. They're thinking stuff like, "The room on eleven needs soap, the room on eight has a heater that won't work, the room service cart on four needs to be moved . . ."

Then I happened upon a whore. Now, *she* was interesting. Most of the whores I knew were of the amateur variety, but this woman was a thorough professional. I was curious enough to make eye contact. She was fairly attractive in the face department, but would never have been a candidate for Miss America or even homecoming queen—definitely not the girl next door, unless you lived in a red-light district. Her platinum hair was in a tousled, bedtime hairdo, and she had rather narrow brown eyes, an allover tan, enhanced breasts, big earrings, stiletto heels, bright lipstick, a dress that was mostly red spangles—you couldn't say she didn't advertise. She was accompanying a man who'd been made vamp when he was in his forties. She held on to his arm as if she couldn't walk without help, and I wondered if the stiletto heels were responsible for that, or if she held on because he liked it.

I was so interested in her—she was projecting her sexuality so strongly, she was so very much a prostitute—that I slipped through the crowd to track her more closely. Absorbed in my goal, I didn't think about her noticing me, but she seemed to feel my eyes on her and she looked over her shoulder to watch me approach. The man she was with was talking to another vampire, and she didn't have to kowtow to him just for the moment, so she had time to eye me with sharp suspicion. I stood a few feet away to listen to her, out of sheer ill-bred curiosity.

*Freaky girl, not one of us, does she want him? She can have him; I can't stand that thing he does with his tongue, and after he does me he'll want me to do him and that other guy—geez, do I have some spare batteries? Maybe she could go away and stop staring?*

"Sure, sorry," I said, ashamed of myself, and plunged back into the crowd. Next I went over the servers hired by the hotel, who were busy circulating through the crowd with trays of glasses filled with blood and a few actual drinks for the humans scattered around. The servers were all preoccupied with dodging the milling crowd, not spilling, sore backs and tender feet, things like that. Barry and I exchanged nods, and I caught a trailing thought that had Quinn's name embedded, so I followed that trail until I found it led to an employee of E(E)E. I knew this because she was wearing the company T-shirt. This gal was a young woman with a very short haircut and very long legs. She was talking to one of the servers, and it was definitely a one-sided conversation. In a crowd that was noticeably dressed up, this woman's jeans and sneakers stood out.

"—and a case of iced soft drinks," she was saying. "A tray of sandwiches, and some chips. Okay? In the ballroom, within an hour." She swung around abruptly and came face-to-face with me. She scanned me up and down and was little impressed.

"You dating one of the vamps, blondie?" she asked. Her voice was harsh to my ears, a northeastern clipped accent.

"No, I'm dating Quinn," I said. "Blondie, yourself." Though at least I was naturally blond. Well, *assisted* natural. This gal's hair looked like straw . . . if straw had dark roots.

She didn't like that at all, though I wasn't sure which

part of it displeased her most. "He didn't say he had a new woman," she said, and of course she said it in the most insulting way possible.

I felt free to dip into her skull, and I found there a deep affection for Quinn. She didn't think any other women were worthy of him. She thought I was a slow southern girl who hid behind men.

Since this was based on our conversation of less than sixty seconds, I could excuse her for being wrong. I could excuse her for loving Quinn. I couldn't forgive her overwhelming contempt.

"Quinn doesn't have to tell you his personal information," I said. What I really wanted was to ask her where Quinn was now, but that would definitely hand the advantage to her, so I was going to keep that question to myself. "If you'll excuse me, I have to get back to work, and I assume you do, too."

Her dark eyes flashed at me, and she strode off. She was at least four inches taller than me, and very slim. She hadn't bothered with a bra, and she had little plum-like boobs that jiggled in an eye-catching way. This was a gal who'd always want to be on top. I wasn't the only one who watched her cross the room. Barry had jettisoned his fantasy about me for a brand-new one.

I returned to the queen's side because she and Andre were moving into the convention hall from the lobby. The wide double doors were propped open by a really beautiful pair of urns that held huge arrangements of dried grasses.

Barry said, "Have you ever been to a real convention, a normal one?"

"No," I said, trying to keep my scan of the surrounding crowd up. I wondered how Secret Service agents coped. "Well, I went to one with Sam, a bartending supplies convention, but just for a couple of hours."

"Everyone wore a badge, right?"

"If you can call a thing on a lanyard around your neck a badge, yeah."

"That's so workers at the door can be sure you've paid your admittance, and so that unauthorized people won't come in."

"Yeah, so?"

Barry went silent. *So, you see anyone with a badge? You see anyone checking?*

*No one but us. And what do we know? The whore might be an undercover spy for the northeastern vampires. Or something worse,* I added more soberly.

*They're used to being the strongest and scariest,* Barry said. *They might fear each other, but they don't seriously fear humans, not when they're together.*

I took his point. The Britlingen had already aroused my concern, and now I was even more worried.

Then I looked back at the doors to the hotel. They were guarded, now that it was dark, by armed vampires instead of armed humans. The front desk, too, was staffed with vampires wearing the hotel uniform, and those vampires were scanning each and every person who walked in the doors. This building was not as laxly protected as it might seem. I relaxed and decided to check out the booths in the convention hall.

There was one for prosthetic fangs that you could have implanted; they came in natural ivory, silver, or gold, and the really expensive ones retracted by means of a tiny motor when your tongue pressed a tiny button in your mouth. "Undetectable from the real thing," an elderly man was assuring a vampire with a long beard and braided hair. "And sharp, oh goodness, yes!" I couldn't figure out who would want a pair. A vamp with a broken tooth? A vamp wannabe who wanted to pretend? A human looking for a little role-playing?

The next booth sold CDs of music from various historical eras, like *Russian Folk Songs of the Eighteenth Century* or *Italian Chamber Music, the Early Years*. It was doing a brisk business. People always like the music of their prime, even if that prime was centuries past.

The next booth was Bill's, and it had a large sign arching over the temporary "walls" of the enclosure. VAMPIRE IDENTIFICATION, it said simply. TRACK DOWN ANY VAMPIRE, ANYWHERE, ANYTIME. ALL YOU NEED IS A COMPUTER-SMART MINION, said a smaller sign. Bill was talking to a female vamp who was extending her credit card to him, and Pam was popping a CD case into a little bag. Pam caught my eye and winked. She was wearing a campy harem outfit, which I would have supposed she'd refuse to do. But Pam was actually smiling. Maybe she was enjoying the break in her routine.

HAPPY BIRTHDAY PRESS PRESENTS: SANGUINARY SOUP FOR THE SOUL was the sign over the next booth, at which sat a bored and lonely vampire with a stack of books in front of her.

The next exhibit took up several spaces and needed no explanation. "You should definitely upgrade," an earnest salesman was telling a black vampire whose hair was braided and tied with a thousand colored strings. She listened intently, eyeing one of the sample miniature coffins open in front of her. "Certainly, wood's biodegradable and it's traditional, but who needs that? Your coffin is your home; that's what my daddy always said."

There were others, including one for Extreme(ly Elegant) Events. That one was a large table with several price brochures and photo albums lying open to tempt the passersby. I was ready to check it out when I noticed that the booth was being "manned" by Miss Snooty Long-Legs. I didn't want to talk to her again, so I sauntered on, though I never lost sight of the queen. One of the human waiters was admiring Sophie-Anne's ass, but I figured that wasn't punishable by death, so I let it go.

By that time the queen and Andre had met with the sheriffs Gervaise and Cleo Babbitt. The broad-faced Gervaise was a small man, perhaps five foot six. He appeared to be about thirty-five, though you could easily add a hundred years to that and be closer to his true age. Gervaise had borne the burden of Sophie-Anne's maintenance and amusement for the past few weeks, and the wear and tear was showing. I'd heard he'd been renowned for his sophisticated clothing and debonair style. The only time I'd seen him before, his light hair had been combed as smooth as glass on his sleek round head. Now it was definitely disheveled. His beautiful suit needed to go to the cleaner, and his wing tips needed polishing. Cleo was a husky woman with broad shoulders and coal black hair, a wide face with a full-lipped mouth. Cleo was modern enough to want to use her last name; she'd been a vampire for only fifty years.

"Where is Eric?" Andre asked the other sheriffs.

Cleo laughed, the kind of deep-throated laugh that made men look. "He got conscripted," she said. "The priest didn't show up, and Eric's taken a course, so he's going to officiate."

Andre smiled. "That'll be something to watch. What's the occasion?"

"It'll be announced in a second," Gervaise said.

I wondered what church would have Eric as a priest. The Church of High Profits? I drifted over to Bill's booth and attracted Pam's attention.

"Eric's a priest?" I murmured

"Church of the Loving Spirit," she told me, bagging three copies of the CD and handing them to a fangbanger sent by his master to pick them up. "He got his certificate from the online course, with Bobby Burnham's help. He can perform marriage services."

A waiter somehow outmaneuvered all the guests around the queen and approached her with a tray full of wineglasses brimming with blood. In the blink of an eye Andre was between the waiter and the queen, and in the blink of another eye, the waiter swiveled and walked in another direction.

I tried to look in the waiter's mind but found it perfectly blank. Andre had grabbed control of the guy's will and sent him on his way. I hoped the waiter was okay. I followed his progress to a humble door set in a corner until I was sure that he was going back to the kitchen. Okay, incident averted.

There was a ripple in the currents of the display hall, and I turned to see what was happening. The King of Mississippi and the King of Indiana had come in together hand in hand, which seemed to be a public signal that they'd concluded their marriage negotiations. Russell Edgington was a slight, attractive vampire who liked other men—exclusively and extensively. He could be good company, and he was a good fighter, too. I liked him. I was a little anxious about seeing Russell, since a few months before I'd left a body in his pool. I tried to look on the bright side. The body was a vampire's, so it should have disintegrated before the pool covering had been removed in the spring.

Russell and Indiana stopped in front of Bill's booth. Indiana, incidentally, was a big bull-like guy with brown curly hair and a face I thought of as no-nonsense.

I drifted closer, because this could be trouble.

"Bill, you look good," Russell said. "My staff tells me you had a hard time at my place. You seem to have recovered nicely. I'm not sure how you got free, but I'm glad." If Russell was pausing for a reaction, he didn't get one. Bill's

face was just as impassive as if Russell had been comment-
ing on the weather, not Bill's torture. "Lorena was your sire,
so I couldn't interfere," Russell said, his voice just as calm as
Bill's face. "And here you are, selling your own little computer thing that Lorena was trying so hard to get from you.
As the Bard said, 'All's well that ends well.'"

Russell had been too verbose, which was the only indication that the king was anxious about Bill's reaction. And
sure enough, Bill's voice was like cold silk running over
glass. But all he said was, "Think nothing of it, Russell.
Congratulations are in order, I understand."

Russell smiled up at his groom.

"Yes, Mississippi and I are tying the knot," the King of
Indiana said. He had a deep voice. He would look at home
beating up some welsher in an alley or sitting in a bar with
sawdust on the floor. But Russell did everything but blush.

Maybe this was a love match.

Then Russell spotted me. "Bart, you have to meet this
young woman," he said immediately. I about had a panic attack, but there was no way out of the situation without simply turning tail and running. Russell pulled his intended
over to me by their linked hands. "This young woman was
staked while she was in Jackson. Some of those Fellowship
thugs were in a bar, and one of them stabbed her."

Bart looked almost startled. "You survived, obviously,"
he said. "But how?"

"Mr. Edgington here got me some help," I said. "In fact,
he saved my life."

Russell tried to look modest, and he almost succeeded.
The vampire was trying to look good in front of his intended,
such a human reaction that I could scarcely believe it.

"However, I believe you took something with you when
you left," Russell said severely, shaking a finger at me.

I tried to glean something from his face that would tell me which way to jump with my answer. I'd taken a blanket, sure enough, and some loose clothes the young men in Russell's harem had left lying around. And I'd taken Bill, who'd been a prisoner in one of the outbuildings. Probably Russell was referring to Bill, huh?

"Yessir, but I left something behind in return," I said, since I couldn't stand this verbal cat and mouse. All right, already! I'd rescued Bill and killed the vampire Lorena, though that had been more or less by accident. And I'd dumped her evil ass in the pool.

"I did think there was some sludge at the bottom when we got the pool ready for the summer," Russell said, and his bitter chocolate eyes examined me thoughtfully. "What an enterprising young woman you are, Miss . . ."

"Stackhouse. Sookie Stackhouse."

"Yes, I remember now. Weren't you at Club Dead with Alcide Herveaux? He's a Were, honey," Russell said to Bart.

"Yessir," I said, wishing he hadn't remembered that little detail.

"Didn't I hear Herveaux's father was campaigning for packleader in Shreveport?"

"That's right. But he . . . ah, he didn't get it."

"So that was the day Papa Herveaux died?"

"It was," I said. Bart was listening intently, his hand running up and down Russell's coat sleeve all the while. It was a lusty little gesture.

Quinn appeared at my side just then and put his arm around me, and Russell's eyes widened. "Gentlemen," Quinn said to Indiana and Mississippi, "I believe we have your wedding ready and waiting."

The two kings smiled at each other. "No cold feet?" Bart asked Russell.

"Not if you keep them warm," Russell said with a smile that would have melted an iceberg. "Besides, our lawyers would kill us if we reneged on those contracts."

They both nodded at Quinn, who loped to the dais at one end of the exhibit hall. He stood at the highest level and stretched out his arms. There was a microphone up there, and his deep voice boomed out over the crowd. "Your attention, ladies and gentlemen, kings and commoners, vampires and humans! You are all requested and invited to attend the union of Russell Edgington, King of Mississippi, and Bartlett Crowe, King of Indiana, in the Ritual Room. The ceremony will begin in ten minutes. The Ritual Room is through the double doors in the east wall of the hall." Quinn pointed regally at the double doors.

I'd had time to appreciate his outfit while he spoke. He was wearing full trousers that gathered at the waist and the ankle. They were deep scarlet. He had cinched the trousers with a wide gold belt like a prizefighter's, and he was wearing black leather boots with the trouser legs tucked in. He wasn't wearing a shirt. He looked like a genie who'd just popped out of a really big bottle.

"This is your new man?" Russell said. "Quinn?"

I nodded, and he looked impressed.

"I know you got things on your mind right now," I said impulsively. "I know you're about to get married. But I just want to say I hope that we're even-steven, right? You're not mad at me, or holding a grudge at me, or anything?"

Bart was accepting the congratulations of assorted vampires, and Russell glanced his way. Then he did me the courtesy of concentrating on me, though I knew he had to turn away and enjoy his evening in a very short time, which was only right.

"I hold no grudge against you," he said. "Fortunately,

I have a sense of humor, and fortunately, I didn't like Lorena worth a damn. I lent her the room in the stable because I'd known her for a century or two, but she always was a bitch."

"Then let me ask you, since you're not mad at me," I said. "Why does everyone seem so in awe of Quinn?"

"You really don't know, and you've got the tiger by his tail?" Russell looked happily intrigued. "I don't have time to tell you the whole story, because I want to be with my husband-to-be, but I'll tell you what, Miss Sookie, your man has made a lot of people a lot of money."

"Thanks," I said, a bit bewildered, "and best wishes to you and, ah, Mr. Crowe. I hope you'll be very happy together." Since shaking hands was not a vampire custom, I bowed and tried to sort of back away quickly while we were still on such good terms with each other.

Rasul popped up at my elbow. He smiled when I jumped. Those vamps. Gotta love their sense of humor.

I'd only seen Rasul in SWAT gear, and he'd looked good in that. Tonight he was wearing another uniform, but it was also pretty military looking, in a kind of Cossack way. He wore a long-sleeved tunic and tailored pants in a deep plum with black trim and bright brass buttons. Rasul was deeply brown, quite naturally, and had the large, dark liquid eyes and black hair of someone from the Middle East.

"I knew you were supposed to be here, so it's nice to run into you," I said.

"She sent Carla and me ahead of time," he said lightly in his exotic accent. "You are looking lovelier than ever, Sookie. How are you enjoying the summit?"

I ignored his pleasantries. "What's with the uniform?"

"If you mean, whose uniform is it, it's the new house uniform of our queen," he said. "We wear this instead of the armor when we're not out on the streets. Nice, huh?"

"Oh, you're stylin'," I said, and he laughed.

"Are you going to the ceremony?" he said.

"Yeah, sure. I've never seen a vampire wedding. Listen, Rasul, I'm sorry about Chester and Melanie." They'd been on guard duty with Rasul in New Orleans.

For a second, all the humor left the vampire's face. "Yes," he said after a moment of stiff silence. "Instead of my comrades, now I have the Formerly Furred." Jake Purifoy was approaching us, and he was wearing the same uniform as Rasul. He looked lonely. He hadn't been a vampire long enough to maintain the calm face that seemed to be second nature to the undead.

"Hi, Jake," I said.

"Hi, Sookie," he said, sounding forlorn and hopeful.

Rasul bowed to both of us and set off in another direction. I was stuck with Jake. This was too much like grade school for my taste. Jake was the kid who'd come to school wearing the wrong clothes and packing a weird lunch. Being a combo vamp-Were had ruined his chances with either crowd. It was like trying to be a Goth jock.

"Have you had a chance to talk to Quinn yet?" I asked for lack of anything better to say. Jake had been Quinn's employee before his change had effectively put him out of a job.

"I said hello in passing," Jake said. "It's just not fair."

"What?"

"That he should be accepted no matter what he's done, and I should be ostracized."

I knew what *ostracized* meant, because it had been on my Word of the Day calendar. But my brain was just snagging on that word because the bigger meaning of Jake's comment was affecting my equilibrium. "No matter what he's done?" I asked. "What would that mean?"

"Well, of course, you know about Quinn," Jake said, and I thought I might jump on his back and beat him around the head with something heavy.

"The wedding begins!" came Quinn's magnified voice, and the crowd began streaming into the double doors he'd indicated earlier. Jake and I streamed right along with them. Quinn's bouncy-boobed assistant was standing just inside the doors, passing out little net bags of potpourri. Some were tied with blue and gold ribbon, some with blue and red.

"Why the different colors?" the whore asked Quinn's assistant. I appreciated her asking, because it meant I didn't have to.

"Red and blue from the Mississippi flag, blue and gold from the Indiana," the woman said with an automatic smile. She still had it pasted on her face when she handed me a red-and-blue tied bag, though it faded in an almost comical way when she realized who I was.

Jake and I worked our way to a good spot a bit to the right of center. The stage was bare except for a few props, and there were no chairs. They weren't expecting this to take very long, apparently. "Answer me," I hissed. "About Quinn."

"After the wedding," he said, trying not to smile. It had been a few months since Jake had had the upper hand on anyone, and he couldn't hide the fact that he was enjoying it. He glanced behind us, and his eyes widened. I looked in that direction to see that the opposite end of the room was set up as a buffet, though the main feature of the buffet was not food but blood. To my disgust, there were about twenty men and women standing in a line beside the synthetic blood fountain, and they all had name tags that read simply, "Willing Donor." I about gagged. Could that be legal? But they were all free and unrestrained and could walk out if they chose, and most of them looked pretty eager to begin their donation. I did a quick scan of their brains. Yep, willing.

I turned to the platform, only eighteen inches high, which Mississippi and Indiana had just mounted. They'd put on elaborate costumes, which I remembered seeing before in a photo album at the shop of a photographer who specialized in recording supernatural rituals. At least these were easy to put on. Russell was wearing a sort of heavy brocade, open-fronted robe that fit over his regular clothes. It was a splendid garment of gleaming gold cloth worked in a pattern of blue and scarlet. Bart, King of Indiana, was wearing a similar robe in a copper brown color, embroidered with a design in green and gold.

"Their formal robes," Rasul murmured. Once again, he'd drifted to my side without me noticing. I jumped and saw a little smile twitch the corners of his generous mouth. To my left, Jake sidled a little closer to me, as if he were trying to hide from Rasul by concealing himself behind my body.

But I was more interested in this ceremony than I was in vampire one-upmanship. A giant ankh was the prop at the center of the group onstage. Off to one side, there was a table bearing two thick sheaves of paper with two plumed pens arranged between them. A female vampire was standing behind the table, and she was wearing a business suit with a knee-length skirt. Mr. Cataliades stood behind her, looking benevolent, his hands clasping each other across his belly.

Standing on the opposite side of the stage from the table, Quinn, my honey (whose background I was determined to learn pretty shortly), was still in his Aladdin's genie outfit. He waited until the crowd's murmur died to nothing and then he made a great gesture to stage right. A figure came up the steps and onto the platform. He was wearing a cloak of black velvet, and it was hooded. The hood was drawn well forward. The ankh symbol was embroidered in gold on the shoulders of the cloak. The figure took its position between Mississippi and Indiana, its back to the ankh, and raised its arms.

"The ceremony begins," Quinn said. "Let all be silent and witness this joining."

When someone tells a vampire to be quiet, you can be sure the silence is absolute. Vampires don't have to fidget, sigh, sneeze, cough, or blow their nose like people do. I felt noisy just breathing.

The cloaked figure's hood fell back. I sighed. Eric. His wheat-colored hair looked beautiful against the black of the cloak, and his face was solemn and commanding, which was what you want in an officiant.

"We are here to witness the joining of two kings," he said, and every word carried to the corners of the room. "Russell and Bart have agreed, both verbally and by written covenant, to ally their states for a hundred years. For a hundred years, they may not marry any other. They may not form an alliance with any other, unless that alliance is mutually agreed and witnessed. Each must pay the other a conjugal visit at least once a year. The welfare of Russell's kingdom shall come second only to his own in Bart's sight, and the welfare of Bart's kingdom shall come second only to his own in Russell's sight. Russell Edgington, King of Mississippi, do you agree to this covenant?"

"Yes, I do," Russell said clearly. He held out his hand to Bart.

"Bartlett Crowe, King of Indiana, do you agree to this covenant?"

"I do," Bart said, and took Russell's hand. Awwww.

Then Quinn stepped forward and knelt, holding a goblet under the joined hands, and Eric whipped out a knife and cut the two wrists with two movements too quick to separate.

Oh, *ick.* As the two kings bled into the chalice, I chided myself. I might have known that a vampire ceremony would include a blood exchange.

Sure enough, when the wounds closed, Russell took a sip from the chalice, and then handed it to Bart, who drained it dry. Then they kissed, Bart holding the smaller man tenderly. And then they kissed some more. Evidently the mingled blood was a real turn-on.

I caught Jake's eye. *Get a room*, he mouthed, and I looked down to hide my smile.

Finally, the two kings moved on to the next step, a ceremonious signing of the contract they'd agreed upon. The business-suit woman turned out to be a vampire lawyer from Illinois, since a lawyer from another state had to draw up the contract. Mr. Cataliades had been a neutral lawyer, too, and he signed the documents after the kings and the vampire lawyer.

Eric stood in his black-and-gold glory while all this was done, and once the pens were back on their elaborate stands, he said, "The marriage is sacred for one hundred years!" and a cheer went up. Vampires aren't big on cheering, either, so it was mostly the humans and the other supes in the crowd who did the hurrahing, but the vampires all made an appreciative murmur—not as good, but the best they could do, I guess.

I sure wanted to find out more about how Eric had qualified as a priest, or whatever they called the officiant, but first I was going to make Jake tell me about Quinn. He was trying to wriggle away in the crowd, but I caught up with him pretty quick. He wasn't a good enough vampire yet to get away from me.

"Spill," I said, and he tried to act like he didn't know what I was talking about, but he saw from my face I wasn't buying it.

So, while the crowd eddied around us, trying not to speed toward the open bar, I waited for Quinn's story.

"I can't believe he hasn't told you this himself," Jake said, and I was tempted to slap him upside the head.

I glared at him to let him know I was *waiting.*

"Okay, okay," he said. "I heard all this when I was still a Were. Quinn is like a rock star in the shifter world, you know. He's one of the last weretigers, and he's one of the most ferocious."

I nodded. So far, that paralleled my knowledge of Quinn.

"Quinn's mom was captured one full moon when she changed. A bunch of hunters were out camping, set up a trap because they wanted a bear for their illegal dogfights. Something new to bet on, you know? A pack of dogs versus a bear. This was somewhere in Colorado, and snow was on the ground. His mom was out on her own, and somehow she fell into the trap, didn't sense it."

"Where was his dad?"

"He had died when Quinn was little. Quinn was about fifteen when this happened."

I had a feeling worse was coming, and I was right.

"He changed, of course, the same night, soon as he found she was missing. He tracked them to the camp. His mom had turned back into a woman under the stress of the capture, and one of them was raping her." Jake took a deep breath. "Quinn killed them all."

I looked down at the floor. I couldn't think of anything to say.

"The campsite had to be cleaned up. There wasn't a pack around to step in—course, tigers don't hang in packs—and his mother was hurt bad and in shock, so Quinn went to the local vampire nest. They agreed to do the job, if he'd be indebted to them for three years." Jake shrugged. "He agreed."

"What exactly did he agree to do?" I asked.

"To fight in the pits for them. For three years or until he died, whichever came first."

I began to feel cold fingers moving up my spine, and this time it wasn't creepy Andre . . . it was just fear. "The pits?" I said, but if he hadn't had vampire hearing, he wouldn't have been able to make my words out.

"There's a lot of bets placed on pit fighting," Jake said. "It's like the dogfights the hunters wanted the bear for. Humans aren't the only ones who like to watch animals kill each other. Some vamps love it. So do some other supes."

My lips curled in disgust. I felt almost nauseated.

Jake was looking at me, troubled by my reaction, but also giving me time to understand the sad story was not at an end. "Obviously Quinn survived his three years," Jake said. "He's one of the few who've lived that long." He looked at me sideways. "He kept winning and winning. He was one of the most savage fighters anyone's ever seen. He fought bears, lions, you name it."

"Aren't they all really rare?" I asked.

"Yeah, they are, but I guess even rare Were creatures need money," Jake said with a toss of his head. "And you can make big bucks pit fighting, when you've earned enough to bet on yourself."

"Why did he stop?" I asked. I regretted more than I could say that I had been curious about Quinn. I should have waited until he volunteered all this. He would have, I hoped. Jake caught a human servant walking by and snagged a glass of synthetic blood off the tray. He drained it in one gulp.

"His three years ended, and he had to take care of his sister."

"Sister?"

"Yeah, his mom got pregnant that night, and the result was the dyed blonde who gave us the potpourri bags at the door. Frannie gets into trouble from time to time, and Quinn's mother can't handle her, so she sends her to stay with Quinn for a while. Frannie turned up here last night."

I'd had as much as I could stomach. I turned in one quick movement and walked away from Jake. And to his credit, he didn't try to stop me.

# 11

I WAS SO ANXIOUS TO GET OUT OF THE CROWD IN THE wedding hall that I collided with a vampire, who whirled and grabbed my shoulders in a blur of darkness. He had a long Fu Manchu mustache and a mane of hair that would have done a couple of horses credit. He was wearing a solid black suit. At another time, I might have enjoyed the total package. Now I just wanted him to move.

"Why in such a hurry, my sweet maid?" he asked.

"Sir," I said politely, since he must be older than I, "I really am in a hurry. Excuse me for bumping into you, but I need to leave."

"You're not a donor, by any chance?"

"Nope, sorry."

Abruptly he let go of my shoulders and turned back to the conversation I'd interrupted. With a great wave of relief,

I continued to pick my way through the assemblage, though with more care now that I'd already had one tense moment.

"There you are!" Andre said, and he almost sounded cross. "The queen needs you."

I had to remind myself that I was there to work, and it really didn't matter how much inner drama I was experiencing. I followed Andre over to the queen, who was in conversation with a knot of vamps and humans.

"Of course I am on your side, Sophie," said a female vampire. She was wearing an evening gown of pink chiffon joined at one shoulder with a big broach sparkling with diamonds. They might be Swarovski crystals, but they looked real to me. What do I know? The pale pink looked real pretty against her chocolate skin. "Arkansas was an asshole, anyway. I was only astonished that you married him in the first place."

"So if I come to trial, you will be kind, Alabama?" Sophie-Anne asked, and you would have sworn she wasn't a day over sixteen. Her upturned face was smooth and firm, her big eyes gleamed, her makeup was subtle. Her brown hair was loose, which was unusual for Sophie-Anne.

The vamp seemed to soften visibly. "Of course," she said.

Her human companion, the designer-clad fangbanger I'd noticed earlier, thought, *That'll last ten minutes, until she turns her back on Sophie-Anne. Then they'll be plotting again. Sure, they all say they like crackling fires and long walks on the beach by moonlight, but whenever you go to a party, it's maneuver, maneuver, maneuver, and lie, lie, lie.*

Sophie-Anne's gaze just brushed mine, and I gave a tiny shake of my head. Alabama excused herself to go congratulate the newlyweds, and her human tagged along. Mindful of all the ears around us, most of which could hear far better than I could, I said, "Later," and got a nod from Andre.

Next to court Sophie-Anne was the King of Kentucky, the man who was guarded by Britlingens. Kentucky turned out to look a lot like Davy Crockett. All he needed was a ba'ar and a coonskin cap. He was actually wearing leather pants and a suede shirt and jacket, fringed suede boots, and a big silk kerchief tied around his neck. Maybe he needed the bodyguards to protect him from the fashion police.

I didn't see Batanya and Clovache anywhere, so I assumed he'd left them in his room. I didn't see what good it was to hire expensive and otherworldly bodyguards if they weren't around your body to guard it. Then, since I didn't have another human to distract me, I noticed something odd: there was a space behind Kentucky that stayed constantly empty, no matter what the flow of the crowd might be. No matter how natural it would be for someone passing behind Kentucky to step in that area, somehow no one ever did. I figured the Britlingens were on duty, after all.

"Sophie-Anne, you're a sight for sore eyes," said Kentucky. He had a drawl that was thick as honey, and he made a point of letting Sophie-Anne see his fangs were partially out. Ugh.

"Isaiah, it's always good to see you," Sophie-Anne said, her voice and face smooth and calm as always. I couldn't tell whether or not Sophie-Anne knew the bodyguards were right behind him. As I drew a little closer, I found that though I couldn't see Clovache and Batanya, I could pick up their mental signatures. The same magic that cloaked their physical presence also muffled their brain waves, but I could get a dull echo off both of them. I smiled at them, which was really dumb of me, because Isaiah, King of Kentucky, picked up on it right away. I should have known he was smarter than he looked.

"Sophie-Anne, I want to have a chat with you, but you gotta get that little blond gal out of here for the duration," Kentucky said with a broad grin. "She pure-dee gives me the willies." He nodded toward me, as if Sophie-Anne had lots of blond human women trailing her.

"Of course, Isaiah," Sophie-Anne said, giving me a very level look. "Sookie, please go down to the lower level and fetch the suitcase the staff called about earlier."

"Sure," I said. I didn't mind a humble errand. I'd almost forgotten the gruff voice on the phone earlier in the evening. I thought it was stupid that procedure required us to come down to the bowels of the hotel, rather than allowing a bellman to bring us the suitcase, but red tape is the same everywhere you go, right?

As I turned to go, Andre's face was quite blank, as usual, but when I was almost out of earshot, he said, "Excuse me, your majesty, we didn't tell the girl about your schedule for the night." In one of those disconcerting flashes of movement, he was right beside me, hand on my arm. I wondered if he'd gotten one of those telepathic communications from Sophie-Anne. Without a word, Sigebert had moved into Andre's place beside Sophie-Anne, a half step back.

"Let's talk," said Andre, and quick as a wink he guided me to an EXIT sign. We found ourselves in a blank beige service corridor that extended for maybe ten yards, then made a right-angle turn. Two laden waiters came around the corner and passed us, giving us curious glances, but when they met Andre's eyes they hurried away on their task.

"The Britlingens are there," I said, assuming that was why Andre had wanted to talk to me in private. "They're trailing right behind Kentucky. Can all Britlingens become invisible?"

Andre did another movement that was so fast it was a blur, and then his wrist was in front of me, dripping blood. "Drink," he said, and I felt him pushing at my mind.

"No," I said, outraged and shocked at the sudden movement, the demand, the blood. "Why?" I tried to back away, but there was no place to go and no help in sight.

"You have to have a stronger connection to Sophie-Anne

or me. We need you bound to us by more than a paycheck. Already you've proved more valuable than we'd imagined. This summit is critical to our survival, and we need every advantage we can get."

Talk about brutal honesty.

"I don't want you to have control over me," I told him, and it was awful to hear my voice going wavery with fear. "I don't want you to know how I'm feeling. I got hired for this job, and after it, I'm going back to my real life."

"You don't have a real life anymore," Andre said. He didn't look unkind; that was the weird, and most frightening, thing. He looked absolutely matter-of-fact.

"I do! You guys are the blip on the radar, not me!" I wasn't totally sure what I meant by that, but Andre got my drift.

"I don't care what your plans are for the rest of your human existence," he said, and shrugged. *Phooey for your life.* "Our position will be strengthened if you drink, so you must. I've explained this to you, which I wouldn't bother to do if I didn't respect your ability."

I pushed at him, but it was like shoving an elephant. It would work only if the elephant felt like moving. Andre didn't. His wrist came closer to my mouth, and I clamped my lips together, though I was sure Andre would break my teeth if he had to. And if I opened my mouth to scream, he'd have that blood in my mouth before you could say Jack Robinson.

Suddenly there was a third presence in the stark beige corridor. Eric, still wearing the black velvet cape, hood thrown back, was standing right by us, his face uncharacteristically uncertain.

"Andre," he said, his voice sounding deeper than usual. "Why are you doing this?"

"Are you questioning the will of your queen?"

Eric was in a bad place, because he was definitely interfering with the execution of the queen's orders—at least, I assumed the queen knew about this—but I could only pray he stayed to help me. I begged him with my eyes.

I could name several vamps I'd rather have a connection to than Andre. And, stupidly, I couldn't help but feel hurt. I'd given Andre and Sophie-Anne such a good idea about him being King of Arkansas, and this was the way I got repaid. That would teach me to keep my mouth shut. That would teach me to treat vampires like they were people.

"Andre, let me offer a suggestion," Eric said in a much cooler, calmer voice. Good. He was keeping his head together. One of us needed to. "She must be kept happy, or she won't cooperate anymore."

Oh, crap. Somehow I knew his suggestion wasn't going to be, "Let her go or I'll break your neck," because Eric was way too canny for that. Where was John Wayne when you needed him? Or Bruce Willis? Or even Matt Damon? I would be glad to see Jason Bourne right now.

"We've exchanged blood several times, Sookie and I," Eric said. "In fact, we've been lovers." He took a step closer. "I think she wouldn't be so balky if I were the blood giver. Would that suit your purposes? I'm under oath to you." He bowed his head respectfully. He was being careful, so careful. That made me more frightened of Andre.

Andre let me go while he pondered. His wrist had almost healed up, anyway. I took a few long, shaky breaths. My heart was racing.

Andre looked at Eric, and I thought I could detect a certain amount of distrust in his gaze. Then he looked at me.

"You look like a rabbit hiding under a bush while the fox tracks her," he said. There was a long pause. "You did do my queen and me a large service," he said. "More than once. If the end result will be the same, why not?"

I started to say, "And I'm the only witness to Peter Threadgill's death," but my guardian angel shut my mouth to seal in the words. Well, maybe it wasn't my *actual* guardian angel, but my subconscious, which told me not to speak. Whatever. I was grateful.

"All right, Eric," Andre said. "As long as she's bonded to someone in our kingdom. I've only had a drop of her blood, to find out if she was part fae. If you've exchanged blood with her more than once, the bond is already strong. Has she answered well to your call?"

What? What call? When? Eric had never called me. In fact, I'd out and out defied him before.

"Yes, she heels nicely," Eric said without a blink of an eye. I about choked, but that would have ruined the effect of Eric's words, so I looked down at my chest as if I was embarrassed by my thralldom.

"Well, then," Andre said with an impatient gesture of his hand. "Go on."

"Right here? I'd prefer somewhere more private," Eric said.

"Here and now." Andre was not going to compromise any further.

Eric said, "Sookie." He looked at me intently.

I looked right back at him. I understood what that one word was saying. There was no way out of this. No struggling or screaming or refusal would prevent this procedure. Eric might have spared me from submitting to Andre, but that was as far as he could go.

Eric raised one eyebrow.

With that arched eyebrow, Eric was telling me that this was my best bet, that he would try not to hurt me, that being tied to him was infinitely preferable to being tied to Andre.

I knew all this not only because I wasn't stupid, but because we *were* bound together. Both Eric and Bill had had my blood, and I theirs. For the first time, I understood there was a real connection. Didn't I see the two of them as more human than vampire? Didn't they have the power to wound me more than any others? It wasn't only my past relationships with the two that kept me tied to them. It was the blood exchange. Maybe because of my unusual heritage, they couldn't order me around. They didn't have mind control over me, and they couldn't read my thoughts; and I couldn't do any of those things to them. But we did share a tie. How often had I heard their lives humming away in the background, without realizing what I was listening to?

It takes way longer to tell this than it did to think it.

"Eric," I said, and tilted my head to one side. He read as much from the gesture and word as I had from his. He stepped over to me and extended his arms to hold the black cloak out as he leaned over me, so the cloak and the hood could give us some illusion of privacy. The gesture was hokey, but the idea was nice. "Eric, no sex," I said in a voice as hard as I could make it. I could tolerate this if it wasn't like a lovers' blood exchange. I *wouldn't* have sex in front of another person. Eric's mouth was in the bend of my neck and shoulder, and his body pressed against mine. My arms slid around him, because that was simply the easiest way to stand. Then he bit, and I couldn't choke back a gasp of pain.

He didn't stop, thank God, because I wanted to get this over with. One of his hands stroked my back as if he was trying to soothe me.

After a long few seconds, Eric licked my neck to be sure his coagulant-laden saliva had coated the little wounds. "Now, Sookie," he said right into my ear. I couldn't reach his neck unless we were lying down, not without him bending over awkwardly. He started to hold his wrist up to my mouth, but we'd have to rearrange ourselves for that to work. I unbuttoned his shirt and pushed it open. I hesitated. I always hated this part, because human teeth are not nearly as sharp as vampire teeth, and I knew it would be messy when I bit. Eric did something that surprised me, then; he produced the same small ceremonial knife he'd used in marrying Mississippi and Indiana. With the same quick motion he'd used on their wrists, Eric sliced a cut in his chest right below his nipple. The blood oozed out sluggishly, and I took advantage of the flow to latch on. This was embarrassingly intimate, but at least I didn't have to look at Andre, and he couldn't see me.

Eric moved restlessly, and I realized he was getting aroused. There was nothing I could do about it, and I held our bodies apart that crucial couple of inches. I sucked hard, and Eric made a small noise, but I was strictly trying to get this over with. Vampire blood is thick and almost sweet, but when you think about what you're actually doing and you're not sexually aroused, it's not pleasant at all. When I thought I'd done it long enough, I let go and rebuttoned Eric's shirt with unsteady hands, thinking this little incident was over and I could hide somewhere until my heart stopped pounding.

And then Quinn flung open the door and stepped into the corridor.

"What the hell are you doing?" he roared, and I wasn't sure if he meant me, or Eric, or Andre.

"They are obeying orders," Andre said sharply.

"My woman doesn't have to take orders from you," Quinn said.

I opened my mouth to protest, but under these circumstances, it was hard to hand Quinn the line that I could take care of myself.

There was no social guideline to cover a calamity like this, and even my grandmother's all-purpose rule of etiquette ("Do what will make everyone most comfortable") could not remotely stretch to encompass my situation. I wondered what Dear Abby would say.

"Andre," I said, trying to sound firm instead of cowed and scared, "I'll finish the job I undertook to do for the queen here, because I shook on it. But I'll never work for you two again. Eric, thank you for making that as pleasant for me as you could." (Though *pleasant* hardly seemed the right word.)

Eric had staggered a step over to lean against the wall. He'd allowed the cloak to fall open, and the stain on his pants was clearly visible. "Oh, no problem," Eric said dreamily.

*That* didn't help. I suspected he was doing it on purpose. I felt heat rise in my cheeks. "Quinn, I'll talk to you later, as we agreed," I snapped. Then I hesitated. "That is, if you're still willing to talk to me." I thought, but couldn't say because it would have been too grossly unfair, that it would have been more help to me if he'd come ten minutes earlier . . . or not at all.

Looking neither to the right nor the left, I made myself march down that hall, took the right-angle turn, and walked through a swinging doorway directly into the kitchen.

This clearly wasn't where I wanted to be, but at least it was away from the three men in the hall. "Where's the baggage area?" I asked the first uniformed staff person I saw. She was a server loading glasses of synthetic blood onto a huge round tray, and she didn't pause in her task but nodded her head toward a door in the south wall marked EXIT. I was taking a lot of those this evening.

This door was heavier and led to a flight of stairs descending to a lower level, which I figured was actually under the ground. We don't have basements where I come from (the water table's too high), so it gave me a little frisson to be below street level.

I'd been walking as if something was chasing me, which in a nonliteral way was absolutely true, and I'd been thinking about the damn suitcase so I wouldn't have to think about anything else. But when I reached the landing, I came a complete stop.

Now that I was out of sight and truly alone, I took a moment to stand still, one hand resting against the wall. I let myself react to what had just happened. I began shaking, and when I touched my neck, I realized my collar felt funny. I pulled the material out and away and did a sort of sideways downward squinch to have a look at it. The collar was stained with my blood. Tears began flooding my eyes, and I sank to my haunches on the landing of that bleak staircase in a city far from home.

# 12 ～

I SIMPLY COULDN'T PROCESS WHAT HAD JUST HAP-
pened; it didn't jibe with my inner picture of myself or how
I behaved. I could only think, *You had to be there.* And even
then that didn't sound convincing.

*Okay, Sookie,* I said to myself. *What else could you have
done?* It wasn't the time to do a lot of detailed thinking, but
a quick scan of my options came up zero. I couldn't have
fought off Andre or persuaded him to leave me alone. Eric
could have fought Andre, but he chose not to because he
wanted to keep his place in the Louisiana hierarchy, and also
because he might have lost. Even if he'd chanced to win, the
penalty would have been incredibly heavy. Vampires didn't
fight over humans.

Likewise, I could have chosen to die rather than submit
to the blood exchange, but I wasn't quite sure how I would
have achieved that, and I was quite sure I didn't want to.

There was simply nothing I could have done, at least nothing that popped to my mind as I squatted there in the beigeness of the back stairway.

I shook myself, blotted my face with a tissue from my pocket, and smoothed my hair. I stood up straighter. I was on the right track to regaining my self-image. I would have to save the rest for later.

I pushed open the metal door and stepped into a cavernous area floored with concrete. As I'd progressed farther into the working area of the hotel (beginning with the first plain beige corridor), the decor had scaled back to minimal. This area was absolutely functional.

No one paid the least attention to me, so I had a good look around. It's not like I was anxious to hurry back to the queen, right? Across the floor, there was a huge industrial elevator. This hotel had been designed with as few openings onto the outside world as possible, to minimize the chance of intrusion, both of humans and the enemy sun. But the hotel had to have at least one large dock to load and unload coffins and supplies. This was the elevator that served that dock. The coffins entered here before they were taken to their designated rooms. Two uniformed men armed with shotguns stood facing the elevator, but I have to say that they looked remarkably bored, not at all like the alert watchdogs in the lobby.

In an area by the far wall, to the left of the huge elevator, some suitcases were slumped together in a forlorn sort of suitcase corral, an area delineated by those posts that contain retractable strips that are used to direct crowds in airports. No one appeared to be in charge of them, so I walked over—and it was a long walk—and began reading labels. There was already another lackey like me searching through the luggage, a young man with glasses and wearing a business suit.

"What are you looking for?" I asked. "If I see it while I'm looking, I can pull it out for you."

"Good idea. The desk called to say we had a suitcase down here that hadn't made it to the room, so here I am. The tag should say 'Phoebe Golden, Queen of Iowa' or something like that. You?"

"Sophie-Anne Leclerq, Louisiana."

"Wow, you work for her? Did she do it?"

"Nope, and I know because I was there," I said, and his curious face got even more curious. But he could tell I wasn't going to say any more about it, and he resumed looking.

I was surprised at the number of suitcases in the corral.

"How come," I asked the young man, "they can't just bring these up and leave them in the rooms? Like the rest of the luggage?"

He shrugged. "I was told it's some kind of liability issue. We have to identify our suitcases personally, so they can say we were the ones who picked them out. Hey, this is the one I want," he said after a moment. "I can't read the name of the owner, but it does say Iowa, so it must belong to someone in our group. Well, bye, nice to talk to you." He set off briskly with a black rolling bag.

Immediately after that, I hit luggage pay dirt. A blue leather suitcase was tagged with "Sheriff, Area"—well, that was too scribbled to make out. The vampires used all kinds of scripts, depending on the education they'd had in the age they were born. "Louisiana": the label did say that. I picked up the old suitcase and lifted it over the barrier. The writing wasn't any clearer closer to my eyes. Like my opposite number in Iowa, I decided the best course would be to take it upstairs and show it around until someone claimed it.

One of the armed guards had turned halfway from his post to figure out what I was doing. "Where you going with that, beautiful?" he called.

"I work for the Queen of Louisiana. She sent me down to get it," I said.

"Your name?"

"Sookie Stackhouse."

"Hey, Joe!" he called to a fellow employee, a heavy guy who was sitting behind a really ugly desk on which sat a battered computer. "Check out the name Stackhouse, will ya?"

"Sure thing," Joe said, wrenching his gaze from the young Iowan, who was just barely visible over on the other side of the cavernous space. Joe regarded me with the same curiosity. When he saw that I'd noticed, he looked guilty and tapped away at the keyboard. He eyed the computer screen like it could tell him everything he needed to know, and for the purposes of his job, maybe he was right.

"Okay," Joe called to the guard. "She's on the list." His was the gruff voice that I remembered from the phone conversation. He resumed staring at me, and though all the other people in the cavernous space were having blank, neutral thoughts, Joe's were not blank. They were shielded. I'd never encountered anything like it. Someone had put a metaphysical helmet on his head. I tried to get through it, around, under it, but it stayed in place. While I fumbled around, trying to get inside his thoughts, Joe was looking at me with a cross expression. I don't think he knew what I was doing. I think he was a grouch.

"Excuse me," I asked, calling so my question could reach Joe's ears. "Is my picture by my name on your list?"

"No," he said, snorting as if I'd asked a strange question. "We got a list of all the guests and who they brought with them."

"So, how do you know I'm me?"

"Huh?"

"How do you know I'm Sookie Stackhouse?"

"Aren't you?"

"Yeah."

"Then what you bitching about? Get outta here with the

damn suitcase." Joe looked down at his computer, and the guard swung around to face the elevator. *This must be the legendary Yankee rudeness,* I thought.

The bag didn't have a roller mechanism; no telling how long the owner had had it. I picked it up and marched back over to the door to the stairs. There was another elevator close to the door, I noticed, but it wasn't half as large as the huge one that had access to the outside. It could take up coffins, true, but perhaps only one at a time.

I'd already opened the stair door when I realized that if I went up that way I'd have to pass through the service corridor again. What if Eric, Andre, and Quinn were still there? What if they'd ripped each other's throats out? Though just at the moment such a scenario wouldn't have devastated me, I decided to forgo the chance of an encounter. I took the elevator instead. Okay, cowardly, but a woman can handle only so much in one night.

This elevator was definitely for the peons. It had pads on the walls to prevent cargo from being damaged. It serviced only the first four floors: basement levels, lobby, mezzanine, human floor. After that, the shape of the pyramid dictated that to rise, you had to go to the center to catch one of elevators that went all the way up. This would make taking the coffins around a slow process, I thought. The staff of the Pyramid worked hard for their money.

I decided to take the suitcase straight to the queen's suite. I didn't know what else to do with it.

When I stepped off at Sophie-Anne's floor, the lobby area around the elevator was silent and empty. Probably all the vampires and their attendants were downstairs at the soiree. Someone had left a discarded soda can lying in a large, boldly patterned urn holding some kind of small tree. The urn was positioned against the wall between the two elevators. I think the tree was supposed to be some kind of short palm tree, to maintain the Egyptian theme. The stupid soda can bothered me. Of course, there were maintenance people in the hotel whose job it was to keep everything clean, but the habit of picking up was ingrained in me. I'm no neat freak, but still. This was a nice place, and some idiot was strewing garbage around. I bent over to pick the darn thing up with my free right hand, intending to toss it into the first available garbage can.

But it was a lot heavier than it should have been.

I set down the suitcase to look at the can closely, cradling it in both my hands. The colors and the design made the cylinder look like a Dr Pepper can in almost every respect, but it just wasn't. The elevator doors whooshed open again, and Batanya stepped off, a strange-looking gun in one hand, a sword in the other. Looking over the bodyguard's shoulder into the elevator car, I saw the King of Kentucky, who looked back at me curiously.

Batanya seemed a bit surprised to see me standing there, smack-dab in front of the door. She scanned the area, then pointed her gunlike weapon carefully at the floor. The sword remained ready in her left hand. "Could you step to my left?" she asked very courteously. "The king wants to visit in that room." Her head nodded toward one of the rooms to the right.

I didn't move, couldn't think of what to say.

She took in the way I was standing and the expression on my face. She said in a sympathetic way, "I don't know why you people drink those carbonated things. They give me gas, too."

"It's not that."

"Is something wrong?"

"This isn't an empty can," I said.

Batanya's face froze. "What do you think it is?" she asked very, very calmly. That was the voice of Big Trouble.

"It might be a spy camera," I said hopefully. "Or, see, I'm thinking it might be a bomb. Because it's not a real can. It's full of something heavy, and that heaviness is not fluid." Not only was the tab top not on the can, but the innards didn't slosh.

"I understand," Batanya said. Again with the calm. She pressed a little panel on the armor over her chest, a dark blue area about the size of a credit card. "Clovache," she said. "Unknown device on four. I'm bringing the king back down."

Clovache's voice said, "How large is the device?" Her accent was sort of like Russian, at least to my untravelled ears. ("Hau larch . . . ?")

"The size of one of those cans of sweetened syrup," Batanya answered.

"Ah, the burping drinks," Clovache said. *Good memory, Clovache,* I thought.

"Yes. The Stackhouse girl noticed it, not me," Batanya said grimly. "And now she is standing with it in her hand."

"Tell her to put it down," advised the invisible Clovache with the simplicity of one who was stating an obvious fact.

Behind Batanya, the King of Kentucky was beginning to look very nervous. Batanya glanced over her shoulder at him. "Get a bomb team up here from the local policing unit," Batanya said to Clovache. "I'm bringing the king back down."

"The tiger is here, too," Clovache said. "She is his woman."

Before I could say, "For God's sake, don't send him up," Batanya pressed the rectangle again, and it went dark.

"I have to protect the king," Batanya said with an apology in her voice. She stepped back into the elevator, punched a button, and gave me a nod.

Nothing had scared me as much as that nod. It was a good-bye look. And the door swooshed shut.

There I stood, alone on the silent hotel floor, holding an instrument of death. Maybe.

Neither of the elevators gave any signs of life. No one came out of the doors on the fourth floor, and no one went into them. The stair door didn't budge. There was a long, dead time in which I did nothing but stand and hold a fake Dr Pepper can. I did a little breathing, too, but nothing too violent.

With an explosion of sound that startled me so much I nearly dropped the can, Quinn burst onto the floor. He'd taken the stairs in a huge hurry if his breathing was any indication. I couldn't spare the brainpower to find out what was going on in his head, but his face was showing nothing but the same kind of calm mask that Batanya wore. Todd Donati, the security guy, was right on Quinn's heels. They stopped dead about four feet away from me.

"The bomb squad is coming," Donati said, leading off with the good news.

"Put it down where it was, babe," Quinn said.

"Oh, yeah, I *want* to put it back where it was," I said. "I'm just scared to." I hadn't moved a muscle in what felt like a million years, and I was becoming tired already. But still I stood looking down at the can I was holding in both hands. I promised myself I would never drink another Dr Pepper as long as I lived, and I'd been real fond of them before tonight.

"Okay," Quinn said, holding out his hand. "Give it to me."

I'd never wanted to do anything more in my life.

"Not till we know what it is," I said. "Maybe it's a camera. Maybe some tabloid is trying to get insider shots of the big vampire summit." I tried to smile. "Maybe it's a little computer, counting vampires and humans as they go by. Maybe it's a bomb Jennifer Cater planted before she got offed. Maybe she wanted to blow up the queen." I'd had a couple of minutes to think about this.

"And maybe it'll take your hand off," he said. "Let me take it, babe."

"You sure you want to do that, after tonight?" I asked dismally.

"We can talk about that later. Don't worry about it. Just give me the damn can."

I noticed Todd Donati wasn't offering, and he already had a fatal disease. Didn't he want to go out as a hero? What was wrong with him? Then I was ashamed of myself for even thinking that. He had a family, and he'd want every minute with them.

Donati was sweating visibly, and he was white as a vampire. He was talking into the little headset he wore, relaying what he was seeing to . . . someone.

"No, Quinn. Someone with one of those special suits on needs to take it," I said. "I'm not moving. The can's not moving. We're okay. Till one of those special guys gets here. Or special gal," I added in the interest of fairness. I was feeling a little light-headed. The multiple shocks of the night were taking their toll on me, and I was beginning to tremble. Plus, I thought I was nuts for doing this; and yet here I was, doing it. "Anyone got X-ray vision?" I asked, trying to smile. "Where's Superman when you need him?"

"Are you trying to be a martyr for these damn things?" Quinn asked, and I figured the "damn things" were the vampires.

"Ha," I said. "Oh, ha-ha. Yeah, 'cause they *love* me. You see how many vampires are up here? Zero, right?"

"One," said Eric, stepping out of the stairwell. "We're bound a bit too tightly to suit me, Sookie." He was visibly tense; I couldn't remember ever seeing Eric so notably anxious. "I'm here to die right along with you, it seems."

"Good. To make my day absolutely effing complete, here's Eric again," I said, and if I sounded a little sarcastic, well, I was due. "Are you all completely nuts? Get the hell out of here!"

In a brisk voice, Todd Donati said, "Well, *I* will. You won't let anyone take the can, you won't put it down, and you haven't blown up yet. So I think I'll go downstairs to wait for the bomb squad."

I couldn't fault his logic. "Thanks for calling in the troops," I said, and Donati took the stairs, because the elevator was too close to me. I could read his head easily, and he felt deep shame that he hadn't actually offered to help me in any more concrete way. He planned to go down a floor to where no one could see him and then take the elevator to save his strength. The stairwell door shut behind him, and then we three stood by ourselves in a triangular tableau: Quinn, Eric, and me. Was this symbolic, or what?

My head was feeling light.

Eric began to move very slowly and carefully—I think so I wouldn't be startled. In a moment, he was at my elbow. Quinn's brain was throbbing and pulsating like a disco ball farther to my right. He didn't know how to help me, and of course, he was a bit afraid of what might happen.

Who knew, with Eric? Aside from being able to locate him and determine how he was oriented to me, I couldn't see more.

"You'll give it to me and leave," Eric said. He was pushing his vampire influence at my head with all his might.

"Won't work, never did," I muttered.

"You are a stubborn woman," he said.

"I'm *not*," I said, on the verge of tears at being first accused of nobility, then stubbornness. "I just don't want to move it! That's safest!"

"Some might think you suicidal."

"Well, 'some' can stick it up their ass."

"Babe, put it down on the urn. Just lay it down re-a-a-llll

easy," Quinn said, his voice very gentle. "Then I'll get you a big drink with lots of alcohol. You're a real strong gal, you know that? I'm proud of you, Sookie. But if you don't put that down now and get out of here, I'm gonna be real mad, hear me? I don't want anything to happen to you. That would be nuts, right?"

I was saved from further debate by the arrival of another entity on the scene. The police sent up a robot in the elevator.

When the door swooshed open we all jumped, because we'd been too wrapped up in the drama to notice the noise of the elevator. I actually giggled when the stubby robot rolled off the elevator. I started to hold the bomb out to it, but I figured the robot wasn't supposed to take it. It seemed to be operating on remote control, and it turned slightly right to face me. It remained motionless for a couple of minutes to have a good look at me and what was in my hand. After a minute or two of examination, the robot retreated onto the elevator, and its arm jerkily reached up to punch the correct button. The doors swished shut, and it left.

"I hate modern technology," Eric said quietly.

"Not true," I said. "You love what computers can do for you. I know that for a fact. Remember how happy you got when you saw the Fangtasia employee roster, with all the work hours filled in?"

"I don't like the impersonality of it. I like the knowledge it can hold."

This was just too weird a conversation for me to continue under the circumstances.

"Someone's coming up the stairs," Quinn said, and opened the stair door.

Into our little group strode the bomb disposal guy. The homicide squad might not have boasted any vampire cops, but the bomb squad did. The vampire wore one of those space suit–looking outfits. (Even if you can survive it, I

guess getting blown up is not a good experience.) Someone
had written "BOOM" on his chest where a name tag would
normally be. Oh, that was *so funny*.

"You two civilians need to leave the floor to the lady and
me," Boom said, moving slowly across the floor to me. "Take
a hike, guys," he said when neither man moved.

"No," said Eric.

"Hell, no," said Quinn.

It isn't easy to shrug in one of those suits, but Boom
managed. He was holding a square container. Frankly, I was
in no mood to have a look at it, and all I cared about was
that he opened the lid and held it out, carefully placing it
under my hands.

Very, very carefully I lowered the can into the padded interior of the container. I let it go and brought my hands out
of the container with a relief that I can't even describe, and
Boom closed the container, still grinning merrily through
his clear face guard. I shuddered all over, my hands trem-
bling violently from the release of the position.

Boom turned, slowed by the suit, and gestured to Quinn
to open the stairwell door again. Quinn did, and down the
stairs the vampire went: slowly, carefully, evenly. Maybe he
smiled all the way. But he didn't blow up, because I didn't
hear a noise, and I've got to say we all stood frozen in our
places for a good long while.

"Oh," I said, "Oh." This was not brilliant, but I was in
about a thousand emotional pieces. My knees gave way.

Quinn pounced on me and wrapped his arms around me.
"You idiot," he said. "You idiot." It was like he was saying,
"Thank you, God." I was smothered in weretiger, and I
rubbed my face against his E(E)E shirt to wipe up the tears
that had leaked from my eyes.

When I peered under his arm, there was no one else in the
area. Eric had vanished. So I had a moment to enjoy being

held, to know that Quinn still liked me, that the thing with Andre and Eric hadn't killed all feeling he had begun to have for me. I had a moment to feel the absolute relief of escaping death.

Then the elevator and the stair door opened simultaneously, and all manner of people wanted to talk to me.

# 13

"IT WAS A BOMB," TODD DONATI SAID. "A QUICK, crude bomb. The police will be telling me more, I hope, after they've finished their examination." The security chief was sitting in the queen's suite. I had finally gotten to stow the blue suitcase by one of her couches, and, boy, was I glad to be rid of it. Sophie-Anne hadn't bothered to thank me for its return, but I hadn't really expected her to, I guess. When you had underlings, you sent them on errands and you didn't have to thank them. That's why they were underlings. For that matter, I wasn't sure the stupid thing was even hers.

"I expect I'll get fired over it, especially after the murders," the security chief said. His voice was calm, but his thoughts were bitter. He needed the health insurance.

Andre gave the security chief one of his long, blue gazes. "And how did the can come to be on the queen's floor, in

that area?" Andre couldn't have cared less about Todd Donati's job situation. Donati glared back, but it was a weary
kind of glare.

"Why on earth would you be fired, just because someone
was able to bring a bomb in and plant it? Maybe because
you are in charge of the safety of everyone in the hotel?"
Gervaise asked, definitely on the cruel side. I didn't know
Gervaise very well, and I was beginning to feel that was just
fine with me. Cleo slapped him on the arm hard enough to
make Gervaise wince.

Donati said, "That's it in a nutshell. Obviously someone
brought that bomb up and put it on the potted plant by
the elevator door. It might have been meant for the queen,
since it was closest to her door. Almost equally, it might
have been meant for anyone else on the floor, or it might have
been planted at random. So I think the bomb and the murder of the Arkansas vampires are two different cases. In our
questioning, we're finding Jennifer Cater didn't have a lot of
friends. Your queen isn't the only one with a grudge against
her, though your queen's is the most serious. Possibly Jennifer planted the bomb, or arranged to have someone else do
it, before she was murdered." I saw Henrik Feith sitting in a
corner of the suite, his beard quivering with the shaking of
his head. I tried to picture the one remaining member of the
Arkansas contingent creeping around with a bomb, and I
just couldn't feature it. The small vampire seemed convinced
that he was in a nest of vipers. I was sure he was regretting
his acceptance of the queen's protection, because right now
that was looking like it wasn't a very reliable prospect.

"There is much to do here and now," Andre said. He
sounded just a shade concerned, and he was riding his own
conversational train. "It was rash of Christian Baruch to
threaten to fire you now, when he needs your loyalty the
most."

"The guy's got a temper on him," Todd Donati said, and I knew without a doubt that he wasn't a native of Rhodes. The more stressed he got, the more he sounded like home; not Louisiana, maybe, but northern Tennessee. "The ax hasn't fallen yet. And if we can get to the bottom of what's happening, maybe I'll get reinstated. Not too many people would cotton to this job. Lots of security people don't like—"

*Working with the damn vampires,* Donati completed his sentence silently to everyone but me and him. He reminded himself harshly to stick to the immediate present. "Don't like the hours it takes to run security in a big place like this," he finished out loud, for the vampires' benefit. "But I enjoy the work." *My kids will need the benefits when I die. Just two more months and coverage will stay with them after I pass.*

He'd come to the queen's suite to talk to me about the Dr Pepper incident (as had the police, and the ever-present Christian Baruch), but he was staying to chat. Though the vampires didn't seem to notice, Donati was so chatty because he had taken some heavy pain medication. I felt sorry for him, and at the same time I realized that someone with so many distractions wasn't likely to be doing a good job. What had gotten by Donati in the past couple of months, since his illness had begun affecting his daily life?

Maybe he'd hired the wrong people. Maybe he'd omitted some vital step in protecting the guests of the hotel. Maybe— I was distracted by a wave of warmth.

Eric was coming.

I'd never had such a clear sense of his presence, and my heart sank as I knew the blood exchange had been an important one. If my memory was clear, it was the third time I'd taken Eric's blood, and three is always a significant number. I felt a constant awareness of his presence when he was anywhere near me, and I had to believe it was the same for him. There might be even more to the tie now, more that I just hadn't experienced yet. I closed my eyes and leaned over to rest my forehead on my knees.

There was a knock at the door, and Sigebert answered it after a careful look through the peephole. He admitted Eric. I could scarcely bring myself to look at him or to give him a casual greeting. I should be grateful to Eric, and I knew it; and on one level I was. Sucking blood from Andre would have been intolerable. Scratch that: I would've had to tolerate it. It would have been disgusting. But exchanging blood at all had not been a choice I got to make, and I wasn't going to forget it.

Eric sat on the couch beside me. I jumped up as if I'd been poked by a cattle prod and went across the room to the bar to pour myself a glass of water. No matter where I went, I could feel Eric's presence; to make that even more unsettling, I found his nearness was somehow comforting, as if it made me more secure.

Oh, just *great*.

There wasn't anywhere else for me to sit. I settled miserably by the Viking, who now owned a piece of me. Before this night, when I'd seen Eric, I'd felt simply a casual pleasure— though I had thought of him perhaps more often than a woman ought to think about a man who would outlive her for centuries.

I reminded myself that this was not Eric's fault. Eric might be political, and he might be focused on looking out for number one (which was spelled E-R-I-C), but I didn't see how he could have surmised Andre's purpose and caught up with us to reason with Andre, with any degree of premeditation. So I owed Eric a big thank-you, no matter how you looked at it, but that wasn't going to be a conversation we had anywhere in the vicinity of the queen and the aforesaid Andre.

"Bill is still selling his little computer disk downstairs," Eric remarked to me.

"So?"

"I thought perhaps you were wondering why I showed up when you were in dire straits, and he didn't."

"It never crossed my mind," I said, wondering why Eric was bringing this up.

"I made him stay downstairs," Eric said. "After all, I'm his area sheriff."

I shrugged.

"He wanted to hit me," Eric said with only the hint of a smile on his lips. "He wanted to take the bomb from you and be your hero. Quinn would have done that, too."

"I remember that Quinn offered," I said.

"I did, too," Eric said. He seemed a bit shocked at the fact.

"I don't want to talk about it," I said, and I hoped my tone made it clear I was serious. It was getting close to dawn, and I'd had a stressful night (which was the mildest way I could put it). I managed to catch Andre's eye and give him the tiny nod toward Todd Donati. I was trying to clue him in that Donati was not entirely okay. In fact, he was as gray as a snow sky.

"If you'll excuse us, Mr. Donati. . . . We've enjoyed your company, but we have much to discuss about our plans for tomorrow night," Andre said smoothly, and Donati tensed, since he knew quite well he'd been dismissed.

"Of course, Mr. Andre," the security chief said. "I hope all of you sleep well this day, and I'll see you tomorrow night." He rose to his feet with a lot more effort than it should have taken, and he suppressed a flinch at the pain. "Miss Stackhouse, I hope you get over your bad experience real soon."

"Thank you," I said, and Sigebert opened the door for Donati to leave.

"If you'll excuse me," I said the minute he was gone, "I'll just go to my room now."

The queen gave me a sharp look. "Are you unhappy about something, Sookie?" she said, though she sounded like she didn't really want to hear my answer.

"Oh, why would I be unhappy? I *love* having things done to me without my will," I said. The pressure had built up and up, and the words came out like lava erupting from a volcano, even though my more intelligent self kept telling me to put a plug in it. "And then," I said very loudly, not listening to myself one little bit, "I like hanging around the ones responsible. That's *even better*!" I was losing coherence and gaining momentum.

There was no telling what I would have said next if Sophie-Anne hadn't held up one little white hand. She seemed a weensy bit perturbed, as my grandmother would have put it.

"You are assuming I know what you are talking about, and that I want to hear a human yelling at me," Sophie-Anne said.

Eric's eyes were glowing as if a candle burned behind them, and he was so lovely I could have drowned in him. God help me. I made myself look at Andre, who was examining me as if he was deciding where the best cut of meat was. Gervaise and Cleo just looked interested.

"Excuse me," I said, returning to the world of reality with a thud. It was so late, and I was so tired, and the night had been filled with so many incidents that I thought for a split second that I might actually faint. But the Stackhouses don't produce fainters, and neither do the fairies, I guess. It was time I gave a nod to that little percentage of my heritage. "I'm very tired." I had no fight left in me all of a sudden. I really wanted to go to bed. Not a word was spoken as I trudged to the door, which was almost a miracle. Though, as I closed it behind me, I heard the queen say, "Explain, Andre."

Quinn was waiting by the door to my room. I didn't know if I even had the energy to be glad or sad to see him. I got out the plastic rectangle and opened the door, and after I'd scanned the interior and seen that my roommate was gone (though I wondered where, since Gervaise had been by himself ), I jerked my head to tell Quinn he could come in.

"I have an idea," he said quietly.

I raised my eyebrows, too exhausted to speak.

"Let's just climb in the bed and sleep."

I finally managed to smile at him. "That's the best offer I've had all day," I said. At that second, I saw how I could come to love Quinn. While he visited the bathroom, I pulled off my clothes, folded them, and slipped into my pajamas, short and pink and silky to the touch.

Quinn came out of the bathroom in his briefs, but I was just too worn out to appreciate the view. He got into the bed while I brushed my teeth and washed my face. I slid in beside him. He turned on his side and his arms opened, and I just kept on sliding right into them. We hadn't showered, but he smelled good to me: he smelled alive and vital.

"Good ceremony tonight," I remembered to say after I'd switched off the bedside lamp.

"Thanks."

"Got any more coming up?"

"Yeah, if your queen goes on trial. Now that Cater was killed, who knows if that's still on. And tomorrow night is the ball, after the trial."

"Oh, I get to wear my pretty dress." A little pleasure stirred in me at the prospect. "You got to work?"

"No, the ball's being run by the hotel," he said. "You gonna dance with me or the blond vampire?"

"Oh, hell," I said, wishing Quinn hadn't reminded me.

And right on cue, he said, "Forget it now, babe. We're here, now, in bed together like we ought to be."

Like we ought to be. That sounded good.

"You heard about me tonight, right?" he asked.

The night had contained so many incidents it took me a moment to remember that I'd learned about the things he'd had to do to survive.

And that he had a half sister. A troublesome, nutty, dependent half sister who hated me on sight.

He was a little tense, waiting for my reaction. I could feel it in his head, in his body. I tried to think of a sweet, wonderful way to put how I felt. I was too tired.

"Quinn, I've got no problem with you," I said. I kissed his cheek, kissed his mouth. "No problem at all. And I'll try to like Frannie."

"Oh," he said, sounding simply relieved. "Well, then." He kissed my forehead, and we fell asleep.

I slept like a vampire. I didn't wake to make a trip to the bathroom, even, or to turn over. I swam almost up to consciousness once to hear Quinn was snoring, just a faint ruffle of sound, and I snuggled closer to him. He stopped, murmured, and fell silent.

I looked at the bedside clock when I finally, really, woke up. It was four in the afternoon; I'd slept for twelve hours. Quinn was gone, but he'd drawn a big pair of lips (with my lipstick) on a piece of hotel stationery and laid it on his pillow. I smiled. My roommate hadn't come in. Maybe she was spending the day in Gervaise's coffin. I shuddered. "He leaves *me* cold," I said out loud, wishing Amelia was there to respond. Speaking of Amelia . . . I fished my cell phone out of my purse and called her.

"Hey," she said. "What's up?"

"What are you doing?" I asked, trying not to feel home-sick.

"Brushing Bob," she said. "He had a hair ball."

"Aside from that?"

"Oh, I worked at the bar a little," Amelia said, trying to sound casual.

I was dumbfounded. "Doing what?"

"Well, serving drinks. What else is there to do?"

"How come Sam needed you?"

"The Fellowship is having a big rally in Dallas, and Arlene wanted time off to go with that asshole she's dating. Then Danielle's kid got pneumonia. So Sam was really worried, and since I happened to be in the bar, he asked me if I knew how to do the job. I said, 'Hey, how hard could it be?'"

"Thanks, Amelia."

"Oh, okay, I guess that sounded pretty disrespectful." Amelia laughed. "So, it is a little tricky. Everyone wants to talk to you, but you have to hurry, and you can't spill their drinks on 'em, and you have to remember what everyone was drinking, and who's paying for the round, and who's on a tab. And you have to stand up for hours and hours."

"Welcome to my world."

"So, how's Mr. Stripes?"

I realized she was talking about Quinn. "We're okay," I said, pretty sure that was true. "He did one big ceremony last night; it was so cool. A vampire wedding. You would've loved it."

"What's on for tonight?"

"Well, maybe a trial." I didn't feel like explaining, especially over a cell phone. "And a ball."

"Wow, like Cinderella."

"Remains to be seen."

"How's the business part of it going?"

"I'll have to tell you about that when I get back," I said, suddenly not so cheerful. "I'm glad you're busy and I'm glad everything's going okay."

"Oh, Terry Bellefleur called to ask if you wanted a puppy. You remember when Annie got out?"

Annie was Terry's very expensive and much-loved Catahoula. He'd come out to my place looking for Annie when she'd roamed away, and by the time he'd found her, she had had some close encounters.

"What do the puppies look like?"

"He said you had to see them to believe them. I told him you'd come by next week, maybe. I didn't commit you to anything."

"Okay, good."

We chatted a minute more but since I'd been gone from Bon Temps less than forty-eight hours, there really wasn't that much to say.

"So," she said in closing, "I miss you, Stackhouse."

"Yeah? I miss you, too, Broadway."

"Bye. Don't get any strange fangs on you."

Too late for that. "Bye. Don't spill any beer on the sheriff."

"If I do, it'll be on purpose."

I laughed, because I'd felt like dousing Bud Dearborn, too. I hung up feeling pretty good. I ordered room service, very tentatively. That was not something I got to do every day; even every year. Or ever. I was a little nervous about letting the waiter into my room, but Carla wandered in at just the same moment. She was decorated with hickeys and wearing last night's dress.

"That smells good," she said, and I handed her a croissant. She drank my orange juice while I had the coffee. It worked out okay. Carla did the talking for both of us, telling me all about the things I'd experienced. She didn't seem to realize I'd been with the queen when the slaughter of Jennifer Cater's group was discovered, and though she'd heard I'd found the Dr Pepper bomb, she told me all about it anyway, as though I hadn't been there. Maybe Gervaise made her keep silent, and the words just built up.

"What are you wearing to the ball tonight?" I asked, feeling impossibly hokey to even be asking such a question. She showed me her dress, which was black, spangled, and almost nonexistent above the waist, like all her other evening wear. Carla definitely believed in emphasizing her assets.

She asked to see my dress, and we both made insincere noises about what good taste the other had.

We had to take turns in the bathroom, of course, which I wasn't used to doing. I was pretty exasperated by the time Carla emerged. I hoped the entire city hadn't run out of hot water. Of course, there was plenty left, and despite the scattering of her cosmetics on the bathroom counter, I managed to get clean and get made-up on time. In honor of my beautiful dress, I tried to put my hair up, but I'm no good with anything more complex than a ponytail. The hair would be down. I went a little heavier on the makeup than I do in the daytime, and I had some big earrings that Tara had told me were just right. I turned my head experimentally and watched them swing and glitter. They were silvery and white, just like the beading on the bodice of my evening dress. *Which it is now time to put on,* I told myself with a little jolt of anticipation.

Oh, boy. My dress was ice blue, and had silver and white beads, and was cut just the right depth in the front and back. It had a built-in bra so I didn't have to wear one, and I pulled on some blue panties that would never leave a line on me. Then thigh-high hose. Then my shoes, which were high heeled and silvery.

I'd done my nails while Water Woman was in the shower, and I put on my lipstick and had a final look in the mirror.

Carla said, "You look real pretty, Sookie."

"Thanks." I knew I was smiling a big smile. There's nothing like dressing up once in a while. I felt like my prom date was picking me up with a corsage to pin to my dress. JB had taken me to my senior prom, though other girls had asked him because he would look so good in the photographs. My aunt Linda had made my dress.

No more homemade dresses for me.

A knock at the door had me looking anxiously in the mirror. But it was Gervaise, checking to see if Carla was ready. She smiled and turned around to garner the admiration due her, and Gervaise gave her a kiss on the cheek. I wasn't too impressed with Gervaise's character, and he wasn't my cup of tea physically, either, with his broad, bland face and his light mustache, but I had to hand it to him for generosity: he fastened a diamond tennis bracelet around Carla's wrist then and there, with no further ado than if he were giving her a bauble. Carla tried to restrain her excitement, but then she cast that to the winds and threw her arms around Gervaise's neck. I was embarrassed to be in the room, because some of the pet names she used while thanking him were sort of anatomically correct.

After they left, well pleased with each other, I stood in the middle of the bedroom. I didn't want to sit down in my dress until I had to, because I knew it would wrinkle and lose that perfect feeling. That left me with very little to do, other than trying not to get miffed about the chaos Carla had left on her side and feeling a bit at a loss. Surely Quinn had said he'd come by the room to get me? We hadn't been supposed to meet downstairs, right?

My purse made a noise, and I realized I'd stuck the queen's pager in there. Oh, surely not!

"Get down here," read the message. "Trial is now."

At the same moment, the room phone rang. I picked it up, trying to catch my breath.

"Babe," said Quinn. "I'm sorry. In case you hadn't heard, the council has decided that the queen will have to go on trial, right now, and you gotta hustle down here. I'm sorry," he said again, "I'm in charge of setting up. I gotta work. Maybe this won't take long."

"Okay," I said weakly, and he hung up.

So much for my glamorous evening with my new guy.

But, dammit, I wasn't going to change into anything less festive. Everyone else would have party clothes on, and even if my role in the evening had altered, I deserved to look pretty, too. I rode down on the elevator with one of the hotel employees, who couldn't tell if I was a vampire or not. I made him very nervous. It always tickles me when people can't tell. To me, vampires sort of glow, just a bit.

Andre was waiting for me when I got off the elevator. He was as flustered as I'd ever seen him; I could tell because his fingers were clenching and unclenching, and his lip was bloody where he'd bitten it, though it healed as I watched. Before last night, Andre had just made me nervous. Now I loathed him. But it was evident I had to put personal issues aside until another time.

"How could this happen?" he asked. "Sookie, you need to learn everything you can about this. We have more enemies than we knew."

"I thought there wouldn't be a trial after Jennifer got killed. Since she was the queen's chief accuser—"

"That's what we all thought. Or, if there was a trial, it would be an empty form, staged simply so the charges could be dismissed. But we got down here tonight and they were waiting for us. They've put off the start of the ball to do this. Take my arm," he said, and I was so taken by surprise that I slid my arm through his.

"Smile," he said. "Look confident."

And we walked into the convention hall with bold faces—me and my good buddy Andre.

It was lucky I'd had plenty of practice in insincere smiling, because this was like the marathon of Saving Face. All the vampires and their human entourages parted way for us. Some of them were smiling, too, though not pleasantly, and some looked concerned, and some just looked mildly anticipatory, as if they were about to watch a movie that had gotten good buzz.

And the rush of thoughts engulfed me. I smiled and walked on automatic while I listened in. *Pretty . . . Sophie-Anne'll get what's coming to her . . . maybe I can call her lawyer, see if she's open to an approach from our king . . . nice boobs . . . my man needs a telepath . . . hear she's fucking Quinn . . . hear she's fucking the queen and Baby Boy Andre . . . found her at a bar . . . Sophie-Anne's washed up, serves her right . . . hear she's fucking Cataliades . . . stupid trial, where's the band? . . . hope they have some food at the dance, people food . . .*

And on and on. Some of it pertaining to me, the queen, and/or Andre, some of it the simple thoughts of people who are tired of waiting and want to get the party started.

We strolled the gauntlet until it terminated in the room where the wedding had been held. The crowd in this room was almost 100 percent vampire. A notable absence: human servers, and any other human hotel staff. The only ones circulating with drinks trays were vampires. Things were going to happen in this room that weren't for human consumption. If it was possible for me to feel more anxious, I did.

I could see Quinn had been busy. The low platform had been rearranged. The giant ankh had been put away, and two lecterns had been added. On the spot where Mississippi and his loved one had taken their vows, about midway between the two lecterns, there sat a thronelike chair. In it was an ancient woman with wild white hair. I had never seen a vampire who had been turned when she was so old, and though I'd sworn I wasn't going to speak to him, I said as much to Andre.

"That is the Ancient Pythoness," he said absently. He was scanning the crowd, trying to find Sophie-Anne, I supposed. I spotted Johan Glassport, who was going to get his moment in the limelight after all, and the rest of the Louisiana contingent was with the murderous lawyer—all except the queen and Eric and Pam, whom I'd glimpsed standing near the stage.

Andre and I took our seats at the right front. On the left front was a clump of vampires who were no fans of ours. Chief among them was Henrik Feith. Henrik had transformed himself from a panicky scaredy-cat to a ball of wrath. He glowered at us. He did everything but throw spitballs.

"What crawled up his ass and died?" muttered Cleo Babbitt, dropping into the seat to my right. "The queen offers to take him under her wing when he's alone and defenseless, and this is the thanks she gets?" Cleo was wearing a traditional tuxedo, and she looked pretty darn good in it. The severity of it suited her. Her boy toy looked much more feminine than she did. I wondered at his inclusion in the crowd, which was all supe and overwhelmingly vampire. Diantha leaned forward from the row behind us to tap me on the shoulder. She was wearing a red bustier with black ruffles and a black taffeta skirt, also ruffled. Her bustier didn't have much bust to fill it. She was clutching a hand-held computer game. "Goodtoseeya," she said, and I made the effort of smiling at her. She returned her attention to the computer game.

"What will happen to us if Sophie-Anne is found guilty?" Cleo asked, and we all fell silent.

What *would* happen to us if Sophie-Anne were convicted? With Louisiana in a weakened position, with the scandal surrounding Peter's death, we were all at risk.

I don't know why I hadn't thought this through, but I hadn't.

In a moment, I understood that I hadn't even thought about worrying because I'd grown up a free United States human citizen; I wasn't used to worrying about my fate being in question. Bill had joined the little group surrounding the queen, and as I peered across the room at them, he knelt, along with Eric and Pam. Andre leaped up from his seat to my left, and in one of his lightning moves he crossed the room to kneel with them. The queen stood before them like a Roman goddess accepting tribute. Cleo followed my gaze, and her shoulder twitched. Cleo wasn't going to go do any kneeling.

"Who's on the council?" I asked the dark-haired vamp, and she nodded to the group of five vampires seated right before the low stage, facing the Ancient Pythoness.

"The King of Kentucky, the Queen of Iowa, the King of Wisconsin, the King of Missouri, the Queen of Alabama," she said, pointing to them in order. The only one I'd met was Kentucky, though I recognized the sultry Alabama from her conversation with Sophie-Anne.

The lawyer for the other side joined Johan Glassport on the stage. Something about the Arkansans' lawyer reminded me of Mr. Cataliades, and when he nodded in our direction, I saw Mr. Cataliades nod back.

"They related?" I asked Cleo.

"Brothers-in-law," Cleo said, leaving me to imagine what a female demon would look like. Surely they didn't all look like Diantha.

Quinn leaped up on the stage. He was wearing a gray

suit, white shirt, and tie, and he carried a long staff covered with carvings. He beckoned to Isaiah, King of Kentucky, who floated onto the stage. With a flourish, Quinn handed the staff to Kentucky, who was dressed much more stylishly than he had been earlier. The vampire thudded the staff against the floor, and all conversation ceased. Quinn retreated to the back of the stage.

"I am the elected master-at-arms of this judicial session," Kentucky announced in a voice that carried easily to the corners of the room. He held the staff up so it could not be ignored. "Following the traditions of the vampire race, I call you all to witness the trial of Sophie-Anne Leclerq, Queen of Louisiana, on the charge that she murdered her signed and sealed spouse, Peter Threadgill, King of Arkansas."

It sounded very solemn, in Kentucky's deep, drawling voice.

"I call the lawyers for the two parties to be ready to present their cases."

"I am ready," said the part-demon lawyer. "I am Simon Maimonides, and I represent the bereaved state of Arkansas."

"I am ready," said our murderous lawyer, reading from a pamphlet. "I am Johan Glassport, and I represent the bereaved widow, Sophie-Anne Leclerq, *falsely* charged with the murder of her signed and sealed spouse."

"Ancient Pythoness, are you ready to hear the case?" Kentucky asked, and the crone turned her head toward him.

"Is she blind?" I whispered.

Cleo nodded. "From birth," she said.

"How come she's the judge?" I asked. But the glares of the vampires around us reminded me that their hearing hardly made whispering worthwhile, and it was only polite to shut up.

"Yes," said the Ancient Pythoness. "I am ready to hear the case." She had a very heavy accent that I couldn't begin to identify. There was a stirring of anticipation in the crowd.

Okay. Let the games begin.

Bill, Eric, and Pam went to stand against the wall, while Andre sat by me.

King Isaiah did a little staff-pounding again. "Let the accused be brought forth," he said with no small amount of drama.

Sophie-Anne, looking very delicate, walked up to the stage, escorted by two guards. Like the rest of us, she'd gotten ready for the ball, and she was wearing purple. I wondered if the royal color had been a coincidence. Probably not. I had a feeling Sophie-Anne arranged her own coincidences.

The dress was high-collared and long-sleeved, and it actually had a train.

"She is beautiful," said Andre, his voice full of reverence.

Yeah, yeah, yeah. I had more on my mind than admiring the queen. The guards were the two Britlingens, probably pressed into service by Isaiah, and they had packed some dress armor in their interdimensional trunks. It was black, too, but it gleamed dully, like slowly moving dark water. It was just as figure-hugging as the first set of armor. Clovache and Batanya lifted Sophie-Anne onto the low platform and then retreated a bit. This way, they were close to both the prisoner and their employer, so it worked out great, I suppose, from their point of view.

"Henrik Feith, state your case," Isaiah said with no further ado.

Henrik's case was long and ardent and full of accusations. Boiled down, he testified that Sophie-Anne had married his king, signed all the usual contracts, and then immediately began maneuvering Peter into his fatal fight, despite the king's angelic temperament and his adoration of his new queen. It sounded like Henrik was talking about Kevin and Britney, rather than two ancient and crafty vampires.

Blah blah blah. Henrik's lawyer let him go on and on, and Johan did not object to any of Henrik's highly colored statements. Johan thought (I checked) that Henrik would lose sympathy by being so fervent and immoderate—and boring—and he was quite right, if the slight movements and shifts in body language in the crowd were anything to go by.

"And now," Henrik concluded, faint pink tears running down his face, "there are only a handful of us left in the whole state. She, who killed my king and his lieutenant Jennifer, she has offered me a place with her. And I was almost weak enough to accept, for fear of being rogue. But she is a liar and she will kill me, too."

"Someone told him that," I murmured.

"What?" Andre's mouth was right by my ear. Keeping a conversation private in a group of vampires is not an easy thing.

I held up a hand to request his silence. No, I wasn't listening to Henrik's brain but to Henrik's lawyer's, who didn't have as much demon blood as Cataliades. Without realizing I was doing it, I was leaning forward in my seat and craning toward the stage to hear better. Hear with my head, that is.

Someone had told Henrik Feith that the queen planned to kill him. He had been willing to let the lawsuit slide, since Jennifer Cater's murder had taken out the chief complainant. He had never rated high enough in the ranks to take up the mantle of leadership; he didn't have the wit or the desire. He would rather go into the service of the queen.

But if she really meant to kill him . . . he would try to kill her first by the only means he might survive, and that was through the law.

"She doesn't want to kill you," I called, hardly knowing what I was doing.

I wasn't even aware I'd gotten to my feet until I felt the eyes of everyone in the audience on me. Henrik Feith was staring at me, his face stunned, his mouth still open. "Tell us who told you that, and we'll know who killed Jennifer Cater, because—"

"Woman," said a stentorian voice, and I was drowned out and shut up very effectively. "Be silent. Who are you and what right do you have to intrude on these solemn proceedings?" The Pythoness was surprisingly forceful for someone as frail as she appeared. She was leaning forward on her throne, glaring in my direction with her blind eyes.

Okay, standing in a roomful of vampires and interrupting their ritual was a pretty good way to get bloodstains all over my beautiful new dress.

"I don't have any right in the world, Your Majesty," I said, and from a few yards to my left, I heard Pam snicker. "But I know the truth."

"Oh, then I have no role in these proceedings, do I?" croaked the Ancient Pythoness in her heavily accented English. "Why should I have come forth from my cave to give judgment?"

Why, indeed.

"I may hear the truth, but I don't have the juice to get justice done," I said honestly.

Pam snickered again. I just knew it was her.

Eric had been standing to the side of the room with Pam and Bill, but now he moved forward. I could feel his presence, cold and steady, very near to me. He gave me some courage. I don't know how. I felt it, though, felt a rising strength where there had been only my shaking knees. A shocking suspicion hit me with the force of a Mack truck. Eric had given me enough blood now that I qualified, hemoglobin-wise, as being close to a vampire; and my strange gift had slopped over into fatal territory. I wasn't reading Henrik's lawyer's mind. I was reading *Henrik's*.

"Then come tell me what I must do," said the Ancient Pythoness with a sarcasm so sharp it could have sliced a meat loaf.

I needed a week or two to get over the shock of my terrible suspicion, and I had a renewed conviction that I really ought to kill Andre, and maybe Eric, too, even if a corner of my heart would weep for the loss.

I had all of twenty seconds to process this.

Cleo gave me a sharp pinch. "Cow," she said furiously. "You will ruin everything." I edged left out of the row, stepping over Gervaise as I did so. I ignored his glare and Cleo's pinch. The two were fleas compared to the other powers that might want a piece of me first. And Eric stepped up behind me. My back was covered.

As I moved closer to the platform, it was hard to tell what Sophie-Anne was thinking of this new turn in her unexpected trial. I concentrated on Henrik and his lawyer.

"Henrik thinks that the queen decided to have him killed. He was told that, so he would testify against her in self-defense," I said.

Now I was behind the judges' chairs on the floor, with Eric by my side.

"The queen didn't decide to have me killed?" Henrik said, looking hopeful, confused, and betrayed all at the same time. That was a tall order for a vampire, since facial expressions are not their foremost means of communication.

"No, she didn't. She was sincere in offering you a place." I kept my eyes fixed on his, trying to drill my sincerity into his frightened brain. I'd moved almost squarely in front of him now.

"You're probably lying, too. You're in her pay, after all."

"Perhaps I might have a word?" the Ancient Pythoness said, with acid sarcasm.

Oops. There was a silence that was just chilling.

"Are you a seer?" she asked, speaking very slowly so that I could understand her.

"No, ma'am, I'm a telepath." This close, the Ancient Pythoness looked even older, which I wouldn't have thought possible.

"You can read minds? Vampire minds?"

"No, ma'am, those are the only ones I can't read," I said very firmly. "I pieced all this together from the lawyer's thoughts."

Mr. Maimonides was not happy about that.

"All this was known to you?" the Ancient P. asked the lawyer.

"Yes," he said. "I did know that Mr. Feith felt he was threatened with death."

"And you knew the queen had offered to accept him into her service?"

"Yes, he told me she said so." That was said in so doubtful a tone that you didn't have to be an A.P. to read between the lines.

"And you did not believe the word of a vampire queen?"

Okay, that was a stumper for Maimonides. "I felt it my duty to protect my client, Ancient Pythoness." He struck just the right note of humble dignity.

"Hmmm," said the A.P., sounding as skeptical as I felt. "Sophie-Anne Leclerq, it is your turn to present your side of the story. Will you proceed?"

Sophie-Anne said, "What Sookie has said is true. I offered

Henrik a place with me and protection. When we get to call witnesses, Ancient One, you will hear that Sookie is my witness and was there during the final fight between Peter's people and mine. Though I knew that Peter married me with a secret agenda, I didn't lift a hand against him until his people attacked on the night of our celebratory feast. Due to many circumstances, he didn't get to pick his best moment to go after me, and as a result, his people died and most of mine lived. He actually began the attack when there were others there not of our blood." Sophie-Anne managed to look shocked and saddened. "It has taken me all these months to be sure the accounts were hushed."

I thought I'd gotten most of the humans and Weres out before the slaughter started, but apparently there'd been some around.

Probably they weren't "around" anymore.

"In the time since that night, you have suffered many other losses," the Ancient Pythoness observed. This sounded quite sympathetic.

I began to sense that the deck had been stacked in Sophie-Anne's favor. Was it significant that Kentucky, who'd been courting Sophie-Anne, was the council member in charge of the proceedings?

"As you say, I've had many losses—both in terms of my people and in terms of my income," Sophie-Anne agreed. "This is why I need my inheritance from my husband, to which I'm entitled as part of our marriage covenant. He thought he would inherit the rich kingdom of Louisiana. Now I will be glad if I can get the poor one of Arkansas."

There was a long silence.

"Shall I call our witness?" Johan Glassport said. He sounded very hesitant and uncertain, for a lawyer. But in this courtroom, it wasn't hard to understand why. "She's already right here, and she was witness to Peter's death." He held out his hand to me, and I had to mount the platform. Sophie-Anne looked relaxed, but Henrik Feith, a few inches to my left, was gripping the arms of his chair.

Another silence. The wild white hair of the ancient vampire hung forward to hide her face as she stared at her own lap. Then she looked up, and her sightless eyes went unerringly to Sophie-Anne. "Arkansas is yours by law, and now yours by right. I declare you innocent of conspiring to murder your husband," the Ancient Pythoness said, almost casually.

Well . . . *yippee.* I was close enough to see that Sophie-Anne's eyes widened with relief and surprise, and Johan Glassport gave a private little grin to his lectern. Simon Maimonides looked down at the five judges to see how they'd take the A.P.'s pronouncement, and when none of them voiced a word of protest, the lawyer shrugged.

"Now, Henrik," croaked the Ancient Pythoness, "your safety is assured. Who has told you lies?"

Henrik hardly looked assured. He looked scared witless. He rose to his feet to stand by me.

Henrik was smarter than we were. There was a flash through the air.

The next time an expression crossed his face, it was utter horror. He looked down, and we all followed his eyes. There was a thin wooden shaft protruding from his chest, and as soon as his eyes identified it, Henrik's hand rose to touch it, and he swayed. A human crowd would have erupted in chaos, but the vampires threw themselves on the floor in near silence. The only person who shrieked was the blind Ancient Pythoness, who demanded to know what had happened and why everyone was so tense. The two Britlingens leaped across the stage to Kentucky and stood in front of him, their weapons in their hands and ready. Andre literally flew out of his seat in the audience to land in front of Sophie-Anne. And Quinn leaped across the stage to knock me down, and he took the second arrow, the insurance arrow, that was meant for Henrik. It was quite unnecessary. Henrik was dead when he hit the floor.

# 14 ～

BATANYA KILLED THE ASSASSIN WITH A THROWING star. She was facing the crowd, so she saw the vampire left standing after all the others had prudently hit the floor. This vampire wasn't firing the arrows from a bow; he was *throwing* them, which was why he'd managed to remain inconspicuous. Even in that group, someone carrying in a bow would have attracted a certain amount of attention.

Only a vampire could throw an arrow and kill someone. Perhaps only a Britlingen could throw a razor-sharp star in such a way as to decapitate a vampire.

I've seen vampires decapitated before, and it's not as messy as you'd think; not like cutting off the head of a human. But it's not pleasant, either, and as I watched the head topple off the shoulders, I had a moment of knee-knocking nausea from my position on the floor. I scrambled to my knees to check on Quinn.

"I'm not bad," he said instantly. "Not bad. It's in my shoulder, not my heart." He rolled over to lie on his back. The Louisiana vamps had all leaped up to the platform to circle the queen, just a second behind Andre. Once they were sure the threat was over, they clustered around us.

Cleo threw off her tuxedo jacket and ripped off the pleated white shirt. She folded it into a pad in movements so fast I could hardly follow them. "Hold this," she said, pressing it into my hand and placing my hand close to the wound. "Prepare to press hard." She didn't wait for me to nod. "Hold on," she said to Quinn. And she put her strong hands on his shoulders to hold him still while Gervaise pulled the arrow out.

Quinn bellowed, not too surprisingly. The next few minutes were pretty bad. I pressed the pad against the wound, and while Cleo pulled on the tuxedo jacket over her black lace bra, she directed Herve, her human squeeze, to donate his shirt, too. I've got to say, he whipped it right off. There was something really shocking about seeing a bare hairy chest in the middle of all this evening finery. And it was beyond weird that I would note that, after I'd just seen a guy's head separated from his body.

I knew Eric was beside me before he spoke, because I felt less terrified. He knelt down to my level. Quinn was concentrating on not yelling, so his eyes were shut as though he was unconscious and there was still lots of action going on all around me. But Eric was next to me, and I felt . . . not exactly calm, but not as upset. Because he was there.

I just hated that.

"He's going to heal," Eric said. He didn't sound especially happy about it, but not sad, either.

"Yes," I said.

"I know. I didn't see it coming."

"Oh, would you have flung yourself in front of me?"

"No," Eric said simply. "Because it might have hit me in the heart, and I would die. But I would have dived in and tackled you to take you out of the arrow's path if there had been time."

I couldn't think of a thing to say.

"I know you may come to hate me because I spared you the bite of Andre," he said quietly. "But I really am the lesser of two evils."

I glanced sideways at him. "I know that," I said, Quinn's blood staining my hands as it soaked through the makeshift pad. "I wouldn't have rather died than get bit by Andre, but it was a close thing."

He laughed, and Quinn's eyes flickered. "The weretiger is regaining consciousness," Eric said. "Do you love him?"

"Don't know yet."

"Did you love me?"

A team of stretcher bearers came over. Of course, these weren't regular paramedics. Regular paramedics wouldn't have been welcome in the Pyramid of Gizeh. These were Weres and shifters who worked for the vamps, and their leader, a young woman who looked like a honey bear, said, "We'll make sure he gets healed in record time, lady."

"I'll check on him later."

"We'll take care of him," she said. "Among us, he'll do better. It's a privilege to take care of Quinn."

Quinn nodded. "I'm ready to be moved," he said, but he was clenching the words between his teeth.

"See you later," I said, taking his hand in mine. "You're the bravest of the brave, Quinn."

"Babe," he said, biting his lower lip from the pain. "Be careful."

"Don't you be worrying about her," said a black guy with a short, clipped Afro. "She's got guardians." He gave Eric a cool look. Eric held out his hand and I took it to stand up.

My knees were aching a little after their acquaintance with the hard floor.

As they got him onto the stretcher and lifted him, Quinn seemed to lose consciousness. I started forward, but the black guy held out his arm. It looked like carved ebony, the muscles were so defined. "Sister, you just stay here," he said. "We're on the job now."

I watched them carry him off. Once he was out of sight, I looked down at my dress. Amazingly, it was all right. Not dirty, not bloody, and the wrinkles were at a minimum.

Eric waited.

"Did I love you?" I knew Eric wasn't going to give up, and I might as well figure out an answer. "Maybe. Sort of. But I knew all along that whoever was with me, it wasn't the real you. And I knew sooner or later you'd remember who you were and what you were."

"You don't seem to have yes or no answers about men," he said.

"You don't exactly seem to know how you feel about me, either," I said.

"You're a mystery," he said. "Who was your mother, and who was your father? Oh, I know, you'll say they raised you from a child and died when you were a little girl. I remember you telling me the story. But I don't know if it's exactly true. If it is, when did the fairy blood enter your family tree? Did it come in with one of your grandparents? That's what I'm supposing."

"And what business is it of yours?"

"You know it is my business. Now we are tied."

"Is this going to fade? It will, right? We won't always be like this?"

"I like being like this. You'll like it, too," he said, and he seemed mighty damn sure.

"Who was the vampire who tried to kill us?" I asked, to

change the subject. I was hoping he wasn't right, and anyway, we'd said everything there was to say on the subject, as
far as I was concerned.

"Let's go find out," he said, and took my hand. I trailed
along with him, simply because I wanted to know.

Batanya was standing by the vampire's body, which had
begun the rapid disintegration of its kind. She'd retrieved
her throwing star, and she was polishing it on her pants leg.

"Good throw," Eric said. "Who was he?"

She shrugged. "I dunno. The guy with the arrows, was
all I know. All I care."

"He was the only one?"

"Yes."

"Can you tell me what he looked like?"

"I was sitting next to him," said a very small male vampire. He was perhaps five feet tall, and slim besides. His hair
trailed down his back. If he went to jail, he'd have guys
knocking on his cell door within thirty minutes. They'd be
sorry, of course, but to the unobservant eye, he did look like
the world's easiest target. "He was a rough one, and not
dressed for the evening. Khakis and a striped dress shirt . . .
well, you can see."

Though the body was blackening and flaking away as
vamp corpses did, naturally the clothes were intact.

"Maybe he had a driver's license?" I suggested. That was
almost a given with humans, but not with vampires. However, it was worth a shot.

Eric squatted and inserted his fingers into the man's
front pocket. Nothing came out, or from the other front
pocket, so without further ado Eric rolled him over. I took a
couple of steps back to avoid the flurry of flakes of ash.
There was something in the rear pocket: a regular wallet.
And inside it, sure enough, was a driver's license.

It had been issued by Illinois. Under blood type was the

designation "NA." Yep, a vamp, for sure. Reading over Eric's shoulder, I could see that the vamp's name had been Kyle Perkins. Perkins had put "3V" as his age, so he had been a vamp for only three years.

"He must have been an archer before he died," I said. "Because that's not a skill you'd pick up right away, especially that young."

"I agree," Eric said. "And in the daytime, I want you to check all the local places you can practice archery. Throwing arrows is not a skill you can improvise. He trained. The arrow was specially made. We need to find out what happened to Kyle Perkins, and why this rogue accepted the job to attend this meeting and kill whomever necessary."

"So he was a . . . vampire hit man?"

"Yes, I think so," Eric said. "Someone is maneuvering us very carefully. Of course, this Perkins was simply backup in case the trial went wrong. And if it hadn't been for you, the trial might well have gone wrong. Someone went to a lot of trouble to play on Henrik Feith's fears, and stupid Henrik was about to give that someone up. This Kyle, he was planted to prevent just that."

Then the cleanup crew arrived: a group of vampires with a body bag and cleaning supplies. The human maids would not be asked to mop up Kyle. Luckily, they were all occupied in refreshing the vampire rooms, which were off-limits to them during the day.

In very short order, the residue of Kyle Perkins was bagged up and taken away, with one vampire remaining behind to wield a little handheld vacuum. Let Rhodes CSI try to get ahold of *that*.

I sensed a lot of movement and looked up to see that the service doors were open and staff was pouring into the large room to pack away the chairs. In less than fifteen minutes, Quinn's judicial paraphernalia was being stored away, his sister directing the work. Then a band set up on the platform, and the room was cleared for dancing. I'd never seen anything like it. First a trial, then a few murders, then dancing. Life goes on. Or, in this case, death continues.

Eric said, "You had better check in with the queen."

"Oh. Yeah, she might have a few words to say to me." I glanced around and spotted Sophie-Anne pretty quickly. She was surrounded by a crowd of people congratulating her on the favorable verdict. Of course, they would have been just as glad to see her executed, or whatever would have happened if the Ancient Pythoness had turned thumbs down. Speaking of the A.P. . . .

"Eric, where'd the old gal go?" I asked.

"The Ancient Pythoness is the original oracle that Alexander consulted," he said, his voice quite neutral. "She was considered so revered that even in her old age, she was converted by the very primitive vampires of her time. And now she has outlasted all of them."

I didn't want to think about how she'd fed before the advent of the synthetic blood that had changed the vampire world. How'd she hobble after her human prey? Maybe they'd brought people to her, like snake owners bring live mice to their pets?

"To answer your question, I would guess her handmaidens have removed her to her suite. She is brought out for special occasions."

"Like the good silver," I said seriously, and then burst into giggles. To my surprise, Eric smiled, too, that big smile that made multiple little arcs appear in the corners of his mouth.

We took our places behind the queen. I wasn't sure she'd even registered my presence, she was so busy being the belle of the ball. But in a momentary lull in the chitchat, she reached behind her and took my hand, squeezing it very lightly. "We'll talk later," she said, and then greeted a stout female vampire in a sequined pantsuit. "Maude," Sophie-Anne said, "how good to see you. And how are things going in Minnesota?"

Just then a tap on the music stand drew everyone's attention to the band. It was all vampire, I noticed with a start. The slick-haired guy at the podium said, "If all you hot vamps and vampesses are ready to rumble, we're ready to play! I'm Rick Clark, and this is . . . the Dead Man Dance Band!"

There was a polite smattering of applause.

"Here to open the evening are two of Rhodes's finest dancers, courtesy of Blue Moon Productions. Please welcome . . . Sean and Layla!"

The pair who stepped out into the middle of the dance floor were striking, whether you were human or vamp. They were both of the cold-blooded variety themselves, though he was very old and she was freshly turned, I thought. She was one of the most beautiful women I'd ever seen, and she was wearing a beige lace dress that drifted around her world-class legs like snow falling around trees. Her partner was maybe the only vampire I'd ever seen with freckles, and his dusty red hair was as long as hers.

They only had eyes for each other, and they danced together as if they were gliding through a dream.

I had never seen anything like it, and from the rapt attention of the audience, no one else had, either. As the music drew to a conclusion—and to this day, I can't remember what they danced to—Sean flung Layla back over his arm, bent over her, and bit. I was shocked, but the others seemed to expect it, and it turned them on no little amount. Sophie-Anne smoldered up at Andre (though she didn't have far to smolder, since he wasn't much taller than she), and Eric looked down at me with that hot light in his eyes that made me wary.

I turned my attention to the dance floor with determination and clapped like a maniac when the two took their bow and more couples began to join them as the music started up again. From habit I looked around for Bill, who was nowhere to be seen.

Then Eric said, "Let's dance," and I found I couldn't say no.

We took the floor along with the queen and her potential king, and I saw Russell Edgington and his husband, Bart, step out to dance, too. They looked almost as enthralled with each other as the two exhibition dancers.

I can't sing, but by golly, I can dance. And Eric had had a few ballroom lessons along the way, some century or other. My hand rested on his back, his on mine, our free hands clasped, and off we went. I wasn't sure exactly what the dance was, but he was a strong leader, so it was easy to follow along. More like the waltz than anything else, I decided.

"Pretty dress," said the dancer Layla as we swung by them.

"Thank you," I said, and beamed at her. From someone as lovely as she was, that was a great compliment. Then her partner leaned over to give her a kiss, and they swirled away into the crowd.

"That *is* a pretty dress," Eric said. "And you are a beautiful woman."

I was oddly embarrassed. I'd gotten compliments before—you can't be a barmaid and not get compliments—but most of them had consisted of (various degrees of drunk) guys telling me I was really cute—or, in one man's case, how impressive my "rack" was. (Somehow, JB du Rone and Hoyt Fortenberry had managed to stomp on that guy's toes and spill a drink all over him at the same time, just accidentally.)

"Eric," I said, but I couldn't finish the sentence because I couldn't think of what to say next. I had to concentrate on

the speed with which my feet were moving. We were dancing so fast I felt like I was flying. Suddenly Eric dropped my
hand to grip my waist, and as we turned, he swung me up,
and then I was really flying, with a little help from a Viking.
I laughed like a loon, my hair billowing out around my
head, and then he let me go and caught me, just inches away
from the floor, and then he did it again and again, until at
last I was standing on the floor and the music was over.

"Thank you," I said, knowing I must look like I'd been
standing in a high gale. "Excuse me while I go to the ladies'
room."

I scooted off through the crowd, trying not to grin like
an idiot. I should be with—oh, yeah—*my boyfriend.* Instead
of dancing with another guy until I felt tingly with happiness. And it didn't do any good, excusing myself on account
of our blood tie.

Sophie-Anne and Andre had stopped dancing, and they
were standing with a group of other vampires. She couldn't
need me, then, since there were no humans for me to "listen" to. I spotted Carla dancing with Gervaise, and they
seemed happy enough. Carla was getting lots of admiring
looks from other vampires, and that would make Gervaise
swell with pride. Having his fellow vampires craving what
he was already getting was sweet.

I knew how Gervaise felt.

I stopped in my tracks.

Had I . . . I wasn't really reading his mind, was I? No, I
couldn't. The only times I'd caught a fragment of vampire
thought prior to tonight, that fragment had felt cold and
snaky.

But I knew how Gervaise felt, for sure, just as I'd read
Henrik's thoughts. Was it just my knowledge of men and
their reactions or my knowledge of vampires, or could I really

follow vampire emotions better since I'd had Eric's blood for a third time? Or had my skill, or my talent, or my curse— whatever I called it—broadened to include vampires since I was closer to being one myself?

No. No, no, no. I felt like myself. I felt human. I felt warm. I was breathing. I had to use the bathroom. I was hungry, too. I thought about old Mrs. Bellefleur's famous chocolate cake. My mouth watered. Yep, human.

Okay, then, this new affinity for vamps would fade, like my extra strength would fade, in time. I'd had two drinks from Bill, I thought; maybe more. And three from Eric. And every time I'd had their blood, two or three months had seen the waning of the strength and acuity I'd gained from the intake. So that would happen this time, too, right? I shook myself briskly. Sure, it would.

Jake Purifoy was leaning against the wall, watching the couples dance. I'd glimpsed him earlier steering a young vampire woman around the floor, and she'd been laughing. So it wasn't all melancholy for Jake, and I was glad.

"Hey," I said.

"Sookie, that was quite some action at the trial."

"Yeah, it was scary."

"Where'd that guy come from?"

"Rogue, I guess. Eric's got me looking at archery ranges tomorrow to track him down, try to find out who hired him."

"Good. That was a close call for you. I'm sorry," he said awkwardly. "I know you must have been frightened."

I'd really been too worried about Quinn to think about the arrow being aimed at me. "I guess I was. You have a good time, now."

"Something's got to make up for not being able to change anymore," Jake said.

"I didn't know you'd tried." I couldn't think of anything else to say.

"Over and over," he said. We looked at each other for a long, long moment. "Well, I'm off to find another partner," he told me, and headed purposefully in the direction of a vampire who'd come with Stan Davis's group from Texas. She looked glad to see him coming.

By that time I was ducking into the ladies' room, which was small, of course; most of the females at the Pyramid of Gizeh wouldn't need to use such a facility, except to comb their hair. There was an attendant, a nicety I'd never seen before though I'd read about it in books. I was supposed to tip her. I still had my little evening purse with my room key in it, and I was relieved to recall I'd slipped a few dollars in there, along with some tissues and breath mints and a tiny brush. I nodded to the attendant, a squatty, dark-skinned woman with an unhappy face.

I took care of business in the nice clean stall and then emerged to wash my hands and to try to smooth out my hair. The attendant, wearing a name tag that read "Lena," turned on the water for me, which kind of weirded me out. I mean, I can turn a faucet. But I washed my hands and used the towel she extended to me, figuring this was the routine and I shouldn't act ignorant. I dropped two dollars in the tip bowl, and she tried to smile at me, but she looked too unhappy to manage it. She must be having a bad night.

"Thanks," I said, and turned to leave. I don't know why, but I glanced into the mirror on the inside of the door before I pulled on the handle. There Lena was, staring a hole into my back. She'd looked so unhappy because she'd been having to suppress how much she loathed me.

That's always a bad feeling, when you know someone hates you; especially when it's for no good reason. But her problems were not mine, and if she didn't want to turn on the faucet for women who dated vampires, she could find another job. I didn't want her damn faucet-turning-on, anyway, by God.

So I forged my way through the crowd, checking with the queen to see if she had any humans around who needed scanning (no), checking to see if I could find a Were or shifter to give me an update on Quinn (no).

By a stroke of luck, I did find the weather witch, the male witch I'd spotted earlier. I confess it made me a little proud to find my conjecture had actually been right. His being here tonight was his reward for good service, though I couldn't detect who his patron was. The weather witch had a drink in his hand and a middle-aged woman on his arm. Mrs. Witch, I discovered with another quick dip into his mental pool. He was hoping she hadn't observed that he was very interested in the beautiful vampire dancer and the pretty blond human coming toward him, the one who'd looked at him earlier like she knew him. Oh . . . that would be me.

I couldn't pick up his name, which would have greased the skids, and I didn't know what to say to him. But this was a person who should be brought to Sophie-Anne's attention. Someone had used him against her.

"Hello," I said, giving them my biggest smile. The wife smiled back, a little cautiously, because the sedate couple weren't normally approached by young single women (she'd glanced at my left hand) during glamorous parties. The weather witch's smile was more on the frightened side. "Are you all enjoying the party?" I asked.

"Yes, quite an evening," the wife said.

"My name is Sookie Stackhouse," I said, oozing charm.

"Olive Trout," she replied, and we shook hands. "This is my husband, Julian." She had no idea what her husband was.

"Are you all from around here?" I was scanning the crowd as unobtrusively as possible. I had no idea what to do with them now that I'd found them.

"You haven't watched our local stations," Olive said proudly. "Julian is the Channel 7 weatherman."

"How interesting," I said, with absolute sincerity. "If you two would just come with me, I know someone who'd just love to meet you." As I dragged the two through the crowd, I began to have second thoughts. What if Sophie-Anne intended retribution? But that wouldn't make sense. The important fact was not that there *was* a weather witch; the important fact was that someone had hired Julian Trout to predict the weather outlook for Louisiana and had somehow postponed the summit until Katrina had wreaked its havoc.

Julian was bright enough to figure out something was wrong with my enthusiasm, and I was afraid they'd both balk. I was mighty relieved to spot Gervaise's blond head. I called his name in a hearty voice as if I hadn't talked to him in a coon's age. By the time I reached him I was almost out of breath from herding the Trouts with such speed and anxiety.

"Gervaise, Carla," I said, depositing the Trouts in front of the sheriff as if I'd drug them out of the water. "This is Olive Trout and her husband, Julian. The queen's been anxious to meet someone like Julian. He's *really into the weather.*" Okay, not subtle. But Julian's face turned white. Yeah, a little knowledge of wrongdoing definitely present in Julian's conscience.

"Honey, are you sick?" Olive asked.

"We need to go home," he said.

"No, no, no," Carla said, leaping into the conversation. "Gervaise, honey, you remember Andre said if we heard of anyone who was really a weather authority, he and the queen especially wanted to have a word with 'em?" She tucked her arms around the Trouts and beamed at them. Olive looked uncertain.

"Of course," said Gervaise, the lightbulb finally switching on above his head. "Thank you, Sookie. Please, come with us." And they guided the Trouts away.

I felt a little giddy with the pleasure of having been proved right.

Looking around, I spotted Barry sticking a little plate on an empty tray.

"You wanna dance?" I asked, because the Dead Man Dance Band was playing a great cover of an old Jennifer Lopez song. Barry looked reluctant, but I pulled him by his hand, and pretty soon we were shaking our bonbons all over the place and having a great time. Nothing's like dancing for relaxing tension and losing yourself, just for a little while. I wasn't as good as Shakira at muscle control, but maybe if I practiced once in a while . . .

"What are you doing?" Eric asked, and he wasn't being facetious. He was glacial with disapproval.

"Dancing, why?" I gave a wave to signal Eric to scoot. But Barry had stopped, already, and given me a little good-bye wave.

"I was having a good time," I protested.

"You were twitching your assets in front of every male in the room," he said. "Like a . . ."

"You hold up, buddy! You stop right there!" I held up a finger, warning him.

"Take your finger out of my face," he said.

I inhaled to say something unforgivable, welcoming the tide of anger with actual delight—I was *not* tied to him at the waist—when a strong, wiry arm clamped around me, and an unfamiliar Irish-accented voice said, "Dance, darling?" As the red-haired dancer who'd opened the night's shindig swung me off in a more sedate but complicated set of steps, I spotted his partner seizing Eric's wrist to do the same.

"Just follow while you calm down, girl. I'm Sean."

"Sookie."

"Pleased to meet you, young woman. You're a fine dancer."

"Thank you. That's a high compliment, coming from you. I really enjoyed your routine earlier." I could feel the rush of anger draining away.

"It's my partner," he said, smiling. It didn't look easy for him, that smile, but it transformed him from a thin-faced freckled man with a blade of a nose to a man with sexiness to spare. "My Layla is a dream to dance with."

"She's very beautiful."

"Oh, yes, inside and out."

"How long have you been partners?"

"In dancing, two years. In life, over a year."

"From your accent, I guess you came here in a round-about way." I glimpsed Eric and the beautiful Layla. Layla had an easy smile on her lips, and she was talking to Eric, who was still looking sort of grim. But not angry.

"You could say so," he agreed. "Of course, I'm from Ireland, but I've been over here for . . ." His brow furrowed in thought, and it was like watching marble ripple. "Been here for a hundred years, anyway. From time to time, we think about moving back to Tennessee, where Layla's from, but we haven't made up our minds."

This was a lot of conversation from a quiet-looking guy. "You're just getting tired of living in the city?"

"Too much anti-vampire stuff going around lately. The Fellowship of the Sun, the Take the Night from the Dead movement: we seem to breed 'em here."

"The Fellowship is everywhere," I said. The very name made me feel gloomy. "And what'll happen when they get to hear about Weres?"

"Aye. And I think that'll be soon. I keep hearing from Weres that it's just around the corner."

You'd think, that out of all the supes I knew, one of them would let me know what was up. Sooner or later the Weres and the shifters would have to let the world in on their big secret, or they'd get outed by the vampires, either intentionally or unintentionally.

"There might even be a civil war," Sean said, and I forced my mind back to the topic at hand.

"Between the Fellowship and the supes?"

He nodded. "I'm thinking that could happen."

"What would you do in that case?"

"I've been through a few wars, and I don't want to go through another one," he said promptly. "Layla hasn't seen the Old World, and she would enjoy it, so we'd go to England. We could dance there, or we could just find a place to hide out."

As interesting as this was, it wasn't getting me any closer to solving the numerous problems facing me right at the moment, which I could count off on my fingers. Who had paid Julian Trout? Who had planted the Dr Pepper bomb? Who had killed the rest of the Arkansas vampires? Was it the same person who'd had Henrik killed, the employer of the rogue vamp?

"What was the result?" I said out loud, to the red-haired vamp's confusion.

"I beg your pardon?"

"Just talking to myself. It's been a pleasure to dance with you. Excuse me; I have to go find a friend."

Sean danced me to the edge of the crowd, and we parted ways. He was already looking for his mate. Vampire couples didn't stay together for long, as a rule. Even the hundred-year marriages of kings and queens required only a once-a-year nuptial visit. I hoped Sean and Layla would prove to be the exception.

I decided I should check on Quinn. That might be a lengthy process, since I had no idea where the Weres had taken him. I was so confused by the effect Eric was having on me, all mixed up with the beginnings of affection for Quinn. But I knew whom I was beholden to. Quinn had saved my life tonight. I started my search by calling his room but got no answer.

If I was a Were, where would I take a wounded tiger? Well, nowhere public, because Weres were secretive. They wouldn't want the hotel staff to catch a word or a phrase that would tip them off to the existence of the other supes. So they'd take Quinn to a private room, right? So, who had a private room and was sympathetic to the Weres?

Jake Purifoy, of course—former Were, current vamp. Quinn could be there—or he could be down in the hotel garage somewhere, or in the security chief's room, or in the infirmary, if there was such a thing. I had to start somewhere. I inquired at the front desk, where the clerk didn't seem to have any problem releasing the room number to me, though it's true Jake and I were flagged as being members of the same party. The clerk was not the one who'd been so rude when we'd checked in. She thought my dress was very pretty, and she wanted one just like it.

Jake's room was a floor up from mine, and as I raised my hand to knock on the door, I casually scanned inside to count the brains. There was the hole in the air that marked a vampire brain (that's the best way I can describe it), and a couple of human signatures. But I picked up on a thought that froze my fist before it had a chance to touch the door.

. . . *they should all die*, came the faint fragment of thought. Nothing followed it, though—no other thought that clarified or elaborated on that malign idea. So I knocked, and the pattern in the room changed instantly. Jake answered the door. He didn't look welcoming.

"Hi, Jake," I said, making my smile as bright and innocent as I could. "How you doing? I came by to check if Quinn was with you."

"With me?" Jake sounded startled. "Since I turned, I've hardly talked to Quinn, Sookie. We just don't have anything to talk about." I must have looked disbelieving, because he said in a rush, "Oh, it's not Quinn; it's me. I just can't bridge the chasm between who I was and who I am now. I'm not even sure who I am." His shoulders slumped.

That sounded honest enough. And I felt a lot of sympathy for him. "Anyway," Jake said, "I helped carry him to the infirmary, and I bet he's still there. There's a shifter called Bettina and a Were called Hondo with him."

Jake was holding the door shut. He didn't want me to see his companions. Jake didn't know that I could tell that he had people in his room.

It wasn't any of my business, of course. But it was disquieting. Even as I thanked him and turned to leave, I was thinking the situation over. The last thing in the world I wanted to do was to cause the troubled Jake any more problems, but if he was somehow involved in the plot that seemed to be snaking through the halls of the Pyramid of Gizeh, I had to find out.

First things first. I went down to my room and called the desk to get directions to the infirmary, and I carefully wrote them on the phone pad. Then I sneaked back up the stairs to stand outside Jake's door again, but in the time I'd been gone, the party had begun to disperse. I saw two humans from the rear. Strange; I couldn't be certain, but one of them looked like the surly Joe, the computer-consulting employee from the luggage area. Jake had been meeting with some of the hotel staff in his room. Maybe he still felt more at home with humans than he did with vampires. But surely Weres would have been his choice. . . .

As I stood there in the corridor, feeling sorry for him, Jake's door opened and he stepped out. I hadn't checked for blank spots, only live signatures. My bad. Jake looked a bit suspicious when he saw me, and I couldn't blame him.

"Do you want to go with me?" I asked.

"What?" He looked startled. He hadn't been a vampire long enough to get the inscrutable face down pat.

"To see Quinn?" I said. "I got directions to the infirmary, and you said you hadn't talked to him in a while, so I thought you might want to go with me if I'd kind of smooth the way?"

"That's a nice idea, Sookie," he said. "I think I'll pass. The fact is, most shifters don't want me around anymore. Quinn is better than most, I'm sure, but I make him uneasy. He knows my mom, my dad, my ex-girlfriend; all the people in my former life, the ones who don't want to hang with me now."

I said impulsively, "Jake, I'm so sorry. I'm sorry Hadley turned you if you would rather have passed on. She was fond of you, and she didn't want you to die."

"But I did die, Sookie," Jake said. "I'm not the same guy anymore. As you know." He picked up my arm and looked at the scar on it, the one he'd left with his teeth. "You won't ever be the same, either," he said, and he walked away. I'm not sure he knew where he was going, but he just wanted to get away from me.

I watched him until he was out of sight. He didn't turn to look back at me.

My mood had been fragile anyway, and that encounter pretty much started it on the downslope. I trudged to the elevators, determined to find the damn infirmary. The queen hadn't buzzed me, so presumably she was hobnobbing with other vampires, trying to find out who had hired the weather witch, and generally reveling in her relief. No more trial, a clear inheritance, the chance to put her beloved

Andre in power. Things were coming up roses for the Queen of Louisiana, and I tried not to be bitter. Or did I have a right to be? Hmmm, let's see. I'd helped stop the trial, though I hadn't counted on it stopping as finally and completely as it had for, say, the hapless Henrik. Since she'd been found innocent, she'd get the inheritance as promised in her marriage contract. And who'd had the idea about Andre? And I'd been proved right about the witch. Okay, maybe I could be a little bitter at my own unbenevolent fortune. Plus, sooner or later I'd have to choose between Quinn and Eric, through no fault of my own. I'd stood holding a bomb for a very long time. The Ancient Pythoness was not a member of my fan club, and she was an object of reverence to most of the vampires. I'd almost been killed with an arrow.

Well, I'd had worse nights.

I found the infirmary, which was easier to locate than I'd thought, because the door was open and I could hear a familiar laugh coming from the room. I stepped in to find that Quinn was talking to the honey bear–looking woman, who must be Bettina, and the black guy, who must be Hondo. Also, to my astonishment, Clovache was there. Her armor was not off, but she managed to give the impression of a guy who'd loosened his tie.

"Sookie," said Quinn. He smiled at me, but the two shapechangers didn't. I was definitely an unwelcome visitor.

But I hadn't come to see them. I'd come to see the man who'd saved my life. I walked over to him, letting him watch me, giving him a little smile. I sat on the plastic chair by the bed and took his hand.

"Tell me how you're feeling," I said.

"Like I had a real close shave," he said. "But I'm gonna be fine."

"Could you all excuse us a moment, please?" I was at my most polite as I met the eyes of the three others in the room.

Clovache said, "Back to guarding Kentucky," and took off. She might have winked at me before she vanished. Bettina looked a bit disgruntled, as if she'd been student teaching on her own and now the teacher had returned and snatched back her authority.

Hondo gave me a dark look that held more than a hint of threat. "You treat my man right," he said. "Don't give him no hard time."

"Never," I said. He couldn't think of a way to stay, since Quinn apparently wanted to talk to me, so he left.

"My fan base just gets bigger and bigger," I said, watching them go. I got up and shut the door behind them. Unless a vampire, or Barry, stood outside the door, we were reasonably private.

"Is this where you dump me for the vampire?" Quinn asked. All trace of good humor had vanished from his face, and he was holding very still.

"No. This is where I tell you what happened, and you listen, and then we talk." I said this as if I was sure he'd go along with it, but that was far from the case, and my heart was thudding in my throat as I waited for his reply. Finally he nodded, and I closed my eyes in relief, clutching his left hand in both of mine. "Okay," I said, bracing myself, and then I was off and running with my narrative, hoping that he would see that Eric really was the lesser of two evils.

Quinn didn't pull his hand away, but he didn't hold mine, either. "You're bound to Eric," he said.

"Yes."

"You've exchanged blood with him at least three times."

"Yes."

"You know he can turn you whenever he feels like it?"

"Any of us could be turned whenever the vampires feel like it, Quinn. Even you. It might take two of them to hold you down and one to take all your blood and give you his, but it still could happen."

"It wouldn't take that long if he made up his mind, now that you two have swapped so often. And this is Andre's fault."

"There's nothing I can do about that now. I wish there were. I wish I could cut Eric out of my life. But I can't."

"Unless he gets staked," Quinn said.

I felt a pang in my heart that almost had me clapping a hand to my chest.

"You don't want that to happen." Quinn's mouth was compressed in a hard line.

"No, of course not!"

"You care about him."

Oh, *crap.* "Quinn, you know Eric and I were together for a while, but he had amnesia and he doesn't remember it. I mean, he knows it's a fact, but he doesn't remember it at all."

"If anyone besides you told me that story, you know what I'd think."

"Quinn. I'm not anybody else."

"Babe, I don't know what to say. I care about you, and I love spending time with you. I love going to bed with you. I like eating at the table with you. I like cooking together. I like almost everything about you, including your gift. But I'm not good at sharing."

"I don't go with two guys at the same time."

"What are you saying?"

"I'm saying, I'm going with you, unless you tell me different."

"What will you do when Mr. Big and Blond tells you to hop in bed with him?"

"I'll tell him I'm spoken for . . . if you're going to speak."

Quinn shifted restlessly on the narrow bed. "I'm healing, but I'm hurting," he admitted. He looked very tired.

"I wouldn't trouble you with all this if it didn't seem pretty important to me," I said. "I'm trying to be honest with you. Absolutely honest. You took the arrow for me, and it's the least I can do in return."

"I know that. Sookie, I'm a man who almost always knows his own mind, but I have to tell you . . . I don't know what to say. I thought we were just about ideal for each other until this." Quinn's eyes blazed in his face suddenly. "If he died, we'd have no problems."

"If you killed him, I'd have a problem," I said. I couldn't get any plainer than that.

Quinn closed his eyes. "We have to think about this again when I'm all healed and you've had sleep and time to relax," he said. "You gotta meet Frannie, too. I'm so . . ." To my horror, I thought Quinn was going to choke up. If he cried, I would, too, and the last thing I needed was tears. I leaned over so far I thought I was going to fall on top of him, and I kissed him, just a quick pressure of my mouth on his. But then he held my shoulder and pulled me back to him, and there was much more to explore, his warmth and intensity . . . but then his gasp drew us out of the moment. He was trying not to grimace with pain.

"Oh! I'm sorry."

"Don't ever apologize for a kiss like that," he said. And he didn't look teary anymore. "We definitely have something going on, Sookie. I don't want Andre's vampire crap to ruin it."

"Me, either," I said. I didn't want to give Quinn up, not the least because of our sizzling chemistry. Andre terrified me, and who knew what his intentions were? I certainly didn't. I suspected Eric didn't know, either, but he was never averse to power.

I said good-bye to Quinn, a reluctant good-bye, and began finding my way back to the dance. I felt obliged to check in with the queen to make sure she didn't need me, but I was exhausted, and I needed to get out of my dress and collapse on my bed.

Clovache was leaning against a wall in the corridor ahead, and I had the impression she was waiting for me. The younger Britlingen was less statuesque than Batanya, and while Batanya looked like a striking hawk with dark curls, Clovache was lighter altogether, with feathery ash-brown hair that needed a good stylist and big green eyes with high, arched brows.

"He seems like a good man," she said in her harsh accent, and I got the strong feeling that Clovache was not a subtle woman.

"He seems that way to me, too."

"While a vampire, by definition, is twisty and deceptive."

"By definition? You mean, without exception?"

"I do."

I kept silent as we walked. I was too tired to figure out the warrior's purpose in telling me this. I decided to ask. "What's up, Clovache? What's the point?"

"Did you wonder why we were here, guarding the King of Kentucky? Why he had decided to pay our truly astronomical fees?"

"Yes, I did, but I figured it wasn't my business."

"It's very much your business."

"Then tell me. I'm not up to guessing."

"Isaiah caught a Fellowship spy in his entourage a month ago."

I stopped dead, and Clovache did, too. I processed her words. "That's really bad," I said, knowing the words were inadequate.

"Bad for the spy, of course. But she gave up some information before she went to the vale of shadows."

"Wow, that's a pretty way to put it."

"It's a load of crap. She died, and it *wasn't* pretty. Isaiah is an old-fashioned guy. Modern on the surface, a traditional vampire underneath. He had a wonderful time with the poor bitch before she gave it up."

"You think you can trust what she said?"

"Good point. I'd confess to anything if I thought it would spare me some of the things his cronies did to her."

I wasn't sure that was true. Clovache was made of pretty stern stuff.

"But I think she told him the truth. Her story was, a splinter group in the Fellowship got wind of this summit and decided it would be a golden opportunity to come out in the open with their fight against the vampires. Not simply protests and sermons against the vamps, but out-and-out warfare. This isn't the main body of the Fellowship . . . the leaders are always careful to say, 'Oh, gosh, no, we don't condone violence against anyone. We're only cautioning people to be aware that if they consort with vampires, they're consorting with the devil.'"

"You know a lot about things in this world," I said.

"Yes," she agreed. "I do a lot of research before we take a job."

I wanted to ask her what her world was like, how she got from one to the other, how much she charged, if all the warriors on (in?) her world were women or could the guys kick butt, too; and if so, what they looked like in the wonderful pants. But this wasn't the time or the place.

"So, what's the bottom line on this?" I asked.

"I think maybe the Fellowship is trying to mount some major offensive here."

"The bomb in the soda can?"

"Actually, that baffles me. But it was outside Louisiana's room, and the Fellowship has to know by now that their operative didn't succeed, if it was their work."

"And there are also the three murdered vampires in the Arkansas suite," I pointed out.

"Like I say, baffled," Clovache said.

"Would they have killed Jennifer Cater and the others?"

"Certainly, if they had a chance. But to tip their hand in such a small way when according to the spy they have planned something really big—that seems very unlikely. Also, how could a human get into the suite and kill three vampires?"

"So, what was the result of the Dr Pepper bomb?" I asked, trying hard to figure out the thinking behind it. We'd resumed walking, and now we were right outside the ceremonies room. I could hear the orchestra.

"Well, it gave you a few new white hairs," Clovache said, smiling.

"I can't think that was the goal," I said. "I'm not that egocentric."

Clovache had made up her mind. "You're right," she said, "because the Fellowship wouldn't have planted it. They wouldn't want to draw attention to their larger plan with the little bomb."

"So it was there for some other purpose."

"And what was that purpose?"

"The end result of the bomb, if it had gone off, would have been that the queen got a big scare," I said slowly.

Clovache looked startled. "Not killed?"

"She wasn't even in the room."

"It should have gone off earlier than it did," Clovache said.

"How do you know that?"

"Security guy. Donati. That's what the police told him.

Donati sees us as fellow professionals." Clovache grinned. "He likes women in armor."

"Hey, who doesn't?" I grinned back.

"And it was a weak bomb, if any bomb can be called weak. I'm not saying there wouldn't have been damage. There would have. Maybe even someone killed, like you could have been. But the episode seems to be ineffective and ill-planned."

"Unless it was designed only to scare. Designed to be spotted. Designed to be disarmed."

Clovache shrugged.

"I don't understand," I said. "If not the Fellowship, who? What does the Fellowship plan to do? Charge the lobby armed with sharpened baseball bats?"

"The security here is not so good," Clovache said.

"Yeah, I know. When I was down in the basement, getting a suitcase for the queen, the guards were pretty lazy, and I don't think the employees are searched as they come in, either. And they got a lot of suitcases mixed up."

"And the vampires hired these people. Unbelievable. On one level vampires realize they're not immortal. They can be killed. On another, they've survived for so long, it makes them feel omnipotent." Clovache shrugged. "Well, back to duty." We'd reached the ballroom. The Dead Man Dance Band was still playing.

The queen was standing very close to Andre, who no longer stood behind her but to her side. I knew this was significant, but it wasn't plain enough to cause Kentucky to give up hope. Christian Baruch was also in close attendance. If he'd had a tail, it would have been wagging, he was so anxious to please Sophie-Anne. I glanced around the room at the other kings and queens, recognizable by their entourages. I hadn't seen them in a room all together before, and I counted. There were only four queens. The other twelve rulers were males. Of the four queens, Minnesota appeared to be mated with the King of Wisconsin. Ohio had his arm around Iowa, so they were a couple. Besides Alabama, the only unmated queen was Sophie-Anne.

Though many vampires tend to be elastic about the gender of their sexual partner, or at least tolerant of those who prefer something different, some of them definitely aren't. No wonder Sophie-Anne was shining so brightly, even from under the lifted cloud of Peter Threadgill's death. Vampires didn't seem to be afraid of merry widows.

Alabama's boy toy scuttled his fingers up her bare back, and she shrieked in pretended fear. "You know I hate spiders," she said playfully, looking almost human, clutching him close to her. Though he'd played at frightening her, she clung closer.

*Wait,* I thought. *Wait just a minute.* But the idea wouldn't form.

Sophie-Anne noticed me lurking, and she beckoned. "I think most of the humans are gone for the night," she said.

A glance around the room told me that was true. "What did you think of Julian Trout?" I asked, to allay my fear that she'd do something awful to him.

"I think he doesn't understand what he did," Sophie-Anne said. "At least to some extent. But he and I will come to an understanding." She smiled. "He and his wife are quite all right. I don't need you anymore tonight. Go amuse yourself," she said, and it didn't sound condescending. Sophie-Anne really wanted me to have a good time, though, granted, she wasn't too particular about how I did it.

"Thanks," I said, and then recalled that I'd better dress that up a bit. "Thank you, ma'am, and you have a good night. See you tomorrow evening."

I was glad to get out of there. With the room chock full o' vampires, the glances I was getting were a little on the pointy-toothed side. Individual bloodsuckers had an easier time of it sticking to the artificial blood than a group did. Something about the memory of the good ole days just made them want something warm from the source, rather than a liquid created in a lab and heated up in a microwave. Right on schedule, the crowd of Willing Donors returned through a back door and lined up, more or less, against the back wall. In very short order, they were all occupied, and (I suppose) happy.

After Bill had taken my blood during lovemaking, he'd told me blood from the neck of a human—after a diet of TrueBlood, say—was like going to Ruth's Chris Steak House after many meals at McDonald's. I saw Gervaise nuzzling Carla off in a corner, and I wondered if she needed help; but when I saw her face, I decided not.

Carla didn't come in that night, either, and without the distraction of Quinn, I was kind of sorry. I had too much to think about. It seemed that trouble was looking for me in the corridors of the Pyramid of Gizeh, and no matter which turn I took, it was going to find me.

# 15 ～

I'D FINALLY GONE TO BED AT FOUR IN THE MORNING, and I woke at noon. That eight hours wasn't a good eight hours. I kept starting half awake, and I couldn't regulate my temperature, which might have had something to do with the blood exchange . . . or not. I had bad dreams, too, and twice I thought I heard Carla entering the room, only to open my eyes enough to see she wasn't there. The weird light that entered through the heavily colored glass of the human-only floor was not like real daylight, not at all. It was throwing me off.

I felt a tad bit better after a long shower, and I lifted the phone to call room service to get something to eat. Then I decided to go down to the little restaurant. I wanted to see other humans.

There were a few there; not my roommate, but a human playmate or two, and Barry. He gestured to the empty chair at his table, and I dropped into it, looking around for the waiter to signal for coffee. It came right away, and I shuddered with pleasure at the first sip. After I'd finished the first cup, I said—in my way—*How are you today? Were you up all night?*

*No, Stan went to bed early with his new girlfriend, so I wasn't needed. They're still in the honeymoon stage. I went to the dance for a while, then I hung out with the makeup girl the Queen of Iowa brought with her.* He waggled his eyebrows to tell me that the makeup girl was hot.

*So, what's your program for today?*

*Did you get one of these slid under your door?* Barry pushed a stapled sheaf of papers across the table to me just as the waiter brought my English muffin and eggs.

*Yeah, I stuffed it in my purse.* Wow, I could talk to Barry while I ate, the neatest answer to talking with your mouth full I could ever devise.

*Take a look.*

While Barry cut open a biscuit to slather it with butter, I scanned the pages. An agenda for the night, which was very helpful. Sophie-Anne's trial had been the most serious case that had to be adjudicated, the only one involving royalty. But there were a couple of others. The first session was set for 8:00, and it was a dispute over a personal injury. A Wisconsin vampire named Jodi (which seemed unlikely in and of itself) was being sued by an Illinois vampire named Michael. Michael alleged that Jodi had waited until he had dozed off for the day and then broken off one of his canines. With pliers.

*Wow. That sounds . . . interesting.* I raised my eyebrows. *How come the sheriffs aren't handling this?* Vampires really didn't like airing their dirty laundry.

"Interstate," Barry said succinctly. The waiter had just brought a whole pot of coffee, so Barry topped off my cup and filled his own.

I flipped over a page. The next case involved a Kansas City, Missouri, vampire named Cindy Lou Suskin, who'd turned a child. Cindy Lou claimed that the child was dying of a blood disorder anyway, and she'd always wanted a child; so now she had a perpetual vampire preteen. Furthermore, the boy had been turned with his parents' consent, gotten in writing. Kate Book, the Kansas City, Kansas, lawyer appointed by the state to supervise the child's welfare, was complaining that now the child refused to see his human parents or to have any interaction with them, which was contrary to the agreement between the parents and Cindy Lou.

Sounded like something on daytime television. *Judge Judy*, anyone?

*So, tonight is court cases,* I summarized after scanning the remaining sheets. "I guess we're needed?"

"Yes, I guess so. There'll be human witnesses for the second case. Stan wants me to be there, and I'm betting your queen will want you there, too. Her subject Bill is one of the appointed judges. Only kings and queens can judge other kings and queens, but for cases involving lesser vampires, the judges are picked from a pool. Bill's name came out of the hat."

"Oh, goody."

*You got a history with him?*

*Yeah. But I think he'd probably be a good judge.* I wasn't sure why I believed this; after all, Bill had shown he was capable of great deception. But I thought he would try to be fair and dispassionate.

I had noticed that the "court" cases would take up the hours between eight and eleven. After that, midnight to four a.m. was blocked out as "Commerce." Barry and I looked at each other and shrugged.

"Swap meet?" I suggested. "Flea market?"

Barry had no idea.

The fourth night of the conference was the last, and the first half of it was marked "Free Time for Everyone in Rhodes." Some of the suggested activities: seeing the Blue Moon dancers again, or their more explicit division, Black Moon. The difference wasn't spelled out, but I got the definite idea that the Black Moon employees did much more sexually oriented performances. Different dance teams from the studio were listed as appearing at different venues. The visiting vampires were also advised to visit the zoo, which would be open at night by special arrangement, or the city museum, ditto. Or they could visit a club "for the particular enjoyment of those who enjoy their pleasures on the darker side." It was called Kiss of Pain. *Remind me to walk down the other side of the street from that one,* I told Barry.

*You never enjoy a little bite?* Barry touched his tongue to his own blunt canines so I couldn't miss the implication.

*There's lots of pleasure in that,* I said, because I could hardly deny it. *But I think this place probably goes a little beyond a nip in the neck. Are you busy right now? Because I have to do some legwork for Eric, and I could use some help.*

"Sure," Barry said. "What's up?"

"We need to find archery places," I said.

"This was left for you at the desk, miss," said our waiter, who dropped a manila envelope on the table and retreated as if he suspected we had rabies. Evidently our silent exchanges had freaked someone out.

I opened the envelope to find a picture of Kyle Perkins inside. There was a note paper-clipped to it in Bill's familiar cramped handwriting. "Sookie: Eric says you need this to do some detective work, and that this picture is necessary. Please be cautious. William Compton." And just when I was thinking about asking the waiter for a phone book, I saw there was a second sheet. Bill had searched the Internet and made a list of all the archery practice places in the city.

There were only four. I tried not to be impressed by Bill's thoughtfulness and assistance. I'd done with being impressed by Bill.

I called the hotel garage to get one of the cars brought by the Arkansas contingent. The queen had assumed ownership of them, and Eric had offered me one of them.

Barry had run up to his room to get a jacket, and I was standing by the front door, waiting for the car to be brought around and wondering how much I should tip the valet when I spotted Todd Donati. He came over to me, walking slowly and somehow heavily, though he was a thin man. He looked bad today, the scalp exposed by his receding hairline gray and damp looking, even his mustache sagging.

He stood facing me for a moment, not speaking. I thought he was gathering his courage, or his hopelessness. If ever I saw death riding on a man's shoulder, it was on Todd Donati's.

"My boss is trying to interest your boss in hooking up," he said abruptly. If I'd imagined how he'd open our conversation, it had never included that line.

"Yeah, now that she's a widow, she's attracting quite a lot of interest," I said.

"He's an old-fashioned guy in a lot of ways," Todd Donati said. "Comes from an old family, doesn't like modern thinking."

"Um-hum," I said, trying to sound neutral but encouraging.

"He don't believe in women making up their own minds, being able to fend for themselves," the security chief said.

I couldn't look like I understood what Donati was talking about, because I sure didn't.

"Even vampire women," he said, and looked at me squarely and directly.

"Okay," I said.

"Think about it," Donati said. "Get your queen to ask him where the security tape is that shows that area in front of her room."

"I will," I said, having no idea why I was agreeing. Then the ailing man spun on his heel and walked away with an air of having discharged his duty.

Then the car came around, Barry hurried out of the elevator and came over to join me, and any thinking I might have done about the encounter faded in my fear of driving in the city. I don't think Eric ever considered how hard it would be for me to drive in Rhodes, because he just didn't think about stuff like that. If I hadn't had Barry with me, it would have been nearly impossible. I could cope with the driving, or I could look at the map the parking attendant loaned us, but not both.

I didn't do too bad, though the traffic was heavy and the weather was cold and raining. I hadn't been out of the hotel since we'd arrived, and it was kind of refreshing to see the outside world. Also, this was probably the only glimpse of the rest of the city I would get. I did as much looking as I could. Who knew if I'd ever come back? And this was so far north.

Barry plotted our course, and we began our archery tour of Rhodes.

We started with the farthest business, called Straight Arrow. It was a long, narrow place on a very busy avenue. It was gleaming, well-lit—and had qualified instructors behind the counter who were heavily armed. I knew this, because a big sign said so. The men there were not impressed by Barry's southern accent. They thought it made him sound stupid. Though when I talked, they thought I was cute. Okay, how insulting is that? The subtext, which I read very clearly from their minds, was: women sound stupid anyway, so a southern accent just enhances that adorable dimness. Men are supposed to sound crisp and direct, so southern men sound stupid and weak.

Anyway, aside from their built-in prejudices, these men were not helpful. They'd never seen Kyle Perkins at any of their night classes, and they didn't think he'd ever rented time to practice at their place.

Barry was fuming at the disrespect he'd endured, and he didn't even want to go in the second place. I trotted in by myself with the picture, and the one guy at work at the second archery supply store, which had no range, said, "No," immediately. He didn't discuss the picture, ask me why I wanted to know about Kyle Perkins, or wish me a nice day. He didn't have a sign to tell me how formidable he was. I figured he just ruded people to death.

The third place, housed in a building that I thought might at one time have been a bowling alley, had a few cars in the parking lot and a heavy opaque door. STOP AND BE IDENTIFIED a sign said. Barry and I could read it from the car. It seemed a little ominous.

"I'm tired of being in the car anyway," he said gallantly, and got out with me. We stood where we could be seen, and I alerted Barry when I spotted the camera above our heads. Barry and I both looked as pleasant as we could. (In Barry's case, that was pretty pleasant. He just had a way about him.) After a few seconds, we heard a loud click, and the door unlocked. I glanced at Barry, and he pulled open the heavy door while I stepped inside the room and to one side so he could enter, too.

We were faced with a long counter extending the length of the opposite wall. There was a woman about my age behind the counter, with coppery hair and skin, the product of an interesting racial blend. She'd dyed her eyebrows black, which added a touch of the bizarre to the whole uni-color effect.

She looked us over just as carefully in person as she had

over the camera, and I could read the thought that she was much happier to see Barry than she was to see me. I told Barry, *You better take this one.*

*Yeah, I'm getting the idea,* he answered, and while I laid Kyle's picture on the counter, he said, "Could you tell us if this guy ever came in here to buy arrows or to practice?"

She didn't even ask why we wanted to know. She bent over to look at the picture, maybe a little farther than necessary to give Barry the benefit of her neckline. She scanned Kyle's picture and immediately made a face. "Yeah, he came in here right after dark yesterday," she said. "We'd never had a vampire customer, and I didn't really want to serve him, but what are you gonna do? He had the money, and the law says we can't discriminate." She was a woman who was ready and willing to discriminate, no doubt about it.

"Was anyone with him?" Barry asked.

"Oh, let me think." She posed, her head thrown back, for Barry's benefit. *She* didn't think his southern accent sounded stupid. She thought it was adorable and sexy. "I just can't remember. Listen, I'll tell ya what I'll do. I'll get the security tape for last night; we've still got it. And I'll let you have a look at it, okay?"

"Can we do that right now?" I asked, smiling sweetly.

"Well, I can't leave the counter right now. There's no one else here to watch the store if I have to go to the back. But if you'll come to look tonight after my replacement gets here"—she cast a very pointed glance at Barry, to make sure I realized I need not come—"I'll let you have a peek."

"What time?" Barry said, rather reluctantly.

"Shall we say seven? I get off right after that."

Barry didn't touch the hint, but he agreed to be back at seven.

"Thanks, Barry," I said as we buckled up again. "You're really helping me out." I called the hotel and left a message for the queen and Andre, explaining where I was and what I was doing, so they wouldn't get mad when I wasn't at their disposal the moment they woke, which should be very soon. After all, I was following Eric's orders.

"You gotta come in with me," Barry said. "I'm not seeing that woman by myself. She'll eat me alive. That was the War of Northern Aggression, for sure."

"Okay. I'll stay out in the car, and you can yell to me from your head if she climbs on top of you."

"It's a deal."

To fill the time, we had a cup of coffee and some cake at a bakery. It was great. My grandmother had always believed that northern women couldn't cook. It was delightful to find out exactly how untrue that conviction had been. My appetite was also delightful. It was a continuing relief to find that I was just as hungry as I normally was. Nothing vampy about me, no sir!

After we filled up the tank and checked our route back to the Pyramid, it was finally time to return to the archery range to talk to Copper. The sky was full dark, and the city glowed with light. I felt sort of urban and glamorous, driving around such a large and famous city. And I'd been given a task and performed it successfully. No country mouse, me.

My feeling of happiness and superiority didn't last long.

Our first clue that all was not well at the Monteagle Archery Company was the heavy metal door hanging askew.

"Shit," said Barry, which summed up my feelings in a nutshell.

We got out—very reluctantly—and, with many glances from side to side, we went up to the door to examine it.

"Blown or ripped?" I said.

Barry knelt on the gravel to have a closer look.

"I'm no 007," he said, "but I think this was ripped off."

I looked at the door doubtfully. But when I bent over to look more closely, I saw the twisted metal of the hinges. Chalk one up for Barry.

"Okay," I said. *Here's the part where we actually have to go in.*

Barry's jaw tightened. *Yeah,* he said, but he didn't sound too sure. Barry was definitely not into violence or confrontations. Barry was into money, and he had the best-paying employer. Right now, he was wondering if any amount of money would be enough to compensate for this, and he was thinking if he weren't with a woman, he'd just get in the car and drive away.

Sometimes male pride can be a good thing. I sure didn't want to do this by myself.

I shoved the door, which responded in a spectacular way by falling off its hinges and crashing to the gravel.

"Hi, we're here," Barry said weakly. "Anyone who didn't know before . . ."

After the noise had stopped and nothing had leaped out of the building to eat us, Barry and I straightened up from our instinctive crouching positions. I took a deep breath. This was my task, since this had been my errand. I stepped into the stream of light coming from the empty doorway. I took one big step forward over the threshold of the building. A quick scan hadn't given me a brain signal, so I pretty much figured what I was going to find.

Oh, yeah, Copper was dead. She was on top of the counter, laid out in a sprawl of limbs, her head canting off to one side. There was a knife protruding from her chest. Someone had been sick about a yard to the left of my foot—not blood—so there'd been at least one human on-site. I heard Barry step into the building and pause, just as I had.

I'd noted two doors from the room on our earlier visit.

There was a door to the right, outside the counter, that would admit customers to the range. There was a door behind the counter that would allow employees to duck back for breaks and to attend customers in the range area. I was sure the tape we'd come to watch had been back there, because that would be the natural place for the security equipment. Whether it was still back there, that was the big question.

I wanted to turn around and leave without a backward glance, and I was scared out of my mind, but she'd died because of that tape, I figured, and it seemed like I'd be discarding her unwilling sacrifice if I discarded the tape. That didn't really make much sense, but that was how I felt.

*I'm not finding anyone else in the area,* Barry told me.

*Me, either,* I said, after I'd performed my second, more thorough, scan.

Barry, of course, knew exactly what I planned to do, and he said, *Do you want me to come with you?*

*No, I want you to wait outside. I'll call you if I need you.* In truth, it would have been nice to have him closer, but it smelled too bad in the room for anyone to stand around for more than a minute, and our minute was up.

Without protesting, Barry went back outside, and I crept down the counter to a clear area. It felt indescribably creepy to scramble over, avoiding Copper's body. I was glad her sightless eyes were not aimed in my direction as I used a tissue to wipe the area my hands had gripped.

On the employee side of the counter, there was evidence of a considerable struggle. She'd fought hard. There were smears of blood here and there, and paperwork had gotten knocked to the floor. There was a panic button clearly visible, below the top of the counter, but I guess she hadn't had time to punch it.

The lights were on in the office behind the counter, too,

as I could see through the partially open door. I pushed it with my foot, and it swung away from me with a little creak. Again, nothing leaped out at me. I took a deep breath and stepped through.

The room was a combination security room/office/break-room. There were counters built around the walls with rolling chairs pulled up to them, and there were computers and a microwave and a little refrigerator: the usual stuff. And there were the security tapes, heaped in a pile on the floor and smoldering. All the other smells in the outer room had been so bad we simply hadn't gotten around to this one. There was another door leading out; I didn't go check to see where it led to, because there was a body blocking it. It was a man's body, and it was lying facedown, which was a blessing. I didn't need to go over to check to see if he was dead. He was surely dead. Copper's replacement, I assumed.

"Well, crap," I said out loud. And then I thought, *Thank God I can get the hell out of here.* One thing about the security tapes having been burned: any record of our earlier visit was gone, too.

On my way, I pressed the panic button with my elbow. I hoped it was ringing somewhere at a police station, and that they'd get here soon.

Barry was waiting for me outside, as I'd been 99 percent sure he would be. Though I confess I wouldn't have been completely surprised if he'd left. "Let's book! I set off the alarm," I said, and we jumped into the car and got the hell out of there.

I was driving, because Barry was looking green. We had to pull over once (and in Rhodes traffic that wasn't easy) for him to be sick. I didn't blame him one little bit. What we'd seen was awful. But I've been blessed with a strong stomach, and I'd seen worse.

We got back to the hotel in time for the judicial session.

Barry looked at me with gaping astonishment when I commented that I'd better get ready for it. He hadn't had an inkling what I'd been thinking, so I knew he was really feeling bad.

"How can you think of going?" he said. "We have to tell someone what happened."

"I called the police, or at least a security company who'll report it," I said. "What else can we do?" We were in the elevator rising from the parking garage to the lobby.

"We have to talk to them."

"Why?" The doors opened and we stepped out into the hotel lobby.

"To tell them."

"What?"

"That someone tried to kill you last night here by . . . okay, throwing an arrow at you." He fell silent.

"Right. See?" I was getting his thoughts now, and he'd come to the correct conclusion. "Would it help solve her murder? Probably not, because the guy is dead and the tapes are destroyed. And they'd come here asking questions of the master vampires of a third of the United States. Who would thank me for that? No one, that's who."

"We can't stand by and do nothing."

"This isn't perfect. I know that. But it's realistic. And practical."

"Oh, so now you're *practical?*" Barry was getting shrieky.

"And you're yelling at my—at Sookie," said Eric, earning another shriek (this one wordless) from Barry. By that time, Barry didn't care if he ever saw me again in his life. Though I didn't feel quite that drastic, I didn't think we were going to become pen pals, either.

If Eric didn't know how to pick a term for what I was to him, I was equally stumped. "Do you need something?" I

asked him in a voice that warned him I wasn't in the mood
for any double entendres.

"What did you find out today?" he asked, all business,
and the starch ran out of me in a stream.

"You go on," I told Barry, who didn't need telling twice.

Eric looked around for a safe place to talk, didn't see one.
The lobby was busy with vampires who were going to the judicial proceedings, or chatting, or flirting. "Come," he said,
not as rudely as it sounds, and we went to the elevators and
up to his room. Eric was on the ninth floor, which covered a
much larger area than the queen's. There were twenty rooms
on nine, at least. There was a lot more traffic, too; we passed
quite a few vamps on the way to Eric's room, which he told
me he was sharing with Pam.

I was a little curious about seeing a regular vampire
room, since I'd seen only the living room of the queen's
suite. I was disappointed to find that aside from the traveling coffins, it looked quite ordinary. Of course, that was
kind of a big "aside." Pam's and Eric's coffins were resting
on fancy trestles covered with fake hieroglyphics in gilt on
black-painted wood, which gave them a neat atmospheric
touch. There were two double beds, too, and a very compact
bathroom. Both towels were hung up, which I could see because the door was open. Eric had never hung up his towels
when he lived with me, so I was willing to bet that Pam had
folded them and hung them on the rack. It seemed oddly
domestic. Pam had probably picked up for Eric for over a
century. Good God. I hadn't even managed two weeks.

What with the coffins and the beds, the room was a bit
crowded, and I wondered what the lower echelon vamps had
to put up with, say, on floor twelve. Could you arrange
coffins in a bunk configuration? But I was just waffling, trying not to think about being alone with Eric. We sat down,

Eric on one bed and I on another, and he leaned forward. "Tell me," he said.

"Well, it's not good," I said, just to put him on the right track.

His face darkened, the blond brows drawing in to meet, his mouth turning down.

"We did find an archery range that Kyle Perkins visited. You were right about that. Barry went with me to be nice, and I really appreciated it," I said, getting my opening credits in. "To condense the whole afternoon, we found the right range at our third stop, and the gal behind the counter said we could look at the security tape from the night Kyle visited. I thought we might see someone we knew coming in with him. But she wanted us to come back at the end of her shift, seven o'clock." I paused to take a deep breath. Eric's face didn't change at all. "We came back at the appointed time, and she was dead, murdered, in the store. I went past her to look in the office, and the tapes had been burned."

"Killed how?"

"She'd been stabbed, and the knife was left in her chest, and the killer or someone with him had thrown up food. Also, a guy who worked at the store was killed, but I didn't check him out to see how."

"Ah." Eric considered this. "Anything else?"

"No," I said, and got to my feet to leave.

"Barry was angry with you," he observed.

"Yeah, he was, but he'll get over it."

"What's his problem?"

"He doesn't think I handled the . . . He doesn't think we should've left. Or . . . I don't know. He thinks I was unfeeling."

"I think you did exceptionally well."

"Well, *great*!" Then I clamped down on myself. "Sorry," I said. "I know you meant to compliment me. I'm not feeling all that good about her dying. Or leaving her. Even if it was the practical thing to do."

"You're second-guessing yourself."

"Yes."

A knock at the door. Since Eric didn't shift himself, I got up to answer it. I didn't think it was a sexist thing; it was a status thing. I was definitely the lower dog in the room.

Completely and totally not to my surprise, the knocker was Bill. That just made my day complete. I stood aside to let him enter. Darn if I was going to ask Eric if I should let him in.

Bill looked me up and down, I guess to check that my clothes were in order, then strode by me without a word. I rolled my eyes at his back. Then I had a brilliant idea: instead of turning back into the room for further discussion, I stepped out of the open door and shut it behind me. I marched off quite briskly and grabbed the elevator with hardly any wait. In two minutes, I was unlocking my door.

End of problem.

I felt quite proud of myself.

Carla was in our room, naked again.

"Hi," I said. "Please put on a robe."

"Well, hey, if it bothers you," she said in a fairly relaxed manner, and pulled on a robe. Wow. End of another problem. Direct action, straightforward statements; obviously, those were the keys to improving my life.

"Thanks," I said. "Not going to the judicial stuff?"

"Human dates aren't invited," she said. "It's Free Time for us. Gervaise and I are going out nightclubbing later. Some really extreme place called Kiss of Pain."

"You be careful," I said. "Bad things can happen if there are lots of vamps together and a bleeding human or two."

"I can handle Gervaise," Carla said.

"No, you can't."

"He's nuts about me."

"Until he stops being nuts. Or until a vamp older than Gervaise takes a shine to you, and Gervaise gets all conflicted."

She looked uncertain for a second, an expression I felt sure Carla didn't wear too often.

"What about you? I hear you're tied to Eric now."

"Only for a while," I said, and I meant it. "It'll wear off."

*I will never go anywhere with vampires again,* I promised myself. *I let the lure of the money and the excitement of the travel pull me in. But I won't do that again. As God is my witness . . .* Then I had to laugh out loud. Scarlett O'Hara, I wasn't. "I'll never be hungry again," I told Carla.

"Why, did you eat a big supper?" she asked, focused on the mirror because she was plucking her eyebrows.

I laughed. And I couldn't stop.

"What's up with you?" Carla swung around to eye me with some concern. "You're not acting like yourself, Sookie."

"Just had a bad shock," I said, gasping for breath. "I'll be okay in a minute." It was more like ten before I gathered my control back around me. I was due at the judicial meeting, and frankly, I wanted to have something to occupy my mind. I scrubbed my face and put on some makeup, changed into a bronze silk blouse and tobacco-colored pants with a matching cardigan, and put on some brown leather pumps. With my room key in my pocket and a relieved good-bye from Carla, I was off to find the judicial sessions.

# 16

THE VAMPIRE JODI WAS PRETTY FORMIDABLE. SHE PUT me in mind of Jael, in the Bible. Jael, a determined woman of Israel, put a tent peg through the head of Sisera, an enemy captain, if I was remembering correctly. Sisera had been asleep when Jael did the deed, just as Michael had been when Jodi broke off his fang. Even though Jodi's name made me snicker, I saw in her a steely strength and resolve, and I was immediately on her side. I hoped the panel of judges could see past the vampire Michael's whining about his damn tooth.

This wasn't set up like the previous evening, though the session took place in the same room. The panel of judges, I guess you'd call them, were on the stage and seated at a long table facing the audience. There were three of them, all from different states: two men and a woman. One of the males was Bill, who was looking (as always) calm and collected. I didn't know the other guy, a blond. The female was a tiny, pretty vamp with the straightest back and longest rippling black hair I ever saw. I heard Bill address her as "Dahlia." Her round little face whipped back and forth as she listened to the testimony of first Jodi, then Michael, just as if she was watching a tennis match. Centered on the white tablecloth before the judges was a stake, which I guess was the vampire symbol of justice.

The two complaining vampires were not represented by lawyers. They said their piece, and then the judges got to ask questions before they decided the verdict by a majority vote. It was simple in form, if not in fact.

"You were torturing a human woman?" Dahlia asked Michael.

"Yes," he said without blinking an eye. I glanced around. I was the only human in the audience. No wonder there was a certain simplicity to the proceedings. The vampires weren't trying to dress it up for a warm-blooded audience. They were behaving as they would if they were by themselves. I was sitting by those of my party who'd attended—Rasul, Gervaise, Cleo—and maybe their closeness masked my scent, or maybe one tame human didn't count.

"She'd offended me, and I enjoy sex that way, so I abducted her and had a little fun," Michael said. "Then Jodi goes all ballistic on me and breaks my fang. See?" He opened wide enough to show the judges the fang's stump. (I wondered if he'd gone by the booth that was still set up out in the vendors' area, the one that had such amazing artificial fangs.)

Michael had the face of an angel, and he didn't get that what he'd done was wrong. He had wanted to do it, so he did it. Not all people who've been brought over to be vampires are mentally stable to start with, and some of them are utterly conscienceless after decades, or even centuries, of disposing of humans as they damn well please. And yet, they enjoy the openness of the new order, getting to stride around being themselves, with the right not to be staked. They don't want to pay for that privilege by adhering to the rules of common decency.

I thought breaking off one fang was a very light punishment. I couldn't believe he'd had the gall to bring a case against anyone. Apparently, neither did Jodi, who was on her feet and going for him again. Maybe she meant to snap off his other fang. This was way better than *The Peoples' Court* or *Judge Judy*.

The blond judge tackled her. He was much larger than Jodi, and she seemed to accept that she wasn't going to heave him off. I noticed Bill had moved his chair back so he could leap up if further developments required quick action.

The tiny Dahlia said, "Why did you take such exception to Michael's actions, Jodi?"

"The woman was the sister of one of my employees," Jodi said, her voice shaking with anger. "She was under my protection. And stupid Michael will cause all of us to be hunted again if he continues his ways. He can't be corrected. Nothing stops him, not even losing the fang. I warned him three times to stay away, but the young woman spoke back to him when he propositioned her yet again on the street, and his pride was more important than his intelligence or discretion."

"Is this true?" the little vamp asked Michael.

"She insulted me, Dahlia," he said smoothly. "A human publicly insulted me."

"This one's easy," said Dahlia. "Do you both agree?" The blond male restraining Jodi nodded, and so did Bill, who was still perched on the edge of his chair to Dahlia's right.

"Michael, you will bring retribution on us by your unwise

actions and your inability to control your impulses," Dahlia said. "You have ignored warnings, and you ignored the fact that the young woman was under the protection of another vampire."

"You can't mean this! Where is your pride?" Michael was yelling and on his feet.

Two men stepped forward out of the shadows at the back of the stage. They were both vampires, of course, and they were both good-sized men. They held Michael, who put up quite a fight. I was a little shocked by the noise and the violence, but in a minute they'd take Michael off to some vampire prison, and the calm proceedings would continue.

To my absolute astonishment, Dahlia nodded to the vamp sitting on Jodi, who got up and assisted her to rise. Jodi, smiling broadly, was across the stage in one leap, like a panther. She grabbed up the stake lying on the judges' table, and with one powerful swing of her lean arm, she buried the stake in Michael's chest.

I was the only one who was shocked, and I clapped both hands over my mouth to keep from squeaking.

Michael looked at her with utter rage, and he even kept struggling, I suppose to free his arms so he could pull the stake out, but in a few seconds it was all over. The two vamps holding the new corpse hauled it off, and Jodi stepped off the stage, still beaming.

"Next case," called Dahlia.

The next was the one about the vampire kid, and there were humans involved in this one. I felt less conspicuous when they came in: the hangdog parents with their vampire representative (was it possible that humans couldn't testify before this court?) and the "mother" with her "child."

This was a longer, sadder case, because the parents' suffering over the loss of their son—who was still walking and talking, but not to them—was nearly palpable. I wasn't the only one who cried, "For shame!" when Cindy Lou revealed the parents were giving her monthly payments for the boy's upkeep. The vampire Kate argued for the parents ferociously, and it was clear she thought Cindy Lou was a trailer-trash vampire and a bad mother, but the three judges—different ones this time, and I didn't know any of them—abided by the written contract the parents had signed and refused to give the boy a new guardian. However, they ruled, the contract had to be equally enforced on the parents' behalf, and the boy was required to spend time with his biological parents as long as they chose to enforce the right.

The head judge, a hawk-faced guy with dark, liquid eyes, called the boy up to stand before them. "You owe these people respect and obedience, and you signed this contract, too," he said. "You may be a minor in human law, but to us, you are as responsible as . . . *Cindy Lou.*" Boy, it just killed him, having to admit there was a vampire named Cindy Lou. "If you try to terrorize your human parents, or coerce them, or drink their blood, we will amputate your hand. And when it grows back, we'll amputate it again."

The boy could hardly be whiter than he was, and his human mother fainted. But he'd been so cocky, so sure of himself, and so dismissive of his poor parents, I thought the strong warning was necessary. I caught myself nodding.

Oh, yeah, this was fair, to threaten a kid with having his hand amputated.

But if you'd seen this kid, you might have agreed. And Cindy Lou was no prize; whoever had turned her must have been mentally and morally deficient.

I hadn't been needed after all. I was wondering about the rest of the evening when the queen came through the double doors at the end of the room, Sigebert and Andre in close attendance. She was wearing a sapphire blue silk pantsuit with a beautiful diamond necklace and small diamond earrings. She looked classy, absolutely smooth, sleek, and perfect. Andre made a beeline to me.

"I know," he said, "that is, Sophie-Anne tells me that I have done wrong to you. I'm not sorry, because I will do anything for her. Others don't mean anything to me. But I do regret that I have not been able to refrain from causing something that distresses you."

If that was an apology, it was the most half-assed one I'd ever received in my life. It left almost everything to be desired. All I could do was say, "I hear you." It was the most I'd ever get.

By then, Sophie-Anne was standing in front of me. I did my head-bob thing. "I will need you with me during the next few hours," she said, and I said, "Sure." She glanced up and down my clothes, as if wishing I had dressed up a little more, but no one had warned me that a part of the night marked off for Commerce meant fancy clothes were appropriate.

Mr. Cataliades steamed up to me, wearing a beautiful suit and a dark red-and-gold silk tie, and he said, "Good to see you, my dear. Let me brief you on the next item on the schedule."

I spread my hands to show I was ready. "Where's Diantha?" I asked.

"She is working something out with the hotel," Cataliades said. He frowned. "It's most peculiar. There was an extra coffin downstairs, apparently."

"How could that be?" Coffins belonged to somebody. It's not like a vampire was going to be traveling with a spare, like you had to have a dress coffin and an everyday coffin. "Why did they call you?"

"It had one of our tags on it," he said.

"But all of our vamps are accounted for, right?" I felt a tingle of anxiety in my chest. Just then, I saw the usual waiters moving among the crowd, and I saw one spot me and turn away. Then he saw Barry, who'd come in with the King of Texas. The waiter turned away yet again.

I actually started to call to a nearby vampire to hold the guy so I could have a look into his head, and then I realized I was acting as high-handed as the vampires themselves. The waiter vanished, and I hadn't had a close look at him, so I wasn't sure I could even identify him in a crowd of other servers in the same outfit. Mr. Cataliades was talking, but I held up a hand. "Hold it for a sec," I murmured. The waiter's quick turn had reminded me of something, something else that had seemed odd.

"Please pay attention, Miss Stackhouse," the lawyer said, and I had to stow the thread of thought away. "Here's what you need to do. The queen will be negotiating for a few favors she needs to help rebuild her state. Just do what you do best to discover if everyone dealing with her is honorable."

This was not a very specific guideline. "Do my best," I said. "But I think you should go find Diantha, Mr. C. I think there's something really strange and wrong about this extra coffin they're talking about. There was that extra suitcase, too," I said. "I carried it up to the queen's suite."

Mr. Cataliades looked at me blankly. I could see that he considered the small problem of extra items turning up in a hotel to be a small one and below his concern. "Did Eric tell you about the murdered woman?" I asked, and his attention sharpened.

"I haven't seen Master Eric this evening," he said. "I'll be sure to track him down."

"Something's up; I just don't know what," I muttered more or less to myself, and then I turned away to catch up with Sophie-Anne.

Commerce was conducted in a sort of bazaar style. Sophie-Anne positioned herself by the table where Bill was sitting, back at work selling the computer program. Pam was helping him, but she was in her regular clothes, and I was glad the harem costume was getting a rest. I wondered what the procedure was, but I adopted a wait-and-see attitude, and I found out soon enough. The first to approach Sophie-Anne was the big blond vampire who'd served as a judge earlier. "Dear madam," he said, kissing her hand. "I am charmed to see you, as always, and devastated by the destruction of your beautiful city."

"A small portion of my beautiful city," Sophie-Anne said with the sweetest of smiles.

"I am in despair at the thought of the straits you must be in," he continued after a brief pause to register her correction. "You, the ruler of such a profitable and prestigious kingdom . . . now brought so low. I hope to be able to assist you in my humble fashion."

"And what form would that assistance take?" Sophie-Anne inquired.

After much palaver, it turned out that Mr. Flowery was willing to bring a gazillion board feet of lumber to New Orleans if Sophie-Anne would give him 2 percent of her next five years' revenue. His accountant was with him. I looked into his eyes with great curiosity. I stepped back, and Andre slithered to my side. I turned so that no one could read my lips.

"Quality of the lumber," I said as quietly as a hummingbird's wings.

That took forever to hammer out, and it was boring, boring, boring. Some of the wannabe providers didn't have humans with them, and I was no help with those; but most of them did. Sometimes the human had paid the vampire a substantial sum to "sponsor" him, so he could just be in the hall and pitch his woo in a one-on-one setting. By the time vendor number eight simpered to a stop in front of the queen,

I was unable to suppress my yawns. I'd noticed Bill was doing a landmark business selling copies of his vampire database. For a reserved kind of guy, he did a good job of explaining and promoting his product, considering some of the vampires were very mistrustful of computers. If I heard about the "Yearly Update Package" one more time, I was gonna puke. There were lots of humans clustering around Bill, because they were more computer savvy than the vamps as a whole. While they were absorbed, I tried to get a scan in here and there, but they were just thinking megahertz and RAM and hard drives—stuff like that.

I didn't see Quinn. Since he was a wereanimal, I figured he'd be completely over his wound of the night before. I could only take his absence as a signal. I was heart-heavy and weary.

The queen invited Dahlia, the little, pretty vampire who'd been so direct in her judgment, up to her suite for a drink. Dahlia accepted regally, and our whole party moved up to the suite. Christian Baruch tagged along; he'd been hovering around Sophie-Anne all evening.

His courtship of Sophie-Anne was heavy-handed, to say the least. I thought again of the boy toy I'd watched the previous evening, tickling the back of his ladylove in imitation of a spider, because he knew she was frightened of them, and how he'd gotten her to snuggle closer to him. I felt a lightbulb come on over my head and wondered if it was visible to anyone else.

My opinion of the hotelier plummeted. If he thought such a strategy would work on Sophie-Anne, he had a lot of thinking to do.

I didn't see Jake Purifoy anywhere around, and I wondered what Andre had him doing. Something innocuous probably, like checking to make sure all the cars were gassed up. He wasn't really trusted to handle anything more taxing, at least not yet. Jake's youth and his Were heritage counted against him, and he'd have to bust his tail to earn points. But Jake didn't have that fire in him. He was looking to the past, to his life as a Were. He had a backlog of bitterness.

Sophie's suite had been cleaned; all the vampire suites had to be cleaned at night, of course, while the vamps were out of them. Christian Baruch started telling us about the extra help he'd had to take on to cope with the summit crowd and how nervous some of them were about cleaning rooms occupied by vampires. I could tell Sophie-Anne was not impressed by Baruch's assumption of superiority. He was so much younger than her, he must seem like a swaggering teenager to the centuries-old queen.

Jake came in just then, and after paying his respects to the queen and meeting Dahlia, he came to sit by me. I was slumping in an uncomfortable straight chair, and he pulled a matching one over.

"What's up, Jake?"

"Not much. I've been getting the queen and Andre tickets to a show for tomorrow night. It's an all-vampire production of *Hello, Dolly!*"

I tried to imagine that, found I couldn't. "What are you going to be doing? It's marked as free time on the schedule."

"I don't know," he said, a curiously remote tone in his voice. "My life has changed so much I just can't predict what will happen. Are you going out tomorrow in the day, Sookie? Shopping, maybe? There are some wonderful stores on Widewater Drive. That's down by the lake."

Even I had heard of Widewater Drive, and I said, "I guess it's possible. I'm not much of a shopper."

"You really should go. There're some great shoe stores, and a big Macy's—you'd love Macy's. Make a day of it. Get away from this place while you can."

"I'll sure think about it," I said, a little puzzled. "Um, have you seen Quinn today?"

"Glimpsed him. And I talked to Frannie for a minute. They've been busy getting props ready for the closing ceremonies."

"Oh," I said. Right. Sure. That took loads of time.

"Call him, ask him to take you out tomorrow," Jake said.

I tried to picture me asking Quinn to take me shopping. Well, it wasn't totally out of the question, but it wasn't likely, either. I shrugged. "Maybe I'll get out some."

He looked pleased.

"Sookie, you can go," Andre said. I was so tired I hadn't even noticed him glide up.

"Okay. Good night, you two," I said, and stood to stretch. I noticed the blue suitcase was still where I'd dropped it two nights ago. "Oh, Jake, you need to take that suitcase back down to the basement. They called me and told me to bring it up here, but no one's claimed it."

"I'll ask around," he said vaguely, and took off for his own room. Andre's attention had already returned to the queen, who was laughing at the description of some wedding Dahlia had attended.

"Andre," I said in a very low voice, "I gotta tell you, I think Mr. Baruch had something to do with that bomb outside the queen's door."

Andre looked as if someone had stuck a nail up his fundament. "What?"

"I'm thinking that he wanted Sophie-Anne scared," I said. "I'm thinking that he thought she'd be vulnerable and need a strong male protector if she felt threatened."

Andre was not Mr. Expressive, but I saw incredulity, disgust, and belief cross his face in quick order.

"And I'm also thinking maybe he told Henrik Feith that

Sophie-Anne was going to kill him. Because he's the hotel owner, right? And he'd have a key to get into the queen's room, where we thought Henrik was safe, right? So Henrik would continue the queen's trial, because he'd been persuaded she would do him in. Again, Christian Baruch would be there, to be her big savior. Maybe he had Henrik killed, after he'd set him up, so he could do a tah-*dah* reveal and dazzle Sophie-Anne with his wonderful care of her."

Andre had the strangest expression on his face, as if he was having trouble following me. "Is there proof?" he asked.

"Not a smidge. But when I talked to Mr. Donati in the lobby this morning, he hinted that there was a security tape I might want to watch."

"Go see," Andre said.

"If I go ask for it, he'll get fired. You need to get the queen to ask Mr. Baruch point-blank if she can see the security tape for the lobby outside during the time the bomb was planted. Gum on the camera or not, that tape will show something."

"Leave first, so he won't connect you to this." In fact, the hotelier had been absorbed in the queen and her conversation, or his vampire hearing would have tipped him off that we were talking about him.

Though I was exhausted, I had the gratifying feeling that I was earning the money they were paying me for this trip. And it was a load off my mind to feel that the Dr Pepper thing was solved. Christian Baruch would not be doing any more bomb planting now that the queen was on to him. The threat the splinter group of the Fellowship posed . . . well, I'd only heard of that from hearsay, and I didn't have any evidence of what form it would take. Despite the death of the woman at the archery place, I felt more relaxed than I had since I'd walked into the Pyramid of Gizeh, because

I was inclined to attribute the killer archer to Baruch, too. Maybe when he saw that Henrik would actually take Arkansas from the queen, he'd gotten greedy and had the assassin take out Henrik, so the queen would get everything. There was something confusing and wrong about that scenario, but I was too tired to think it through, and I was content to let the whole tangled web lie until I was rested.

I crossed the little lobby to the elevator and pressed the button. When the doors dinged open, Bill stepped out, his hands full of order forms.

"You did well this evening," I said, too tired to hate him. I nodded at the forms.

"Yes, we'll all make a lot of money from this," he said, but he didn't sound particularly excited.

I waited for him to step out of my way, but he didn't do that, either.

"I would give it all away if I could erase what happened between us," he said. "Not the times we spent loving each other, but . . ."

"The times you spent lying to me? The times you pretended you could hardly wait to date me when it turns out you were under order to? Those times?"

"Yes," he said, and his deep brown eyes didn't waver. "Those times."

"You hurt me too much. That's not ever gonna happen."

"Do you love any man? Quinn? Eric? That moron JB?"

"You don't have the right to ask me that," I said. "You don't have any rights at all where I'm concerned."

JB? Where'd that come from? I'd always been fond of the guy, and he was lovely, but his conversation was about as stimulating as a stump's. I was shaking my head as I rode down in the elevator to the human floor.

Carla was out, as usual, and since it was five in the morning the chances seemed good that she'd stay out. I put on my pink pajamas and put my slippers beside the bed so I wouldn't have to grope around for them in the darkened room in case Carla came in before I awoke.

# 17

My eyes snapped open like shades that were wound too tight.

*Wake up, wake up, wake up! Sookie, something's wrong.*

*Barry, where are you?*

*Standing at the elevators on the human floor.*

*I'm coming.* I pulled on last night's outfit, but without the heels. Instead, I slid my feet into my rubber-soled slippers. I grabbed the slim wallet that held my room key, driver's license, and credit card, and stuffed it in one pocket, jammed my cell phone into the other, and hurried out of the room. The door slammed behind me with an ominous thud. The hotel felt empty and silent, but my clock had read 9:50.

I had to run down a long corridor and turn right to get to the elevators. I didn't meet a soul. A moment's thought told me that was not so strange. Most humans on the floor would still be asleep, because they kept vampire hours. But there weren't even any hotel employees cleaning the halls.

All the little tracks of disquiet that had crawled through my brain, like slug tracks on your back doorstep, had coalesced into a huge throbbing mass of uneasiness.

I felt like I was on the *Titanic,* and I'd just heard the hull scrape against the iceberg.

I finally spotted someone, lying on the floor. I'd been woken so suddenly and sharply that everything I did had a dreamlike quality to it, so finding a body in the hall was not such a jolt.

I let out a cry, and Barry came bounding around the corner. He crouched down with me. I rolled over the body. It was Jake Purifoy, and he couldn't be roused.

*Why isn't he in his room? What was he doing out so late?* Even Barry's mental voice sounded panicked.

*Look, Barry, he's lying sort of pointing toward my room. Do you think he was coming to see me?*

*Yes, and he didn't make it.*

What could have been so important that Jake wasn't prepared for his day's sleep? I stood up, thinking furiously. I'd never, ever heard of a vampire who didn't know instinctively that the dawn was coming. I thought of the conversations I'd had with Jake, and the two men I'd seen leaving his room.

"You *bastard*," I hissed through my teeth, and I kicked him as hard as I could.

"Jesus, Sookie!" Barry grabbed my arm, horrified. But then he got the picture from my brain.

"We need to find Mr. Cataliades and Diantha," I said. "They can get up; they're not vamps."

"I'll get Cecile. She's human, my roommate," Barry said, and we both went off in different directions, leaving Jake to lie where he was. It was all we could do.

We were back together in five minutes. It had been surprisingly easy to raise Mr. Cataliades, and Diantha had been sharing his room. Cecile proved to be a young woman with a no-nonsense haircut and a competent way about her, and I wasn't surprised when Barry introduced her as the king's new executive assistant.

I'd been a fool to discount, even for a minute, the warning that Clovache had passed along. I was so angry at myself I could hardly stand to be inside my own skin. But I had to shove that aside and we had to act now.

"Listen to what I think," I said. I'd been putting things together in my head. "Some of the waiters have been avoiding Barry and me over the past couple of days, as soon as they found out what we were."

Barry nodded. He'd noticed, too. He looked oddly guilty, but that had to wait.

"They know what we are. They didn't want us to know what they're about to do, I'm assuming. So I'm also assuming it must be something really, really bad. And Jake Purifoy was in on it."

Mr. Cataliades had been looking faintly bored, but now he began to look seriously alarmed. Diantha's big eyes went from face to face.

"What shall we do?" Cecile asked, which earned her high marks in my book.

"It's the extra coffins," I said. "And the blue suitcase in the queen's suite. Barry, you were asked to bring up a suitcase, too, right? And it didn't belong to anyone?"

Barry said, "Right. It's still sitting in the foyer of the king's suite, since everyone passes through there. We thought someone would claim it. I was going to take it back to the luggage department today."

I said, "The one I went down for is sitting in the living room of the queen's suite. I think the guy who was in on it was Joe, the manager down in the luggage and delivery area.

He's the one who called me down to get the suitcase. No one else seemed to know anything about it."

"The suitcases will blow up?" Diantha said in her shrill voice. "The unclaimed coffins in the basement, too? If the basement goes, the building will collapse!" I'd never heard Diantha sound so human.

"We have to wake them up," I said. "We have to get them out."

"The building's going to blow," said Barry, trying to process the idea.

"The vamps won't wake up." Cecile the practical. "They can't."

"Quinn!" I said. I was thinking of so many things at once that I was standing rooted in place. Fishing my phone from my pocket, I punched his number on speed dial and heard his mumble at the other end. "Get out," I said. "Quinn, get your sister and get out. There's going to be an explosion." I only waited to hear him sound more alert before I shut the phone.

"We have to save ourselves, too," Barry was saying.

Brilliantly, Cecile ran down the hall to a red fixture and flipped the fire alarm. The clamor almost split our eardrums, but the effect was wonderful on the sleeping humans on this floor. Within seconds, they began to come out of the rooms.

"Take the stairs," Cecile directed them in a bellow, and obediently, they did. I was glad to see Carla's dark head among them. But I didn't see Quinn, and he was always easy to spot.

"The queen is high up," said Mr. Cataliades.

"Can those glass panels be busted from the inside?" I asked.

"They did it on *Fear Factor*," Barry said.

"We could try sliding the coffins down."

"They'd break on impact," Cecile said.

"But the vamps would survive the explosion," I pointed out.

"To be burned up by the sun," Mr. Cataliades said. "Diantha and I will go up and try to get out the queen's party, wrapped up in blankets. We'll take them . . ." He looked at me desperately.

"Ambulances! Call 911 now! They can figure out where to take them!"

Diantha called 911 and was incoherent and desperate enough to get ambulances started to an explosion that had not happened yet. "The building's on fire," she said, which was like a future truth.

"Go," I told Mr. Cataliades, actually shoving the demon, and off he sped to the queen's suite.

"Go try to get your party out," I said to Barry, and he and Cecile ran for the elevator, though at any minute it might be unworkable.

I'd done everything about getting humans out that I could. Cataliades and Diantha could take care of the queen and Andre. Eric and Pam! I knew where Eric's room was, thank God. I took the stairs. As I ran up, I met a party coming down: the two Britlingens, both with large packs on their backs, carrying a wrapped bundle. Clovache had the feet, Batanya the head. I had no doubt that the bundle was the King of Kentucky, and that they were doing their duty. They both nodded as I hugged the wall to let them by. If they weren't as calm as if they were out for a stroll, they were close to it.

"You set off the fire alarm?" Batanya said. "Whatever the Fellowship is doing, it's today?"

"Yes," I said.

"Thanks. We're getting out now, and you should, too," Clovache said.

"We'll go back to our place after we deposit him," Batanya said. "Good-bye."

"Good luck," I told them stupidly, and then I was running

upstairs as if I'd trained for this. As a result, I was huffing like a bellows when I flung open the door to the ninth floor. I saw a lone maid pushing a cart down a long corridor. I ran up to her, frightening her even more than the fire alarm already had.

"Give me your master key," I said.

"No!" She was middle-aged and Hispanic, and she wasn't about to give in to such a crazy demand. "I'll get fired."

"Then open this door"—I pointed to Eric's—"and get out of here." I'm sure I looked like a desperate woman, and I was. "This building is going to blow up any minute."

She flung the key at me and made tracks down the hallway to the elevators. Dammit.

And then the explosions began. There was a deep, resounding quiver and a boom from way below my feet, as if some gargantuan sea creature were making its way to the surface. I staggered over to Eric's room, thrusting the plastic key into the slot and shoving open the door in a moment of utter silence. The room was in complete darkness.

"Eric, Pam!" I yelled. I fumbled for a light switch in the pitch-black room, felt the building sway. At least one of the upper charges had gone off. Oh, shit! Oh, shit! But the light came on, and I saw that Eric and Pam had gotten in the beds, not the coffins.

"Wake up!" I said, shaking Pam since she was closest. She didn't stir at all. It was exactly like shaking a doll stuffed with sawdust. "Eric!" I screamed right in his ear.

This got a bit of a reaction; he was much older than Pam. His eyes opened a slit and tried to focus. "What?" he said.

"You have to get up! You have to! You have to go out!"

"Daytime," he whispered. He began to flop over on his side.

I slapped him harder than I've ever hit anyone in my life. I screamed, "Get up!" until my voice would hardly work.

Finally Eric stirred and managed to sit up. He was wearing black silk pajama bottoms, thank God, and I spied the ceremonial black cloak tossed over his coffin. He hadn't returned it to Quinn, which was huge luck. I arranged it over him and fastened it at the neck. I pulled the hood over his face. "Cover your head!" I yelled, and I heard a burst of noise above my head: shattering glass, followed by shrieks.

Eric would drop back to sleep if I didn't keep him awake. At least he was trying. I remembered that Bill had managed to stagger, under dire circumstances, at least for a few minutes. But Pam, though roughly the same age as Bill, simply could not be roused. I even pulled her long pale hair.

"You have to help me get Pam out," I said finally, despairing. "Eric, you just have to." There was another roar and a lurch in the floor. I screamed, and Eric's eyes went wide. He staggered to his feet. As if we'd shared thoughts like Barry and I could, we both shoved his coffin off its trestle and onto the carpet. Then we slid it over to the opaque slanting glass panel forming the side of the building.

Everything around us trembled and shook. Eric's eyes were a little wider now, and he was concentrating so heavily on keeping himself moving that his strength was pulling on mine.

"Pam," I said, trying to push him into more action. I opened the coffin, after some desperate fumbling. Eric went over to his sleeping child, walking like his feet were sticking to the floor with each step. He took Pam's shoulders and I took her feet, and we picked her up, blanket and all. The floor shook again, more violently this time, and we lurched over to the coffin and tossed Pam into it. I shut the lid and latched it, though a corner of Pam's nightgown was sticking out.

I thought about Bill, and Rasul flashed across my mind, but there was nothing I could do, and there wasn't any time left. "We have to break the glass!" I shrieked at Eric. He nodded very slowly. We knelt to brace ourselves against the end of the coffin and we pushed as hard as we could till it slammed into the glass, which cracked into about a thousand pieces. They hung together, amazingly—the miracle of safety glass. I could have screamed from frustration. We needed a *hole*, not a curtain of glass. Crouching lower, digging our toes into the carpet, trying to ignore the rumbling noises in the building below us, Eric and I shoved with all our strength.

Finally! We punched the coffin all the way through. The window let go of its frame and cascaded down the side of the building.

And Eric saw sunlight for the first time in a thousand years. He screamed, a terrible, gut-wrenching noise. But in the next instant, he pulled the cloak tight around him. He grabbed me and hopped astride the coffin, and we pushed off with our feet. For just a fraction of a minute, we hung in the balance, and then we tilted forward. In the most awful moment of my life, we went out the window and began tobogganing down the building on the coffin. We would crash unless—

Suddenly we were off the coffin and kind of staggering through the air, Eric holding me to him with dogged persistence.

I exhaled with profound relief. Of course, Eric could fly.

In his light-stunned stupor, he couldn't fly very well. This was not the smooth progress I'd experienced before; we had more of a zigzag, bobbing descent.

But it was better than a free fall.

Eric could delay our descent enough to keep me from being dashed to my death on the street outside the hotel. However, the coffin with Pam inside had a bad landing, and Pam came catapulting out of the remains of the wood and into the sunlight where she lay motionless. Without making a sound, she began to burn. Eric landed on top of her and used the blanket to cover both of them. One of Pam's feet was exposed, and the flesh was smoking. I covered it up.

I also heard the sound of sirens. I flagged down the first ambulance I saw, and the medics leaped out.

I pointed to the blanketed heap. "Two vampires—get them out of the sun!" I said.

The pair of EMTs, both young women, exchanged an incredulous glance. "What do we do with them?" asked the dark one.

"You take them to a nice basement somewhere, one without any windows, and you tell the owners to keep that basement open, because there are gonna be more."

High up, a smaller explosion blew out one of the suites. A suitcase bomb, I thought, wondering how many Joe had talked us into carrying up into the rooms. A fine shower of glass sparkled in the sun as we looked up, but darker things were following the glass out of the window, and the EMTs began to move like the trained team they were. They didn't panic, but they definitely moved with haste, and they were already debating which building close at hand had a large basement.

"We'll tell everyone," said the dark woman. Pam was now in the ambulance and Eric halfway there. His face was bright red and steam was rising from his lips. Oh, my God. "What you going to do?"

"I have to go back in there," I said.

"Fool," she said, and then threw herself in the ambulance, which took off.

There was more glass raining down, and part of the bottom floor appeared to be collapsing. That would be due to some of the larger explosive-packed coffin bombs in the shipping and receiving area. Another explosion came from about the sixth floor, but on the other side of the pyramid.

My senses were so dulled by the sound and the sight that I wasn't surprised when I saw a blue suitcase flying through the air. Mr. Cataliades had succeeded in breaking the queen's window. Suddenly I realized the suitcase was intact, had not exploded, and was hurtling straight at me.

I began to run, flashing back to my softball days when I had sprinted from third to home and had to slide in. I aimed for the park across the street, where traffic had come to a stop because of the emergency vehicles: cop cars, ambulances, fire engines. There was a cop just ahead of me who was facing away, pointing something out to another cop. "Down!" I yelled. "Bomb!" and she swung around to face me and I tackled her, taking her down to the ground with me. Something hit me in the middle of the back, whoosh, and the air was shoved out of my lungs. We lay there for a long minute, until I pushed myself off of her and climbed unsteadily to my feet. It was wonderful to inhale, though the air was acrid with flames and dust. She might have said something to me, but I couldn't hear her.

I turned around to face the Pyramid of Gizeh.

Parts of the structure were crumbling, folding in and down, all the glass and concrete and steel and wood separating from the whole into discrete parts, while most of the walls that had created the spaces—of rooms and bathrooms and halls—collapsed. That collapse trapped many of the bodies that had occupied these arbitrarily divided areas. They were all one now: the structure, its parts, its inhabitants.

Here and there were still bits that had held together. The human floor, the mezzanine, and the lobby level were partially intact, though the area around the registration desk was destroyed.

I saw a shape I recognized, a coffin. The lid had popped clean off with the impact of its fall. As the sun hit the creature inside, it let out a wail, and I rushed over. There was a hunk of drywall by it, and I hauled that over the coffin. There was silence as soon as the sun was blocked from touching the vampire inside.

"Help!" I yelled. "Help!"

A few policemen moved toward me.

"There are people and vamps still alive," I said. "The vamps have to be covered."

"People first," said one beefy veteran.

"Sure," I agreed automatically, though even as I said it, I thought, *Vampires didn't set these bombs.* "But if you can cover the vamps, they can last until ambulances can take them to a safe place."

There was a chunk of hotel still standing, a bit of the south part. Looking up, I saw Mr. Cataliades standing at an empty frame where the glass had fallen away. Somehow, he had worked his way down to the human floor. He was holding a bundle wrapped in a bedspread, clutching it to his chest.

"Look!" I called, to get a fireman's attention. "Look!"

They leaped into action at seeing a live person to rescue. They were far more enthusiastic about that than about rescuing vamps who were possibly smoldering to death in the sunlight and could easily be saved by being covered. I tried to blame them, but I couldn't.

For the first time I noticed that there was a crowd of regular people who had stopped their cars and gotten out to help—or gawk. There were also people who were screaming, "Let them burn!"

I watched the firemen go up in a bucket to fetch the demon and his burden, and then I turned back to working my way through the rubble.

After a time, I was flagging. The screams of the human survivors, the smoke, the sunlight muted by the huge cloud of dust, the noise of the groaning structure settling, the hectic noise of the rescue workers and the machinery that was arriving and being employed . . . I was overwhelmed.

By that time, since I'd stolen one of the yellow jackets and one of the hard hats all the rescuers were wearing, I'd gotten close enough to find two vampires, one of whom I knew, in the ruins of the check-in area, heavily overlaid by debris from the floors above. A big piece of wood survived to identify the reception desk. One of the vampires was very burned, and I had no idea if he'd survive it or not. The other vamp had hidden beneath the largest piece of wood, and only his feet and hands had been singed and blackened. Once I yelled for help, the vamps were covered with blankets. "We got a building two blocks away; we're using it for the vampire repository," said the dark-skinned ambulance driver who took the more seriously injured one, and I realized it was the same woman who'd taken Eric and Pam.

In addition to the vampires, I uncovered a barely alive Todd Donati. I spent a few moments with him until a stretcher got there. And I found, near to him, a dead maid. She'd been crushed.

I had a smell in my nose that just wouldn't go away, and I hated it. It was coating my lungs inside, I thought, and I'd spend the rest of my life breathing it in and breathing it out. The odor was composed of burning building materials, scorched bodies, and disintegrating vampires. It was the smell of hatred.

I saw some things so awful I couldn't even think about them then.

Suddenly, I didn't feel I could search anymore. I had to sit down. I was drawn to a pile created by the chance arrangement of a large pipe and some drywall. I perched on it and wept. Then the whole pile shifted sideways, and I landed on the ground, still weeping.

I looked into the opening revealed by the shifted debris.

Bill was crouched inside, half his face burned away. He was wearing the clothes I'd last seen him in the night before. I arched myself over him to keep the sun off, and he said, "Thanks," through cracked and bloody lips. He kept slipping in and out of his comatose daytime sleep.

"Jesus God," I said. "Come help!" I called, and saw two men start toward me with a blanket.

"I knew you'd find me," Bill said, or did I imagine that?

I stayed hunched in the awkward position. There just wasn't anything near enough to grab that would cover as much of him as I did. The smell was making me gag, but I stayed. He'd lasted this long only because he'd been covered by accident.

Though one fireman threw up, they covered him and took him away.

Then I saw another yellow-jacketed figure tear off across the debris field toward the ambulances as fast as anyone could move without breaking a leg. I got the impression of a live brain, and I recognized it at once. I scrambled over piles of rubble, following the signature of the brain of the man I wanted most to find. Quinn and Frannie lay half-buried under a pile of loose rubble. Frannie was unconscious, and she'd been bleeding from the head, but it had dried. Quinn was dazed but coming to full awareness. I could see that fresh water had cut a path in the dust on his face, and I realized the man who'd just dashed away had given Quinn some water to drink and was returning with stretchers for the two.

He tried to smile at me. I fell to my knees beside him. "We might have to change our plans, babe," he said. "I may have to take care of Frannie for a week or two. Our mom's not exactly Florence Nightingale."

I tried not to cry, but it was like, once turned to "on," I

couldn't tell my tear ducts to switch off. I wasn't sobbing anymore, but I was trickling steadily. Stupid. "You do what you have to do," I said. "You call me when you can. Okay?" I hated people who said "Okay?" all the time, like they were getting permission, but I couldn't help that, either. "You're alive; that's all that matters."

"Thanks to you," he said. "If you hadn't called, we'd be dead. Even the fire alarm might not have gotten us out of the room in time."

I heard a groan from a few feet away, a breath on the air. Quinn heard it, too. I crawled away from him, pushing aside a large chunk of toilet and sink. There, covered with dust and debris, under several large bits of drywall, lay Andre, completely out of it. A quick glance told me he had several serious injuries. But none of them was bleeding. He would heal them all. Dammit.

"It's Andre," I told Quinn. "Hurt, but alive." If my voice was grim, I felt grim. There was a nice, long wood splinter right by his leg, and I was so tempted. Andre was a threat to my freedom of will, to everything I enjoyed about my life. But I'd seen so much death that day already.

I crouched there beside him, hating him, but after all . . . I knew him. That should have made it easier, but it didn't.

I duckwalked out of the little alcove where he lay, scuttled back to Quinn.

"Those guys are coming back to get us," he told me, sounding stronger every minute. "You can leave now."

"You want me to leave?"

His eyes were telling me something. I wasn't reading it.

"Okay," I said hesitantly. "I'll go."

"I've got help coming," he said gently. "You could be finding someone else."

"All right," I said, not knowing how to take this, and pushed to my feet. I'd gone maybe two yards when I heard him begin to move. But after a moment of stillness, I kept walking.

I returned to a big van that had been brought in and parked close to the rescue command center. This yellow jacket had been a magic pass, but it might run out any minute. Someone would notice I was wearing bedroom slippers, and they were ripping up, since they'd hardly been intended for ruin-scrambling. A woman handed me a bottle of water from the van, and I opened it with unsteady hands. I drank and drank, and poured the rest of the water over my face and hands. Despite the chill in the air, it felt wonderful.

By then, two (or four, or six) hours must have passed since the first explosion. There were now scores of rescuers there who had equipment, machinery, blankets. I was casting around for someone who looked authoritative, intending to find out where the other human survivors had been taken, when a voice spoke in my head.

*Sookie?*

*Barry!*

*What kind of shape are you in?*

*Pretty rocky, but not much hurt. You?*

*Same. Cecile died.*

*I'm so sorry.* I couldn't think of anything else to say.

*I've thought of something we can do.*

*What?* I probably didn't sound very interested.

*We can find living people. We'll be better, together.*

*That's what I've been doing,* I told him. *But you're right, together we'll be stronger.* At the same time, I was so tired that something inside of me cringed at the thought of making further effort. *Of course we can,* I said.

If this pile of debris had been as horrifyingly huge as the Twin Towers, we couldn't have done it. But this site was smaller and more contained, and if we could get anyone to believe us, we had a chance.

I found Barry close to the command center, and I took his grimy hand. He was younger than me, but now he didn't look it, and I didn't think he'd ever act it again. When I scanned the line of bodies on the grass of the little park, I saw Cecile, and I saw what might have been the maid I'd accosted in the hallway. There were a few flaking, vaguely manlike shapes that were disintegrating vampires. I could have known any of them, but it was impossible to tell.

Any humiliation would be a small thing to pay if we could save someone. So Barry and I prepared to be humiliated and mocked.

At first, it was hard to get anyone to listen. The professionals kept referring us to the casualty center or to one of the ambulances parked nearby ready to take survivors to one of Rhodes's hospitals.

Finally, I was face-to-face with a thin, gray-haired man who listened to me without any expression on his face at all.

"I never thought I'd be rescuing vampires, either," he said, as though that explained his decision, and maybe it did. "So, take these two men with you, and show 'em what you can do. You have fifteen minutes of these men's valuable time. If you waste it, you might be killing someone."

Barry had had the idea, but now he seemed to want me to speak for us. His face was blackened with smears of soot. We had a silent conference about the best way to go about our task, and at the end of it, I turned to the firemen and said, "Put us up in one of those bucket things."

For a wonder, they did, without further argument. We were lifted out over the debris, and yes, we knew it was dangerous, and yes, we were prepared to take the consequences. Still holding hands, Barry and I shut our eyes and *searched*, flinging our minds open and outward.

"Move us left," I said, and the fireman in the bucket with us gestured to the man in the cab of the machine. "Watch me," I said, and he looked back. "Stop," I said, and the bucket stopped. We searched again. "Directly below," I said. "Right below here. It's a woman named something Santiago."

After a few minutes, a roar went up. They'd found her alive.

We were popular after that, and there were no more questions about how we did it, as long as we kept it up. Rescue people are all about rescuing. They were bringing dogs, and they were inserting microphones, but Barry and I were quicker and more articulate than the dogs, and more precise than the microphones. We found four more live people, and we found a man who died before they could get to him, a waiter named Art who loved his wife and suffered terribly right up until the end. Art was especially heartbreaking, because they were trying like hell to dig the guy out, and I had to tell them it was no good. Of course, they didn't take my word for it; they kept excavating, but he had passed. By that time, the searchers were really excited about our ability and wanted us to work through the night, but Barry was failing and I wasn't much better. Worse, dark was closing in.

"The vampires'll be rising," I reminded the fire chief. He nodded and looked at me for further explanation. "They'll be hurt bad," I said. He still didn't get it. "They'll need blood instantly, and they won't have any control. I wouldn't send any rescue workers out on the debris alone," I said, and his face went blank with thought.

"You don't think they're all dead? Can't you find them?"

"Well, actually, no. We can't find vamps. Humans, yes. But not undead. Their brains don't give off any, ah, waves. We've got to go now. Where are the survivors?"

"They're all in the Thorne Building, right down there," he said, pointing. "In the basement." We turned to walk away. By this time, Barry had slung his arm around my shoulders, and not because he was feeling affectionate. He needed the support.

"Let me get your names and addresses, so the mayor can thank you," the gray-haired man said, holding a pen and clipboard at the ready.

*No!* Barry said, and my mouth snapped shut.

I shook my head. "We're going to pass on that," I said. I'd had a quick look in his head, and he was greedy for more of our help. Suddenly I understood why Barry had stopped me so abruptly, though my fellow telepath was so tired he couldn't tell me himself. My refusal didn't go over big.

"You'll work for vamps, but you don't want to stand and be counted as someone who helped on this terrible day?"

"Yes," I answered. "That's just about right."

He wasn't happy with me, and I thought for a minute he was going to force the issue: grab my wallet out of my pants, send me to jail, or something. But he reluctantly nodded his head and jerked it in the direction of the Thorne Building.

*Someone will try to find out,* Barry said. *Someone will want to use us.*

I sighed, and I hardly had the energy to take in more air. I nodded. *Yeah, someone will. If we go to the shelter, someone will be watching for us there, and they'll ask for our names from someone who recognizes us, and after that, it's only a matter of time.*

I couldn't think of a way to dodge going in there. We had to have help, we had to find our parties and discover how and when we could leave the city, and we had to find out who had lived and who hadn't.

I patted my back pocket, and to my amazement, my cell phone was still in it and still had bars. I called Mr. Cataliades. If anyone besides me had come out of the Pyramid of Gizeh with a cell phone, the lawyer would be the one.

"Yes," he said cautiously. "Miss St—"

"Shhh," I said. "Don't say my name out loud." It was sheer paranoia talking.

"Very well."

"We helped them out down here, and now they really want to get to know us better," I said, feeling very clever for talking so guardedly. I was very tired. "Barry and I are outside the building where you are. We need to stay somewhere else. Too many people making lists in there, right?"

"That is a popular activity," he said.

"You and Diantha okay?"

"She has not been found. We were separated."

I didn't speak for a few seconds. "I'm so sorry. Who were you holding when I saw them rescue you?"

"The queen. She is here, though badly injured. We can't find Andre."

He paused, and because I couldn't help it, I said, "Who else?"

"Gervaise is dead. Eric, Pam, Bill . . . burned, but here. Cleo Babbitt is here. I haven't seen Rasul."

"Is Jake Purifoy there?"

"I haven't seen him, either."

"Because you might want to know he's at least partially responsible if you do see him. He was in on the Fellowship plot."

"Ah." Mr. Cataliades registered that. "Oh, yes, I certainly did want to know that. Johan Glassport will be especially interested, since he has several broken ribs and a broken collarbone. He's very, very angry." It said something about Johan Glassport's viciousness, that Mr. Cataliades thought him capable of exacting as much vengeance as a vampire would. "How did you come to know there was a plot at all, Miss Sookie?"

I told the lawyer the story Clovache had told me; I figured now that she and Batanya had gone back to wherever they came from, that would be okay.

"Hiring them proved to be worth the money for King Isaiah." Cataliades sounded thoughtful rather than envious. "Isaiah is here and completely uninjured."

"We need to go find somewhere to sleep. Can you tell Barry's king that he's with me?" I asked, knowing I needed to get off the phone and make a plan.

"He is too injured to care. He is not aware."

"All right. Just someone from the Texas party."

"I see Joseph Velasquez. Rachel is dead." Mr. Cataliades couldn't help himself; he had to tell me all the bad news.

"Cecile, Stan's assistant, is dead," I told him.

"Where are you going to go?" Cataliades asked.

"I don't know what to do," I said. I felt exhausted and hopeless, and I'd had too much bad news and gotten too battered to rally one more time.

"I will send a cab for you," Mr. Cataliades offered. "I can get a number from one of the nice volunteers. Tell the driver you are rescue workers and you need a ride to the nearest inexpensive hotel. Do you have a credit card?"

"Yeah, and my debit card," I said, blessing the impulse that had led me to stuff the little wallet in my pocket.

"No, wait, they'll track you very easily if you use it. Cash?"

I checked. Thanks largely to Barry, we had a hundred ninety dollars between us. I told Mr. Cataliades we could swing it.

"Then spend the night in a hotel, and tomorrow call me again," he said, sounding unutterably weary.

"Thanks for the plan."

"Thanks for your warning," the courtly demon said. "We would all be dead if you and the Bellboy hadn't wakened us."

I ditched the yellow jacket and the hard hat. Barry and I tottered along, more or less holding each other up. We found a concrete barricade to lean against, our arms around each other. I tried to tell Barry why we were doing this, but he didn't care. I was worried that at any minute some fire-fighter or cop from the scene would spot us and stop to find out what we were doing, where we were going, who we were. I was so relieved that I felt sick when I spied a cab cruising slowly, the driver peering out the window. Had to be for us. I waved my free arm frantically. I had never hailed a cab before in my life. It was just like the movies.

The cab driver, a wire-thin guy from Guyana, wasn't too excited about letting filthy creatures like us get into his cab, but he couldn't turn down people as pitiful as we were. The nearest "inexpensive" hotel was a mile back into the city, away from the water. If we'd had the energy, we could have walked it. At least the cab ride wasn't too pricey.

Even at the mid-range hotel, the desk clerks were less than thrilled with our appearance; but after all, it was a day for charity to people who were involved in the blast. We got a room at a price that would have made me gasp if I hadn't seen the room rates at the Pyramid. The room itself wasn't much, but we didn't need much. A maid knocked on the door right after we got in and said she'd like to wash our clothes for us, since we didn't have any more. She looked down when she said that, so she wouldn't embarrass me. Trying not to choke up at her kindness, I looked down at my shirt and slacks and agreed. I turned to Barry to find he was absolutely out cold. I maneuvered him into the bed. It was unpleasantly like handling one of the vampires, and I held my lips pressed together in a tight line the whole time I undressed his limp body. Then I shucked my own clothes, found a plastic bag in the closet to hold them, and handed the soiled clothes out to her. I got a washcloth and wiped off Barry's face and hands and feet, and then I covered him up.

I had to shower, and I thanked God for the complimen-tary shampoo and soap and cream rinse and skin lotion. I also thanked God for hot and cold running water, particularly hot. The kind maid had even handed me two toothbrushes and a little packet of toothpaste, and I scrubbed my mouth clean of the flavor of ashes. I washed my panties and bra in the sink and rolled them up in a towel before I hung them up to dry. I'd given the lady every stitch of Barry's clothes.

Finally, there was nothing else to do, and I crawled into the bed beside Barry. Now that I smelled so good, I noticed that he didn't, but that was just tough for me, right? I wouldn't have woken him for anything. I turned on my side away from him, thought about how frightening that long, empty corridor had been—isn't it funny that that was what I picked out as scary, after such a horrific day?

The hotel room was so very quiet after the tumult of the scene of the explosions, and the bed was so very comfortable, and I smelled so much better and hardly hurt at all.

I slept and didn't dream.

# ~ 18

I KNOW THERE ARE MANY WORSE THINGS THAN WAKing up naked in a bed with someone you don't know very well. But when my eyes fluttered open the next day, I couldn't think of any, for five long minutes. I knew Barry was awake. You can tell when a brain pops into awareness. To my relief, he slipped out of the bed and into the bathroom without speaking, and I heard the drumming of the water in the shower stall soon after.

Our clean clothes were in a bag hanging on our inside doorknob, and there was a *USA Today*, too. After hastily donning my clothes, I spread the newspaper out on the small table while I brewed a pot of the free coffee. I also extended the bag with Barry's clothes in it into the bathroom and dropped it on the floor, waving it a little first to attract his attention.

I'd looked at the room service menu, and we didn't have enough cash to get anything on it. We had to reserve some of our funds for a cab, because I didn't know what our next move would be. Barry came out, looking as refreshed as I'd been last night. To my surprise, he kissed me on the cheek, and then sat opposite me with his own insulated cup that contained something that bore a faint relationship to brewed coffee.

"I don't remember much about last night," he said. "Fill me in on why we're here."

I did.

"That was good thinking on my part," he said. "I'm in awe of myself."

I laughed. He might be feeling a little male chagrin that he had wilted before I did, but at least he could make fun of himself.

"So, I guess we need to call your demon lawyer?"

I nodded. It was eleven by then, so I called.

He answered right away. "There are many ears here," he said without preamble. "And I understand these phones aren't too secure. Cell phones."

"All right."

"So I will come to you in a while, bringing some things you'll need. You are where?"

With a twinge of misgiving, since the demon was a guy people would notice, I told him the name of the hotel and our room number, and he told me to be patient. I'd been feeling fine until Mr. Cataliades said that, and all of a sudden I began to twitch inwardly. I felt like we were on the run now, when we in no way deserved to be. I'd read the newspaper, and the story about the Pyramid said the catastrophe was due to "a series of explosions" that Dan Brewer, head of the state terrorist task force, attributed to several bombs. The fire chief was less committal: "An investigation is underway." I should damn well hope so.

Barry said, "We could have sex while we wait."

"I liked you better unconscious," I said. I knew Barry was only trying not to think about stuff, but still.

"You undress me last night?" he said with a leer.

"Yeah, that was me, lucky me," I said. I smiled at him, surprising myself.

A knock at the door had us both staring at it like startled deer.

"Your demon guy," said Barry after a second of mental checking.

"Yep," I said, and got up to answer it.

Mr. Cataliades hadn't had the kindness of a maid, so he was still in the soiled clothes of the day before. But he managed to look dignified, anyway, and his hands and face were clean.

"Please, how is everyone?" I asked.

"Sophie-Anne has lost her legs, and I don't know if they'll come back," he said.

"Oh, geez," I said, wincing.

"Sigebert fought free of the debris after dark," he continued. "He'd hidden in a safe pocket in the parking garage, where he landed after the explosions. I suspect he found someone to feed off, because he was healthier than he ought to have been. But if that's the case, he shoved the body into one of the fires, because we would have heard if a drained body had been found."

I hoped the donor had been one of the Fellowship guys.

"Your king," Mr. Cataliades said to Barry, "is so injured it may take him a decade to recover. Until the situation is clear, Joseph leads, though he'll be challenged soon. The king's child Rachel is dead; perhaps Sookie told you?"

"Sorry," I said. "I just had too much bad news to finish getting through it all."

"And Sookie has told me the human Cecile perished."

"What about Diantha?" I asked, hesitating to do so. It had to be significant that Mr.Cataliades hadn't mentioned his niece.

"Missing," he said briefly "And yet that piece of filth, Glassport, has only bruises."

"I'm sorry for both things," I said.

Barry seemed numb. All traces of his flippant mood had vanished. He looked smaller, sitting on the edge of the bed. The cocky sharp dresser I'd met in the lobby of the Pyramid had gone underground, at least for a while.

"I told you about Gervaise," Mr. Cataliades said. "I identified his woman's body this morning. What was her name?"

"Carla. I can't remember her last name. It'll come to me."

"The first name will probably be enough for them to identify her. One of the corpses in hotel uniform had a computer list in his pocket."

"They weren't all in on it," I said with some certainty.

"No, of course not," Barry said. "Only a few."

We looked at him.

"How do you know?" I asked.

"I overheard them."

"When?"

"The night before."

I bit the inside of my mouth, hard.

"What did you hear?" Mr. Cataliades asked in a level voice.

"I was with Stan in the, you know, the buy-and-sell thing. I had noticed the waiters and so on were dodging me, and then I watched to see if they were avoiding Sookie as well. So I thought, 'They know what you are, Barry, and there's something they don't want you to know. You better check it out.' I found a good place to sort of skulk behind some of those fake palm trees, close by the service door, and I could get a reading on what they were thinking inside. They didn't spell it out or anything, okay?" He had gotten an accurate reading on our thoughts, too. "It was just, like, 'Okay, we're gonna get those vamps, damn them, and if we take some of their human slaves, well, that's just too bad, we'll live with it. Damned by association.'"

I could only sit there and look at him.

"No, I didn't know when or what they were going to do! I went to bed finally kind of worrying about them, what the plan was, and when I couldn't settle into a good sleep, I finally quit trying and called you. And we tried to get everyone out," he said, and began crying.

I sat beside him and put my arm around him. I didn't know what to say. Of course, he could tell what I was thinking.

"Yes, I wish I'd said something before I did," he said in a choked voice. "Yes, I did the wrong thing. But I thought if I spoke up before I knew something for sure, the vamps would fall on them and drain them. Or they'd want me to point out who knew and who didn't. And I couldn't do that."

There was a long silence.

"Mr. Cataliades, have you seen Quinn?" I asked to break the silence.

"He's at the human hospital. He couldn't stop them from taking him."

"I have to go see him."

"How serious is your fear that the authorities will try to coerce you into doing their bidding?"

Barry raised his head and looked at me. "Pretty serious," we said simultaneously.

"It's the first time I've ever shown anyone, aside from local people, what I can do," I said.

"Me, too." Barry wiped his eyes with the back of his hand. "You should have seen that guy's face when he finally believed that we could find people. He thought we were psychics or something, and he couldn't understand that what we were doing was registering a live brain signature. Nothing mystical about it."

"He was all over the idea once he believed us," I said. "You could hear in his head that he was thinking of the hundred different ways we could be of use to rescue operations, to the government at conferences, police interrogations."

Mr. Cataliades looked at us. I couldn't pick out all his snarly demon thoughts, but he was having a lot of them.

"We'd lose control over our lives," Barry said. "I like my life."

"I guess I could be saving a lot of people," I said. I'd just never thought about it before. I'd never been faced with a situation like the one we'd faced the previous day. I hoped I never was again. How likely was it I would ever be on-site again at a disaster? Was I obligated to give up a job I liked, among people I cared about, to work for strangers in far away places? I shivered when I thought of it. I felt something harden within me when I realized that the advantage Andre had taken of me would only be the beginning, in situations like that. Like Andre, everyone would want to own me.

"No," I said. "I won't do it. Maybe I'm just being selfish and I'm damning myself, but I won't do it. I don't think we're exaggerating how bad that would be for us, not a bit."

"Then going to the hospital is not a good idea," Cataliades said.

"I know, but I have to, anyway."

"Then you can stop by on your way to the airport."

We sat up straighter.

"There's an Anubis plane flying out in three hours. It'll go to Dallas first, then Shreveport. The queen and Stan are paying for it jointly. It'll have all the survivors of both parties on it. The citizens of Rhodes have donated used coffins for the trip." Mr. Cataliades made a face, and honestly, I couldn't blame him. "Here's all the cash we can spare," he continued, handing me a short stack of bills. "Make it to the Anubis terminal in time, and you'll both go home with us. If you don't make it, I'll assume something happened to stop you and you'll have to call to make some other arrangement. We know we owe you a great debt, but we have wounded to get home ourselves, and the queen's credit cards and so on were lost in the fire. I'll have to call her credit company for emergency service, but that won't take much time."

This seemed a little cold, but after all, he wasn't our best friend, and as the daytime guy for the queen, he had a lot to do and many more problems to solve.

"Okay," I said. "Hey, listen, is Christian Baruch at the shelter?"

His face sharpened. "Yes. Though somewhat burned, he's hanging around the queen in Andre's absence as if he would take Andre's place."

"He wants to, you know. He wants to be the next Mr. Queen of Louisiana."

"Baruch?" Cataliades could not have been more scornful if a goblin had applied for the job.

"No, he's gone to extreme lengths." I already told Andre about this. Now I had to explain again. "That's why he planted that Dr Pepper bomb," I said about five minutes later.

"How do you know this?" Mr. Cataliades asked.

"I figured it out, from this and that," I said modestly. I sighed. Here came the yucky part. "I found him yesterday, hiding underneath the registration desk. There was another vampire with him, badly burned. I don't even know who that one was. And in the same area was Todd Donati, the security guy, alive but hurt, and a dead maid." I felt the exhaustion all over again, smelled the awful smell, tried to breathe the thick air. "Baruch was out of it, of course."

I was not exactly proud of this, and I looked down at my hands. "Anyway, I was trying to read Todd Donati's mind, to find out how hurt he was, and he was just hating Baruch and blaming him, too. He was willing to be frank, this time. No more job to worry about. Todd told me he'd watched all the security tapes over and over again, and he'd finally figured out what he was seeing. His boss was leaping up to block the camera with gum so he could plant the bomb. Once he'd figured that out, Donati knew that Baruch had wanted to alarm the queen, make her insecure, so she'd take a new husband. And that would be Christian Baruch. But guess why he wants to marry her?"

"I can't imagine," said Mr. Cataliades, thoroughly shocked.

"Because he wants to open a new vampire hotel in New Orleans. Blood in the Quarter got flooded and closed, and Baruch thought he could rebuild and reopen."

"But Baruch didn't have anything to do with the other bombs?"

"I sure don't think so, Mr. Cataliades. I think that was the Fellowship, just like I said yesterday."

"Then who killed the vampires from Arkansas?" Barry asked. "I guess the Fellowship did that, too? No, wait . . . why would they? Not that they'd quibble at killing some vampires, but they'd know the vampires would probably get killed in the big explosion."

"We have an overload of villains," I said. "Mr. Cataliades, you got any ideas about who might have taken out the Arkansas vampires?" I gave Mr. Cataliades a straight-in-the-eyes stare.

"No," Mr. Cataliades said. "If I did, I would *never* say those ideas out loud. I think you should be concentrating on your man's injuries and getting back to your little town, not worrying about three deaths among so many."

I wasn't exactly worried about the deaths of the three Arkansas vampires, and it seemed like a really good idea to take Mr. Cataliades's advice to heart. I'd had the odd moment to think about the murders, and I'd decided that the simplest answer was often the best.

Who'd thought she had a good chance of skipping a trial altogether, if Jennifer Cater was silenced?

Who'd prepared the way to be admitted to Jennifer's room, by the simple means of a phone call?

Who'd had a good long moment of telepathic communication with her underlings before she began the artificial flurry of primping for the impromptu visit?

Whose bodyguard had been coming out of the stairway door just as we were exiting the suite?

I knew, just as Mr. Cataliades knew, that Sophie-Anne had ensured Sigebert would be admitted to Jennifer Cater's room by calling down ahead and telling Jennifer she herself was on her way. Jennifer would look out the peephole, recognize Sigebert, and assume the queen was right behind him. Once inside, Sigebert would unsheath his sword and kill everyone in the place.

Then he would hurry back up the stairs to appear in time to escort the queen right back down to the seventh floor.

He'd enter the room again so there'd be a reason for his scent to be on the air.

And at the time I'd suspected absolutely nothing.

What a shock it must have been to Sophie-Anne when Henrik Feith had popped up alive; but then the problem had been solved when he accepted her protection.

The problem reasserted itself when someone talked him into accusing her anyway.

And then, amazingly, problem solved again: the nervous little vampire had been assassinated in front of the court.

"I do wonder how Kyle Perkins was hired," I said. "He must have known he was on a suicide mission."

"Perhaps," Mr. Cataliades said carefully, "he had decided to meet the sun anyway. Perhaps he was looking for a spectacular and interesting way to go, earning a monetary legacy for his human descendants."

"It seems strange that I was sent looking for information about him by a member of our very own party," I said, my voice neutral.

"Ah, not everyone needs to know everything," Mr. Cataliades said, his voice just as neutral.

Barry could hear my thoughts, of course, but he wasn't getting what Mr. Cataliades was saying, which was just as well. It was stupid that it made me feel better, Eric and Bill not knowing the queen's deep game. Not that they weren't capable of playing deep games themselves, but I didn't think Eric would have sent me on the wild goose chase for the archery range where Kyle Perkins had trained if Eric had known the queen herself had hired Perkins.

The poor woman behind the counter had died because the queen hadn't told her left hand what her right hand was doing. And I wondered what had happened to the human, the one who'd thrown up on the murder scene, the one who'd been hired to drive Sigebert or Andre to the range . . . after

I'd so thoughtfully left a message to tell them when Barry and I were going back to collect the evidence. I'd sealed the woman's fate myself by leaving that phone message.

Mr. Cataliades took his departure, shaking our hands with his beaming smile, almost normal. He urged us once again to get to the airport.

"Sookie?" said Barry.

"Yeah."

"I really want to be on that plane."

"I know."

"What about you?"

"I don't think I can do it. Sit on the same plane with them."

"They all got hurt," Barry said.

"Yeah, but that isn't payback."

"You took care of that, didn't you?"

I didn't ask him what he meant. I knew what he could pick up out of my head.

"As much as I could," I said.

"Maybe I don't want to be on the same plane with *you*," Barry said.

Of course it hurt, but I guess I deserved it.

I shrugged. "You gotta decide that on your own. All of us have different things we can live with."

Barry considered that. "Yeah," he said. "I know. But for right now, it's better that we go our separate ways, here. I'm leaving for the airport to hang around until I can leave. Are you going to the hospital?"

I was too wary now to tell him. "I don't know," I said. "But I'm finding a car or a bus to take me home."

He hugged me, no matter how upset he was about the choices I'd made. I could feel the affection and regret in his heart. I hugged him back. He'd made his own choices.

I left the maid ten dollars when I departed on foot about

five minutes after Barry got in a cab. I waited until I got two blocks from the hotel, and then I asked a passerby how to get to St. Cosmas. It was a long ten-block hike, but the day was beautiful, cool and crisp with a bright sun. It felt good to be by myself. I might be wearing rubber-soled slippers, but I was dressed nicely enough, and I was clean. I ate a hot dog on my way to the hospital, a hot dog I'd bought from a street vendor, and that was something else I'd never done before. I bought a shapeless hat from a street vender, too, and stuffed all my hair up under it. The same guy had some dark glasses for sale. With the sky being so bright and the wind blowing in off the lake, the combination didn't look too odd.

St. Cosmas was an old edifice, with lots of ornate architectural embellishment on the outside. It was huge, too. I asked about Quinn's condition, and one of the women stationed at the busy visitors' desk said she couldn't give out that information. But to see if he was registered at the hospital, she'd had to look up his records, and I plucked his room number from her thoughts. I waited until all three of the women were occupied with other queries, and I slipped into the elevator and rode up.

Quinn was on the tenth floor. I'd never seen a hospital so large, and I'd never seen one so bustling. It was easy to stride around like I had a purpose and knew where I was going.

There was no one on guard outside his room.

I knocked lightly, and there wasn't a sound from inside. I pushed open the door very gently and stepped inside. Quinn was asleep in the bed, and he was attached to machines and tubes. And he was a fast-healing shifter, so his injuries must have been grievous. His sister was by his side. Her bandaged head, which had been propped on her hand, jerked up as she became aware of my presence. I pulled off the sunglasses and the hat.

"You," she said.

"Yeah, me, Sookie. What's Frannie short for, anyway?"

"It's really Francine, but everyone calls me Frannie." She looked younger as she said it.

Though I was pleased at the decreased hostility, I decided I'd better stay on my side of the room. "How is he?" I asked, jerking my chin at the sleeping man.

"He fades in and out." There was a moment of silence while she took a drink from a white plastic cup on the bed-side table. "When you woke him up, he got me up," she said abruptly. "We started down the stairs. But a big piece of ceiling fell on him, and the floor went out from beneath us, and the next thing I knew, some firemen are telling me some crazy woman found me while I was still alive, and they're giving me all kinds of tests, and Quinn's telling me he was going to take care of me until I was well. Then they told me he had two broken legs."

There was an extra chair, and I collapsed onto it. My legs just wouldn't hold me. "What does the doctor say?"

"Which one?" Frannie said bleakly.

"Any. All." I took one of Quinn's hands. Frannie almost reached out as if she thought I'd hurt him, but then she subsided. I had the hand that was free of tubes, and I held it for a while.

"They can't believe how much better he is already," Frannie said just when I'd decided she wasn't going to answer. "In fact, they think it's something of a miracle. Now we're gonna have to pay someone to get his records out of the system." Her dark-rooted hair was in clumps, and she was still filthy from the blast site.

"Go buy some clothes and come back and have a shower," I said. "I'll sit with him."

"Are you really his girlfriend?"

"Yes, I am."

"He said you had some conflicts."

"I do, but not with him."

"So, okay. I will. You got any money?"

"Not a lot, but here's what I can spare."

I handed her seventy-five dollars of Mr. Cataliades's money.

"Okay, I can stretch it," she said. "Thanks." She said it without enthusiasm, but she said it.

I sat in the quiet room and held Quinn's hand for almost an hour. In that time, his eyes had flickered open once, registered my presence, and closed again. A very faint smile curved his lips for a moment. I knew that while he was sleeping, his body was healing, and when he woke, he might be able to walk again. I would have found it very comforting to climb on that bed and snuggle with Quinn for a while, but it might be bad for him if I did that; I might jostle him or something.

After a while, I began talking to him. I told him why I thought the crude bomb had been left outside the queen's door, and I told him my theory about the deaths of the three Arkansas vampires. "You gotta agree, it makes sense," I said, and then I told him what I thought about the death of Henrik Feith and the execution of his murderer. I told him about the dead woman in the shop. I told him about my suspicions about the explosion.

"I'm sorry it was Jake that was in with them," I told him. "I know you used to like him. But he just couldn't stand being a vamp. I don't know if he approached the Fellowship or the Fellowship approached him. They had the guy at the computer, the one who was so rude to me. I think he called a delegate from each party to have them come pick up a suitcase. Some of them were too smart or too lazy to pick them up, and some of them returned the suitcases when no one claimed them. But not me, oh no, I put it in the queen's effing living room." I shook my head. "I guess not too many of the staff were in on it, because otherwise Barry or I would've picked up on something way before Barry did."

Then I slept for a few minutes, I think, because Frannie was there when I looked around, and she was eating from a McDonald's bag. She was clean, and her hair was wet.

"You love him?" she asked, sucking up some Coke through a straw.

"Too soon to tell."

"I'm going to have to take him home to Memphis," she said.

"Yeah, I know. I may not get to see him for a while. I've got to get home, too, somehow."

"The Greyhound station is two blocks away."

I shuddered. A long, long bus ride was not a prospect that I could look forward to.

"Or you could take my car," Frannie said.

"What?"

"Well, we got here separately. He drove here with all the props and a trailer, and I left out of my mama's in a hurry in my little sports car. So there are two cars here, and we only need one. I'm going to have to go home with him and stay for a while. You have to get back to work, right?"

"Right."

"So, drive my car home, and we'll pick it up when we're able."

"That's very nice of you," I said. I was surprised by her generosity, because I'd definitely had the impression she wasn't keen on Quinn having a girlfriend, and she wasn't keen on me, specifically.

"You seem okay. You tried to get us out of there in time. And he really cares about you."

"And you know this how?"

"He told me so."

She'd gotten part of the family directness, I could tell.

"Okay," I said. "Where are you parked?"

# 19

I'D BEEN TERRIFIED THE WHOLE TWO-DAY DRIVE: that I'd be stopped and they wouldn't believe I'd gotten permission to use the car, that Frannie would change her mind and tell the police I'd stolen it, that I'd have an accident and have to repay Quinn's sister for the vehicle. Frannie had an old red Mustang, and it was fun to drive. No one stopped me. The weather was good all the way back to Louisiana. I thought I'd see a slice of America, but along the interstate, everything looks the same. I imagined that in any small town I passed through, there was another Merlotte's, and maybe another Sookie.

I didn't sleep well on the trip, either, because I dreamed of the floor shaking under my feet and the dreadful moment we went out the hole in the glass. Or I saw Pam burning. Or other things, things I'd done and seen during the hours we patrolled the debris, looking for bodies.

When I turned into my driveway, having been gone a week, my heart began to pound as if the house was waiting for me. Amelia was sitting on the front porch with a bright blue ribbon in her hand, and Bob was sitting in front of her, batting at the dangling ribbon with a black paw. She looked up to see who it was, and when she recognized me behind the wheel, she leaped to her feet. I didn't pull around back; I stopped right there and jumped out of the driver's seat. Amelia's arms wrapped around me like vines, and she shrieked, "You're back! Oh, blessed Virgin, you're back!"

We danced around and hopped up and down like teenagers, whooping with sheer happiness.

"The paper listed you as a survivor," she said. "But no one could find you the day after. Until you called, I wasn't sure you were alive."

"It's a long story," I said. "A long, long story."

"Is it the right time to tell it to me?"

"Maybe after a few days," I said.

"Do you have anything to carry in?"

"Not a thing. All my stuff went up in smoke when the building went down."

"Oh, my God! Your new clothes!"

"Well, at least I have my driver's license and my credit card and my cell phone, though the battery's flat and I don't have the charger."

"And a new car?" She glanced back at the Mustang.

"A borrowed car."

"I don't think I have a single friend who would loan me a whole car."

"Half a car?" I asked, and she laughed.

"Guess what?" Amelia said. "Your friends got married."

I stopped dead. "Which friends?" Surely she couldn't mean the Bellefleur double wedding; surely they hadn't changed the date yet again.

"Oh, I shouldn't have said anything," Amelia said, looking guilty. "Well, speak of the devil!" There was another car coming to a stop right by the red Mustang.

Tara scrambled out. "I saw you driving by the shop," she called. "I almost didn't recognize you in the new car."

"Borrowed it from a friend," I said, looking at her askance.

"You did *not* tell her, Amelia Broadway!" Tara was righteously indignant.

"I didn't," Amelia said. "I started to, but I stopped in time!"

"Tell me what?"

"Sookie, I know this is going to sound crazy," Tara said, and I felt my brows draw together. "While you were gone, everything just clicked in a strange way, like something I'd known should happen, you know?"

I shook my head. I didn't know.

"JB and I got married!" Tara said, and the expression on her face was full of so many things: anxiety, hopefulness, guilt, wonder.

I ran that incredible sentence through my head several times before I was sure I understood the meaning of it. "You and JB? Husband and wife?" I said.

"I know, I know, it seems maybe a little strange . . ."

"It seems perfect," I said with all the sincerity I could scrape together. I wasn't really sure how I felt, but I owed my friend the happy face and cheerful voice I offered her. At the moment, this was the true stuff, and vampire fangs and blood under the bright searchlights seemed like the dream, or a scene from a movie I hadn't much enjoyed. "I'm so happy for you. What do you need for a wedding present?"

"Just your blessing, we put the announcement in the paper yesterday," she said, burbling away like a happy brook. "And the phone just hasn't stopped ringing off the wall since then. People are so nice!"

She truly believed she'd swept all her bad memories into a corner. She was in the mood to credit the world with benevolence.

I would try that, too. I would do my best to smother the memory of that moment when I'd glanced back to see Quinn pulling himself along by his elbows. He'd reached Andre, who lay mute and stricken. Quinn had propped himself on one elbow, reached out with his other hand, grabbed the piece of wood lying by Andre's leg and jammed it into Andre's chest. And, just like that, Andre's long life was over.

He'd done it for me.

How could I be the same person? I wondered. How could I be happy that Tara had gotten married and yet remember such a thing—not with horror, but with a savage sense of pleasure? I had wanted Andre to die, as much as I had wanted Tara to find someone to live with who would never tease her for her awful past, someone who would care for her and be sweet to her. And JB would do that. He might not be much on intellectual conversation, but Tara seemed to have made her peace with that.

Theoretically, then, I was delighted and hopeful for my two friends. But I couldn't feel it. I'd seen awful things, and I'd felt awful things. Now I felt like two different people trying to exist inside the same space.

*If I just stay away from the vampires for a while*, I told myself, smiling and nodding the whole time as Tara talked on and Amelia patted my shoulder or my arm. *If I pray every night, and hang around with humans, and leave the Weres alone, I'll be okay.*

I hugged Tara, squeezing her until she squeaked.

"What do JB's parents say?" I asked. "Where'd you get the license? Up in Arkansas?"

As Tara began to tell me all about it, I winked at Amelia,

who winked back and bent down to scoop up Bob in her arms. Bob blinked when he looked into my face, and he rubbed his head against my offered fingers and purred. We went inside with the sun bright on our backs and our shadows preceding us into the old house.